Also by Sara Cate

SALACIOUS PLAYERS' CLUB
Praise
Eyes on Me
Give Me More
Mercy

AGE-GAP ROMANCE
Beautiful Monster
Beautiful Sinner

WILDE BOYS DUET
Gravity
Freefall

BLACK HEART DUET
Four
Five

COCKY HERO CLUB
Handsome Devil

BULLY ROMANCE
Burn for Me

WICKED HEARTS
Delicate
Dangerous
Defiant

PRAISE

SARA CATE

sourcebooks
casablanca

Published by Sourcebooks Casablanca, an imprint of Sourcebooks
P.O. Box 4410, Naperville, Illinois 60567–4410
(630) 961-3900
sourcebooks.com

Originally self-published in 2022 by Sara Cate.

Cataloging-in-Publication Data is on file with the Library of Congress.

Printed and bound in the United States of America.
WOZ 10 9 8 7

For all the good girls.

Prologue

Seven Years Ago
Emerson

"SO I HAD A FISTFUL OF HER HAIR IN MY HAND, AND WE WERE both in the moment when I looked her right in the eye and said, 'Suck my cock like a good little girl.' The next thing I knew, she reared back her fist and clocked me right in the face."

"Oh shit!" Garrett curses with a grimace.

"Damn!" Hunter bellows.

Across the table, Maggie, the only woman in our group, looks horrified.

I wince, poking at the raw purple bruise growing around my eye socket.

"I don't think she liked that," Maggie adds with a light chuckle before taking a sip of her white wine.

"You think?" I burst out, grabbing my beer and holding the cold glass against my face to quell the throbbing ache pulsing around my eyeball. It hurts only half as much as my pride. The humiliation from getting my first real shiner from a pretty little brunette I had been flirting with for weeks and was beyond eager to stick my dick into being the worst of my injuries.

"I mean…I thought we were getting along great. She seemed kinky enough, and she definitely appeared into it, but I guess I was wrong. Not a fan of a little sexy degradation, apparently."

The table grows silent for a moment. My three coworkers and I have made these Thursday night happy hours at the bar a little tradition. We collectively hate the entertainment company we work for. When we took these jobs, we did it for the excitement and love of the industry. Now we meet for drinks once a week to rant about how we would run the company differently and how much better we'd do on our own. But we're all talk. None of us are ready to leave our steady positions to start new ones.

And more than occasionally, we talk about sex, each of us dishing out our dirtiest bedroom secrets like a bunch of old men sharing epic war stories. Even our modest Maggie joins in. Aside from Hunter and his long-term girlfriend, Isabel, we're all single, and we all intend to keep it that way. One of the perks of working in the entertainment industry is that we work nights, parties, and drunk soirees, which means we get laid fairly consistently, giving us ample conversation topics, so we don't have to spend *all* of our time together bitching about the company we work for.

"Fuck, man," Garrett replies with a contemplative look. "It's bullshit that there isn't a way to match people up by the kinky shit they like to do in the bedroom."

Immediately, the table breaks out in laughter. Because this is what Garrett does. He makes jokes and expects a roll of amusing reactions after every sentence that comes out of his mouth, something we've come to anticipate.

"I'm fucking serious. How nice would it be if you could meet up with someone who likes the same twisted shit you do? You wouldn't have to hide it or be embarrassed by the kinks that get your panties wet."

"You're fucking crazy, Garrett," Hunter replies, but by the time I set my empty glass down on the table, I can't get the thought out of my head. Why don't dating apps match people by their kinks? Or better yet…what if you could hire someone to fulfill those desires?

And a safe place to indulge in them.

It dawns on me at that moment that a group of people with experience in the entertainment industry might have the right skills to pull something like this off. If only we had the guts to take the leap. It could start with a dating service for more than just booty calls and hookups—but something serious where people didn't have to feel so ashamed for what they enjoy.

It could only grow from there. An app to a service…and then someday, a real kink club.

"I am not," Garrett argues. "Who here doesn't have some freaky bedroom desires you've always wanted to do but are too afraid to ask? I mean, obviously, Emerson isn't afraid to ask."

They laugh again, and Hunter elbows me in the ribs, but I don't reply because I'm still thinking about this idea.

"Come on. I'm serious," Garrett says. "Out of all the shit you've done, what is the one thing you wish you could ask for? You know you have something. So let's hear it."

"You first," Maggie replies with a smug grin. As the only woman, and a slightly reserved one at that, Maggie has mastered the art of spinning conversations around on us, keeping the attention off of her whenever she can.

"Fine," he says.

I sort of tune them out for a minute while they each share their deepest, darkest sexual fantasies because, like Garrett predicted, everyone has one. And they're not all that weird really.

It has me thinking…if everyone at this table has their specific kink they're too afraid to talk about…then does everyone at this bar? Everyone in this town? The country? The world?

"All right, Emerson," Hunter says, nudging me in the shoulder. "Your turn."

"Oh, that's easy," Garrett cuts me off. "Didn't you hear his story? Emerson likes to degrade and get punched in the face for it."

The crowd erupts in laughter, and I join in, but I don't respond. With a smile around my glass, I take a drink, but I don't indulge any more. Because they may think degradation is my style, but that's not it at all.

The next morning, we get the call that the company we work for is going under. They're filing for bankruptcy and we're all out of a job, but before any of us can file for unemployment, we have a business plan. I head the company. Garrett handles the clients. Hunter works with the developers. And Maggie manages all of us. And it's that easy.

Salacious Players' Club is born.

Rule #1: Never put up with a douchebag boyfriend—dump that loser.

Charlie

"What the fuck is wrong with you, Charlie?" Beau snaps when he sees me pull up with my windows down. My jaw clenches as I climb out my car and slam the door behind me. I glance back at my little sister, watching from the passenger seat, and swallow down the humiliation at her hearing my stupid ex-boyfriend berate me on the front lawn of his new house. I don't even bother asking what I've done because, with him, it's always somehow my fault.

"Fuck off, Beau," I mutter through clenched teeth. "Just give me my half of the deposit so I can be on my way."

He stops in his tracks between the pickup truck and the front door of his house with a moving box in his arms. "I wish I could, but you weren't at the final walk-through with the landlord, so they sent the money to my dad. You'll have to pick it up from him."

"Your dad? What? Why?"

Beau carries the box labeled *Xbox shit* into the house and drops it on the floor next to his TV before returning to the truck. He's renting a new place with his best friend, and it would seem

6

SARA CATE

he's still holding a grudge against me for breaking up with him.
Beau and I dated for fifteen months, six of those we spent living
in a shitty rental where we quickly learned that we actually hated
each other. Apparently, we could date and sleep together casually,
but being in a mature live-together relationship was a no-go.

It only took three months in the apartment for him to cheat
on me—or to get caught, I should say.

"Yes, Charlie. My dad. He was listed on the lease as our
cosigner, and when you weren't around to pick up the deposit,
they sent it to him."

"Fuck," I mumble. "Well, I'm sorry I wasn't here, Beau, but I
was busy *working*." I make sure to emphasize the word, since I've
been the one carrying two jobs while he can barely hold down one
for more than a month.

"Frying corn dogs at the skating rink hardly makes you the
responsible one in this relationship."

"At least I could pay the bills."

"Let's not do this again," he shouts as he slams the tailgate of
the truck closed. Beau doesn't have *anger* problems, per se. He's
just an asshole.

"You started it."

I glance back at Sophie, watching from the car. She has a
tight-lipped expression with her eyebrows pinched together. A
look that clearly says she hates everything about the interaction
between me and my ex.

I'll give her credit. Since the beginning, my fourteen-year-old
sister has been the biggest Beau critic. Of course, back then I was
starry-eyed and blinded by love. And at only fourteen, she's still
immune to the sorcery of guys with sandy-brown curls, piercing
blue eyes, six-foot frames, and abs for days.

"So what am I supposed to do?" I ask when Beau continues
on with his unpacking while ignoring my presence.

"Well, if you want your half of the deposit, I guess you're
going to have to get it from my dad."

"Can't you just get it for me?"

For some stupid reason, I feel like *I'm* the one being a pain in the ass. Beau was always like this. He just had a way of making me feel worthless and desperate for any positive attention from him, so much so that I spent more time trying to please him than actually being happy—something that became abundantly clear after we broke up. Sometimes we really can't see the forest for the trees, as they say.

"You know I don't talk to that asshole anymore."

"So you're not going to get your half of the deposit back?"

"Not worth it," he snaps. I follow him back into the house.

"Well, I can't afford to lose that money, Beau."

With a long, annoyed sigh, he spins on me and rolls his eyes. "Fine. Here." He pulls his phone from his back pocket and types something quickly with a furrow in his brow. A moment later, my phone vibrates from my purse. "That's his address. Take it up with him."

Then, he just walks away, leaving me with my jaw hanging open. "Seriously? That's it?"

"If you really wanted the money, you should have met with the landlord yesterday."

"You're an asshole," I mumble, before turning and leaving him to unpack his shit in his new place. Walking down the driveway toward the car where my sister waits with her AirPods in, I do my best to not appear as bothered as I am. But as I climb into the driver's seat and shut the door, I feel the intensity of her sympathetic eyes on me. My forehead drops to the steering wheel as I fight the urge to cry.

"Beau's a dick," she says quietly, and I laugh. Letting Sophie cuss around me is sort of the big-sister deal. My mother has a fit when she hears either of us swearing, so I let Soph do it when we're alone. And in this case, I can't really argue with her.

"I know."

"At least you broke up with him."

"Yeah. Too bad I still don't have my money." Fishing my phone out of my purse, I open the text from Beau.

"Why not?"

"Because I'm an idiot and messed up. So now I have to go pick it up from his dad, and I'm willing to bet that asshole didn't fall far from the asshole tree."

"So let's go get it," she replies, looking a little too pumped to go pick up money from a complete stranger.

"I have no clue where this guy even lives. I'm not taking you." As I click on the address in the text, it pulls up the map app and shows a red pin on a street directly next to the oceanfront. "That can't be right."

"What is it?" she asks, leaning over.

"It says his house is over in the Oceanview district."

"Let's goooo."

I laugh again and ruffle her short, faded blue hair. It's still growing out from the buzz cut she gave herself last summer, so now it hangs just below her ears.

"Nice try, little Smurf, but you have piano lessons, and Mrs. Wilcox will have my head if you're late again."

Sophie rolls her eyes and gives me a dramatic pout as we pull out of Beau's driveway and head across town to the high school where Sophie gets her lessons. The entire way, I replay every moment of the fight with Beau, his harsh tone etched into my memory. And a feeling of dread settles in my gut as I think about having to confront his dad.

Beau rarely spoke about his family when we were together, and whenever I asked about them, he would just change the subject, as if he was ashamed or embarrassed. Getting his dad to cosign for us last year was hard enough, but shortly after, there was a rift between them and Beau stopped talking to him altogether. At first, we bonded over our mutual disdain for our fathers. And if Beau's dad is anything like mine, the whole interaction is sure to be a fucking blast.

Rule #2: No pouting.

Emerson

WHY IS SHE GIVING ME THAT LOOK? THE BETTIE PAGE LOOKALIKE with blunt black bangs and quite lovely curves is kneeling on the floor next to my desk, and she's…pouting. Her ruby-red lips are pursed, and she's just gazing up at me as I drink my coffee. Everything that she should *not* be doing.

This is a cry for attention, which makes sense, considering *my attention* is exactly what brought her here in the first place. I'm literally paying her to earn a soft pat on the head or a little affirmation—*earn* being the operative word. So far, this girl has done nothing but patronize me with all the fucking theatrics, and I'm about two seconds away from tossing her out the door. Literally.

If you want my attention, you have to earn it first. Behave. Do as I say. Otherwise, stay silent. That's not me being a dick; that's literally the scene we're playing, but this girl isn't playing by the rules. She knew exactly what she was signing up for when she took this job.

"Stare at the floor," I command without looking at her.

There's a disgruntled-sounding huff that escapes her lips

before she turns her gaze down to the floor. I sure hope she's not interested in being a brat because that is definitely not my style, and it said so quite clearly in the application.

The next three hours of her shift are practically insufferable, but I'm a gentleman, so I let her stay. She brings me my lunch, rests her opulent tits on my thighs when I kick my feet up during a boring conference call, and even earns a good stroke of her cheek when she manages to be completely silent while I write out an email.

But she's growing restless, and I can tell. Out of the corner of my gaze, I catch her pouting again, and I glance down to see her roll her eyes. That's it. Reaching down, I grab her jaw in my hand and turn her to face me. Her eyes go wide—she's nervous.

"Did you just roll your eyes at me?" I ask through gritted teeth.

"No, sir," she murmurs, and I catch a hint of excitement hidden under the delicate tremble in her voice. Yep, she's definitely a brat.

If punishment was my thing, she'd have earned it by this point, but even I know punishment is exactly what she wants. So instead of laying her over my lap or making her suck my dick for her blatant disrespect, I say, "Stand up. Gather your things. Have a good day."

"But—"

"Goodbye, Rita."

Turning away from her, I focus on my computer, dismissing her entirely.

With a scoff, she marches away, slips on her shoes, grabs her coat, and slams the door as she leaves. The moment she's gone, I dial Garrett's number.

"Let me guess. You didn't like her," he says by way of greeting.

"She just kept pouting. Do men really like girls who pout so much?"

Garrett laughs on the other end of the line. "We don't like what most men like, remember? It makes my job hard, sure, but I'm just trying to find you the right girl, Emerson."

"Apologize to Rita for me, and never send her back to my house."

"You got it."

The line is silent for a moment as I look over the emails from Maggie on the new app update from the developers.

"That's not true, you know," I mumble as I scroll through her messages. I can hear the white noise in the background, which means Garrett is in the car.

"What's not true?" he replies after a moment.

"When you said we don't like what most men like. I think our tastes are very much in line with the majority. We're just unique in that we're not afraid to pursue them."

"We aren't afraid to pursue them in a healthy way."

"Exactly."

"I'll send a new girl for you tomorrow," he says after a moment.

"Don't bother."

He lets out an exasperated sigh. "Are you sure? You seem stressed. We've got the club opening next week and investors to please and the state breathing down our necks."

It's true—I am stressed. On top of everything Garrett just mentioned, my son has not returned my phone calls in four months. But the idea of meeting a new pouty sub only stresses me out more.

"I don't think you even know what you want," he says absently, and I glance at my phone, on speaker.

"I thought I did. These girls want praise, but they don't want to earn it."

"Negative attention is still attention," he replies.

"And you know I don't like brats."

"I know, Emerson. But you're going to have to give someone a chance to impress you before you toss them out. Let me send you another one tomorrow. There are plenty of girls willing to do whatever you want."

"Maybe next week. Keep the application open."

"You got it."

After hanging up with Garrett, I sift through the pile of letters on my desk. It's mostly junk, but there's a handwritten envelope that grabs my attention. Cutting it open, I find a check. It's for two thousand dollars from a name I don't recognize. In the memo portion of the check, it says *Security Deposit for Apartment 623.*

It takes me a minute to realize this is Beau's address. Or at least it was. I had no idea he even moved, let alone had the security deposit sent back to me. Didn't he move in with that girlfriend of his?

The one he never even let me meet because he was too ashamed of me, I think grimly.

This could be good. If he needs the money back, he'll have to come to me to get it. Picking up my phone, I type out a quick text, trying not to sound as desperate as I feel.

Your landlord sent me your security deposit. I'll hold on to it for you. Come over whenever you need it.

Naturally, there's no answer. The entire screen of texts are all outgoing, no responses. I have confirmation from his mother that he's at least alive and doing okay, so I can sleep at night. I just wish he'd talk to me again. Too bad disappointment seems to be the theme of my week.

Rule #3: Always do as you're told—especially when it involves getting on your knees for a hot millionaire daddy.

Charlie

"THIS CAN'T BE RIGHT."

The house I'm looking at is a three-story Spanish-style mansion with manicured palm trees, arched windows, and a cobblestone driveway.

I swear if the guy I was just dating is secretly loaded, I'm going to be so pissed. We literally dug under our couch cushions for enough coins to get Taco Bell for dinner. There's no way *this* was where his dad lived all along.

Climbing out of the car, feeling very out of place in this bougie neighborhood on the coast, I brush the dog hair off my black velvet skirt and walk up the paved steps toward the front door. I can literally hear the ocean from here.

This is ridiculous.

This guy is probably wiping his ass with my thousand-dollar check right now.

I ring the doorbell, but it goes unanswered for about thirty seconds. Usually, I would be relieved that they don't seem to be home, and I'm spared the awkward encounter of having to speak to strangers, but I'm too poor to be relieved. I need the cash.

I promised Sophie I would take her to that Anime Fest in April, and her birthday is right around the corner. Also, I can't bear to live in the casita behind my mother's house forever.

So I knock again.

"Coming!" a sweet voice calls, and I hear high heels click against hard stone floors. When the door is pulled open, I stare into the big blue eyes of a woman with wavy brown hair and full pink lips.

"Hi…I'm here to see Mr. Grant."

She freezes with her eyes wide and her mouth hanging open. Then she glances down at her watch. "Oh, okay…I didn't know you were coming today, but it's fine. Come in, come in."

She didn't know I was coming? I didn't tell anyone I was coming here. Maybe Beau gave his family a heads-up that I would be picking up the check.

"Are you Mrs. Grant?" I ask. Last I knew, Beau told me his parents split when he was still a baby, but I guess it's possible he has a new wife that I never knew about.

A laugh bursts through her lips as she shakes her head. "God, no. I'm just helping him out today. He should be back any minute. You can wait for him in the office."

"Okay, thanks," I mutter, as she guides me through the expansive living room with high ceilings and marble floors to the open french doors on the other side. It leads to a large office with bay windows overlooking the ocean. I'm struck speechless for a moment as I gaze out at the open water.

"Wow…" I whisper, freezing in the doorway.

"That is a cute outfit," the woman says, looking down at my all-black ensemble. It's a sheer long sleeve top with a Peter Pan collar, a black velvet pencil skirt, and tights with black Docs to finish it off.

"Thanks," I reply with a smile.

"It's different, but I think he'll like it."

"What?" I ask, but her phone rings, so she steps away. While she answers it, rambling on about some business stuff I don't bother paying attention to, I meander around the room, taking in the style. Something feels off to me after that comment about him liking my outfit. Is this how women treat him around here? Like his opinion on our attire matters at all.

As creepy as that comment was, at least his office is beautiful. Unlike the cold, sterile feel of the rest of the house, the floor in the office is covered with a rich, scarlet-red rug and the mahogany desk is large, with two deep gray armchairs facing it. My fingers graze the fabric of each one.

"He's coming," the woman snaps. "You should probably be on your knees."

Assuming I misheard her, I glance back with a look of confusion on my face, but she's already scurrying out of the room, closing the french doors behind her.

Did she seriously just say I should be on my knees?

This place is giving me some seriously weird vibes. I'm glad I didn't bring Sophie. Now I'm starting to understand why Beau didn't want me to meet his dad. I need to just get my check and get the hell out of here.

I turn to leave the office and ask her what's going on, but then *he* steps into view. They are in the foyer, which I can see through the windows of the french doors, and they're talking while the woman moves toward the exit. I can't make out what they're saying, but I'm too stuck on the man she's talking to.

I've never even seen Beau's dad in pictures, so I had no idea what to expect, but it wasn't this. He's tall, with a bulky frame and tan, sun-kissed skin. His dark hair is impeccably styled to the side with hints of white at the temples and a streak at the top. He's wearing a suit, an expensive-looking one in a deep, navy blue.

Only able to make out his profile, I can see enough to tell that his flawless suit and body are paired well with his impeccable face. He has a strong brow, chiseled jawline, and a sandy, cropped beard. I'm staring at him as he turns his head toward me, and my blood practically boils in my cheeks under his gaze. I quickly turn my head, facing the ocean as he walks toward the office.

Once he's entered the room, it's as if everything in it shrinks, including me. After closing the door behind him, he strips off his jacket, hanging it on the tall oak rack. My mouth goes dry as my eyes cascade down his broad shoulders and the muscles of his back through the taut fabric of his shirt.

"Hi, I'm Charlie," I start. My hands are clasped in front of me, and I don't know why I feel so nervous all of a sudden. I'm not normally so skittish.

"You should start on your knees. Never be on your feet when I enter the room. And you don't speak unless I ask you to. When you do, you will address me as 'sir' and nothing else. Is that understood?" His voice is deep and cold, like it comes directly from the depths of the ocean. I'm stuck on his words, trying to make sense of them. My body is suddenly in a panic when I get the eerie feeling I just walked into something I wasn't supposed to.

"Excuse me?" I stammer. He freezes in his spot, his eyes skating over my body head to toe, and I feel a flush of warmth up my spine.

"On your knees," he barks out. My breath is punched out of my body. I should be running and screaming, and I definitely should *not* be considering lowering to the floor for him. Is he some sort of chauvinistic jerk who thinks all women should bow to him or something? And if that idea gets my blood pressure rising with rage, why do I feel so randomly...aroused?

"Why?" I ask.

He reacts like I've slapped him. "Well, you want your money, don't you?"

Jesus fucking Christ.

No, no! Charlotte Marie Underwood, don't you dare even

consider this for one second. This manipulative bastard does not control you, and you do not have to kneel on the carpet for him! That's *your* money, and you don't have to do shit for it.

But he's watching me with fire in his eyes, as if he's waiting for me to obey. Every rational part of my brain is shouting at me to tell this guy to fuck off, get bent, and eat a bag of dicks…but the rational part of my brain is not in control at the moment.

He is.

My knees actually start to bend, and I cannot believe myself. When they hit the carpet, I expect to feel utterly humiliated. I want to be enraged. Instead, I'm still gazing up at his face, waiting to see what this psychopath has in store for me next.

He doesn't want me to…you know…have sex with him just to get my thousand bucks back, does he? I draw the line there.

I think.

Yes, yes, I definitely draw the line there.

"Much better," he says warmly, and a strange sense of calm washes over me.

Then he steps closer, until he's within arm's reach, at which point I get a whiff of his intoxicating cologne. I'm gazing up at this mountain of a man when he reaches out a hand and strokes my jawline before taking my chin in his grip.

Hello, inappropriate, my inner alarm is blaring. This is very, very, very fucking inappropriate, but how the hell am I supposed to get out of it now? I've already kneeled.

"Normally, I'd want your eyes on the floor, but I want to look at you." He tilts my chin up as he examines my face.

I can't breathe. I can't move. I can't do anything because I am defenseless prey in his hands. He's a lion and I'm a meek gazelle caught between his teeth.

His features soften, and the corner of his lip twitches. "Lovely."

That word drips like warm honey trickling down my spine.

When he lets go of my chin, he spins away and walks to the other side of his desk.

"Where did Garrett find you?" he asks.

"Garrett?" I stammer, confused. Does he mean Beau?

"I told him not to send anyone today, and you clearly need more training, but—"

It's like someone snaps in front of my face, waking me up from this hypnosis. "Wait, what?" I bark out, interrupting him.

His head snaps in my direction, looking offended by my audacity to cut him off.

"Who is Garrett? What training are you talking about?"

"What is your name?" he asks slowly.

"Charlotte Underwood. I'm here to pick up a check from you."

"Charlotte? What check—" There is a twitch in his eye at the exact moment he realizes something is wrong, and all of the control and calm melt off his face until he looks scrambled and apologetic. "Jesus, get up."

I jump to my feet.

I watch as he rubs his brow line, looking pensive and distraught. "You're Beau's girlfriend," he says with a groan.

"Ex," I correct. He glances up at me with a hint of surprise on his face.

"You broke up?"

That's what he's focusing on right now?

"Yes."

Letting out an exhale, he reclines in his seat, and I wait for him to say something.

"I just need half of that check. He gave me your address and told me to come get it."

There's a wince in his expression and he goes back to rubbing his forehead. "Of course. How much do you need?"

I watch as he reaches into the drawer of his desk, pulling out a checkbook and a pen.

"The deposit was for two thousand, and half of that was mine."

When his eyes dance up to greet me again, I feel myself almost cower. He's so intimidating, and maybe that's where Beau gets it from, although Beau *acts* more powerful than he really is. This guy just *is* powerful, no denying that.

He scribbles out the check, rips it from its place, and passes it to me. Quickly, I step forward and take it. I should run away right now. I have what I came for, the awkward mix-up is behind us, and I have no further reason to stay, but I feel stuck in my spot.

"Charlotte, I have to apologize. I'm afraid I thought you were someone else when I found you in my office."

He won't look at me as he speaks, just unbuttons his sleeves and begins rolling them up. I'm fixated on the movement of his hands and the way that tight white shirt looks against his tan skin.

I swallow. "Who did you think I was?" I ask, knowing full well I have absolutely no right to that answer, but I'm nothing if not stubborn and reckless.

His eyes are back on my face again. "It's not important."

"Someone who works for you? Or someone you…hire?"

He glares at me, his eyes squinting with intensity as he realizes what I'm implying.

"Like I said, it's not important, and I'd appreciate you not sharing any of this with Beau."

"I don't talk to him anymore, and I don't plan to."

His jaw clenches as he exhales the word "Fine."

Turning on my heel, I head toward the door, reading the check as I go, feeling utterly humiliated and irritable because of it. And just as I reach for the door handle, I picture Sophie's face. And I remember that her birthday is coming up and how those Anime Fest tickets are expensive, and she wanted VIP passes to meet her favorite illustrator.

So I pause.

Oh God, this is stupid, but I have to try.

I turn around to face the person who intimidates me more than anyone I've ever met. And when I see him there, filling up that large chair behind that giant desk in front of floor-to-ceiling bay windows, it makes sense to me why girls would come in here and kneel for him. I bet he's not used to girls who talk back, challenge him, give him hell.

But he owes me. I *got on my fucking knees* for him.

"You know…I might see Beau again, actually," I say carefully.

He glances up at me with a curious notch in his brow.

"I hope I don't accidentally let any of this slip…"

Oh, you are bold, Charlie.

My hands are shaking, and I can't let him see me falter, so I quickly clutch them behind my back. I hold my head up high, shoulders back, and I look him right in the eye.

Without another word, he pulls out his checkbook again, and the look on his face says he is not happy at all, but I remind myself that I don't care. I don't care if he's mad at me or hates me or that I'm making him angry.

Except I do. I do care, and I hate the disappointed scowl on his face as he scrawls out another check. But I need this money, and I'm in the position to get it.

Do it for Sophie, I remind myself.

"What number might help you remember to keep quiet?" he says with a grunt.

I quickly lick my lips. Fuck, I don't know. So I'll just go with the price of the Anime Fest with VIP passes. "Two fifty."

He glances up at me as if he's surprised. Too much? Too little?

"Two hundred and fifty?"

I nod. He seems to contemplate that for a moment before going back to filling it out. Again, he rips it from the book and holds it out for me.

Quickly, I cross the room, and I notice the way he's watching my body as I hurry toward him. Then he meets my eyes, but he doesn't let go of the check right away. Instead, he looks like he wants to say something. I wait, hoping he's not about to argue with me again.

Finally, he lets it go.

"Thank you."

He nods his head, and I turn to run out of his office. I don't stop until I reach my car. Dropping into the driver's seat, I finally let out the heavy breath I was holding.

I glance down at the two checks in my hand. The first for one thousand, and the second for five thousand.

What the...

Is this a mistake? I keep rereading the number written, wondering what exactly I'm missing. For a second, I actually consider running back into the house to tell him he made a huge mistake. Then I notice in the memo of the check, there is a phone number followed by three letters: SPC.

They aren't his initials. But something about that note makes me think he wrote the amount out on purpose. So I don't go back in. I mean, he's loaded. Five thousand might be a mortgage payment for my family *and* tickets to Anime Fest for me, but for him, it's probably nothing.

I let out a squeal of excitement and drop the checks into the passenger seat as I start my car and hurry home.

Was humiliating myself worth five grand? It sure fucking was.

Rule #4: After a humiliating day with your ex's dad, tacos and margaritas are always the answer.

Charlie

SOPHIE IS IN HEAVEN AS THE WAITRESS PLACES A SERVING OF FRIED ice cream bigger than her head on the table. Meanwhile, my mom is next to me sucking down a margarita that's even bigger than hers.

My sister offers me a spoon, and I take it with a smile. We dig in, barely breathing between bites of the sugary caramel-vanilla concoction.

"Wow, Charlie. Thanks for taking us out to dinner," my mother says with a tipsy smile. It's nice to see her so relaxed. With the extra shifts she's been picking up at the hospital, I know she's been stressed.

"My pleasure," I mumble around a mouthful of ice cream.

"Freeze brain!" Sophie shrieks, clutching her forehead. Mom and I laugh at her misspoken phrase, which she's been using since she was a toddler and we never had the heart to correct. So we all call it a *freeze brain* now.

When I came home with five thousand more than I expected to, I immediately told them to get dressed for a dinner out. It's Taco Tuesday, after all.

I didn't bother to mention *how* I came to have the five grand, but it wasn't important. As far as they're concerned, the extra cash was just the security deposit, and that was that.

Why did he leave me his number?

Why would I need to call him?

And what is SPC?

I googled it. I came up with a lot of responses that didn't seem helpful. There's a Sicilian Pizza Café eight miles away from my house, though, so that's good to know.

I zone out while shoveling ice cream into my mouth, thinking about the way he touched my cheek, how strangely gratifying it felt when he said that one word: *lovely.* He didn't call me pretty or say *you look nice.* This was different. It was…approval.

What a ridiculous thing to feel so good about, some stranger's praise. Not even a stranger, really. *Beau's dad.* I get a full-body cringe every time I think about it. I mean, yeah, he's a good-looking guy, but he has to be like…*twenty* years older than me. He's literally my dad's age. Double ick.

And what exactly was he praising? My face. I hate my traitorous body for how turned on I felt in that moment, but that's just a natural reaction, right? Because I am a full-fledged, card-carrying, fist-pumping feminist. The *last* thing I need to be satisfied with my life is a man's approval.

It just felt nice. That doesn't mean anything.

And the fact that being on my knees for him was comforting is just ingrained generational misogyny. Thanks, patriarchy.

After mulling the situation over in my head, I've come to the conclusion that Beau's dad thought I was a prostitute. It's the only thing that makes sense. And apparently, he's into submissive sex workers, which is cool—I mean, to each their kinky own, right?

So why can't I stop thinking about it? Why does my brain seem to think there's something worth hanging on to from this experience? And why did he bother leaving me his phone number?

"To breaking up with Beau," my little sister announces, holding up the last spoonful of ice cream like she's making a toast.

"Sophie!" my mom scolds her.

"It's okay," I reply. Then I clink my spoon against my sister's. "He wasn't any good for me. It's better to be alone than to be with someone who's bad for you."

The table goes silent, and the memory of my dad fills the air like an awkward fog. He left about a year and a half ago because he couldn't let his ignorance go. He didn't approve of the way my sister lives her life, and his own stupidity cost him his family. But we're better without him, something I remind Sophie of as often as I can.

When love becomes toxic, it's not love anymore.

And then I went and stayed with Beau for far longer than I should have, three months after I caught him cheating, letting him talk down to me, making me feel like crap, and questioning everything about myself.

So I can't exactly blame my sister for wanting to raise a spoon to the breakup.

"You deserve better, Charlie."

"I know," I reply, staring at the leftover caramel and chocolate sauce on the plate.

"I think you dated a jerk because you think you deserve a jerk."

I glance up at her, my brow creased in confusion. "Dude, you're fourteen! How are you so wise?"

"I read smart books," she replies with a laugh.

"Oh, then I guess I'll have to show Mom your e-reader. Let's see how smart she thinks *Mating the Werewolf* is."

"What?" my mom asks, tearing her tipsy attention away from the ice left in her margarita glass.

"You brat!" Sophie screams, tossing her napkin at me. Her cheeks are tinged pink from embarrassment, and I can't keep my laughter in.

———

Lying in my pool-house room that night, I can't stop thinking about what happened today. Before cashing the check, I scrawled his phone number on an old receipt in my purse. I couldn't seem to part with it yet. It's held tightly between my fingers, and the tone of his voice rings through my ears like an echo.

Lovely.

There's no way I could ever call him. That's insane. I'm sure he was just giving this to me in case I needed help or wanted to keep in contact…because of Beau. It was totally a *dad* move. So I don't know why my brain seems to be stuck on this idea that he wants me to call him for any other reason.

I toss the number into my trash bin next to my bed and turn off the light. But instead of drifting off to sleep, I find myself tossing and turning for almost an hour. I keep reliving that moment over and over, where he called me lovely and stroked my face.

Let it go, Charlie.

But I can't. And a minute later, I'm picking up my phone again. This time instead of googling SPC, I put *Emerson Grant* into the search bar. I don't know why I was so afraid of looking him up earlier, but I think I was too nervous. If I knew too much about him, he'd get under my skin, so the less I knew, the better.

But right now, my curiosity won't let me rest. So I'm going to scratch this itch once and then move on.

Those three letters, *SPC*, pop up first, just under his photo and title: CEO.

I click on the link, and it goes to a black screen with a box in the middle, declaring this site *Members Only*. Well, shit. There's a place to input a password, but I clearly don't have one, so I backtrack.

Scrolling down a little farther, I keep digging. There's information on him and his work history, a lot of vague details about his education, and a few dashing photos of him in his twenties and thirties, mostly in tuxes and at important-looking events. But it's not until page seven of this never-ending Google search that I find what I'm looking for. Apparently, someone else was curious too and posted everything I'm dying to know.

Salacious Players' Club. A dating/escort service, soon-to-be expanding operations to a full-service members-only club in California's Briar Point district.

He owns a…dating service? And what the hell does a members-only club mean?

Clicking through post after post, I nearly drop my phone when I land on what looks like a soft-core porn site. It's a blog titled: *Madame Kink's West Coast Escapades.* The woman on the screen is wrapped in tight leather, holding a whip and wearing a bone-chilling smile. Words like *kink, slave, submission, bondage,* and *exhibitionism* stare back at me from the screen.

"What kind of dating service is this?"

Suddenly, I'm twenty pages deep in a kinky rabbit hole, and I can't stop clicking. Apparently, Madame Kink has some experience with Emerson's…club, er, services or whatever. And she has journaled her way through each interaction.

The SPC is a groundbreaking service in sexual liberation for both men and women. Finally, a place where we can explore our desires in a safe *and healthy (and oh-so fulfilling) manner. Mr. Grant and his team are real pioneers, and I hope to see this club's services spread across the country.*

I have to gulp down the ball of nerves lodged in my throat. Am I dreaming right now? Something about all of this tells me this dating service doesn't pair you up with people who also like to do yoga and take long walks on the beach. According to Madame Kink, people who like to be bound and gagged can easily find other people who like to…bind and gag. Is this really what Beau's dad does? My brain cannot seem to wrap around any of this, but I'm too far in now to discontinue my search.

Can't…stop…clicking.

This blog is like a dummy's guide to kink, and I scroll through a multitude of things I don't understand. There's extensively more to it than I ever thought, and there are a lot of things I'm a little too afraid to read about, but my eyes do catch on one thing in particular.

Praise kink.

Against my better judgment, I click on it. A page pops up with a woman on her knees and a man's hand holding her by the chin. She's staring up at him as if he's God himself, and my stomach churns. That's what I did today, wasn't it? I let him put me in that position, and I *liked* it.

"Nope." Quickly, I swipe the screen away and toss my phone on the nightstand. "Nope, nope, nope." I am *not* that kind of girl, and I have absolutely no interest in finding guys who want to make me get on my knees while they call me pretty. Fuck that.

It's almost two when I finally drift off to sleep, after putting all thoughts of Emerson Grant and Madame Kink and the Salacious Players' Club out of my mind.

But apparently, my mind has other plans because my dreams are filled to the brim, reliving every moment in his office, the man in the suit replaced by Madame Kink herself, who then morphs into Beau. Instead of fighting against the act of kneeling, I actually beg for his attention. I'm clawing at his legs, chasing after him like a dog, but he only makes me feel worse, telling me how pathetic I am instead of how lovely.

It's excruciating, but finally, everything changes when it's Beau's dad looking down at me. Even in my dream, I have some sense of awareness that this isn't real and that it's okay to like it because I will wake up eventually and no one will know.

Except in my dream, I want more. I reach out and touch the soft cotton of his slacks, feeling the muscle of his legs underneath. I fumble with his belt, staring at him from the floor. He strokes my head and overwhelms me with a feeling of euphoria. And I keep struggling with his belt, desperate to get his dick out. And just as I get the zipper down, I wake up.

My alarm blares on my phone, and I let out a groan. My body is a live wire, anxious and horny—not exactly the way I wanted to start my day. I seriously need help. Trying to have sex with my ex-boyfriend's dad in my dreams...just lovely.

Rule #5: When the hot millionaire daddy walks into the skating rink to offer you a better-paying job, you take it.

Charlie

THE ANXIOUS AND HORNY MOOD I WOKE UP IN THIS MORNING stays with me all day, and not even some detachable showerhead time could suppress the way that dream made me feel. At work, the whole thing plays over and over in my mind, making me spacey and a little irritable.

I'm stocking a box of new skates when a deep and oddly familiar voice from the other side of the counter makes me pause, and I'm actually wondering if my sleep-deprived brain just conjured the sound.

"Eleven and a half, please."

I lean back and peer at the customer that made the request and almost scream when I recognize the tall, dark-haired man standing on the brightly colored carpet, his hand resting on the tall lacquered counter. Trying to duck back around the wall, I silently pray he didn't see me. *What is he even doing here?*

"Hello, Charlotte," he says, and my eyes widen.

Nervously, I shove the skates onto the shelf, not even checking to see if I put them in the right place, and gather up my shredding confidence to greet him.

"Hi," I stammer before glancing around to see if anyone is within earshot. It's Wednesday, and we just opened fifteen minutes ago. With the exception of some homeschooled kids and a few regulars, there won't be any actual customers here until tonight.

"Please call me Charlie."

"I was joking about the skates," he adds with a hint of a smile on his face. "I won't be skating."

A forced, awkward laugh bubbles up from my chest as I approach the counter. There goes any hope of trying to act natural.

Seeing his face stirs up memories of my dream and how I was clawing for his dick like a sex-crazed nympho. I cover my cheeks, hoping to hide my blush.

"How did you find me?" I ask.

He holds up his phone, showing me a photo of me in a group of skaters, dancing on the floor in a colorful outfit during our Neon Nights event. "Instagram."

"Oh." Could this be any more mortifying?

He must be here because he realized his mistake writing that check he gave me yesterday and he's here to collect. I've already cashed it and made an extra payment on my school loan, so this is about to be an awkward conversation.

"Listen…" I say carefully.

"Do you have a moment to talk?" he asks, cutting me off.

"Of course," I stammer.

Turning around, I look for Shelley, the owner of the rink and an old friend of my mom's, but she must be in her office or out back having a cigarette. Instead of going on break, I gesture toward one of the old plastic booths against the wall. He nods and takes a seat, and it's hard not to laugh at the sight.

Beau's dad is huge, bigger than I noticed yesterday. He must be six three, with wide shoulders and a broad body. Like a… muscly dad bod. If that's even a thing.

He also looks ridiculous in the booth because he must be a

bajillionaire who hasn't stepped foot in a roller rink or sat in a booth in his entire life. I'm sure if he takes women on dates, it's on a yacht or to Montenegro, not to a cheap roller rink to eat pizza and drink beer. That's far more *my* reality, which is fine. I mean… dates to Montenegro wouldn't be terrible, but it's just a sliver out of my league.

"What can I do for you?" I ask as I take the seat opposite him.

He opens his mouth and then shuts it, and it dawns on me that he's about to bring up something that could be mildly uncomfortable, and I'm already dreading that it's going to be about what happened yesterday. Especially after looking through everything on his website.

I quickly save him the discomfort. "If this is about yesterday, it's okay. You don't have to say anything. It's fine."

"It's not about yesterday," he replies. "At least, not really."

"About Beau then?"

His attention piques and it feels like our conversation takes a hard left the moment his son is brought up. "Have you spoken to him?"

My shoulders fall and I tighten my lips. "Mr. Grant, I told you. We broke up. I'm not going to talk to Beau anymore."

It feels like a harsh line to deliver, but I think he needs to understand that Beau is out of my life for good. I can no longer be a lifeline to his son.

Something in him deflates, and his brow furrows as he leans back in his seat. Then he just comes out with it, like ripping off a Band-Aid. "Ms. Underwood, I'd like to offer you a job."

For a split second, I get excited. A job? A real paying, adult job. Something I would actually want to put on a résumé. No more corn dogs or antibacterial shoe spray.

Then I remember what I found last night—what he thought I was there to do—and heat floods my cheeks. "Oh…"

He clears his throat. "It's a secretary job, Ms. Underwood. A *regular* secretary job."

"Oh," I repeat, this time with less hesitation. I keep my eyes completely averted from his gaze. "So…"

"Do you have a question?" he asks after a long awkward moment.

"There won't be any…kneeling in this job?"

A hint of a smile tugs at the corner of his mouth. "No kneeling. Mostly paperwork."

I clear my throat, still keeping my eyes on the walls, the rink, the skaters…literally anywhere but at the handsome and intimidating man on the other side of this table.

He crosses his arms, furrowing his brow. "Is there something else you want to ask me, Charlotte?"

The way he says my name sends tingles up my spine. It's the only reason I don't correct him. No one calls me Charlotte. It's Charlie and has been Charlie since I was about eight years old.

It's the only reason I finally draw my eyes toward him, letting our gazes meet. He's so handsome, it's almost hard to look at him, but he doesn't shy away from the contact. In fact, he almost seems to stare at me longer than is generally accepted.

"Did you think I was a…prostitute?" I ask, hovering over the table and whispering the last word, as if anyone could hear anything while "Groove Is in the Heart" blares over a strobe lit rink.

He leans forward to match my position, his watch clanging against the linoleum table. "No. I didn't think you were a prostitute."

We simply stare at each other for a moment, both of us hunching over the booth and our faces so close it probably looks like we're either sharing dirty secrets or about to kiss.

"Are you going to expand on that or make me use my imagination?" I ask when he doesn't give me any more information.

There's a hint of mischief in his eyes as he licks his lower lip and leans away from me. "I think I want you to use your imagination. What exactly are you imagining?" That sounded flirtatious, but I don't call him on it. Instead, I answer his question.

Except, I have no clue what I'm imagining, and I'm not sure how dirty I feel comfortable getting. This feels way too intimate. To counteract the sudden tension between us, I force myself to sound as casual as possible. I could tell him that I've already researched everything about his company, but I sort of want to make him explain it to me as if I know nothing.

"Well…do you have a lot of random women just show up in your office ready for you to bark orders at them and get on their knees for you?"

"Sometimes," he replies confidently, as if that wasn't the craziest thing he's ever confessed to. *Seriously, who is this guy?*

My mouth goes dry.

"And you pay them…"

"Yes, I do."

"Well, I hate to break it to you, but that sounds a lot like prostitution."

"Prostitution involves sex, Ms. Underwood. I don't have sex with women for money."

My eyes widen. He said sex—*twice*—and it stirs up a mixture of arousal and unease in my belly. I clench my thighs together.

"Well, then what exactly do you do with them?" I ask.

"That sounds like a personal question." He's toying with me again. "I told you to use your imagination, so go ahead then. If I'm not having sex with them, what do you think I hire them to do?"

I have no earthly idea. I didn't really get that far into the website. So I gnaw on my bottom lip as I run through what I know so far.

"You can't possibly just pay women to kneel in your office for you."

"Why not?"

"Because that's ridiculous. What's the point?"

"The point is I like it, and they are willing to do it."

I'm speechless. This can't be real. The confusion on my face morphs into a smile that pulls on my cheeks. This should really be humiliating for him, but he's not embarrassed at all. And it really has me wondering something very wicked. "So…"

But I stop myself. I can't finish the sentence. It's too close to flirting, too…intimate.

Fuck it.

"So?" he echoes, impatiently waiting for me to finish.

"So how did I do?" I desperately want to bury my face in my hands or hide under the table or even pull the fire alarm, but if he's going to be so flippant and nonchalant about this, then so will I. Because I'm actually dying to know now. If he lives this secretive kinky life, then I want a peek behind the curtain. It's enticing, the idea of just dipping my toe into whatever forbidden, yet *exciting*, life he leads.

So instead of hiding, I force my body not to betray me, and I keep my spine straight and expression relaxed. As if I just asked him what the soup of the day is and not how well I performed as a kinky secretary slave.

After a moment of prolonged silence and a deep exhale, he says, "You did exceptional, Charlotte."

Wait, what?

"You seemed pretty exasperated with me," I reply. "I didn't do anything right."

"Well, in your defense, you didn't even know what you were doing."

A laugh bubbles out of my chest. "So how was that exceptional?"

He's pensive again, clearly at war with himself inside his head as he weighs his options, probably thinking that as the adult-ier adult here, he should really put an end to this inappropriate discussion. "I really shouldn't say…"

"Oh, come on. You started it." It takes some effort, but I manage to keep my casual tone and lazy approach.

And suddenly, there is no hesitation. The words just travel effortlessly across the table straight from his lips to my ears. "Ms. Underwood, you looked exquisite on your knees."

Even if I had a voice at this moment, I wouldn't know what to say. Instead, I'm rendered completely and utterly speechless, sitting across from him like a fish with my jaw hanging open, wondering how I went from a fight with Beau on his front lawn a couple days ago to this—his father telling me that I look good *on my knees.*

No, not just good. *Exquisite.* That word has lost all meaning to me now. Not a day will go by in my long life when I will hear those three syllables and not think of a man twenty years my senior, using that exact designation when referring to how well I kneeled for him.

It's ludicrous. Ridiculous. Narcissistic and sexist and demeaning and sensuous and flattering and…so many more words I can't seem to find at the moment.

And somehow the only words I manage to utter in response are "I did?"

"Yes," he replies, and it sounds hungry, like a lion growling before the kill.

Sitting here in my dumbfounded silence, I implore my brain to manifest a coherent thought outside *oh, that felt nice.* Finally, it settles on a question.

"And this kneeling job…is something your company hires girls for?"

"Yes, we do."

"And you thought I was one of those girls."

"Correct."

"Is that the job you're offering me now?"

"That would be highly inappropriate, considering your relationship with my son."

"Past relationship," I add because all of this sounds insane, it really does, but I'm not so sure I want him to exclude me from it all just yet. My curiosity has gotten the better of me.

"Still."

"You're not hiring me as one of your kneeling girls because of Beau…"

"No, Charlotte. I'm not hiring you as one of my *kneeling girls* because I need a secretary, and you seem like you need the money."

"That felt like an insult," I reply, and he laughs again.

"So you don't need the money?"

"Very funny. You know I do. But why would you hire me to be your secretary? You don't know anything about me."

"I know you lived with my son, now you don't. He won't talk to me, so let me help you instead. The job isn't much. Help out around my office, bring me coffee and lunch. That sort of thing." He glances around the rink. "And I'm assuming the pay will be better. With benefits."

There's really not much to think about, is there? He's offering me a real job with undoubtedly better pay. And I'm not going to lie, this company intrigues me. It sounds a lot more exciting than being a secretary for a banker or Realtor.

"You can take some time to think about it," he adds.

My head tilts and my lips press into a thin line as if to say *don't be ridiculous*. If he thinks I really need to think about it, he's crazy or just being condescending. As he moves to stand, I think of an important question that's just a little uncomfortable to ask, but I have to.

"Wait," I say, grabbing his arm. "Random question, but is your company Sal...vatious...club whatever—"

"Salacious Players' Club."

"Yeah." I nod, swallowing down my nerves. "Is it inclusive?"

He settles back into his seat. "Inclusive?"

"Yeah, LGBTQ friendly?"

His brow furrows and a sly smile lifts one side of his mouth. "Very. Why do you ask?"

"It's important to me," I reply, shutting down the conversation there. I'm sure he's now wondering if I'm secretly a member of the community, and if so, how, but I don't expand. He doesn't need to know that I'm the world's most fiercest ally because I have the world's cutest little cub to protect.

"Then in that case," I add as I stand up and put out my hand…
which I realize now is awkward and pretty much uncalled for.
That crooked smile stays on his face as he eyes my outstretched
arm and follows suit, standing up and taking my hand in his. His
bear paw dwarfs my little hand as he shakes it. But it's warm, and
his grip is firm enough to send butterflies down my spine.

"I assume this means you'll take the job," he replies.

As we stand here, shaking hands in a roller rink, I wonder
who has signed up for the weirder position here. Does Emerson
Grant know what he has committed to with me? Surely by now
he's picked up on the fact that I'm not some girly-girl chick, soft-
spoken and appropriate, and I'm not going to behave like a regular
secretary, *Mad Men* style.

But at the same time, I'm signing up to work at a company
that deals in freaky kinks and shit. I'm pretty sure neither of us are
cut out for normal.

Rule #6: Avoid malls for the risk of running into your ex while holding bags of lingerie you fantasize wearing for his dad.

Charlie

"Nine a.m. tomorrow," he says, all back to business. It's interesting, watching him change from serious to casual and back again. He seems like a man who hides himself behind a suit and his desk. It makes me wonder if he ever lets loose and relaxes. Does he crack jokes, watch trashy TV, get so drunk he says something really embarrassing? I'd pay to see that.

Beau is nothing like him. Beau is unfiltered, real, and raw. He's rough around the edges, and maybe that's what drew me to him in the first place. We met at the coffee shop I worked at, where he also held a job for a small amount of time before he went through something at home, which he never really confided in me about. He stopped coming to work and got fired.

But I stuck with him. I wanted the broken parts of him because I thought if I could love him through the storm, I would be rewarded with a love that was more intense and intoxicating. I was wrong. Instead of appreciating me for staying with him at his worst, he blamed me for little things when his life seemed to be going right. I wasn't the glue that held him together; I was the glue that held him in his pain and reminded him of his past.

After work, I head straight for the mall because I don't own a damn thing a secretary would wear. I'm imagining a silk shirt and pencil skirt, so that's what I'm going for. It's actually a lot harder to find than I expected.

But I do eventually find something. A black polyester pencil skirt that even I have to admit makes my ass look like a million bucks. An almost see-through white sheer blouse, and then, just for fun, I pop into the lingerie store to get a smoking hot black bra with panties and those little clips that hold up my thigh-high tights. Buying lingerie for a new secretary job is gratuitous, but I'm just in that kind of mood. Also…with what I know about his business, I kind of want to feel sexy under my clothes.

I stand in front of the mirror in the dressing room, looking at myself. I never considered myself sexy before, but as I stare at my full curves and the fleshy softness of my belly, I love the way I look in this. I see something sexy I never saw before. My ass is tight and round, and the fullness of my thighs looks hot in these stockings.

Then I start to think about Emerson and the women he hires. What could possibly be so bad about being someone's pet, sub, or slave? In the playful sense, of course. As long as it's consensual and everyone has something to gain, I don't see why it's so taboo.

I'm not going to beat myself up for wanting to feel the way I felt on my knees for him. A man like Emerson…I could be that girl. I mean…in the fantasies in my head, of course. He's just hiring me to do paperwork—he'd never really want a girl like me for that.

For one thing, he's so far out of my league, he might as well be in space. Emerson Grant probably dates women who don't live in their mother's pool house. He's so mature and handsome and rich, I bet they breed girls especially for him. They probably don't bite their nails or eat fried food and definitely don't take their little sister roller-skating every Saturday night. Meanwhile, I get my underwear from Target, and I don't buy shampoo that costs more than six dollars.

For another thing, he's Beau's dad. That's weird. And wrong. Beau would lose his mind if he knew. I'm pretty sure he'd go apeshit if he found out I was even taking this job, but I'm no longer subscribing to "things Beau cares about."

Wait, does he know about his father's company at all? Surely he does. Maybe that's why he doesn't like him. Maybe he doesn't approve. Makes sense, I guess.

After buying the underwear in both black and white, I spend my whole check from the coffee shop on clothes for my new job.

As I'm walking across the mall with about eight bags in my hands, I spot a familiar gait walking in front of me. Beau is crossing the aisle from the food court to the video game store. He's with…a girl.

And try as I might to stop and turn the other way, he spots me. Then it becomes an awkward stare-off where we both wish we hadn't just locked eyes. At this point, it would be too weird to turn around and avoid each other altogether. So I keep walking until we are standing just a foot apart.

"Beau, hi," I stammer, readjusting the bags cutting off the circulation to my hands.

"Hey, Charlie," he says very unenthusiastically. "Uh, this is Ella."

I give her an awkward wave.

"You did some shopping," he says, and I look down to notice the huge lingerie bag in front.

"Yeah, well, I got a new job," I say proudly. You're damn right I'm going to brag about it a little bit, even if I choose to omit where it is or who I'm working for.

"What is it?"

"Umm…a secretary position," I say.

He scoffs, a half laugh, and I feel a cool breeze of disappointment trickle over me. Then he eyes the pink lingerie bag again, his eyebrows lifting. "You need something from that store for your new secretary job?"

"Nope. That's just for me," I reply.

The girl on his arm is looking very uncomfortable, but I don't care. She probably doesn't even know that Beau was mine last week. Or maybe she does.

"Hey, did you pick up that check from my dad?" he asks.

"Yeah," I mutter quickly, searching his facial expression as if he could somehow know from that little bit of information that I am also going to be his dad's new secretary.

"Well?" he asks, looking at me like he's waiting for something.

"Well, what?"

"Well where's my half?"

You've got to be fucking kidding me.

"Your dad has it, Beau. If you want it, then go get it."

His jaw clenches as he glares at me, looking as if he's already lost his patience, and I want to run. I hate the way Beau makes me feel—like I've already failed before I've even tried. Like I am nothing but a constant disappointment, regardless of whether or not I was even attempting to impress him.

Then, he grabs my arm and guides me to the side, so we're out of the way of the mall's foot traffic. "Charlie, you know I don't talk to my dad. If you went and got the money from him, then where is mine?"

"He gave me *half* of the deposit, Beau. That's what I was owed, so that's what I took. You can be responsible for your own half."

"Beau." Ella calls for him from the middle of the wide aisle, but he just holds up a hand to her.

"Jesus, Charlie! You were supposed to take the *whole* check, so I could get mine. You just—ugh!"

It occurs to me about halfway through this sentence that I don't have to stand around and listen to him anymore. I no longer belong to him and I don't owe him anything. So before he even finishes what he's saying, I turn and walk away. I don't cuss at him or tell him how little and stupid he makes me feel. But I do have to fight back the tears as I reach the exit of the mall, hearing him yell after me.

The minute I'm alone, I feel a little bit lighter. His voice is still in my head, though, constantly reminding me what a fuckup I am.

Rule #7: Don't stare too long at your new secretary's cleavage.

Emerson

I was prepared for Charlotte to show up at my house in those same black boots I've seen her in twice now. I was prepared for her to be clumsy and nervous. I was even prepared for her to be late.

What I was *not* prepared for is her showing up five minutes early in a nearly see-through blouse and a black pencil skirt that makes my hands itch because of the way her ass fills it.

Highly inappropriate to look at my secretary and son's ex-girlfriend like that, I know, but in my defense, I'm not used to having a platonic employee in my office. The craving to see her on her knees in that outfit is damn near painful.

"Good morning," she says as she walks into my house at 8:55 a.m.

My eyes land on her deep red lipstick—is she trying to fuck with me?

"Morning," I grumble. Her heels click against the marble floor as she follows me into the house. Pointing to the entryway closet, I show her where to put her things.

"Jacket?"

"Oh," she stammers, starting to shrug out of the heavy wool peacoat. Putting a hand on her shoulder, I stop her and gently guide her to turn around. With her back to me, I lift the coat from her tiny frame, letting my gaze linger on the soft hairs brushing the back of her neck. After I hang her jacket up on the hanger, she turns around, and my eyes immediately fall downward, landing on her chest.

I was wrong. The shirt isn't almost transparent...it's *entirely* transparent, and she is wearing a black lacy bra underneath. What happened to the roller-skate girl or the one dressed in all black the other day? This feels like an ambush I wasn't ready for.

"Coffee?" I ask because my mind seems to be caught on lame one-word phrases.

"No, thank you."

"Come in then," I reply, placing a hand lightly at the small of her back and using the other to point toward my office.

I keep having to check myself. Her surprising appearance today has thrown me off. As hard as I try to stay natural and behave as I normally would, I keep seeing my actions as being too forward and too sexual. Which is *not* what I'm going for. She's *just* a secretary. Not a sub. This is not a scene. *Clear your head, dammit.*

After directing her to the chair in front of my desk, I hand her the packet Garrett gave me to have her fill out for payroll. Maggie had a small fit over me hiring a new employee, but I have faith we'll find room in the budget. I need a secretary, after all—an *actual* secretary, and Maggie is too busy managing all of us to do the work I need around here.

"So you work from home?" Charlotte asks.

"Yes, I do. We all do at the moment. The new building is in construction right now."

"Oh, that's exciting."

I fight back a smirk, picturing the blueprint for the new

building with the cages, stage, and fully-equipped private rooms. Yes, it is exciting, but I'm not going to hit her with all of that right now. Best to ease her into things.

"Do you have any questions about the company?" I ask.

Her eyes go wide. "Tons. I have tons of questions."

I have to bite back my smile again. "Well, go ahead then. Ask one."

"Umm…" She twists up her ruby-red lips and furrows her brow seemingly in thought. "So you hire girls to kneel and serve you. Is that what everyone does?"

"Not at all. That's just my style. There is an array of fantasies that our employees will fulfill."

"But no sex?"

"Not exactly."

"What does that mean?" she asks with a curious expression.

"It means that the money exchanged is not for sex. What they do behind closed doors is their business." Best to leave it at that. We find a lot of loopholes and loose language in the law books to work around, but that's what we have Xander for—the best lawyer in Briar Point.

The look on her face, tight-lipped and skeptical, says she doesn't quite believe what I'm saying, so I pry her some more. "What other questions do you have?"

"What other…*things* do people do?" she asks with a sort of curious delight in her eyes.

I have to give her credit. She doesn't look as uncomfortable as I expected her to be, and I love her open curiosity. There is still so much stigma attached with sexual fantasies and pleasure, it's ridiculous. But Charlotte doesn't seem bothered by that.

Standing from my desk, I walk around to the front, where I lean against its surface and cross my arms. "Anything and everything. As long as it's consensual and everyone is of age, anything goes."

"Like…tying people up and whipping them?"

I shrug. "Sure. If that's what they like. We also have clients who just like to watch...or *be watched*. Role-play. Degradation. Age-play, edging, objectification, bondage..."

With each word that comes out of my mouth, I watch Charlotte's eyes widen and her shoulders tighten, so I stop, giving her a moment to say whatever it is she's thinking, or rather, wondering. I mean...it's only nine in the morning. We might need coffee for this conversation.

"I don't know what half of those are," she replies.

"Well, it's not something you need to know for this job, but if you are curious, you can learn. There's no reason to be intimidated by all of it. I know it seems strange, but you'd be surprised how normal it really is."

A laugh escapes her lips.

"What?" I ask.

"Nothing, it's just...normal?"

"Everyone has a desire they think is kinky, Ms. Underwood. Thinking what we like is abnormal is the one thing we all seem to have in common."

Her grin relaxes, and she leans forward, giving me a full view of her tits that I have to force myself to look away from.

"Okay, then," she replies, resting her chin on her clenched fists. "What is *yours*?"

My head snaps back in her direction, and I glare at her in shock. Not because I'm offended by her asking that. I can't give a speech about how normal kinks are and then act like it's an affront to be interrogated to reveal mine. But I'm shocked because Charlotte is nothing like any girl I've had in my office. She's blunt in a way I'm not used to.

"You should already know," I reply, biting back my grin.

"The whole secretary on her knees thing?"

This time I do grin. "It's called a Dominant-submissive relationship."

She seems to deliberate for a moment, as if she's trying to tell if she likes the taste of something. I use the approximately three seconds of silence to imagine her in that role for me, and it's the most appealing vision I've had in a while. Isn't life grand like that? The forbidden fruit always tastes sweetest.

"What about me?"

I nearly choke, clearing my throat and waiting for her to elaborate. "What about you?"

Please, God, don't let her tempt me more than she already has.

"What do you think my kink is?"

She bites her bottom lip, and I can't resist the urge to mirror her actions, tugging mine between my teeth as well. Charlotte is beautiful in a mysterious and unique way. Her eyes are large and innocent looking, and her nose has a high ridge, making her look a little more regal than her attitude suggests. It's those wide red lips of hers that keep my attention, though.

"I don't know you well enough yet. Besides, that's really up to you to decide, isn't it?"

"I thought that was your job," she replies with a smile that shows her bright teeth in contrast to her scarlet lips. "You're supposed to help people find their deepest, darkest desires, aren't you?"

I can't tell if she's patronizing me or not, but I don't reprimand her for it. I think she's taking this as seriously as Charlotte can, assuming she's not an overtly austere person. It makes me wonder if she was this way with Beau.

Garrett is really better at this than me. It's his job, anyway. He can read people so well, much better than I can. It's something I'm sure stems from how much he likes to *watch*.

But I take a shot at it anyway, running through the things I know about Charlotte so far...

She's bold, fearless, outspoken with a healthy sense of humor. She would hate impact play, anything age-related or bondage. She might like to be watched, considering how see-through that shirt is and how prominently she displays her breasts for me now.

48 SARA CATE

Then I remember a certain expression on her face the other day while she knelt on the floor for me—to my own utter humiliation. But there was a blip of a moment when I held her softly by the chin and called her lovely. Her gaze softened and her posture almost melted into my touch. It seemed too natural to be fake.

When she notices my pensive expression change to amused, she speaks up.

"What?" she asks eagerly. "You look like you figured it out. What is it?"

Yes, I definitely figured it out. But I don't quite know if I want to disclose it to her. I don't know why, but I have a strange desire to keep this one to myself, like a small treasure. If I tell Charlotte she most likely has a strong praise kink, she'll share it with other people. Someday, it could be another man whispering all the dirty things I want to tell her, like how well she swallows his cock or how beautiful she looks while he pumps into her.

It's selfish of me, especially considering it can never be me doing and saying those things, and it would only benefit her in the future to know this about herself, but I want to hold on to it for just a little while longer.

"Nothing," I mutter as I stand up and walk back around to my chair.

"Oh, come on, tell me!"

"I told you," I reply sternly. "I don't know enough about you yet to determine that. If you'd really like to know, then talk to Garrett. You can ask him when you drop this paperwork off to him later today. For now, get to work."

My tone has gone cold, and the expression on her face sinks as she picks up the clipboard and pen, starting to fill them out with a new wrinkle between her brows.

If this week has proven anything to me, it's that I need to watch myself around this girl. She's too perfect to ignore and too forbidden to be mine.

Rule #8: It is possible to be dressed too provocatively even when you work for a sex club.

Charlie

"ALL DONE?" EMERSON IS TOWERING OVER ME FROM BEHIND AS I fill out the hundredth page of boring-as-hell paperwork.

"Was having to rewrite my name on each page of this packet really necessary?" I joke. When I glance up at him with a smile, he glares down at me, looking mostly unamused.

"Unfortunately, yes. Now, gather your things. I can drive you over to the club, give you a tour, and introduce you to everyone."

My spine straightens. Everyone? Club? I sort of thought this was going to be a one-location sort of job. I mean, I read about the club being built, but I didn't really expect to be going there. And meeting people—kinky people. My palms begin to sweat immediately, and I glance down at my outfit.

Now I know that when dressing for a new administrative job, you should really be wearing the world's most appropriate outfit ever, but for some reason, when choosing my garments this morning, I was out of sorts. I mean, it's not like I put on a see-through blouse and black bra by accident, but I was still so fixated on my first encounter in this office that I sort of went for something a little more…risqué than normal.

I wanted to…I don't know, impress him. No, impress isn't the right word.

Turn him on? Ick, no.

Please him. That's it. I wanted to wear an outfit that didn't just fit me but him too.

Not sure how I feel about that, but it is what it is.

"Now?" I ask.

"Yes, now. Come on. I'll drive."

He turns on his heel, grabbing his blue jacket and throwing it over his large frame. I follow him through his house toward the garage. While he walks, I can't help but stare at his broad shoulders that fit so well in that tight cotton shirt. It's light gray with a subtle damask design.

My gaze drifts downward and I notice the way he fills out those deep gray slacks, tight around his butt and thick thighs. I can see a resemblance in his and Beau's build. Beau is big too, but I've never seen him fill out a pair of pants like this before.

Straight to hell, Charlie. Straight to hell.

When we reach the garage, he opens the door and ushers me in. It's a nice garage, big enough to fit four cars, two wide and two deep, but he only has one parked in here. It's black and expensive looking. The car beeps to signal it's unlocked as the garage opens, and I cringe when I realize he's about to see my car.

He takes a moment to acknowledge my beat-up Subaru sedan with duct tape on the side-view mirror. His eyes linger for a moment on the embarrassing patch job.

"I'm not a bad driver," I say. "My little sister and I were just playing red-light fire drill and I got a little too excited."

His brow creases as he stares at me curiously. "Red-light fire drill?"

"Yeah. It's where you pull up to a red light and someone yells 'fire drill' and everyone has to get out and run around the car and get back into their seat before it turns green. Well, this one time, I got out and ran straight into my mirror. It went flying and I had to crawl under a truck to get it."

The wrinkle in his forehead deepens. "That sounds a little dangerous."

"It was, but it was fun." I wish he'd smile or something, but he's so broody. Those intense, dark green eyes stare at me without an ounce of humor. It makes me instantly uncomfortable.

"Can't say I've ever played," he replies, opening his driver side door.

"Yeah, well, I guess you just play different games."

His eyes flash in my direction, so I quickly duck into my seat to avoid that haunting gaze. When he climbs in next to me, I swear I catch a hint of a smile painted on his face before it vanishes.

The ride is silent, and I'm a little surprised to find out the location of this new building is actually downtown. It's not really a new building at all but an old brick warehouse that looks to be under renovation. The windows and doors are covered with brown paper and there are scaffoldings and trucks parked around the exterior. Just above the door is the company logo, sleek in black iron, a circle with the letters *SPC*.

Emerson parks the car on the opposite side of the street, away from the dirt and debris of the construction site. As we climb out of the car, I try to pull my skirt down a couple inches and cross my arms over my chest to hide the bra underneath.

Stupid, stupid, stupid.

As soon as we shut the doors of the car, a tall blond man in dusty jeans and a tight flannel shirt exits the building and marches in our direction. He has a hard hat on his head and two in his hand. There's a mildly disgruntled look on his face as he approaches us, but when he lifts his head and locks eyes with me, his expression suddenly changes. A smile stretches across his stubbled cheeks as his blue eyes skate up and down my body. When he turns his head, I spot a blond ponytail hanging under his hat, and when I get closer, I find myself staring at those chiseled cheekbones and full, pink lips. He's freaking gorgeous.

"Well, hello there," he crooned with his disarming gaze on me.

Emerson clears his throat, putting the attention back on him. "Drake, this is my new secretary, Charlotte Underwood. Charlotte, this is our general contractor, Drake Nielsen."

"A new *secretary*," Drake says with a sexy, low-tone drawl as he takes my hand and lifts it to his lips. There's something strange about the way he says *secretary*, but I'm too hypnotized by his attention to pick out what it is.

"Drake," Emerson snaps as if he's scolding the man. Drake doesn't even flinch, but he does give me a subtle wink. I finally realize, because my brain is moving a little slow with this Greek god staring at me like we're about to fuck, that Drake thinks I am one of Emerson's *special* secretaries.

And you know what? I don't hate it.

I almost don't want Emerson to correct him, but of course, he does.

"She's my *actual* secretary, Drake. Knock it off."

There's a hint of disappointment on the contractor's face as he lets my hand go. There must be some unwritten rule that people who *know of* and *partake in* the kinky stuff can be kinky and flirtatious around each other. But to the rest of us, they have to modify their behavior. Like we're the muggles and they're the wizards.

And right now, I hate being a muggle.

"That's me," I reply. "A boring secretary." I twist my lips into a knot and do my best to look downhearted.

Drake's rough hand runs along the length of my forearm like he's trying to enchant me. "We'll have to see about changing that."

Suddenly, a softer hand latches around my waist and I'm

tugged abruptly away from the contractor. "That's enough. We have work to do."

There's laughter from Drake as he follows behind us. "Don't forget your hats."

With a scowl on his face, Emerson grabs them out of the man's hands, keeping his body between mine and Drake's. The contractor doesn't follow us inside though. Instead, he begins barking orders at a team of workers on the scaffolding outside.

Emerson mutters in my ear, keeping my body close to his, "Stay away from him. He has no boundaries."

"What's his kink?" I ask, and Emerson's head snaps in my direction.

With his arm still around my waist, he stops me before we reach the door. "You can't just go around asking people what their kinks are."

"But you said—"

He's so close now, hovering over me like a shadow. "I know what I said. I just don't want you…" His voice trails off.

"You don't want me what?"

"You're just my secretary, all right? And you're my son's ex, remember? I don't want you getting involved in this stuff. So don't ask people their kinks and don't flirt with the men. Or women," he adds as an afterthought.

I feel my jaw clench and my shoulders tighten as I glare up at him. "You know I'm twenty-one, right? And remember that big speech you gave about this stuff being so…normal?"

The hand around my waist tightens, and I feel the eyes of other workers on us.

"Will you just listen to me, please? You're not ready for this, Charlotte."

In that moment, I hear Beau. I hear him telling me what I can and can't handle, making decisions for me and taking away my right to think for myself. So I snap, tearing my body away from Emerson's grasp.

"*I* will decide what I'm ready for. And my name is Charlie, not Charlotte." My tone is harsh, biting out each word with anger before I stomp away, tearing open the front door with abandon. He's quick on my heels, but I don't dare look at him, even after he approaches me from behind, not touching me this time.

I'm too fired up to really absorb what's happening around me. There are people working everywhere. They are laying tile and painting the walls while drills and other machines buzz loudly, echoing through the empty space.

"Emerson," a male voice calls from the other side of the build-ing. We pass through a lobby area with a tall desk and black tiles on the floor. Then we enter the main room, which reminds me of a dance club. There's even a stage at the front, and a team of guys are installing the tallest stripper pole I've ever seen.

Along the sides of the room are doors and two hallway entrances, one on either side of the stage. There's also a second floor with a wraparound balcony that lets those above look down at the club below. I can't seem to stop looking at everything, trying to imagine what would go on here, what all the rooms are for and what is down those hallways.

"This must be Charlotte," a male voice says as we approach a slender man in a suit.

He takes my hand and shakes it delicately, keeping his eyes on my face and not my breasts like the god of thunder outside.

"Charlotte, this is my partner, Garrett Porter."

"Nice to meet you," I reply.

Unlike Emerson, Garrett has a warm smile, showing his teeth as he grins. With honey-brown hair and a clean-shaven face, he has the look of someone who does a lot of business. He looks like a salesman, but with those scrutinizing eyes on me, I get the feeling he's reading me.

Yep, he's a salesman, all right.

"Is Maggie around? She has paperwork to give her," Emerson asks.

"Yep, in the office."

A broad, soft hand lands at the small of my back, but I'm still a little pissed at him, so I quickly step away, instantly missing the comforting touch.

"I'll find it," I mutter darkly. I turn back to find him clenching his jaw as he glares at me, and I'm overcome with a wave of disappointment, but I quickly brush it off.

Leaving him with the other men, I cross the open space, stepping over beams and tools, my shoes echoing with each step. Emerson doesn't say anything as I head down the hallway that leads toward the back of the building, so I assume I'm going the right way.

But this isn't just a regular hallway. It's broad with doors on each side and large windows. As I pass the rooms, I take a peek in, but they are still empty, each about the size of a bedroom, and I find myself gulping down my nerves. Will they really let people just go into those rooms and…

I freeze, peering into one. The walls are painted a deep red and it's still mostly bare, except for one large chair raised on a dais with gold decorative embellishments framing the red velvet seat. "Is that…" I say to myself, or at least I thought it was to myself.

A warm voice that is definitely *not* Emerson's finishes my sentence as he approaches me from behind.

"A throne," Garrett answers plainly. I quickly spin around and stare at him. He has a sly grin on his face, as if he's daring me to go inside. I glance down the hall for Emerson, and when I notice he hasn't followed and is still talking to the crew in the main room, I take Garrett up on his dare and step tentatively into the room.

"Why a throne?" I ask. It seems a little weird for a sex club. This isn't a Renaissance faire.

"Why not?" he replies casually, like it's obvious.

I swallow again. The chair is ginormous, and the platform it sits on has cushioned edges and plenty of space for…movement. I feel Garrett lean closer, his warm breath against my ear as he whispers, "Try it."

"Me? No. I'm not really a 'sit in a throne' type of girl."

"How can you know if you've never tried it?"

I pause, looking back at him. He's challenging me, and I can't quite tell if I really like this guy or sort of hate him. But I never turn down a challenge.

"Go ahead," he continues. His hand is soft against my back as he presses me toward the chair.

"What is even the point?" I ask, relenting to his nudges. Crossing the room, I climb up the step and touch the golden arms of the broad chair. The first thought in my head is that this throne is for kings, larger-than-life men, monarchs and masters. But as my fingers glide along the ridges and peaks of the decor, I correct my train of thought.

Why *can't* I sit in it?

Why have I let my own mind be groomed into believing this inferiority?

Turning around, I settle my weight into the seat, and the moment the backs of my thighs hit the crushed red velvet, it feels good. Crossing my legs, I stare down at the room, Garrett leaning against the doorframe watching me with a look of approval on his face.

"How do I look?" I ask. Judging by the way he's staring at me, I expect another compliment, and he opens his mouth as if to deliver one. But he stops, closing his lips, almost as if he isn't allowed. Instead, he ambles forward, stopping at the platform and circling around me.

"Now imagine how it would feel to have someone kneeling at your feet. Worshiping you, bowing to your presence."

I try to imagine it, but it feels so wrong. I can't seem to shake this idea that a man belongs here and I belong at his feet. Fucking patriarchy.

"Well, go ahead," I say with a wry smile as he steps in front of me. Let's see how he likes to be challenged.

He lets out a laugh. "Yes, ma'am." Then he faces me and drops to his knees on the velvet cushions with his eyes on my face. As he lowers his gaze, I watch him bend his head downward and bow down to me, his lips near my black stilettos.

There is no chemistry between us, but there is still a warm buzz of arousal coursing down my spine at the sensation. This big, powerful man is bowing to me, and it is intoxicating. I let myself imagine someone else in his place, someone I shouldn't think about.

As Garrett lifts up, he touches my leg, sliding his fingers up the side of my calf, and I can't seem to breathe at all. This feels forbidden, and not the good kind. Almost as if I'm...cheating?

"Now imagine what someone could do from this position," he says quietly. The raspy tone of his voice feels like it's echoing through my bones. And when I look down at him, I imagine another pair of eyes looking back.

His attention moves downward to the apex of my crossed legs. My mouth goes dry, and I have the undeniable urge to leave.

"What are you doing?" a voice thunders from the doorway, and I jump about three feet in the air. Emerson is glaring at us as I erupt from the chair. His arms are crossed, his fists clenched, and those wolflike eyes are trained on me with so much vitriol, I feel like I'm going to cry.

"Emerson," I stammer, waltzing across the room and trying to remain as casual as I can. I'm not interested in Garrett. I mean, he's gorgeous, but I just met him and I don't even know him... and why am I defending myself? I didn't do anything wrong.

"Your assistant was curious," Garrett replies as if the room isn't drenched in tension. "This room was my idea, you know," he adds.

"Naturally," Emerson replies through clenched teeth. Then his gaze lands on me and I swallow, trying not to shrink in his presence.

"The window can be adjusted for viewers or privacy, and the stockade will go off to the right."

"The stockade?" I ask, my mind reeling as I try to picture it. As my mind settles on the wooden plank with three holes and a lock, my cheeks flush hot. "Oh."

Garrett chuckles. The smile that plays on his lips is wicked, and there's a mischievous gleam in his eye.

It makes me wonder—what's *his* kink?

Does everyone really have one? Like an astrological sign, aligned with their personality and built into their identity. A secret, dirty astrological sign.

I feel Emerson's hot gaze on my face, and when neither of us move toward the door, Garrett excuses himself, leaving me alone with my fuming boss. What is his deal?

Garrett's footsteps disappear down the hall, and Emerson strikes, slamming the door and cornering me against the crimson red wall. "I thought I told you I don't want you involved with this stuff."

"Then why did you bring me? Why did you even hire me?" I ask, forcing my voice to hide the shake. He's towering over me, and I am momentarily overwhelmed with his proximity. Those hard pecs in my face, that intoxicating cologne, the deep rumble of his voice.

"At the moment, I'm not exactly sure."

The cold, harsh expression on his face makes me want to crumble to my knees. I'm not even sure what I did wrong, but I'm tired of feeling scolded.

"I don't think this is going to work out," I say in a quivering whisper, but when I try to escape from this place, he has me cornered; his warm grasp on my arm stops me.

"No," he barks.

"No?" He can't tell me I can't quit. Not when everything I do seems to infuriate him.

His chest rises and falls with a heavy breath before a softer expression settles on his face.

"No, you can't quit. But when we're at the club, I don't

want you leaving my side or talking to anyone other than me, understand?"

"That's not fair!"

"I'm not saying this as your boss, Charlotte."

The argument dies on my lips as I stare up at him.

"Then, what…"

"You're my son's…friend, and it's my job to protect you. No one will hurt you here, but I don't feel comfortable throwing you into the lion's den on your first day. Understand?"

My body temperature cools about a hundred degrees. Here I am thinking about Emerson's hot pecs and big hands while he sees me as a kid, as one of his son's friends. I feel like an idiot.

Why couldn't Beau's dad be ugly?

"Let's go see Maggie," Emerson says, letting go of my arm and turning his back to me. I'm frozen in place for a moment, and when he gets to the door, he waits for me to follow. Once I reach his side, his hand returns to that comforting place at the small of my back. I hate myself for how much I love that, but I can't stand the idea of him being angry at me. He nudges me gently out the door and down the hall. This time, I just keep my eyes forward instead of letting them trail into the various open rooms we pass on the way to the office.

Rule #9: Dressing like a hooker comes in handy.

Charlie

"I WAS ONLY TRYING TO PROTECT YOU," HE MUMBLES QUIETLY ON the drive home.

"What?"

I can't stop picking at the chipped black polish on my nails since that incident in the throne room. I hate how naive I feel. I hate how controlling Emerson is and how small I am in his presence when he tells me what to do. And dammit, I want him to acknowledge that.

"You have to be careful around those guys, especially Drake." His eyes glance over to my body, and I realize he's referring to my scandalous outfit.

"Is he bad?" I ask, knowing full well I have no interest in him. He was handsome beyond words, but he just didn't feel like my type. Of course, after Beau, I'm not quite sure I know what my type is.

"Drake isn't bad at all. He's a good friend, but he'll fuck anything that moves and you're too young, Charlotte."

I clench my jaw and turn away. "If you're going to keep treating me like a child, then you really shouldn't have hired me."

When I glance back, I spot the muscles of his jaw clench in unison with mine. We stay silent for the rest of the drive. After he pulls into the garage, he climbs out and turns toward me.

"Have you spoken to Beau lately?"

I catch his expression over the top of the car, and I see a hint of desperation on his face. "I saw him at the mall yesterday."

His eyebrows lift, and his spine straightens. "How was he?"

I consider my answer for a moment. Should I sugarcoat it and tell him Beau is great and not the overgrown man-child without direction that he is? Would that make him feel better? I settle on cutting to the chase instead. "He wants his half of the security deposit. He was pretty mad at me for not getting it for him."

Emerson's brow flinches at my words. "Mad at you?"

"Yeah, in Beau's eyes, I'm nothing but a fuckup. A loser and an idiot." I don't know why I'm telling him this, the words just seem to pour out of my mouth.

His expression hardens from confusion to anger. "He does not think that."

"Yes, he does."

I circle around the car, meeting him near the trunk. He's silent, as if he's deliberating. And I'm sure he's thinking of ways of getting Beau here to get his half of the check. It's really a great piece of bait if he wants to see his son.

I'm a little surprised by his next words. "You're none of those things, Charlotte."

I scoff. "You barely know me."

His hand grips me tenderly just above my elbow, drawing my attention to his face. "Stop it," he commands me, his voice deep and jarring as I nearly stumble backward, his grip on my arm keeping me upright.

Somehow I'm closer to him, nearly pressed against his chest and staring up at him. Did he pull me closer?

"You are not a loser or a fuckup or an idiot, do you understand

me?" He seems almost angry, and if his words weren't so compli-
mentary, I'd be frightened.

"Okay," I mutter.

"I'm sorry he made you feel that way."

"It's okay," I reply. The neurons in my brain have stopped
firing, as I'm overwhelmed by his nearness. His breath is on my
face, warm and masculine, and if I were any other woman, I'd
think he was about to kiss me.

But I'm not any other woman. I'm Charlie. Too naive. Too
clumsy and immature and insignificant.

"And I'm sorry for reprimanding you today at the club.
Garrett and Drake were out of line. That wasn't your fault."

What happened to Mr. Bossy Asshole? He was easier to deal
with than Mr. Compliments and Apologies. I'm not sure how to
respond to this, so I back away, pulling my arm from his grasp. "I
understand. Yes. Thank you," I stammer.

"If Beau wants his money, he can come get it himself,"
Emerson adds with a bite to each syllable as he marches into the
house. I follow after him, feeling a little shaken.

Somewhere between the garage and the kitchen, where
Emerson shows me the coffee maker and the water and where I
can find everything I need, I think about my own father.

Emerson probably hasn't spoken to Beau in four months. I
haven't spoken to mine in almost five times as long. He doesn't
call or text or hire my exes to try and get me back. He's never
forcibly made me accept that I wasn't a screwup.

And later, as I'm filing paperwork, I let my gaze linger on
Emerson as he works. And I wonder what he sees when he looks
at me. Does he really see a girl young enough to be his daughter?

Then I mentally try on what it would feel like to have a man
like Emerson Grant look at me as a woman good enough for him.
Warmth floods my lower belly as I think about him in that way, to
be *his* woman. To feel his hands on my body, his lips on my skin. To
walk into a building on his arm and know that no matter who is in

that building, *I* am the most important one to *him*. And everything shifts in my brain from seeing him as a father to seeing him as a man.

———————

After work, I'm pulling up to the curb next to a blue-haired teenager who is so engrossed in her book, she doesn't even see me coming.

"Get in, punk."

My sister turns, her blue hair flying in her face from the harsh winter breeze as she walks home from school. I usually start work around this time and can never pick her up, so it's nice to be able to surprise her during her mile-long hike.

After climbing in, she looks at my outfit and laughs. "You look like a hooker."

"Thanks. You look like a Smurf."

"Thanks. How was your first day at your new job?" she asks as I pull away from the curb and head toward the shopping plaza on the opposite side of town.

"It was...interesting." I'm not really planning on sharing *all* the gritty details of my new job with my fourteen-year-old sister. She may be wise for her years, but she's not ready for all of *that*. I have also decided not to disclose the fact that I'm working for Beau's dad. She was never much a fan of Junior and wouldn't be too keen on me working with Senior.

"Wait, where are we going?" she asks when I miss the turn for our house.

"Didn't that new anime comic come out today?"

Her eyes light up. "It's called manga, and yes, it did...but they probably sold out already."

"Well, it's worth a shot."

As we pull up to the strip mall with Sophie's favorite comic book store, I suddenly wish I had gone home first to change. There's a gaggle of teen boys, all clearly in the throes of puberty, huddled outside. You can tell by the acne, ill-fitting clothes, greasy hair, and metal-filled smiles.

Oh well. *It's for Sophie*, I think as we climb out of the car. She side-eyes me as we walk up to the shop, my heels clicking against the oily, cracked concrete of the parking lot.

"Geez," she mutters under her breath.

I can literally feel their eyes as we pass. Inside the shop, there's a lot of chatter, the excitement from the new release today clearly filling the empty spaces. A group of giggly girls with K-pop T-shirts and Hello Kitty backpacks browse the back wall as Sophie heads toward the empty endcap where the new book should be.

"See." Her shoulders slump and my heart breaks. "They probably sold out hours ago."

"Not today, Satan," I reply, turning toward the heavy-set, bearded man behind the counter. "Excuse me."

When he looks up from the video game console he's currently dismantling, he freezes. His eyes lock, and I mean *lock*, on my breasts. Granted, my shirt is see-through, and my bra is black. It's a display, I know that, but he is looking at my tits like they've put a trance on him and he's incapable of seeing anything else in the room.

"Hi," I bark, trying to tear his attention away from my chest. And just as I'm about to cover it with my folded arms, I realize this might work to my advantage. So instead, I lean forward, letting my cleavage pop as my elbows rest against the glass counter.

"Oh my God," Sophie mumbles quietly behind me.

"Can—Can I help you?" the man asks.

"Yes, my sister and I are looking for the new book in the Wonder Boy Cosmo series. I think it came out today." I flash him a toothy grin.

"Oh, that sold out at ten this morning." He manages to look me in the eye this time, but his gaze dances between my lips and tits like little Ping-Pong balls in his head.

"Really?" I ask with a pout. Then I heave a long sigh, glancing toward the back of the shop behind him, noticing unopened boxes stacked along the wall. Pinching my bottom lip between my teeth, I stare up at him through my lashes as I ask, "Any chance you have just one more back there for us? I really, really wanted it." Then I spy his name tag and add a flirty, "Travis," in for good measure.

He swallows, then forces a tight smile for me. As he seems to deliberate his options for a moment, I consider that this guy is actually pretty handsome. If he trimmed up that unruly beard and combed his hair, it would go a long way. Plus, he has a nice smile.

He must notice me quasi checking him out because he grins. "Let me go check in the back."

He's gone for a while, and I turn toward Sophie, who only shakes her head at me with a blank expression on her face as she scans the Funko Pop wall.

A few minutes later, Mr. Beard returns with his hands behind his back. Leaning toward me on the counter, he passes me a thick book with a bright illustrated cover and what looks like a corgi dressed up like an astronaut. "You didn't get this from me," he whispers.

"Oh my God, you're the best, Travis!"

Leaning forward, I plant a quick kiss on his cheek, leaving the red-lipped stamp there as he blushes. Hiding the book from the girls at the back of the store, I pull out my credit card and hand it to him discreetly. He's still smiling as he gives me my receipt and wishes us a good day.

In the car, Sophie beams at her new book and my heart swells. "Oh my God, you are a hooker, but I'm not complaining!"

"I am not!"

"Well, just keep dressing like one."

My laugh dies down as I think about the throne room today. I've never considered myself a sexual person, but I can't deny that it felt good to sit on that throne, to think about someone—a certain someone—finding ways to pleasure me while I was up there. It excited me to be so admired in the shop, to use my body in a way that worked for me. To be comfortable in my own skin and flaunt that. To know that I may not be a twig or have perfect skin, but that doesn't mean I can't be sexy.

Rule #10: When your friends get nosy, tell them nothing.

Emerson

"How's it going with the new girl?" Garrett and I are sitting at the bar, waiting for the others. We haven't spoken about the incident at the club today, but as far as Garrett and I are concerned, there's really nothing to speak about. To him, Charlotte is just another employee—because that's exactly what she is, and it's not out of line for him to talk to her or even flirt with her a little. I don't usually keep secrets from my best friend, so he doesn't know the details of how I came to find Charlotte—a secret I don't expect to keep for long.

"She's perfect," I reply after taking a sip of my beer.

Garrett makes a big show of looking surprised. Raising his arms in the air, he acts like he's just seen the second coming of Christ or something.

"Knock it off," I mutter.

"Can it be? Emerson Grant is finally satisfied with someone? Drinks are on me tonight."

"Very funny. Besides, she's *just* a secretary, remember? The standards and expectations are considerably lower."

"That's fine. I can get over the fact that I didn't find her myself. I'm just happy I can have twenty hours a week of my time back since that's what I spent trying to find the perfect girl for you. Not to mention all of the paperwork involved in assigning and reassigning each girl. It was exhausting."

"Well, I'm glad you're pleased," I reply.

"No. I'm glad *you're* pleased." He laughs, taking a drink. After setting it down, he throws me a curious look. "Where did you find her anyway?"

I grimace. Best to be out with it, I guess. "Well…"

Just then, Hunter and Drake burst through the door and there's not a word left to be spoken. Our business partner, Hunter, and his best friend are two of the loudest, most foul-mouthed thirty-year-old men I've ever met.

Following behind them are Hunter's wife, Isabel, and Maggie, everyone's right-hand lady. Both of them behaving in an appropriate, suitable for public, composed manner—unlike the two men in front of them.

We all greet each other before taking our seats around the same table we've been inhabiting every Thursday night for the past eight years.

It's really the perfect place for us to meet, since we rarely see each other throughout the week. It's also the only place that will accommodate everyone from Drake in his jeans and boots, straight off the construction site, to me in my business attire. And it's not too seedy that we would feel uncomfortable bringing the girls here.

"What's new?" Hunter asks after they return from the bar with their drinks.

"Well, Emerson was just telling us that his new secretary is *perfect*."

"Hmm…" Maggie says in response, pressing her lips together.

"Ohh, what was that for?" Isabel asks, clearly picking up on the signal Maggie was giving.

"She's not who I expected for Emerson, that's all."

"She's just my secretary," I throw in, although no one seems to hear it.

"What was wrong with her?" Hunter asks.

"There's *nothing* wrong with her," I blurt out quickly.

"Oh, that girl you brought in today? There was definitely *nothing* wrong with her." This time it's Drake who leans in to join the conversation with a suggestive wag of his brows, and I growl quietly into my drink. Drake is Hunter's friend, and except for being the foreman at the construction of our first location, he has nothing to do with our business. He has no real appreciation for the lifestyle, aside from being the biggest man whore in Briar Point. And I meant what I said to Charlotte today: he'll fuck anything over eighteen.

"Enough," I reply quickly.

"What? That's your type, isn't it?" he asks playfully. "Young, hot, follows you around like a puppy."

Garrett answers for me. "Leave him alone, Drake."

I can handle Drake's jokes. It's not his fault he likes it vanilla. He smiles at me from across the table, and I shake my head, finishing off my drink. He can laugh all he wants, but he's never laying a hand on Charlotte. I'll make sure of that.

Standing from the table, I walk over to the bar to order my second drink. After gesturing for the bartender, I let my mind wander back to the interaction with Charlotte today. I'm not sure why I reacted the way I did. I never should have cornered her like that. Fuck, I'm out of my element here. What the hell do I know about working with a twenty-one-year-old girl?

Charlotte is more curious about the business than I expected, and I'm struggling with how fucking adorable that is and how much that shit will get me in trouble. Even I have to admit, unabashed curiosity, especially when it comes to kinks and sex, is a major fucking turn-on. It would do us both a lot of good if she'd be a little more quiet and terrified, and not go exploring and getting into trouble.

Did the image of her on that throne embed itself into my brain? Of course it did. She's a gorgeous girl, and I spent the bulk of my day trying *not* to stare at her tits through that translucent shirt.

But she's my son's girl—past, present, future, doesn't matter. What the fuck is wrong with me?

When I get back to the table, Garrett is watching me. "You look all up in your head," he says. The others are talking about something on their side of the table, so he mutters quietly to me to keep things between us. "Everything okay?"

I rub my hand over my face. "Everything's fine. Just stressed. We open in six weeks and that building didn't look anywhere near done." I glance sideways at Drake, to make sure he didn't hear me, but he's too busy telling some elaborate threesome story loud enough for the whole bar to hear.

Garrett slaps a hand on my shoulder. "Relax. It's not as bad as you think. Once they pull the equipment out of there, it'll look ten times better, you'll see."

I nod, trying to let his words of comfort seep in. "You're right."

His hand stays on my shoulder as he watches me take a sip of my drink. "Hey, we're good, right? I didn't mean to overstep today…"

Quickly shaking my head, I give him a reassuring expression. "Yeah, we're good. She's just my secretary. I was serious."

Holding his hands up in surrender, he nods. "I believe you. I was just having a little fun. I didn't mean to—"

"Garrett, it's fine. She's just…too young for all of this. I didn't really want her getting involved."

I know before the words are out of my mouth that it's a hypocritical thing to say. We have plenty of twenty-one-year-old women working for us. Subs, Dommes, dancers, waitresses, performers, whatever. As long as they are *of age*, then age doesn't matter.

"You were about to tell me where you found her," he says with a quizzical wrinkle in his brow.

A minute ago, I was about to tell him, but suddenly I'm not ready. Once I let it out that I've hired my son's ex-girlfriend, things will get complicated. It's almost like I don't want them judging me for something I haven't even done yet. Nothing sexual can occur between me and Charlotte. I hired her solely for the purpose of trying to get my son back—how, I'm still not quite sure, but it has to work. All that matters is I don't cross that line.

"Another time," I mutter over the rim of my glass.

"Hey," Hunter says, holding up his drink, "can you guys believe we're finally doing this? We need to toast."

"We're still six weeks away," Maggie reminds him. "Don't jinx it."

"I'm not jinxing it. The sign is on the door, the opening event is scheduled. We've hired a staff and have a full membership. You guys…we're opening a fucking sex club."

"Cheers to that," Garrett says, lifting his drink.

The rest of us echo him, clinking our glasses before throwing them back, and then we fall silent as the words settle in. *We're opening a fucking sex club.*

Rule #11: Don't compare your hot boss to your dad moments before touching his heart line.

Charlie

"Oh my God," I stammer, opening my email to find a picture of a woman suspended from the ceiling, naked and wrapped in black cord. She looks like she was caught in a fishing net, and although I can't see her backside clearly, I'm willing to bet it's in a prime location for...access.

Emerson furrows his brow as he glares at me.

"Everything all right?"

"These applications..."

A deep chuckle echoes from his corner of the room, and I look up at him in shock. "I mean, what even is this?"

He stands and walks over to see my computer screen. Resting his hands on the back of my chair, he leans over me and stares at the same image I am. "It's called Shibari," he says quietly, his deep voice rumbling through my body.

"Is that something you...hire people for?" I ask, gulping on a breath.

"It was Garrett's idea to have a rope-bondage presentation, so we need a few experts to demonstrate."

"It looks like it hurts." I grimace. It's difficult to look at, and even more uncomfortable to be scrolling through the various pictures this woman has sent with Beau's dad standing over my shoulder.

"You'd be surprised how many people want to be tied up and…"

I turn my face and gaze up into his eyes. When he looks back down at me, my skin grows hot.

"That's a little more than tied up," I reply in a low whisper.

"Don't knock it until you've tried it," he says.

I drag in a deep breath, inhaling the cedar musk scent of his cologne.

"Have you?" I ask carefully.

"Been tied up like that?" His tone is laced with humor as he leans back. I can no longer smell his cologne, and it's disappointing. "No."

"I meant… Never mind." This is getting uncomfortable. The notion I held two weeks ago about being able to be a sex club owner's secretary without talking about sex is basically out the window. We keep cornering ourselves in conversations that inevitably end up inappropriate. It doesn't help that I don't know when to quit. "I ask too many questions."

"Yes, you do."

It also doesn't help that over the past fourteen days, I've grown more and more attracted to Emerson. Maybe it's curiosity or daddy issues or just a plain old crush, but the fact that he's forty has become attractive instead of sickening. Most guys my age are a mess. Emerson is the epitome of perfection. Everything he owns is upper-echelon expensive and even his skin is clear and perfect. I find myself wanting to run my fingers through his short beard and scratch my nails through his salt-and-pepper hair.

And I bet a man his age has more skills in bed than a guy who's only been doing it for a couple years. *Stop it, stop it, stop it.*

Looking back at the image on the screen, I think about the woman in the photo. She's beautiful, with long black hair and a body most of us would kill for. I wish for one moment I could have the confidence it must have taken to be in the life she's living. And I don't mean tied up, but knowing what she wants and going out and taking it.

Emerson hasn't taken me back to the club since the first day, when he caught me in the throne room with Garrett. Even if he mentions needing to go see Hunter or Maggie, he scowls and adds, "I'll go later." As if to say he'd rather go alone.

I find his overprotectiveness both endearing and annoying. My father was vainly protective in a way that never felt genuine. He tried to tell me the boys I couldn't date but only because he was territorial and stubborn.

Emerson is protective in a different way, although I can't put my finger on how it's different.

The job itself is cake. I go through his emails for him, forwarding the applications to Garrett, the mundane stuff to Maggie, the building stuff to Hunter, and the financial stuff to Emerson. Then I bring him coffee, do lunch runs, file paperwork, and take notes while he's on calls.

And I'm actually starting to get comfortable in my new clothes. I found a boutique online that delivers quickly and has the cutest secretary-style clothing I have ever seen. I love the look on Emerson's face each day as I stroll in, scanning my body with his eyes. I have learned that when he bites his lower lip and looks away, he dislikes it. When he compliments me with a simple, "You look nice," he just thinks it's okay. But when he stares too long, clenching his fists and letting out a deep sigh, then he *really, really* likes it.

He asks me about my personal life a lot more than I expected him to, and I tell him about Sophie—without giving away anything personal or going into too much detail. And I tell him about my mom and how my dad left. He scowls when I bring up my dad, but he doesn't say much, probably feeling like it's really none of his business to assert his opinion.

And he always asks me about Beau, but I can tell it's hard for him to bring him up. He doesn't push me to call him anymore, not after I told him how Beau treated me. And it makes me wonder sometimes if Emerson will still keep me as his secretary when he realizes that I'm not going to lure Beau back home. If I can't bring his son back, I'm basically useless to him—at least where Beau is involved.

"I need your opinion," he says from his desk as I click Send on the roped-up girl, shooting it over to Garrett with a click of a button.

He's sitting at his desk, staring at his computer. I pull up the chair across from him and settle on my knees as I lean over his giant mahogany desk.

"What's up?"

"The club opening party is next month, and I can't decide between these two suits." I pause, glancing at his face before turning toward the screen. Emerson Grant is asking *me* for fashion advice. That would be like me asking a golden retriever to help me do my taxes.

On the screen are two male models, each dressed in formal tuxedos that fit them like they were tailored just for them. The first one is all black, even the tie and undershirt, so it has layers of rich, dark textiles, and I'm certain that it would look dashing as fuck on Emerson.

But the other suit is a deep blue satin with broad lapels and a black tie over a white shirt. My lips twist as I consider the two. Then, I look at him, my face only a few inches away as I stare into his rich green eyes.

The black would be sexy, but the blue over his tan skin and with those colorful pupils would be regal.

"The blue," I whisper, tearing my gaze away from him and looking back at the screen. "What will your date be wearing? I guess you should try and match her." In my mind, his date is some supermodel with a designer gown handmade just for her and this *one* event.

"I don't have one."

I look at him again. "Why not?"

He shrugs, leaning back in his chair. "I don't know. Does it matter?"

"I mean…you're the owner of a sex club. If you walk in there alone, you're not going to be leaving alone," I tease him, but the thought sucks a little bit of the humor out of me. Some lucky bitch is going home with the most important, most handsome, richest man at the party. Must be nice.

He looks mostly unamused. "I'm not hooking up with a random girl at my company's grand opening party." Okay, I guess the boss man doesn't do one-night stands. Interesting…

"And no girlfriend?"

"No girlfriend."

"Then I guess you should take a date." I lean back, settling in the chair. My eyes pause for a moment on his hands resting on the desk, and I get an idea. It's probably going to be embarrassing, but I'm nothing if not stubborn and socially fearless. "Can I see your hand?"

"What?" he asks with a wrinkle in his forehead.

"I can read palms, and I just like to see people's lines."

His confused expression remains as he says, "You are very strange, Charlotte."

I laugh easily as I reach for his giant hand. Laying his open palm out before me, I let my touch drift softly from his wrist to the tips of his fingers. It doesn't take a palm reader to know that Emerson Grant has always been an office man. There are no calluses or scars, and his nails are neatly kept. They're so soft in fact, that I can't seem to stop stroking his skin and the room grows silent.

I feel his eyes on me, so instead of letting myself dwell on my insecurities, I lean forward and let my touch trace the lines of his palm.

His large hand dwarfs my tiny one as I hold it out before me.

"You have a long heart line. That's a good thing," I add, glancing up into his eyes. He's not looking at the lines, though. His gaze is fixed on my face, and I have to swallow down my nerves. *He's your boss, Charlie. And Beau's dad. Get your mind out of the gutter.*

"What does that mean?" he asks.

"People with a long, straight heart line are usually good lovers," I say with a playful smirk.

"Makes sense," he jokes, and I find myself giggling and my cheeks warming.

"It also means you are expressive, romantic, and value true love in your life."

"Hmm…"

"Look, mine is long too." I open my palm for him, showing him where the horizontal line starts at my index finger and stretches all the way across my hand, without any breaks or curves.

"Doesn't everyone have love in their life?" He sounds unimpressed.

Squeezing his open hand in mine, I give him a terse glare. "Not just any love, Emerson. It means you'll have true, all-consuming, intoxicating, life-changing, earth-shattering love. Love you would die for. That you couldn't possibly live without. Love that makes it hard to breathe. Like you can feel it not just in your heart but in your veins and your bones and your muscles. Everywhere."

My hand moves to my chest and I close my eyes and take a deep breath. I didn't mean to get so carried away, but I can literally feel tears sting my eyes, and it's humiliating because there's no way he understands what I'm talking about.

But when I open my eyes, he's staring at me with an expression I haven't seen on his face before. The wrinkle that usually settles between his brows is gone and his eyes are soft. He's studying me as if he's seeing me for the first time.

"Is that what you want, Charlotte?"

I force myself to inhale. "I won't settle for anything less."

"Good." He looks down at my hand still resting on the table, and he takes it, opening my palm the way I held his. "And your lines say you'll have that?"

"Yes."

His fingers trace the creases of my palm, and I forget how to breathe. His touch is so gentle even though he's so much larger than me, and I hate myself for the way I imagine that same touch on my breasts, down my spine, between my legs…

"Someday," I add, breaking the fragile silence.

His eyes meet mine, a moment charged by the intimate touching of hands. I didn't intend for it to get like this. I really thought I could prove to him that he doesn't have to stay so miserably single forever and he would tease me about palm reading, but I didn't expect this. Here I am, stupidly thinking that the mind-blowing love I want so badly could possibly, in any universe, be with Emerson.

"I'll take you to the opening."

At first I think he's saying he'll *take me*, as in, to be his lawfully wedded wife, and I nearly laugh because that would be a joke. Then his words reroute through my brain and I realize he's asking me to go to the club opening with him as his date, and the word, "What?" bursts through my lips.

"You think I need a date, and I don't want to take any chances going home with the wrong girl, so you should go with me."

"You're serious."

A deep chuckle echoes from his chest. "Yes, I'm serious."

"No. *No.*"

"Ouch," he responds, feigning offense.

"Emerson." I level my gaze on him. "Come on. I'm your secretary. And your son's girlfriend."

"Ex."

I pause. Am I seriously considering this? He won't even take me back to the club after what happened last time, and now he wants to take me to the opening *as his date.*

"Will people be…you know?" God, I feel like a child.

"Having sex in the club? Yes, probably. Maybe not on the first night, and not out in the open. You don't have to see anything you don't want to see."

I think I'm sweating. No, I'm *definitely* sweating.

I want to ask him, why me? Why does he want to take me when he has his pick of probably any girl in Briar Point? But I don't. I'll let myself imagine for a moment that he actually *wants* to take me over any of those other girls. Let myself live in the fantasy for a minute.

"I can't afford a dress."

"I'll buy your dress."

When I open my mouth to argue more, I stop myself. Why am I trying to talk him out of this invitation? I am getting invited to an ultra-exclusive, members-only sex club with the freaking *owner*. Why are the first words out of my mouth not *hell yes*?

"Okay. Fine."

"That has to be the most flattering response to a date I've ever received," he replies sarcastically.

"I'm sorry, I mean, I'm excited and of course I want to go with you, but it's just…not really my scene. Come on, Emerson. I work in a skating rink."

"No, you work for Salacious Players' Club as my secretary, remember?"

"Yes, but on the weekends, I still fry corn dogs and lead the crowd in the hokey-pokey on roller skates."

A deliciously handsome grin stretches across his cheeks. "I'd pay to see that."

"You don't have to. Every Saturday night at seven thirty. The black lights come on. We even sell glow sticks, if you'd like to take it up a notch."

"Oh really? I'm not quite versed in roller-skating culture. Do you think I'm ready for glow sticks?"

He's teasing me, and I don't even realize until this moment that he's still holding my hand in his. Or rather, we're just holding hands since he's relaxed his grip.

But I don't let that distract me as I lean in, teasing him as much as he's teasing me. "How would you know if you don't try it? I think you could handle glow sticks. It's the Electric Slide you should probably work your way up to."

"You'll do it with me, so I'm not alone, right?"

I smile, biting the corner of my lip. And because it feels right, I lean forward and say, "Oh, baby, you won't know what hit you when you Electric Slide with me."

It's funny. We're laughing, and it's playful and innocent and *fine*...until it's not. Until the laughter fades, and we're left in the dust of whatever flirtatious thing this was. His eyes are on my face, and mine are on his. Our hands are still linked on the desk.

He swallows, and I swallow.

And I want so badly to kiss him. Just to *see* if I would even like it or if it would be too strange. And to see if these weird feelings in my body are what I think they are. If I'm really growing attached to Emerson in a sexual way or if it's just my imagination getting away with itself.

His fingers squeeze my hand, one finger gently stroking my palm, and it's like a *scream*. It's so subtle, naked to the eye, but I feel it, and it's telling me to lean forward, so I do.

Then he leans forward.

And when I feel his breath on my lips, my body cries for me to kiss him. Close the distance. While my brain has alarms going off, red flags and sirens blaring. *No, no, no, no! This is Beau's dad—his freaking dad, Charlie. What are you doing? You can't kiss him! Because then what? After you kiss him, what if he wants more? Are you going to let him take your clothes off? Have sex with him?*

Okay, that sounds both terrifying and amazing.

But then what? You can't stay in this job after you've fucked him. You'll get emotionally attached and maybe you'll sleep together a couple more times, if you like it, and then he'll move on, and you'll be devastated.

And my rational mind has a point. This is a terrible idea, but his lips are already brushing mine, and it's too late to back out now. It's a soft touch, barely even a kiss, but the moment our lips graze each other, we slide into an intimate space where only we exist, and it's so delicate that I don't dare to move.

His hand slides up my arm and he leans in to deepen the kiss, but before he can, the phone rings.

Compared to the silence we're in, it sounds like a machine gun going off right next to us. I gasp, pulling away in a rush. I don't stop, jumping up from the chair and walking briskly across the room.

The ringing stops, and I turn to see he's silenced the call. His eyes are on me, watching me with concern.

"Charlotte," he calls with that authoritative tone. "What's wrong? Come sit down."

"That was stupid of me. I'm sorry. I got carried away. It was just the heat of the moment, I guess. I don't know—"

"Charlotte," he barks.

"I should go. I'm sorry."

"Don't go," he calls, but I'm already to the foyer, grabbing my jacket from the closet and my purse from the bench. When I spin around again, he's only a foot away.

"I'm really sorry. I'm so embarrassed." My hands fly up to my face, and my cheeks are hot against my hands. And everything just comes barreling to the forefront of my mind.

I kissed Beau's dad. My boss. Beau's dad. A forty-year-old man.

His touch is soft against my wrists as he nudges my hands from my face.

"Are you okay?"

"No!" I shriek.

"Why?"

"Because…" My eyes widen.

"Because we kissed."

"Oh my God," I cry out, trying to cover my face again.

"Charlotte, calm down."

"I'm sorry."

"Stop apologizing. You didn't do anything wrong. Don't leave. Sit down."

He leads me to the formal living room at the front of the house with large bay windows that face the quiet neighborhood. His comforting hand is at the small of my back again, and I relax into the secure way it makes me feel.

It's quiet for so long before he finally speaks. "I think you were right. We just got carried away in the moment, which was not your fault."

There's a *but* hanging on the end of his sentence and I'm sort of dreading it. As much as I hate the idea of kissing him again, I also sort of...love the idea of kissing him again. Which is so, so wrong. And most of all, I don't want him turning me down. It hurts to even think about.

"But the two of us getting involved with each other physically is a very bad idea."

"I agree," I stammer, unable to meet his eyes.

"I don't want you to leave like this. I'm sorry it happened, but if you need to leave, I understand."

I don't want to leave. Suddenly, I find myself glued to his presence, craving that comforting touch again. One little brush of our lips and I'm already attached. *Stupid, stupid Charlie.*

"I'll stay."

In my head is a chorus of self-deprecation walloping my ego. *Why would he want you anyway? Stupid girl. You really tried to kiss Emerson Grant. A handsome millionaire who could have anyone. Why would he want you?*

My eyes are trained on the floor, my hands working anxiously as I let the words have their way, running through my mind until I'm on the verge of tears.

And suddenly, he's touching my chin. And I glance up in surprise as he lifts my gaze upward until we're staring at each other.

"It's *not* because I don't want you. Understand?"

It's eerie how well he reads my mind. He's just being nice, though. Solemnly, I nod.

Then his fingers gently stroke my chin for a moment as he seems to get lost, staring first at my eyes and then my lips.

"You're such a good girl, Charlotte."

My shoulders relax, seeming to melt down at my sides as I gaze up at him, those beautiful words washing over me like warm water. Suddenly, I'm all gooey and compliant, like that one little phrase put me in a trance. He could literally do anything to me in this state.

And I sort of want him to.

Sadly, he releases my hold and moves to stand. "All right then. Let's get back to work and pretend this never happened."

And since I would do just about anything for his praise, that's exactly what I do.

Rule #12: Foot rubs are sexual.

Emerson

MY PALM HAS BEEN ITCHING FOR DAYS. EVERY CHANCE I GET, I stare down at the lines that stretch from my wrist to my fingers and back again, thinking hard about what Charlotte said.

I'm destined for some great love. I laughed at it for the first day or two. Then, the idea began to settle in my mind. After Marie, Beau's mother, I wrote off the idea of love. Truthfully, long before that. What we had was fun, vibrant days of sex and youth when forever felt possible until we had an unexpected pregnancy and had to face the reality of parenting and adulthood.

It's hard to believe it's been twenty years since I gave love a good effort. That was a long time ago, and the idea of a relationship started sounding like more of a hassle than it was worth.

So something about Charlotte's little palm reading changed the course of my thoughts. And I can't stop thinking about how she looked, lips parted and eyes dilated. The hope, the fear, the arousal on her face. Maybe a hint of excitement too, if I'm being honest.

Charlotte has had an effect on me since she started working

here. And not in a good way. At least not if I want to get my son
back and stay out of her pants. Although this plan is falling apart
more and more each day. How can she be of any use to me if she
doesn't speak to him anymore?

While she's out for lunch, I pull out my phone and dial his
number again. Unsurprisingly, it goes to voicemail after only one
and a half rings, which means he declined my call *again*.

And this time, I do something I haven't done yet.

"Hi, Son. I was just talking to Charlotte…er, Charlie, I mean.
I'm sure you know by now she's working for me. She makes a
great secretary, and she talks about you so much. It makes me miss
you. I hope you're well. Please call me."

When I hit the red button, I sit in my silence. I sound so
fucking desperate. Is this what he wants? For me to beg? To make
a fool of myself for him, or does it make him lose respect for me?

A moment later, the front door opens and Charlotte carries in
a bag from the deli down the street.

"It was so beautiful out, I decided to walk. I hope I'm not
late."

"You're fine," I mutter without looking up. When I finally do
trail my eyes upward, I notice her cheeks are bright red, flushed
from the cool wind.

Wait. She walked to the deli? It's almost a mile and a half away.
And it's not nice out. It's February and only forty-five degrees.

"Charlotte," I bark out coldly as I stand. "Why didn't you
drive?"

Rushing toward her, I take the bags and touch her icy hands.
My molars grind. Then I run my thumbs over her cold cheeks,
and she shivers.

"I'm fine!" She pulls away, but as I peer out the window, I
catch a glimpse of her car parked next to mine, and I let out a
heavy sigh.

"Is everything with your car all right?"

She swallows, trying to get around me and walk to the

kitchen, but I block her path. Gripping her chin, I tilt her head up to look at me.

When her shoulders sag, she gives in. "I think it's the battery. I can have a mechanic come out to jump it, so it's not stuck in your driveway, I promise. I'm sorry."

Everything in me tenses as I think about her buried in her coat against the wind as she walked for over forty-five minutes in the cold, because she didn't want to tell me that her car wouldn't start.

"Why didn't you just tell me?"

"It's fine," she replies with a forced smile.

"Charlotte." I take her by the arm, reminding myself to be more gentle than my instincts insist I be. My inner Dom wants to punish her for lying. I'd like to shake her, squeeze her until it hurts, perhaps even put her over my knee—

No. She's only twenty-one, and she has an asshole for a father who never taught her how to jump-start her own car.

I loosen my grip on her arm but keep her close. "Don't do that again. If your car won't start, I want you to tell me and then you can take my car, understand?"

"I'm sorry," she mumbles, and the disappointment in her expression pains me.

I don't bother telling her she didn't do anything worthy of apologizing. Instead, I warm her tiny, cold hands in my large, warm ones. She shivers again as I bring them to my mouth, blowing hot air against her skin.

She avoids my eyes, and I realize I'm getting too intimate again. After her reaction to one kiss last week, I have to be more careful. That kiss was a mistake, but I found myself getting carried away with her. It's too easy to be around her and to feel so comfortable, but if I let myself go there, I'll regret it. She's beautiful, and if she were anyone else, I wouldn't have hesitated to take her to my bedroom to make her feel sublime. But she's not just anyone. She's literally been with my son, and I'll do more damage than good if I cross that line. It's just wrong.

"Let's eat," I say, dropping her hands and guiding her to the dining room.

Normally, I eat at my desk while I work, and she eats alone in here, but today, I feel the need to keep her company.

"After work today, I can help you jump your car."

"You really don't have to," she argues, setting her sandwich down.

"It's easy, Charlotte. Really, it's not necessary to call a mechanic."

She still looks uneasy as she picks at her sandwich, chewing more on her bottom lip than her food. And it occurs to me that she's not comfortable having someone else do things for her.

"Your feet must be hurting."

After taking a bite of her pastrami sandwich, she glances down at her heels.

"Believe it or not, I'm getting used to them. They're actually pretty comfortable."

I look down at her feet again, and they look red and swollen in her black stilettos. Pushing the rest of my sandwich aside, I turn toward her.

"Give me your feet."

"What?" she stammers around a mouthful of food, wiping the napkin across her lips.

"You walked three miles in those to get me lunch. It's the least I can do." Pushing my chair out, I tap my lap. Is this too sexual? I'm not even sure. It's just a foot rub, and I need to do *something*. I'm still so torn between wanting to punish her for lying and nurturing her for going through that for me. Considering I want to do a lot more than massage her feet, I think this is pretty tame.

"Seriously?" she asks before wrapping her sandwich in the deli paper.

"Seriously."

With a nervous swallow, she watches my face as she lifts her feet up to me one at a time. I delicately remove each of her black heels and wince at the painful-looking state of her pinched toes. She has sheer black stockings on her feet, so I pat her foot and say, "Take these off."

Her breath hitches. Pulling her skirt up a couple inches, she unclasps the top of her thigh-highs from the garter, and I say a silent *fuck me* in my head. I don't know what I was expecting but that was not it. I wish I could look away as she unclasps the other side, but those little straps hidden under her clothes are sexy as sin, and I'm only a man after all.

My cock is growing hard in my pants, and what started as an innocent foot rub to help ease her pain and my conscience has turned into a sensual peep show and what will be a rough case of blue balls for me later.

I help her roll the pantyhose down her legs and drape them over the back of her chair. She's quiet, biting her lip and watching my face as I begin rubbing her poor, battered feet.

She lets out a hum as I massage, and I have to shift my growing cock away from her ankle resting on my lap.

"Does that feel good?" I ask, wincing as I hear those words escape my lips. Do I even know how to be nonsexual? Apparently not.

"Yes," she replies softly.

I watch as she melts into her chair, looking relaxed. When I dig my thumbs gently into her arches, her head hangs back, and I know I've won. This was the pleasure I wanted to see, and with nothing in return for myself.

"From now on, take off your shoes when you come into work. Don't wear these all day. Understand?"

"Okay," she replies with a sigh.

Moving to the opposite foot, I do the same, and everything is fine…until her right foot inches too far and brushes against the hard length in my pants. She tenses, her eyes finding mine, and in that moment, I feel like the world's biggest creep. I wasn't doing this to get off or turned on. I was doing this because I wanted her to feel good, but even now that sounds predatory in my head. I'm an HR nightmare waiting to happen.

The moment stretches on between us while I hold her foot in my hand, waiting for her to erupt from her chair and call me out or leave or slap me...because if anyone else touched her the way I'm touching her now, I'd have their fucking head on a stick.

But she doesn't do any of those things. Instead, with her gaze locked on mine, she brushes her foot against my cock again. Or was I imagining that? Nope, she definitely does it again, this time with a little more force, and it feels so fucking good. I resume massaging her foot while the other rests against my aching erection, and this is definitely not so innocent anymore.

"Charlotte," I whisper, but even I don't know what I'm about to say. I should tell her to stop and put her foot down.

"Yes?" Her voice is breathy and inviting. The moment is charged and sexual and very, very fucking dangerous.

Before I can say another word, her phone rings on the table next to her. I almost look away, but my eyes dance back to the screen when I recognize the name.

Beau.

She tears her feet away from me and freezes with her hand over the phone. Then she looks at me.

"Answer it," I command her a bit too enthusiastically.

As she snatches it up and hits the green button, I freeze in my seat. This is because of the message I left him. I knew he'd reach out to her when he found out she's working for me. So now what?

"Hey," she murmurs into the phone, walking across the room but not too far. I can't hear what he's saying on the other end, but I watch her body language. Her shoulders tighten closer to her ears and her other hand wraps around her middle as she speaks. "What?"

She peeks back at me at the exact moment I'm sure she realizes I told him.

"Yeah, I am. Why?" She bites her lip and curls in on herself even more. "Because I needed a job and it pays better than the rink."

A tense pause as I hear his muffled voice rattle on.

"It's not about *you*," she says a bit louder now. "No! I'm not—Beau!"

I stiffen in my seat. She looks noticeably affected and growing more agitated with each second.

"No, I won't quit. I need this job, and what does it even matter to you?"

Then she gasps before turning toward me. "You're wrong," she mumbles quietly, her eyes still on my face. I can't take another moment as I burst out of my seat. I don't even know what I'm doing when I snatch the phone away from her and hold it against my ear.

"Beau?"

He stops talking the second he hears my voice. Then, he responds with just two words. "Fuck you."

And the line goes dead.

Rule #13: Accept change.
Change is good.

Charlie

HE UNBUTTONS HIS SHIRT METHODICALLY WHILE I WAIT
awkwardly by my car. I can't take my eyes off his thick, masculine
fingers as they slip each tiny button through the hole. Underneath
his shirt is a white cotton T-shirt that fits him so snugly, I can
make out the contour of his pecs and the protruding shape of his
nipples.

Jesus, Charlie. His nipples? You're staring at the man's—

"Pop the hood for me," he says, and my mouth goes dry.

"Huh?"

"The hood, Charlotte. I need to reach the battery."

"Oh," I stammer, rushing to the driver's side to find the
latch Sophie showed me last time we had to do this. It pops,
and when I look up through the window, I see that Emerson
has completely removed his long-sleeve shirt and draped it
over the top of his car. I find myself staring at the heavy weight
of his shoulders, marveling at how much more muscular he
looks without the work attire on until he pulls open the hood,
obstructing my view.

He's such a—excuse the cliché—*man*. Not quite *dad* enough but still so much older than me that I find it strange to even look at him like this. And to think I *kissed* him.

And a couple hours ago, I was rubbing my foot against his impressive erection while he massaged my feet. *God, what is happening?* This is all getting out of hand, but I almost don't want it to stop.

I have to stand up to see him again, and I know he can feel me watching. My curiosity is becoming my greatest fault, making me want to do things I know I shouldn't but how can I resist? And he's just jumping my battery, not exactly highly involved mechanical work, but watching him attach those jumper cables is doing something to my heart rate. Warmth pools low in my belly as I imagine running my hands along his chest and abs.

"Okay, start it," he bellows from in front of the car. When I turn the key in the ignition, it stutters for another moment, which is a lot more than it did this morning. And after a moment, it purrs to life.

"Success!" I yell with my hands up. He gives me a curious arched-brow expression before pulling the cables off the battery and closing the hood.

As I move to tell him thank you, he blocks my path, holding a black credit card out to me. "You need a new battery. And you'll need to find a dress for the opening next week. Something that matches with my blue tux."

I stare open-mouthed at the credit card. "I can't take that."

"You have to," he replies so matter-of-factly, like I don't have a choice.

"Why would you buy me a new battery?"

"I'm tempted to buy you a new car."

"Emerson," I say, glaring at him.

"I need to be able to count on you to show up to work, which means you need a reliable vehicle for your job. And the dress is a company event too, so just take it. No spending limit."

"Emerson!"

I stare up at him as he leans on the door of my car. The expression on his face says he'd like to put me in my place for yelling at him, and I let my dirty mind wander, wondering what exactly that would look like.

There's something about the credit card that makes me feel like it has something to do with the call from Beau. As if this is his way of apologizing or making it up to me since I know he must have told Beau about me working here.

I shouldn't take it. I still have no idea why his son isn't talking to him. It only feels minimally like my business, and I don't have the nerve to ask, afraid I might upset Emerson even more. And to be honest, hearing Beau berate me for taking a job with his dad and literally accusing me of sleeping with him really put me in a sour mood since lunch. Not to mention breaking up that hot-as-hell foot rub I was in the middle of getting.

"Are you fucking him? He fucks his secretaries, Charlie. You think you know him, but you have no clue. He's sick."

I had to make sure Emerson didn't hear that last part, which I don't think he did. I wanted to tell Beau that I knew everything about the company and his father's history with secretaries, but it was too strange to try and bring it up in front of Emerson.

Slowly, I close my fingers around the card. "Are you sure? I can afford to fix it myself."

"So can I."

I purse my lips at him, but I take the card anyway. Looking down, we stand in silence for a moment before I quietly mutter, "I'm sorry about that call from Beau today. I didn't expect him to be so angry."

"It's fine. He obviously cares about you. If you're not comfortable working—"

My head snaps up as I stare at him in shock. "I'm perfectly comfortable. I'm not quitting because of *Beau*." Okay, maybe I didn't need to say it like that, but to think of giving up such a good-paying job in an environment I like is ridiculous. It makes me angry just thinking about it.

"Good." His eyes are unfocused as he stares off into the distance, clearly thinking through a lot.

"You're not uncomfortable with me here, are you?"

He hesitates, and my heart sinks. His eyes squint ever so slightly, and I can tell he's not answering very quickly for a reason. He *is* uncomfortable with me here.

Fuck.

"Not because of Beau, no."

What does that mean? It means I do make him uncomfortable in some way, just not in relation to his son.

"Do you feel uncomfortable with me here?" he asks, repeating my question back to me. And suddenly, that foot rub we're not speaking about is standing here between us like a giant, unavoidable elephant. I think what Emerson is asking is if his being turned on around me or attracted to me is crossing a line.

"No," I answer without hesitation. Which is the truth. And it makes me want to know so much more, like if he meant for the foot rub to get so sexual or if he really wants me in the same way I want him.

Before I can ask another question, he says, "Drive safe, Charlotte."

Then I watch him walk away, his white T-shirt stretched across his muscled back, and it feels a little colder without him near me anymore.

"What are we shopping for again?" Sophie whines as we enter the department store of the mall.

"I need a ball gown for the club opening next week."

"What kind of club?"

"Err...like a dance club," I reply awkwardly as we make our way over to the formal section. I'm already discouraged by the selection, nothing but sequined prom dresses and mother-of-the-bride type gowns. Not at all what I want.

"*Like* a dance club or *an actual* dance club?"

"Stop asking questions."

She's trailing behind me in her ripped jeans and black-and-yellow Nirvana tee. We normally spend Friday nights at the rink, and I hate to miss out on the chance to hang out with her, so I figured she'd be a good shopping buddy.

"But I have so many! Like where did you find this new job? Why does it require you to dress like a pricey escort? And since when do you go to dance clubs?"

"Since I started getting paid to. And I found the job through Beau, and it doesn't *require* me to dress the way I do. I choose to."

"Well, you never chose to before, so it had me curious." She won't look me in the eye, and I can feel a little more than judgment coming off her in waves. I think it's concern.

I've pretty much abandoned hope of finding anything here, so I turn toward Sophie and ask what I've been dying to know in the past three weeks.

"Do I seem happy?"

She asked me the same thing two years ago when she opened up to me, exposing her one secret and all of her insecurities. At the time, she seemed anything but happy, and I knew something was up, leading me to fish for information. I was scared to death for her, so we made a pact. Whenever we need a chat, we ask, *Do I seem happy?*

And the other person has to be honest.

When she got her ears pierced, she asked me.

When I started dating Beau, I asked her.

And when she dyed her hair blue and put on makeup for the first time, she asked again.

She seems a little surprised by my question, and maybe she thinks I'm asking because of Beau and not because of the new job, but she looks me up and down for a moment, as if scrutinizing me for signs.

"Yes...but..."

"But what?"

Her face falls a bit and she averts her eyes. "You're changing, that's all."

Am I? I don't feel like I've changed, and aside from the clothes, there's nothing that really feels different. Then I think about the throne room again. And what Emerson said about desires and how normal they are. And the kiss, and the foot rub, and I realize that the way I've been thinking my whole life *has* changed. In ways I'm not really comfortable talking about with my little sister, I think I am in the middle of a major change. Growing into something I've always wanted but never felt confident enough to ask for.

Sexy. *Sexual.*

Like I am the one at the helm of my own experience. Like I can reach for whatever it is that makes me feel good, without shame or embarrassment. Beau never made me feel like that. Sex with him was good, but always on his terms. I haven't even touched a man since, not including that kiss, and I feel like everything has changed.

I just didn't realize that it was showing on the outside too.

"Hey, change is good," I say, tilting my head toward her with a smile.

"Change is scary," she replies, staring at her shoes.

My heart drops. "Oh, little Smurf." I wrap my arms around her, kissing her on the top of the head. I know what she's thinking, that our dad left because he couldn't handle change. That her whole life is changing every day, and the last person she wants to lose is me.

But this change in me isn't scary, not to me. It's exciting. Because I feel like I'm on the brink of something huge, and I can't wait to see what it is.

Rule #14: When in doubt, dance.

Charlie

Emerson: *I will pick you up at eight.*
Charlie: Sounds good. Thanks.

I GOT READY TOO EARLY. MAYBE I WAS JUST EXCITED OR EAGER OR something, but I've been standing outside my mother's house in a shimmery sapphire and gold floor-length gown since seven forty-five. My mom and I got a manicure together and Sophie helped me curl my hair. I don't remember the last time I ever got so dressed up, and I don't understand why my stomach is being assaulted with butterflies.

But when his car pulls up, his windows are too tinted to see his face. I'm a little surprised that he's driving. I thought millionaire business owners were chauffeured around by bald, beefy drivers in black suits, or maybe I've been reading too many of Sophie's books.

When the door opens, and he steps out, walking around the car to open my door for me, I nearly lose my breath. Emerson always looks handsome, but in that blue satin suit, he looks so good it hurts my eyes. His dark brown hair is slicked back, and his beard has been trimmed to perfection.

I keep forgetting he's old enough to be my dad, especially when he looks that good.

His eyes seem to linger on me as long as mine linger on him.

"Charlotte," he says quietly, approaching me.

"Hi," I stammer awkwardly.

"You look…so beautiful."

There is something about his tone, the way he trips over his words and adds *so* in there as if saying I simply look beautiful isn't enough. It tells me he's not just dishing out compliments to be polite. He looks almost shaken as his eyes rake over my body.

"Thank you," I mumble.

Then his gaze casts upward to my house and back to me.

"My mom's on the night shift and Sophie's at a sleepover, or else I'd introduce you to my family."

"You have a nice home," he replies, and I giggle at him. It's a thirty-year-old split-level. The grass needs mowing and I can see the smudgy windows from here. Still, it's nice to hear him call it lovely because it is lovely to me. Although it's not nearly as fancy as his.

"Actually, I live in the guest house in the back." I point to the side gate I use to get to the casita next to the pool. It was a big deal when we bought the house, and I'm pretty sure my dad thought he was pretty hot shit because his house came with a pool house.

"Ready?" He opens the passenger door for me and ushers me inside.

The moment we're alone in the car, I get a whiff of his cologne, headier than his usual scent.

He seems tense as we drive, his knuckles white around the steering wheel.

"Nervous?" I ask.

Emerson handles stress surprisingly well. He's been busy these past few weeks, but he hasn't shown an ounce of anxiety about the club opening.

"About the opening?"

"Yeah."

"Not really. I have a good team. They've handled everything well."

"You're good at delegating," I reply, and the compliment seems to ease some of his nerves. But if he's not worried about the opening, what's his problem?

We make small talk during the rest of the drive, and as we pull up to the valet, there's not a soul outside except for two parking attendants waiting for us. One of them opens the door for me, and I wait for Emerson to round the car to stand next to me. He sticks his elbow out, and I glance up at him nervously before looping my arm through his.

"Don't worry, I'll protect you," I say.

"Protect me?" That wrinkle is back between his brows but so is his smile.

"From the ladies. That's what I'm here for, remember?"

"Oh, that's right. I forgot." Then he leans down until his mouth brushes the lobe of my ear. "I thought you were here as my date."

My lips part and I gaze back up at him. There hasn't been another incident between us since the foot rub a couple weeks ago, and I'll admit, it's been excruciating. Every day I come into work hoping he might brush his hand against my lower back or lean in close enough while reading over my shoulder that I can feel his breath on my neck. My mild curiosity and subtle crush has turned into full-blown infatuation, and I've been looking forward to tonight for weeks.

I squeeze his arm as we stroll toward the door. Just before reaching to open it, he adds with a sly smile, "Besides, in that dress, you'll be the one who needs protecting."

A blush rises to my cheeks, and I squeeze his arm tighter.

It's so quiet outside, but the second we pass through the front doors, that changes.

The lobby is dark with hazy red lights shining over the front desk and loud music echoes through the entire building. People are mingling around the edges of the room, all dressed in formal gowns and tuxedos. The partygoers fall silent when they recognize Emerson, and I cling even closer to him, as if I can actually protect him from anyone who might want to steal him away.

He nods to the woman behind the desk and she greets him with a warm, "Evening, Mr. Grant."

I smile at her as we pass. A heavy black curtain separates the lobby from the main room, and Emerson holds it open for me. It's not as crowded in here as I anticipated, but I guess that's what I should have expected in such an exclusive club.

"Oh my God, Emerson…it's amazing," I say, holding my hand to my lips. There's a crowd of people around the bar and a DJ's playing at the front of the room, on the stage. Dancers twirl around the poles, and quite a few people are dancing in the middle of the dance floor. The private rooms are all open, and it makes me wonder if people will actually have sex in there tonight. Is that even legal? I mean…it's no different than a hotel room, right?

Toward the back is the hallway where I found the throne room, but there's a bouncer standing by the door and a red rope keeping people out. It's ominous, without a sign telling people what is down the hallway, although I know: rooms with windows and plenty of opportunities to live out your wildest fantasies.

"Emerson!" a voice calls from the bar. We both turn to see Garrett heading our way. When his eyes fall on me, he does a double take. Even as he shakes Emerson's hand, he remains staring at me. Then, as he points at me, he says, "Charlotte?"

"Am I that unrecognizable in a dress?"

"You look beautiful," he says as he takes my hand in his and brings it to his lips.

"That's enough," Emerson snaps, pulling me away. Garrett and I laugh in unison.

"Need a drink?" Garrett asks as a server with flutes of

champagne strolls by. He grabs three and hands one to each of us. While I sip on my bubbly, the men chat about the opening. I tune them out, letting my eyes scan the dark room. At first, everything looked normal, but as my eyes adjust, I notice certain things.

Like a woman holding a leash that's connected to a shirtless man's neck beside her.

People browsing the open rooms as if they're picking out their favorites.

And a group of very rich-looking men sitting at one of the tables while someone doles out cards.

My eyes also catch on a girl kneeling next to one of the men gambling. He's stroking her hair as he stares at the cards in his hand. She looks so content, a lazy smile plastered on her face as she nuzzles her cheek against his leg.

I can't take my eyes off of her, thinking about that day in Emerson's office when he told me to kneel. Is this what he does with his girls? Does he pet their heads like they're dogs?

Why does it disgust me in theory? But seeing this man pet her head lovingly, *adoringly*…it seems almost romantic.

My eyes catch on a pair of dark, ominous eyes watching me from across the room, stealing my thoughts away from the woman on her knees. It's an older man, probably in his late fifties, and there's something oddly familiar about him but not in a way my memory can place him. A slight fear settles over me at the thought that he could be someone from my regular life—

"Can I have this dance?" Emerson whispers, clutching my waist and stealing my thoughts. I barely noticed that the music has changed to a sultry, slow dance beat. There are couples scattered across the floor, grinding their bodies together, and I gulp, looking up at Emerson.

He must sense my apprehension because he leans down and adds, "It's not the Electric Slide, but I think you can handle it."

A laugh slips through my lips. Damn, that champagne is kicking in already. I'm such a lightweight. The next thing I know,

I'm electric sliding my hand into his and letting him pull me onto the dance floor. I briefly wonder for a moment if people look at us and think he's too old for me. Then I realize that in this place, there's really nothing too taboo or unacceptable. No wonder people feel comfortable here. It's freeing.

"Relax, Charlotte," he mutters, his deep voice seeping into my bloodstream and making me instantly melt into his hold.

His broad arms engulf me as his hand slides across my ass, pulling me so close I can feel his heartbeat through his chest. It feels as if Emerson is keeping me safe, buried against his body, and even though there's nothing I need protecting from, I like the way it makes me feel.

Our bodies shift together to the music. Every time I look up at him, our faces are so close, we're almost kissing, but as much as I would love to feel Emerson's lips against mine, I'm not sure that's really what he wants to do with me, so I keep my gaze fixed on various places around the room, where I, once again, find myself staring at the woman on her knees.

"What are you looking at?" he whispers next to my ear, and I bite my lip and turn away.

"Nothing," I mumble.

"Liar," he teases.

"Fine." I look up at him. "Is that what you do with your *other* secretaries? Pet them while they kneel at your feet?" My eyes dance toward the kneeling woman, and I watch Emerson glance her way. A gentle smile curves his lips upward.

He doesn't hesitate. "Sometimes."

A flutter of excitement courses through my veins. It's so strange to imagine Emerson in that role. I can't bear to imagine another woman at his feet, so I imagine what it might feel like to gaze up at him like that. To feel him touch my head in such a loving gesture. To think of him like that, playing such a dominant, commanding role...that he claims isn't inherently sexual—it still arouses me.

We stare at each other a moment as I ponder how to phrase this next question. "Do you wish you had a secretary like that now?"

I can't outright ask, *Do you want me to be like that for you?* Because we've already established that it's inappropriate and out of the question—no matter how curious I am. But I am a little worried that he would prefer a girl like that over me. That I'm... not enough for him. The thought actually pains me.

He leans in and I have to shut my eyes because I'm overwhelmed by how close he is to kissing me. Is he actually trying to kill me? "You know they weren't actually my secretaries, right? Or at least they weren't very good ones. Not as good as you."

I force a small laugh, trying to maintain my composure with his nearness. "Too bad you can't have the best of both worlds." I level him with a look that speaks volumes. "A good secretary who's a good sub."

His smile fades as he stares back, his gaze sliding down from my eyes to my mouth. As his hand coasts along my lower back, he pulls me against his hard body even closer.

"Yeah...that's too bad."

Rule #15: In a sex club, it's okay to stare.

Charlie

I SPEND THE NEXT HOUR OR SO AT EMERSON'S SIDE. WHEREVER I try to move, he's there, an affirming hand at the small of my back, and he never misses the chance to introduce me. He does so as his date, not his secretary, with a look of pride on his face.

And after two glasses of champagne, I'm beaming. Every few moments, he checks on me, letting his eyes settle on my face, allowing them to linger for a moment before pulling me closer.

Is this normal? For him to treat me like more than a work date, like a real date? I don't know what's normal and what's not anymore.

I spot the construction worker again, the one who hit on me in front of Emerson and had him so worked up. I barely recognize him in a tux, but that smile gives him away. He's flirting with a woman at the bar, and by the looks of it, those two will be getting a room at any moment.

Emerson introduces me to the rest of the owners. Hunter and his beautiful wife, Isabel. I see Maggie again, but she seems unable to relax and worries about everything until Garrett and Emerson practically force champagne down her throat.

As they all talk, I remain at Emerson's side, but my gaze continues to wander around the room. I notice more than once people going down the dark hallway. The bouncer lifts the rope for them before they disappear into the darkness. There's another black curtain hiding whatever lies behind.

My curiosity is practically killing me. So when Emerson starts talking to the rich man from the poker table, no longer accompanied by the kneeling woman, I excuse myself to use the restroom. I disappear into the crowd and meander my way casually toward the hallway. Being free of Emerson is both liberating and terrifying. I feel like an imposter in a world where I don't fit. I don't belong here, and it's written all over my face.

Eyes linger on me as I pass by. They can tell I'm a fraud.

When I reach the red rope and the black curtain of the forbidden hallway, the bouncer stares at me wordlessly.

"Um…" It's so loud in here, he probably doesn't even hear me. "The bathroom?"

I know well enough that the bathroom isn't down here. His brow furrows at me and I nearly die of embarrassment. I'm about to crawl back into the crowd and try to convince my brain that that didn't just happen when the bouncer looks up for a second and nods at someone across the room. I barely have a moment to turn around and look when he lifts the red rope and anticipation causes the blood to drain out of my body entirely.

It feels like over an hour that I stand there and gape at him in surprise. Though it's probably only a millisecond. Before he can change his mind, I step through the curtain and enter the dark, ominous hallway.

It seems longer than I remember, but it's probably an illusion from the lack of light. There's no crowd back here, but a few people linger along the walls, and unlike in the main room, no one looks at me. They keep to themselves, or each other, and not a single head turns in my direction. Gentle light emits from the large windows on either side, and it takes my brain a few moments to register that the people gathered around the hallway aren't looking at me, because they're busy…with each other.

I don't stare long enough to actually see what they're doing. One man has a woman pressed face-first against the glass as he grinds slowly against her from behind.

Trying to make myself as inconspicuous as possible, I slink into the darker corners, trying not to be a creep. Moving slowly down the hall, my heart is literally pounding so hard in my chest that I can feel it in my ears. *What am I doing here? This is insane.*

But my curiosity is too strong, and I've gotten this far. One slow step at a time, I make my way farther down the hallway. The first window is open to a room that's too dark to see anything. It's a dim blue light, and there's movement on the other side—the quick, pounding motion of someone being…well, pounded.

My throat constricts as I look away, then back again.

And my belly warms.

But I don't stop, turning my head to the other side, where the woman is being dry humped into the window. I can hear the gentle hum of the man's voice as he whispers in her ear. I can only imagine what he's saying…and the filthy thoughts only make me hotter. Beyond the window is what looks like a red room with no one inside. There are a lot of *things* hanging from the wall, a lot of things I can't even assign names to; I'm guessing whips, paddles, cuffs…that sort of thing.

Not my taste, so I keep walking. I pass by a couple standing in the middle of the room, giggling to each other as they enjoy the view. The woman smiles at me and the man says hello in a way that makes me walk a little faster. I nod politely and move on.

The room on the opposite side is blocked by a black curtain with shreds of light peeking through. So people who want to use the rooms, without being exhibitionists, can do so. A little disappointing, actually.

Seriously, who am I?

When I reach the throne room, where I once sat before it was finished, I pause. There are people in it. Three people, unless I'm missing one. It's dimly lit from the inside, enough to see vague figures and movement but not really enough to recognize faces. I then realize that this means we can see them, but they can't really see us.

My gaze still bounces from the dark hallway to the people in the room because, even though I know it's made for watching, it feels strange and wrong to just keep staring.

Plus, there's the awkward sensation of being aroused...in public.

My thin, cotton thong is currently soaked, and every slide of friction when I walk sends sparks up my spine. I have a strong urge to touch myself, which I'm obviously *not going to do*. Not because it wouldn't be appropriate here, I mean...look around. But I just can't. I couldn't. No. That's *too* weird.

Still, I stop at the throne room and force myself to look. I don't know what to do with my hands as I stand here and stare, so I lock my forearms together at my waist.

There's a woman sitting on the giant throne, and another is kneeling in front of her—just as Garrett illustrated for me. She's definitely doing what I think she's doing with her face buried between the other woman's legs.

My mouth goes dry. It feels so wrong to be watching this, but I can't look away.

There's someone standing next to the throne, but I can't quite make out if it's a woman or man. They're just stroking the woman in the chair's shoulders and head. Every few moments, the woman covers her face or lets out a giggle so loud I can make it out over the sound of the music in the main room. She looks almost euphoric, full of smiles and moans, shifting back and forth between embarrassment and pleasure.

The intensity between my legs has grown painful, and I feel myself starting to sweat. I squeeze my thighs together, briefly wondering if I could make myself come without actually touching myself at all. My thighs rub together subtly, and it's like trying to scratch an itch through three layers of wool.

"Enjoying yourself?"

I let out a gasp and move to jump away, but a strong hand wraps around my middle, hauling me against his body, his lips next to my ear.

"Relax, Charlotte."

"You scared me."

"You seem a little jumpy," Emerson replies with a teasing grin.

I feel like I've been caught masturbating or watching porn. Shame washes over me like being doused in ice-cold water.

"I don't think I'm supposed to be back here," I whisper without turning toward him. He's holding me in place, so we're both watching the threesome in the throne room.

"You wouldn't be here if you weren't allowed to. I was hoping you'd find this area." So he did gesture to the bouncer to let me in. I figured, but I'm curious as to why. Last time we were here, Emerson wanted me nowhere near this lifestyle, but now it feels as if he's urging me into it.

"It feels so strange to watch," I whisper.

"They want you to watch." His deep, velvet voice warms me right back up.

We stand in silence for a moment, watching the show in the throne room, my body still humming with arousal.

"No one can see you here, Charlotte. Doesn't it feel liberating? To know you can do anything you want?"

My lips part and I try to force in a breath, even though my chest feels like it weighs a ton. My body has turned into a ticking time bomb, ready to explode, and I want to scream with this need I'm feeling.

Emerson's body is hard against mine and he's still holding me around my waist. In the dark room, the man has moved to the front of the throne with the ladies. He leans over and kisses the kneeling woman. Then, he keeps moving until he's kneeling behind her.

A subtle gasp escapes my lips when I realize what he's doing: pulling up her dress and undoing his pants. And then even in the darkness there's the unmistakable motion of his hips as he enters her.

I turn my head, trying to look away. But a strong hand holds my chin gently, turning my head back to the window.

"Watch them. You know you want to."

I do want to. But the ache between my legs is almost unbearable. My knees begin to buckle, and Emerson holds me tighter.

"What's wrong?" he whispers in my ear.

"Nothing," I stammer, forcing my voice to stay level.

"You can touch yourself back here, Charlotte. No one can see you."

"No," I snap. "I can't."

My hips shift, and I feel something hard against my lower back. As I brush along the length of it, he groans and squeezes me tighter, driving his hips into me.

I take in a sharp inhale, my vision growing blurry. He's hard. Emerson is hard, and he's rubbing his erection against me.

"You feel that?" he whispers. "That's what you do to me."

Me? Not the display of sex all around us? The orgasm cries and sounds of bodies slapping together?

Knowing the effect I have on him drives me to shift my hips back just slightly, and he responds with a growl in my ear.

Maybe because it's dark or because this is just how his business is, but it doesn't feel wrong. It feels...right. We're not crossing a line...just sharing an experience. It's natural and normal, and I'm not ashamed.

His hand glides down my arm until he catches my fingers in his hand, and I'm confused by what he's doing until the other hand gathers my dress, pulling it up until I'm exposed. I can hardly breathe or think when he leads my own hand to the front of my panties.

"Touch yourself, Charlotte."

A whimper escapes my lips. I resist, trying to pull my hand away, but he doesn't let me go. When my fingers reach my clit, even over the cotton of my thong, pleasure radiates through me. At this point, I couldn't pull them away if I tried.

"It's okay. Don't feel ashamed." His lips are touching my ear, and I relax against him, letting my head fall back onto his shoulder as he slides my panties aside and presses my fingers against my clit. I don't even bother fighting anymore.

The man in the throne room has picked up speed, slamming into the kneeling woman at a steady rhythm. Their moans and cries are audible now, and it only urges me deeper and deeper in this steady current toward my climax.

"That's it, Charlotte. Good girl."

His words spur me on, sending bolts of lightning through my body. My own fingers rub my clit in fast circles, and it feels so good; it's a relief. Emerson's hand rests over mine, but he isn't touching me. Instead, he grips my hip with one hand and grinds his erection against my backside.

Any thoughts about this being inappropriate are far away from here—outside of this moment and this dark hallway. Because right now, there's only one thing I want, and that's to come. I don't even care that it's in public anymore.

"You are so fucking beautiful. Make yourself come, baby."

And his words don't stop, like a river of praise I'm coursing down, heading straight for a cliff. My eyes don't leave the throne room for a second, and when my orgasm comes crashing into me, I nearly crumble to the floor. My free hand grips the fabric of Emerson's suit as he wraps his arms around me.

"So perfect." His lips brush my ear, then my cheek, and trail down to my neck. I can't even hear anymore—my ears are ringing, and my skin is buzzing. The orgasm just keeps knocking me down, wave after wave after wave. His hand finds mine again, and I feel his fingers carefully brush my delicate skin. But he doesn't stop as he runs his fingers deeper into my panties, and I stiffen in his grasp when he reaches the evidence of my orgasm.

He moans darkly against my ear. Then, he pulls his wet finger out and lifts it to his mouth. I turn to look up at him just as he slips it past his lips, licking my arousal off of his finger.

"Emerson," I whisper, and our eyes meet. It's a long, heavy moment as we let everything that just happened swim in the tension between us. Does he feel bad for crossing this line? Do I?

No, I don't. I keep waiting for shame or regret to hit me, but it doesn't. Instead, I'm...excited. I feel like I'm on the edge of something big, and I don't want to turn back now.

The threesome in the throne room has come to an end, and when I look back at the window, one of the women is standing just on the other side of the glass. Her gaze catches mine for a moment, and I stare at her with my mouth open. There is something oddly familiar about her, like I've seen her somewhere before. Then, she gives me a small wink and sly smile before pulling the curtain closed.

As soon as Emerson ushers me out of the dark hallway of sin, I scurry off to the bathroom. Suddenly, this dimly lit main room is just too freaking bright. I feel like everyone can see what I just did. They *know* that I just masturbated in *public* while watching Pornhub Live back there.

The bathroom is also dimly lit, which is a blessing. I was afraid it was going to be bright florescent lights in here. I wash my hands at the sink. Even the bathroom is fancy, with ornate gold mirrors and shiny black stone counters.

While rinsing my hands, I glance up at the woman in the mirror's reflection. Do I seem happy?

Happier than I was with Beau, certainly. But something is missing. What, I don't know.

Just then, a woman comes out of the stall and takes her

place at the sink next to me. When I glance up, I'm frozen in place, realizing it's the same woman from the throne room, and I suddenly know why she seemed so familiar. It's Madame Kink.

I almost didn't recognize her without the black leather and whip, but it's definitely the same sable-haired Dominatrix from the blog who told me everything I needed to know about Emerson Grant and the SPC. In fact, she's still teaching me everything I need to know. Her website has gotten more clicks from my browser than probably any other user.

She might as well be a celebrity to me at this point, and I just watched her get publicly railed while she was going down on another woman.

When she notices me, her eyes graze over my body, and she looks up at my face and smiles.

"You are stunning," she says, and my mouth falls open. Me? This woman, this…goddess, is telling me that I'm stunning.

"Thank you," I mumble, feeling stupefied.

As she dries her hands, she keeps her eyes on me. And I know I should leave, but I can't seem to move. Then she looks at me with a bright smile.

"Isn't this place amazing?"

I nod, not quite knowing how to respond. And she continues.

"I mean, to have a place where we can just be ourselves, enjoy what we want to enjoy without feeling bad about it or catching judgment."

"Yeah." I feel so lame because I literally can't think of a single smart thing to say. She steps toward me, letting her fingers dance down my arm to my wrist, where she takes my hand in hers.

"Emerson Grant is a fucking god, and he spent the whole night obsessed with *you*. And you look so nervous."

Hearing his name come out of her mouth sends a shock of ice down my spine. She spoke about him like she knows him or like she *wants* him. *My* Emerson.

"I'm not nervous," I lie. I wish that were true. I wish I were the sexy, confident type of woman she is. The kind Emerson wants.

"Good. Don't be nervous. Just be yourself. That's the beauty of this place. Emerson's given us somewhere to finally be free."

"Us?" I ask.

"Yeah…you don't think this place is just for men, do you?"

I don't respond as I let my mind wander back to everything I saw and experienced tonight. And I realize…she's right.

In the car on the way home, Emerson is silent, which is now awkward, considering everything that happened tonight. While he drives, I take a moment to stare at him, noticing how much he's changed in my perception since we met. I no longer see a man out of my reach. I see a man who makes me feel worthy in a way I didn't know I needed—didn't know I *deserved*.

And I think about what the woman in the bathroom said. Is Emerson really seen as a god? And was he really obsessed with me all night?

A month ago, I might have said she was wrong, that she had me confused with a different type of woman, the kind who could please a man like Emerson.

But I've changed, and I don't feel that way anymore.

He catches me staring. Glancing my way, he asks, "Did you enjoy yourself tonight?"

"Yes," I reply. I'm not sure if he means in general or specifically the time we spent in the hallway. The answer applies to both.

"If you'd like to go back, your membership fees are waived. You'd have to go through the inputting process, though. Provide negative test results, sign some waivers—"

"I don't want to go back without you."

Our eyes meet for a moment, and I wish I knew what he was thinking. Am I being too clingy? Hoping for too much? Or does he feel the same way? I want things with Emerson I don't understand. Things I didn't expect. And it's not sex—although I wouldn't turn that down.

More than anything, I want his attention. I want to live in this world with him and I want him to be my guide—not just for one night. I want to be the only woman on his arm…to be *his*. I'm setting myself up for heartbreak. I know it.

Emerson and I are in this strange limbo where we don't cross lines, but we don't deny ourselves indulgences either. I don't know what we are and I'm still not quite sure what I want. All I know is that when he looks at me the way he is right now, I want whatever I can get.

As we pull up to my house, he gets out to open my door.

"Thank you for taking me," I tell him, and before I walk away, I lean close and press my lips to his cheek. I wish I could thank him for the hallway moment, but I don't quite feel comfortable saying, *Thanks for making me touch myself*, but I wish he knew how big of a moment that was for me. Tonight felt like a turning point, and he may never know that.

Before I can pull away, his hand grasps the back of my neck, holding my face only inches from his. "Just for tonight," he breathes as he touches his lips to mine, and with those three words alone, I understand what this is. Tonight feels special, like it exists outside of our regular Monday-to-Friday, nine-to-five reality. That just for tonight, he can touch me and make me come and kiss me, and it won't have any effect on the rules and lines we've put in place.

I wish he'd kiss me deeper, but his lips only graze mine, so I feel his beard on my face, and I wish it were enough for me, but it's not. I want more. But like the stroke of midnight for Cinderella, this little dream of mine has to end too.

All too soon, he lets me go, and I step back to gaze up into his eyes.

"I'll see you Monday, Charlotte."

"Yes, sir," I reply, and he freezes for a moment, my gaze locked with his as my words echo between us. I didn't really mean to say that, but it just came out, and obviously, it had an effect on him. It's written all over his face. I wonder if he's thinking about that first day. The day he thought I was his new sub, when he told me to kneel and address him as *sir*, because it's exactly what I'm thinking about.

Quickly, I pull away and walk toward the gate that leads to my small guest house in the back. Even as he drives away, I ponder that look on his face and how it felt in that small, minuscule moment. Calling him *sir*, like his "secretaries" before did. How when I asked him if he wanted me to be like that for him, he didn't exactly say no.

I can't stop thinking about it all night, my body still buzzing with excitement.

The next morning, I wake up with a new sense of purpose. Because I know that come Monday morning, everything will be different. Because I *want* everything to be different. So I barely leave my room all day, researching and reading and trying to fully understand what it is that Emerson wants.

No, what *I* want.

Rule #16: Always come prepared.

Charlotte

Sometime on Sunday I receive a text from Emerson.

> I'm meeting with some people at the club at 8:00 tomorrow morning. Let yourself into the house and I'll be back around 10:00.

I type and delete and type and delete my response about ten times before finally hitting Send.

> Yes, sir.

He doesn't respond. And Emerson *always* needs the last word, which means I've left him speechless. Which also means I'm getting what I want.

On Monday, I show up early, using the code he gave me to unlock the front door, and get straight to work. I chose the same pencil skirt and see-through blouse I wore on the first day. I can barely focus on my morning tasks while I wait for him, and when

10:15 rolls around, I hear the garage door open. Quickly, I tidy my desk and rush to the center of the room.

I can do this. I can do this. I can do this.

The internal pep talk is the only thing keeping me from backing out because the more I think about it, the more I realize *this is insane.* And I have no idea how he will react. If he's angry, I'll be humiliated. If he's surprised, I'll be pleased. And if he loves it…God, I don't know how I'll feel.

I hear the garage door close, and I take a deep steadying breath. Then, I drop the pillow on the floor (thanks for the tip, internet) and fall to my knees. Facing the door he's about to walk through, I bow my head and place my hands delicately in my lap.

There's a tremor of nerves traveling all the way down to my bones as I wait for him. His shoes click against the marble floor as he passes through the kitchen—getting closer and closer—and I want to back out. This was stupid. He's going to fire me for being so stupid.

But it's too late. His footsteps reach the office door and they stop. The silence is heavy as he stands there and stares at me, and I don't dare move. Keeping my eyes on my lap, I wait.

"What…are you doing?" he asks.

I expected this question, so I'm prepared.

"Being a good girl," I reply, "sir."

I hear him take in a heavy breath. He's going to say something harsh or tell me to get up or to stop. At least I tried.

Instead, he takes five deafening steps toward me. When he's close enough to touch me, I feel his fingers reach for my chin and tilt my head upward. There's affection in his eyes as he stares down at me, warmth trickling over me. The way that look makes me feel is like gold. If I could bottle it up and sell it, I'd be rich.

"You *are* such a good girl," he says, and I nearly melt into the floor. "You want to learn how to be a good sub?"

"Yes, sir," I reply.

His jaw tenses as he deliberates his response.

"Fine. But not every day, understand?"

I try to fight back my smile, but it slips through anyway. "Yes, sir."

"I want there to be days when you're just Charlotte, okay?"

My shoulders soften as I let his words sink in. Then, I nod.

"And if you don't like it, you don't have to do it. There's a lot more we'll need to discuss, limits and safety and things like that, all right?"

I nod again, knowing from my research this weekend that he would say something like this. I learned that communication is the most important thing and that boundaries have to be set because there are a lot of things that can go wrong.

Which is why I came prepared.

"I wrote down my limits," I reply, staring up at him.

He looks momentarily surprised, stroking my chin. "You did? Can I see them?"

I nod, moving to stand, but he puts gentle pressure on my shoulder to keep me down.

"Ah-ah. Crawl there for me."

My lips part and my body is flooded with heat. "Yes, sir," I reply. He moves out of the way so I can crawl to my desk, where the printed paper sits next to my laptop. Grabbing it off the desk, I hesitate for a moment, not sure how to crawl and carry it at the same time.

"In your teeth," he replies, noticing my uncertainty. And I do as he says, biting down on the paper as I move back onto all fours, carrying it toward him. He's leaning on his desk now, arms crossed and watching me. Once I reach him, I sit back in a kneeling position.

He strokes my head gently and takes the paper from my teeth. Then I wait as he browses through what I wrote. This is the nerveracking part because there were a lot of things on that list that made me a little nervous to admit.

"Where did you get this?" he asks.

"It was a printable list I got online. Is it okay?"

He waits a moment before responding. "It's excellent, Charlotte. I'm proud of you."

I smile to myself. The list has over two hundred items and I had to rank each one from zero, being an absolutely hard limit, to five, being very interested, please do. Most of the list landed at three, which means curious. Naturally.

I know I'm supposed to keep my head down, but I can't resist the urge to watch his face as he reads the list. To be honest, most of the items were hard to rank because they involved sex, and Emerson and I don't have that kind of relationship yet. All I know is that the more I'm with him and the more he pushes me past my limits, the more I want.

He doesn't say a word as he browses, and his poker face doesn't give much away. All I know is he's reading things like...

Paddling, three.

Caning...two.

Serving, five.

Bondage...three.

Boot licking, *zero.*

Sex. No answer.

In fact, everything in the sex category is blank, from hand jobs to fisting—zero on the last one if I had to rank it.

It feels like forever that he reads the papers, and I'm sick with anticipation. I keep waiting to be scolded like a child. And I regret not at least putting a three or four under the sex categories, but how could I?

If I've learned anything this past month and a half, it's that I should ask for what I want and that sex doesn't need to be so serious. It's supposed to be fun and feel good, and that's what I want...so why didn't I ask for it?

From my boss.

Beau's dad.

God, what am I thinking?

"Interesting," he says without looking at me. Then he just sets the paper down on the desk and turns his gaze to me. "I'm not interested in physical punishment, so you don't have to worry about the caning or the paddling. But you left a few of them blank, Charlotte."

I clear my throat. "I didn't know…"

"Sex isn't necessary, you understand that, right?"

"Yes."

"In fact," he adds, "I'm willing to teach you what you need to know to be a proper submissive, but we have to maintain an appropriate relationship. You're still my employee and Beau's…friend."

Disappointment washes over me. "Okay."

"For now, I want you to go back to your desk and do your tasks for the day. You'll be silent and only address me as *sir* if you have a question. Otherwise, you'll stay at your desk, and when I need you, I'll call you over and you'll do what I say. Is that clear?"

I'm hit with another wave of disappointment. Just be silent at my desk? That's it? "Yes, sir," I reply obediently.

"Good girl. On your feet then." He reaches a hand down, and I place my fingers in his as he lifts me to a standing position. Once I'm upright, his gaze drifts down from my face to my blouse, noticing my black bra again like he did on my first day.

"Go ahead, then. Get to work," he says, and his voice sounds a touch strained as if that's not quite what he wanted to say. As if he's holding back.

I'm restless in my chair as I work for the next hour. He asks me to get him coffee and to put in a delivery order for lunch, but for the most part, it's a regular work day. But unlike every other work day, I'm silent and I miss talking to him.

After lunch, he has a videoconference meeting planned with Garrett, Hunter, and Maggie. Apparently, they have something to discuss with their lawyer, and I'm a little nervous about what he expects me to do while he's on the call.

"Charlotte, come here."

Getting up from my desk, I walk over to him, and he gestures for me to come to his side. Once I'm there, he takes my hand.

"I want you to kneel by my side while I'm on the call, okay? No one will see you."

"Okay," I mumble, and he gives me a curious glare. "I mean, yes…sir."

"Very good. Go get your pillow."

When I return with the cushion for my knees, I drop onto the floor. I'm resting in the space just next to his chair but hidden behind his desk…and I hate it. He does a little on his computer while I wait, and I honestly start questioning everything I have chosen to do up to this point. This isn't what I expected at all. I expected him to pay attention to me. I expected for it to be sexy, and at some point, I expected something, anything, to feel good. Where is this beloved *subspace* everyone online raves about?

His meeting starts and he and his co-owners start chatting, but I can't do anything. At least before I would take notes and be useful. This is ridiculous. I'm just staring at his desk, hidden like a dirty secret. But I'm going to see this through. I'll tell him later that I just didn't like being ignored. He'll understand.

When the lawyer gets on the call, Maggie does most of the talking, and I notice Emerson start to tense up. He looks down at me with a furrow between his brows, and I gaze up at him. Everything about this feels wrong. Shouldn't I be doing something?

Just then, he reaches down and brushes my hair out of my face. With his eyes still longingly locked on mine, he strokes my hair again and again.

I want to resist. I'd like to express how demeaning this is and how stupid I feel, but there's something I didn't anticipate with every ounce of his attention. There's this visceral connection between us, and it's stronger than any I've felt before with other guys. He's touching me with adoration, and I can see his shoulders soften as he does, the tension melting off of his face.

In the background, Maggie and the lawyer just keep talking,

but Emerson's not listening and neither am I. Right now we exist in our own separate world.

He gently rolls back his chair and turns toward me, exposing his leg to me, and I instinctually rest my cheek against his thigh.

"Perfect," he whispers almost silently. And I swim in his praise. He's not taking anything I'm not willfully giving. This relationship is symbiotic and wholly powerful. Intoxicating almost.

His large hand brushes through my hair, and I shut my eyes, trying to absorb the way his confidence and calmness washes over me. I wonder if he can feel it too; I have a feeling he can, and I'm almost certain this connection is mutual.

"Emerson," Maggie calls from the computer, and he freezes, looking up at her. It breaks the silence, and I almost hate her for it. "Can you have Charlotte transfer over those files after our meeting? I'm going to go over them tonight."

"Yes, I can," he replies, and I gaze up at him. They can't see me on the camera, and unlike fifteen minutes ago, I suddenly love feeling like his dirty little secret. Because now it feels deliberate. *His attention* is deliberate. And that's what I really want, more than I care to admit.

It makes me wonder if the rest of them suspect I'm down here, doing this for him every day. They know what Emerson likes. They know he hires girls for this, and although he's told them I'm just his secretary, they might suspect that I'm also doing this. For some reason, I really want them to know. Suddenly, I want everyone to know.

I've never had a desire to be *claimed* before, but suddenly, it's like I need the world to know I belong to Emerson Grant. Which is ridiculous.

The meeting comes to an end, and our work day resumes in the same way it started. For the first time in a long time, I'm relieved when five o'clock rolls around. Not because I didn't like certain moments of this very strange day, but because I'm ready to go back to being Charlotte and Emerson again. Just us.

Looking up from my desk at five, I realize that I don't quite know what to do at this point. Do I call *end scene* and say goodbye like nothing weird happened here today?

Almost as if he could read my mind, he looks up at me. "That's enough for today, Charlotte."

"Yes, sir," I reply by habit. Hesitantly, I stand up and start gathering my things. I can feel his eyes on me.

"What did you think?"

I turn toward him with my purse on my shoulder. With a shrug, I say, "It was different. But I liked it."

"What parts did you like?" He leans back in his large chair, those wolflike green eyes on me.

"Umm..." I'm a little torn with my answer because it almost feels like he's testing me. "It's not really about what I like, is it? As your sub, my job is to please you."

He looks impressed as that crooked, sly smile I've come to love over the past six weeks creeps across his face. "You've done your research."

"I don't half-ass anything, Emerson. You should know this about me by now."

His grin grows, reaching his eyes and putting dimples in his cheeks. "Yes, I do." Then, he stands and walks toward me. Keeping a couple feet between us, he says, "But I'm still genuinely curious. What parts of today did you like?"

I let out an exhale, trying to remain casual, as if we're talking about lunch and not BDSM. "I liked being helpful, calming your nerves during the meeting. I like doing things for you."

"I like you doing things for me too."

That gooey, warm feeling is back as I stare up at him.

"How did I do?" I ask in a breathless pant. I'm fishing for compliments, and it's obvious to both of us, but he likes to give them out, so I'm going to take them.

Reaching out, he touches my chin. "You did so good," he replies in a gravelly tone I can feel from the top of my head to the tips of my toes. "You like me telling you that, don't you?"

"Mm-hm."

His thumb strokes my chin. "That's what I thought."

When his fingers leave my face, I let the familiar disappointment wash over me like it does every day. Every time I have to turn away from Emerson without another touch, I feel it. It doesn't get any easier, but there's really no way around it.

Leaving his house, I tell myself the same thing I do every day: I'll never have Emerson the way I want, so I might as well get used to it.

Rule #17: Get her out of your system.

Emerson

MY REFLECTION STARES BACK AT ME IN THE BATHROOM, BUT MY eyes won't focus on the man in front of me. All I see is her on her knees in the middle of my office. The image plays over and over in my mind. How did this happen?

Is it too far? Have I royally fucked things up already?

But there's no room in my mind for regret when it's so damn overwhelmed with desire. The *things I wanted to do to her*. God, I wanted to remove her clothes, touch her face, sit her on my lap, and stroke her perfect body while I worked. With any other girl, that's what I would have done, but I've never wanted it the way I want it now.

For years, I've accepted that these dominant cravings are just a part of who I am. I was happy with that but never fully satisfied with anyone who came along. Now, the craving is stronger than ever, and I have the terrifying notion that Charlotte might actually be perfect for me, and that's a real problem.

She's *Beau's* girl. I can't possibly keep doing this.

Fuck, my brain still can't process *no*, so I strip off my clothes and start the shower. This day fucked with my head and I need to wash it all off so I can refocus on getting my son back.

Apparently, my cock can't process *no* either because it's at full attention, still thinking about the way she hummed with pleasure while I stroked her head during the call.

Not to mention, it's still thinking about what happened Saturday night in the voyeur hall. That's what started all this. I never should have taken her to the club opening, and I definitely shouldn't have followed her into that hall. And I really shouldn't have fucking touched her the way I did.

But it was impersonal. I touched her, *tasted her*, but that's what we do at the club. We shed the personal ties and hang-ups from our daily lives and we experience freely what our body craves to experience. If I hadn't gone back there with her, she never would have had the nerve to touch herself and make herself come the way she did.

My cock twitches at the memory. The way she rubbed herself, the sounds she made, the taste of her arousal, and how good she felt in my arms. Like she belonged there.

I give my dick an easy stroke, but it won't let me let go. And it won't let me think of anything other than Charlotte, conjuring up images of her in my head. Those perfect lips wrapped around my cock.

In my imagination, she's between my legs at my desk, swallowing me down while I work. My perfect little secretary.

Fuck. My hand slaps against the tile wall as my other hand picks up speed. This is so wrong, but maybe this will help me get her out of my system. This is the only way I'll ever have her like this—in my mind. If people knew I was jacking off to my son's girlfriend…

But I'm already too lost to the fantasy. The way she loves my cock. The way she calls me *sir*. That smile as I unload warm jets of cum all over her face, and she licks it up like the good girl she is.

An illicit groan vibrates from my chest as I come onto my

hand. My heart is hammering like crazy in my chest and my cock just won't stop. I obviously need to get laid or something because this is fucking ridiculous.

Tomorrow, I have to tell Charlotte that I can't be the Dom she wants. It's inappropriate, and I need to focus on work and getting my son back. But when I towel off after my shower, I find a message from her on my phone. My eyes nearly bug out of my head when I see a photo come through.

It's a picture of a St. Andrew's cross, a giant wooden frame in the shape of an X with restraints on the end of each post.

She follows the picture up with a text.

I'm doing some research. Have you ever used one of these?

I scrub my hand across my face and force myself to breathe before replying…

You should be sleeping.
And no, I have not. I am not into impact play.

The text bubbles pop up before her response.

I'm googling impact play.

I let out a groan. This should feel wrong, leading her into this lifestyle. But she's an adult. Everything is consensual. I'm not forcing her into anything she isn't interested in. With a shake of my head, I carry my phone to bed with me and climb under the sheets, trying to talk my cock into giving it a rest for the night when I get another alert.

I don't think I'd like that either.
I have a question…
What is it?

Everything is really...sexual. Is it even possible to do this without sex?

I'm about two seconds away from tossing my phone across the bed in frustration. My cock seems to think it was invited to something because it is aching in my boxers, flinching at the sound of each new text that comes through like a puppy waiting for a treat.

I think about my response for a long time. The problem is that I'm not quite sure if Charlotte is asking this because she wants there to be sex and is hopeful it will happen or if she's genuinely afraid of sex being involved and wants to learn about the lifestyle regardless. She is so blunt and open with her questions but so guarded with her emotions.

Finally, I decide to be honest...and careful.

It is possible. It just means our options are limited. Yes, the Dom/sub activities are mostly sexual in nature, but the dynamic is not. And the dynamic is what I like most.

She's typing out her response almost immediately.

So you didn't have sex with your last "secretaries"?

I groan again. Does she even know what she's doing to me? Does she really understand how much I want her and how hard she makes it to deny myself when she asks me stuff like this?

Answering this question is painful, and I hate that I have to be honest.

I had sex with most of them.

Her reply takes a moment longer.

Oh.

There's tension on the line while I wait for another message. I wish I could just tell her how badly I want her, but I can't. Finally, when she does respond, the message nearly breaks me.

I can't believe I'm even saying this, but I like being submissive.
I just want to be enough for you. I want to make you proud.
Even if we can't... :(

The words on the screen course down my spine like a slow drip of lava, and my cock is more than ready for round two. It might actually be the sad face emoji that does me in. The tiny little frown on my screen that makes me want to say *fuck it* and drive over to her pool house right now so I can force her to her knees, slide my cock between those perfect, pink lips, and make her beg me to fuck her. I quickly type out my response before I can overthink it, choosing to ignore the last message she sent altogether.

You made me very proud today.
And you are more than enough.
You are perfect.

The throbbing organ in my chest swells as I hit Send. This is more than arousal. More than wanting to fuck her or hear her call me sir. If I were twenty years younger, she's exactly the kind of girl I'd want. Why Beau let her get away, I have no clue. But I'm finding myself more and more addicted to this girl with each passing day.

And when my phone chimes again with another text, I'm almost too afraid to read it because I'm pretty sure I already know what it's going to say.

Thank you, sir.

God, I'm so fucked.

Rule #18: Wear a remote-controlled vibrator at your own risk.

Charlotte

It's a no-fun day. Which is what I've come to call the days that I have to be just Charlotte and he's Emerson, not sir. There're no *good girls*. No *yes, sirs*. Just a regular secretary. Blah.

We do it every other day, and I find myself more and more disappointed on days like this.

Luckily, we're at the club today. Emerson has a meeting with some sex toy suppliers to stock the store, so I guess I really can't complain about today after all. When we arrive at the club, I follow him to the right where everyone is gathered—Garrett, Maggie, Hunter, and even the construction worker, Drake, who's no longer in his dusty clothes and hard hat but dressed nicely in a pair of tight jeans and V-neck T-shirt, showing off a patch of dark chest hair. My gaze lingers on him for a moment, and he catches me staring, sending me a wink that makes me blush and look away.

My eyes trail to Emerson, who is watching me too, but he doesn't look as happy as Drake. In fact, he's glaring at me with a furrowed brow. Shit…what is that look for? What did I do wrong?

Before I can ask, a woman I don't recognize walks in through the front door. She is a tall redhead dressed all in black and carrying a black tote bag. There is a belted harness over her shoulders and wrapped around her waist. I find myself staring at it. It looks more like a fashion statement than something she utilizes, and I love the way it looks on her. Powerful and dominant and sexy. With a bright smile on her face, she introduces herself to everyone.

Then as her gaze falls on Emerson's face, she pauses. "Hello, Emerson," she says with a bright, flirty smile. Instantly, the hairs on my neck rise in alarm.

"Monica," he replies, biting back his own smile. "How are you?"

They clearly know each other.

"I'm great. You?"

"Good, thanks. Running your own business now?"

"Yes," she says, clutching her bag tighter. "And business is great."

"I'm proud of you," he replies, and the fake smile I was trying to hold fades into a frown. Hearing him praise someone else has me wanting to scream.

"Is this your new secretary?" she asks, glancing at me.

"Yes. This is Charlotte. Charlotte, please greet Monica Taylor. An old employee of mine."

My eyes snap in his direction, but he doesn't give me any signs. Just a blank expression. As her eyes cascade over my body, sizing me up, I shift uncomfortably on my feet.

"Lovely to meet you, Charlotte."

He nods his head subtly as if to remind me of my order. He told me to greet her. Ordered me to. He doesn't do that unless it's a...Dom/sub day. Is he trying to show me off? Because he wants her to see how good his new secretary is?

Well, too bad, because I'm already feeling stubborn.

I don't want to meet his old secretary. Especially not as my imagination sends me images of her on her knees for him. His praise in her ears instead of mine.

Suddenly, I realize I'm replaceable. The truth hits me like a train, and it's excruciating, nearly knocking me off my feet. I mean, I'm not stupid. I know he had other girls before me, but I don't want to fucking meet them. The cruel reminder that she probably got to sleep with him and I don't stings too. And I hate the way he ordered me to greet her, even when he and I both know today is not one of those days. I'm not going to play the part for *her*.

So I grit my teeth, throw her a fake-as-hell smile, and say, "Hey."

Out of the corner of my eye, I see his face fall. His jaw ticks as he glares at me. It feels like standing under a freezing cold rain, his disappointment laser-focused on me. Monica's eyes widen, but she doesn't say anything as she greets the rest of the group.

I refuse to look back at Emerson, out of both obstinance and fear.

Monica displays everything she brought on the glass case and gets started on her presentation. She's brought an array of toys, things customers could use here at the club. Dildos, vibrators, handcuffs, creams, lotions, lube—you name it, she brought it. And I want to pay attention, but I can't make my mind focus on anything but Emerson's frustration with me, so much so that it trumps *my* frustration with *him*.

And it doesn't help that Monica's attention is almost entirely on Emerson. Once she's done, Maggie offers to give Monica a tour of the facility, and I'm momentarily relieved that we're about to be rid of this bitch who just ambushed my perfectly good day.

Then, she turns with a beaming smile at the man next to me and says, "Emerson, I'd love a tour from you." My skin buzzes with fiery hot hatred as I watch her touch his arm. I despise this woman so much I could hit her. I quickly take a step to follow him, but he turns my way, clutching on to my arm and whispering in a dark, low tone, "Stay here."

My mouth falls open. Is he serious?

What is he going to do with her? Take her to one of the private rooms and…

"Fine," I mutter, turning away. If he thinks he's going to get a *yes, sir* out of me now, he's crazy.

As I watch them walk away, tears sting my eyes, and I start to wear circles on the floor from my pacing, trying to convince myself not to be as mad as I feel right now.

What do I care? He's not my boyfriend. We have no claim on each other, and he's certainly never going to touch me like that, so I should really just get over this hang-up. It's dumb. A stupid crush but I'll never be more than his, sometimes, kinky secretary.

Lingering near the side of the great room, I keep my distance from Drake and Hunter, who are the only two left looking at the display of toys Monica left behind. They're talking quietly together, but I don't listen in. I'm too busy stewing about Emerson alone with Monica somewhere in the empty club.

After a few minutes, I hear my name being called.

"Charlie, come here."

When I look up, Drake is smiling at me, waving me toward them. Unlike Emerson, he actually calls me by my preferred name. When I approach them, still feeling a little grumpy, he touches my arm.

"Help Hunter make a choice here."

Hunter immediately shakes his head. "Leave her alone. She doesn't want to help me." Unlike Drake, Hunter is a little more reserved and will barely even look me in the eye. He's the only one of the group who is married, and his wife is a drop-dead gorgeous yoga studio owner, so I can't say I really blame him. I wouldn't jeopardize that either.

"What's up?" I ask.

Drake leans forward. "That lady said these were for us to try…"

He's holding up a U-shaped device. It's bright pink silicone, and my eyebrows lift as I stare at him. "Well, go ahead, Drake. Give it a try."

Hunter laughs, since the toy is clearly meant for a vagina. It's a remote-controlled vibrator with a small black remote.

"It's not for me," he says, staring up at me through thick dark lashes. "But he wants to get one for Isabel."

"So take it. I'm sure she'll love it."

"I think she could wear it in public, while they're out to dinner or something. But Hunter thinks it would be impossible for her to hide it."

He puts the pink vibrator in my hand, letting his fingers linger a moment too long on my skin as he gazes up at me. Drake's flirtation skills are so good, it should be criminal, like some sort of unfair sorcery. I swear, with those eyes and that smile, I would commit arson for him and probably wouldn't remember a thing.

With a push of a button in his hand, the small vibrator comes to life. It's a subtle whirring, but it still sends a jolt of excitement to my core.

"I think it depends on how much vibration you turn on," I reply, my mouth dry as he stares at me, turning up the intensity. It buzzes loudly in my palm.

"How sexy would that be?" he asks. "Sitting in a public place, feeling this between your legs and not being able to react."

"Impossible," I reply in a breathy whisper.

"So try it. I want to know for sure." He's still staring at me with those *fuck me* eyes, and I have to force myself to breathe.

"You can't be serious," I reply with a tilt of my head.

"I *dare* you," Drake says, and it's like he knows me. I'm not the kind of girl to turn down a dare.

Maybe it's because I'm pissed at Emerson or because I've already fucked up once today that I do something I know will piss him off even more. I close my hand around the vibrator and look Drake straight in the eyes, leaning so close to him, it looks like we might kiss. "Fine."

He turns the vibration off and smiles as I grab one of the disinfect wipes and clean off the toy. Then I head toward the bathroom next to us. In my periphery, I see Hunter shake his head at his friend. I really have no intention of doing anything with Drake. As much as I'm sure I'd enjoy it, it would be so wrong. Not only would it drive Emerson completely mad, but it would jeopardize the job I love so much.

In the bathroom, my hands start shaking as I take the vibrator to the stall with me. Once again, I've found myself in another *what the fuck am I doing?* situation. But I said I would, so I'm doing it.

The toy has a thick, bulbous side and a thin, padded one. According to Monica's instructions, the bulbous side goes inside to vibrate against the G-spot. I can't say I've had any experience with guys ever finding the elusive G-spot, so I'm skeptical. Taking a deep breath, I pull up my skirt, pull down my panties, and insert the thick side where it belongs.

Oh. It sort of clamps in place, sitting snug against my clit. And once I pull my panties back up, it's like a hidden little secret under my skirt. It's weird, having something inside me as I walk out of the stall. With every step, it shifts against my clit, and I have to pause at the bathroom door. It's not even turned on and I'm already worried I won't be able to keep a straight face.

Straightening my shoulders and hiding my smile, I strut out of the bathroom toward where Drake and Hunter are waiting. They're both watching me, and I hold back my smile. Then I see movement in Drake's right hand.

Suddenly, the toy hums in my panties, and my eyes widen.

Oh, shit.

It's so good, sensations buzzing inside and out, and I feel myself getting wet already.

"Wait, wait, wait," I call. Drake laughs.

"Come on, that's the lowest setting."

Fuck. I'm about to turn around and run to the bathroom to take it out because there's *no way*. Then, his hand moves again and the damn thing comes to life, buzzing even harder against my clit.

"Drake!" I shriek, bowing toward the floor as I mentally force myself not to come. *No, no, no, no.*

When it stops, I lunge toward him. "Give me that damn thing!" I yell, but he holds it out of my grasp. I'm pressed against his body, reaching for the remote as the toy starts up again.

Against my will, the highest pitch, most humiliating sound slips through my lips. It's like the soundtrack to a porno plays for one second, and Drake howls with laughter.

"You're such a jerk!" I yell clapping my hand over my mouth. I can't believe I just made that sound. Poor Hunter is covering his face with his hand, looking beet red and trying not to watch as I fight Drake for the remote while also trying not to have a very public orgasm against my will.

"You know you like it," Drake replies darkly, and my eyes meet his for a second. Oh, shit. With the way he's looking at me and the way my body is feeling at the moment, we are definitely heading straight for something I don't want, and I'm afraid if I don't stop this right now, I'm going to regret it.

There's only one person I want to cross the line with, and sorry, Drake, but it's not you.

"What is going on?" a dark voice bellows from across the room, and my body turns to ice.

The buzzing stops abruptly, and I pry myself away from Drake's wall of muscle. Quickly turning, I see Emerson walking toward me with a look of horror on his face. Oh God, he's going to find out about the vibrator. I mean, I wanted him to find out, because it would make him mad, and I *wanted* to make him mad. *Does this make me a brat?*

But now that he's staring at me like that, like I've betrayed him and somehow hurt him, I desperately hope he doesn't find out. I can't stand another second of his disappointment.

"Relax. Charlotte and I were just conducting an experiment," Drake says, and my eyes shift toward him. Oh God, he's going to just tell him, isn't he?

"It's nothing," I reply quickly, walking toward Emerson.

"What experiment?" Emerson asks.

Drake holds up the remote. "We wanted to see if she could act natural with that remote control vibrator in."

Emerson's head turns slowly in my direction, and I shrink into a tiny speck of dust next to him. "You're wearing it now?"

I force down a nervous swallow. Drake laughs. "Yeah. And in case you're wondering, she cannot. Couldn't even walk on the lowest setting."

I hate Drake. I hate him so fucking much. More than I hate Monica.

Okay, maybe not more than I hate Monica. But I hate him a lot.

"Ha, ha, ha," I reply snarkily, glaring narrow-eyed at Drake. He winks back at me, and it makes me hate him more. Stupid hot-guy sorcery. I walk toward the bathroom to take the toy out, but Emerson stops me.

"Not so fast." I watch in horror as he steps toward Drake, holding out a hand for the remote. As Drake places it in his palm, I stare, as if waiting for something catastrophic to happen. He wouldn't...would he?

He slips the remote into his pocket. "Let's go, Charlotte."

The look on his face doesn't look playful or kind. His jaw is still clicking as he clenches his teeth. His gaze still hard on me before he turns and marches toward the front door.

I quickly look back at Drake, who doesn't even bother to look apologetic. He snickers to himself.

Yep, I hate him.

With the vibrator snugly in place but still and quiet—thank God—I rush off behind Emerson.

"Where are we going?" I ask.

He gives me one quick, impatient glance before replying, "Out to lunch."

Rule #19: Not all punishments are bad.

Charlotte

I'M SO FUCKED. EMERSON IS SILENT IN THE CAR NEXT TO ME AS WE drive and I still can't really tell if he's mad at me for the way I treated Monica or for flirting with Drake or for wearing the vibrator without his permission. Or all of the above.

The thing is…I don't quite know what's right or wrong anymore, and that doesn't seem fair. If this were a normal secretary job, a normal Dom/sub situation, or a normal romantic relationship, I would at least know what was expected of me. But we're not any of those things. We're a little of everything and it's confusing as hell.

And then there's the nagging fear that Emerson was off doing God knows what with Monica in the club. Would I be upset if I found out they had sex? Yes. Do I have any right to be? No.

It occurs to me as I play possible scenarios over and over in my head that it would actually bother me more if I found out he was treating her like a sub, making her bow to him, being *sir* to her, *praising* her rather than fucking her. Don't get me wrong, they both physically hurt to think about, but the idea that she was being his *good girl* makes me want to go ballistic. That can't be allowed. He would surely know how much that would destroy me, and there's no way he'd do it. Right?

We pull up to a fancy restaurant with valet parking. It's on a golf course, and someone opens my door for me when Emerson parks next to the front door. He gives them his name at the hostess stand, and within minutes, she's walking us to our table. Did he have this planned? We never go out to eat. He pulls out my chair for me, and I try to act natural as I take a seat, letting him push me toward the table. Before walking back to his chair, he leans in and presses his lips against my ear. I stiffen immediately.

"Behave yourself," he whispers, and a chill runs down my spine.

Behave myself? What's that supposed to mean?

Everything is seemingly normal as the waiter takes our drink order. I request a water because honestly, I'm parched. This whole thing has me feeling so unsettled and nervous. It's like I have a time bomb strapped to my chest—or rather, shoved up my vagina—and Emerson is holding the detonator in his pocket.

We don't say a word to each other as we browse the menu, but I can't think. I can barely read, and I swear, I'm sweating.

"Will you order for me?" I ask, setting my menu down.

He gazes at me over the top of his. "What's wrong? Feeling nervous?"

I look up at him. "Yes. Of course."

"Why?"

My brow furrows. "You know why."

"We're in public, Charlotte. You can't expect me to cause a scene here, do you?"

I let out a heavy breath, but I don't answer. He's baiting me, and I want to scream at him. The restaurant is so quiet. There's gentle piano music playing, and delicate chatter fills the room. But I'm still sitting here with a vibrator inside me, and I know at any moment it's going to come to life and I don't know how I can possibly keep my cool when it does.

I just know that I *cannot* let Emerson down.

After the waiter returns, Emerson orders us both today's special, which is pecan-crusted chicken and orzo salad. Meanwhile, I gulp down my ice water like I just ran a mile.

It's silent between us again, and I glare at him, waiting for him to move or say something. Finally, I decide to be the one to start.

"Was she one of your *special* secretaries?" I ask quietly, glancing around to make sure no one is listening.

"Yes," he replies plainly. "Is that why you were so rude to her?"

"I wasn't rude. You asked me to greet her, so I did."

"I didn't ask, Charlotte." He leans back in his chair, looking smug and handsome, making me even more mad at him.

"No, you didn't. You ordered me to, and you don't always do that."

"Do you like it when I order you to?"

I inhale, not sure how he wants me to answer that. "Sometimes."

"Not all the time?"

"I don't know. I just…" I don't even know what I'm trying to say. I'm flustered, feeling too many things I can't seem to put words to.

"Do you know why I ordered you to, Charlotte?"

"Because you knew I didn't like her."

There's a gentle lift at the corner of his lips. "Because I wanted her to know you were more than just a regular secretary. I wanted to make it clear that you are mine."

Oh. My lips open to reply, but no words come out. He was… claiming me? Showing her I was his new girl. Why didn't I pick up on that? How do I even feel about that?

"Why?" I ask when my mouth decides to finally form sounds.

"Because that's what you are, isn't it? Unless you'd like to go back to the way things were before—"

"No," I blurt out. "I just didn't…I don't know why I didn't want to obey you. I just…didn't."

He gives me a subtle smirk again. "Interesting."

"I think I was jealous."

"Why would you be jealous? She was the past. You're the present."

Because deep down, I want to be everything. Past, present... future. But I can't say that. It's too much.

"Did you...sleep with her?" I ask, practically whispering.

There's a moment of hesitation before he answers, "Yes."

Jealousy stings me hard, but I can't reply because the waiter returns, placing our plates on the table. It smells so good I almost forget about the topic of conversation. And I can't stop thinking about him and Monica, and her as his sub and them having sex.

"Eat," he says, and this time, I listen. Because it is really, really delicious.

And I don't shy away from devouring the entire fillet and orzo salad. He looks almost pleased with me as I set down my fork at the end of the meal. It's so good I almost forget about the vibrator still sitting dormant in my panties.

After the waiter takes our plates, I stare at Emerson again. With my belly full and a little relaxed, I get the nerve to finally ask what I really want to know. "Did you sleep with her today?"

He looks shocked. "Today?"

"Yeah. While you were giving her a tour."

"You really think I would do that?"

"I don't know," I reply. We haven't established being exclusive. I mean, we're not even having sex, so why *wouldn't* I think that? But he's right...it does seem wrong to assume he'd do that.

He smiles. "No, I did not have sex with her today."

I let out a heavy breath. Why am I so relieved?

Emerson leans forward, studying me as he says, "Would you be mad at me if I did?"

I swallow. "Yes," I reply with honesty. "Even if I have no right to be, I would."

"Good." He seems pleased. "And what about you?"

"What about me?"

"Flirting with Drake."

"I wasn't—" The breath is stolen from my lungs as the soft humming in my panties racks my body with pleasure. It's surprisingly silent as it quivers inside me. My clit is suddenly wide awake, red hot and filled with blood.

"Behave," he whispers under his breath as he watches me. He's telling me not to cause a scene, and it takes everything in me not to squirm in my seat. Instead, I clutch the napkin in my lap, my knuckles turning white as I squeeze my thighs together. The vibration doesn't stop.

"Then turn it off," I whisper.

"I think this is a fitting punishment, don't you?"

Punishment? "I wasn't flirting," I reply, forcing the words through breathless lips. "And so what if I was? I'm not your—"

He turns up the intensity and I shudder, knocking the table with my leg, the sound of glass clinking echoes through the room. Eyes shift in our direction, and I force myself to keep still when all I want to do is lift my hips from this chair, hump the air, and scream through an orgasm. But even with the constant vibration, without moving my body, I can't seem to come. Instead, I'm forcing myself not to, and strangely, it hurts.

That notorious G-spot I've heard about…well, I think I just found it.

"This is a strange form of *punishment*," I force through tight lips.

"Is it?"

Suddenly, the vibrations are gone, and I should be able to relax, but I feel like the earth has been yanked from under my feet, leaving me to dangle here in excruciating need. I catch my breath without looking visibly bothered. Grabbing the glass of water, I take a long, thirsty drink. As good as the vibrations felt, I don't really want to keep fighting the urge to come in public, so I silently pray he's done torturing me.

"If I was flirting with Drake, I didn't realize it. You should know your general contractor is a natural flirt, and I'm pretty sure he flirts with everyone he speaks to, so it's really not my fault."

"But you put the toy in, didn't you? Did you have permission to do that?"

"Did I need permission?"

The assault returns, this time more powerful than before.

"Emerson!" I gasp. He's wearing a warning on his face as I force myself to relax, but the toy is getting unbearable. "Stop it, please."

But it doesn't go away, and I catch the way Emerson is watching me. His pupils are slightly dilated and his eyes linger on my face as if he's fascinated by me. Then he leans forward again, reaching a hand out to run his fingers along my arm. I freeze, the contact making the arousal coursing through my body even more intense, like a tidal wave of…desire.

"You can take it," he mutters. My lips part and our eyes meet. And I realize what this is. He's punishing me by reminding me who I really belong to.

The vibrator kicks up another notch and I grab Emerson's hand. My thighs are squeezed together so hard, my entire body is locked up. Hot, fiery sensations explode inside me, and I do my best to keep quiet and still. I'm sure if anyone was watching, they would think this looks pretty weird, me staring at him and barely breathing, while our hands are locked, but I don't care. Because right now, nothing exists outside this table. His eyes, his hands, and the violent waves of pleasure rocking through me.

My lips part and I gasp for breath as I come. I have to close my eyes when my climax reaches its peak.

"Atta girl," he whispers. My body trembles and the orgasm just won't stop. Wave after wave after wave knocks me down, and I subtly dig myself against the seat cushion to get more friction.

"Emerson, please," I breathe, begging for relief. My poor sensitive spot is raw, the vibration now feeling more like pain than pleasure.

"I like the way you beg," he whispers. "Tell me what you'll do to make it stop."

With a small gasp, I look around to see if anyone is looking at us.

"Eyes on me," he commands quietly, and I turn my gaze back to him.

"I'll do whatever you want," I reply. "I'll listen to you when you tell me to do something. I'll never flirt with Drake again."

"Good. Are you going to accuse me of being with someone else while I'm with you?"

My gaze intensifies, and I shake my head. "No…"

"You trust me?"

I nod.

"I belong to you as much as you belong to me, Charlotte. If I'm your Dom, I'm no one else's. Don't ever assume I would do that to you. Understand?"

How do his words seem to have such an effect on me, lancing me with heat and arousal and so much longing it's painful?

"Yes, sir."

"Now tell me. What else will you do?"

Our eyes meet in a charged moment. "I'll…"

"Say it," he whispers darkly.

"I'll be good."

A wicked smile stretches across his face. Finally, the vibrations cease. The ringing in my ears quiets. The rattling of my bones and the humming through my veins all stop, and it's like returning to reality. I feel entirely exposed, even though no one is even looking our way.

He pays the check and we leave without another word. This thing is still inside me, but I trust that he won't torture me with it anymore. He seems satisfied with my answers, and I haven't really done anything to warrant more punishment. I can see now just how much give and take there is in this relationship. And trust.

When we get back to his house, I take the toy out, cleaning it off and hiding it in my purse. I have to give it back at some point, but it's not exactly something I want to just hand over before I leave.

While I'm at my desk, my eyes keep tracking Emerson. Watching him work, thinking about Monica and how he smiled at her.

Am I expendable? Will he be tired of me one day and replace me with someone new?

Why does that hurt so much to think about? Because it's more than a job now, isn't it? My stupid, ignorant heart went and got attached, and I can't help the way I feel about Emerson Grant. Someone I really shouldn't have any feelings for.

"See you tomorrow," I call from the door as I ready myself to leave.

He glances up from his computer, his soft, wolflike eyes settling on my face with a new, almost loving expression.

"Here," he says, digging in his pocket. When he pulls out the sleek, black remote, my lips part and I think about what happened today in the restaurant. As excruciating as it was, I loved it.

"Keep it," I reply, knowing the implications of my response. "And I'll keep the other piece."

He tenses for a moment, and I feel like time stretches while I wait for his response. Finally, he nods and lets his eyes crinkle with a delicate smile.

After walking out the door, I sit in my car and let my face rest against the steering wheel. Emerson and I are tiptoeing into dangerous territory. First, the job. Then, the special arrangement. That moment in the hallway at the club. Today, at the restaurant.

We're just toying with this idea of sex, both of us basically expressing that we want it but holding back for Beau's sake. Which I can handle. I never saw that desire coming, but I figured it would pass and I could resist.

But the way Emerson makes me *feel*. The way I feel about

him. How my heart seems to almost expand in his presence, the way I like myself more when I'm around him. How I want to be the only girl in the world he ever sets eyes on again.

I'm falling hard for Emerson Grant.

I'm so fucked.

Rule #20: Establish your limits…and wishes.

Charlotte

THE LIST IS ON MY DESK WHEN I COME IN THE NEXT MORNING—
the list. It's opened to page four, the *unanswered* questions. Words
like *anal, nipple stimulation, threesomes, orgasm denial* stare back at
me, and I haven't even had my coffee yet.

"What's this?" I ask, glancing at Emerson as he walks in. He's
dressed impeccably in tight blue slacks, brown leather shoes, and
a white button-up shirt that looks a couple sizes too small. Has
he always looked this good or is it my lovesick brain starting to
distort reality?

After taking a sip of his black coffee, he sets it down on his
desk and walks over. Standing only a foot or so away from me,
he glances at the paper in my hands. My cheeks start to heat up,
this unspoken thing between us growing more intense by the
second.

"I realized that what we did yesterday was wrong of me. I
should have never used that…toy on you as punishment because
it was an unanswered question on this form. I don't normally
make mistakes like this."

"But I was okay with it," I reply quickly. Is he really worried that he did something to me against my will?

"But I need to know you're okay with it. I need to have your consent beforehand for everything, Charlotte. Not just some things."

His piercing green eyes lift from the paper to my face, and I instantly liquefy from the contact. He wants to know about the sex stuff. Can I really answer these?

"But you said…"

God, I can't say it. I can't bring up sex so casually again. Without a hint of romance between us, treating it like a check mark on a list of activities, like it means nothing.

"I know what I said, and just because you say it's okay for these things to happen, it doesn't mean they will."

My eyes shift downward, hopefully conveying the disappointment I'm feeling from that statement. It's not how I wanted any of this to go down. Where I'm in the position to say, *yes, I'd like you to fuck my brains out*, only for him to tell me he won't. I feel like an idiot.

Should I just save my pride and write a zero next to all of these? How would that make him feel?

"It's better to be safe than sorry," he says gently as if he's trying to spare my feelings.

"Okay."

This whole conversation first thing in the morning puts me in a sour mood. I'm feeling vulnerable and embarrassed, like a stupid young girl pining over her boss, who has no intention of ever reciprocating these feelings. I'm just another Monica.

Stupid, stupid Charlie.

I shove the packet aside as I get started on my tasks for the day, mostly replying to emails and helping to organize the vendor forms for the new store going into the club. I am so distracted by everything that I didn't realize, until almost lunchtime, that today was supposed to be what I like to call our "special" days. I wonder if he even remembered. Does he even care that I'm not kneeling by his side?

Gotta love anxiety, when one paranoid thought spirals into a hundred. Like how I'm suddenly wondering if Emerson even wanted me for a submissive secretary at all, or if I was just a dumbass who threw myself at him and he was too polite to say no.

During my lunch break, I eat alone in the kitchen. With my earbuds in, I pick at the leftovers I packed. I feel his presence behind me before I hear him. Pulling out one of my buds, I turn toward him.

"What's up?" I ask with a touch of attitude that makes his brow twitch.

"Why are you pouting?" He seems strangely unraveled.

"I'm not pouting."

"Yes, you are. Ever since this morning, you've had an attitude. I should be clear that I don't really like the *brat* thing, Charlotte."

My mouth falls open. "Brat thing?"

"Yes. Where you intentionally misbehave and warrant yourself punishment for my attention."

This time I audibly gasp and turn in my chair. "You can't be serious."

He crosses his arms, standing in front of me like a pissed-off statue. "I am serious. You pulled it yesterday at the club, flirting with Drake just to spite me."

For some reason, I stand up. He still towers over me, but at least this time I don't appear to be cowering so much. "I can flirt with whoever I want. That had *nothing* to do with you. You know what…maybe *you* should fill out a form too, so I know exactly what you want and we can settle all of this confusion right now."

"So that's what this is about," he replies with a nod of his head. "You don't want to fill out the form. Charlotte, I'm not forcing you to do anything you don't want to. The form is there for your protection."

I throw my hands up with a scoff. "Yeah, I get it. You want me to lay all of my cards out on the table for you, but what about you, *sir*?" I throw so much sarcastic emphasis on his title that it makes his jaw clench. "Where's your form? Why aren't you obligated to admit to everything you want, even if it means making yourself vulnerable? Come on, Emerson."

I stomp my way out to the office and grab the legal pad on the desk and a pen from the drawer. Shoving them both against his chest, I snap, "Here. Write down everything you want to do with me, just so we're clear." My tone is teasing, chock-full of snark, and I expect him to yell back at me or toss the paper on the floor.

What I don't expect is his body suddenly crowding mine until my ass is against my desk. He presses himself between my legs and leans me backward, so I'm defenseless, letting out a yelp as his face peers only inches from mine.

"You think this is how I want to do this?" he mutters darkly. "You think I'm not dying to know what you'd rate those things on that list, even though I know I'd be the worst father in the world if I ever did any of them?" His hand scoops my lower back as he leans so close to me. I can feel him between my legs.

Staring up into his eyes, my pulse quickens. He wants me. He's basically saying that now.

Before I can even think of a response, he continues, "I'll fill out that form for you if you want, but I don't need to. You want me to tell you that I want to taste you, Charlotte? Because I do. I want to touch you, tease you, fuck you, bend you over my knee and turn that pretty little backside red. There's not a thing on that list I don't want to do with you, so you can put the paper and pen away, little girl. Every single thing would get a five from me."

A small sound escapes my lips.

"You have no idea how hard this is for me, Charlotte. To have you as mine, but not in the way I want."

"I...I don't know what to say," I breathe in response.

"Just fill out the fucking form," he growls, his mouth only inches from mine.

And just like that, he backs up and lets me breathe again. I take in lungfuls of air as I watch him march out of the room, leaving me standing here alone, thinking about what he just said.

This whole time I was so afraid to admit that I wanted more with him, and he basically just admitted that he wanted it too… but also that he would never give in to that want.

There's no sign of him for the next hour as I take the list to the kitchen with me, hovering over each item. A swarm of butterflies assaults my stomach at the mere thought of experiencing these with Emerson.

Exhibitionism…five.

Oral…five.

Sex toys…five.

Anal…*deep breath, Charlie*…five.

Am I going overboard? Putting down a five basically says that not only do I want these things, but I'm practically demanding them. And it's not like I'm saying five for everything. There are a few things on this list that fall deep into the negative one range— hard pass on fisting and golden showers. But how can I possibly hand this paper to him with these fives all over it?

I'm tempting him on purpose, and sure, maybe I am being a little bit of a brat. It's as bad as me using my tits and red lipstick to get my sister a copy of her book at the store. I'm purposefully manipulating Emerson to get what I want…and that's cruel, but I don't feel bad about it. There are so many fun things we could do with me as his submissive servant if sex was on the table, and I don't want to be a PG version of Monica. I want it all.

After lunch, I set the list on Emerson's desk. He's still MIA, but I get back to work anyway. Well, I try. Can't exactly focus on anything with a written confirmation basically proclaiming *I'll be your fuck toy. Bonus: with anal!* just sitting there on his desk, waiting for him. And I have to be here when he does read it. That shouldn't be awkward at all.

It's almost two, and Emerson is still missing. I haven't gotten anything done, and I feel as if we need to have a conversation since he just left me with that truth bomb from earlier. So after setting up the coffeepot to brew his afternoon caffeine fix, I gather up the courage to go investigating. Emerson's house is huge, but I've only really seen the lower level which is the office, kitchen, bathroom, and sitting room. There are large wooden stairs that lead to the second floor.

One quiet step at a time, I sneak my way up. The left side leads to another sitting area, and it has the telltale signs that he actually uses this one. The leather sofa has wear marks; there's a giant flat-screen TV and a couple of books on the nightstand.

He's not in here, so I tiptoe silently to the right, where there's a door open just a crack. It feels like a massive invasion of privacy, but I can't help myself.

Stepping up to the sliver between the door and the frame, I spot his back as he sits on a workout bench, his feet on the floor. So this is how he keeps up that perfect body. It looks like he's turned a spare bedroom into his own personal gym. There are weights, a treadmill, a huge contraption meant for who knows.

And Emerson is shirtless.

Tan skin stretched over muscular shoulders grab my attention and won't let go. Judging by the way his elbows rest on his knees and his head hangs low, Emerson is deep in thought, and something about that bothers me. Like the day I knelt by his side and eased his stress, I want to take it away now.

"Knock, knock," I say, tapping on the door.

He spins and gazes at me with a guarded look of concern written on his face.

"You disappeared," I whisper, stepping into the room. "I didn't even know you had this up here."

He grabs a towel and brushes it against his sweaty brow. Still sitting away from me, he replies, "I had to work out some... aggression."

After our encounter at the desk, he had to come work out to let off some steam?

Walking over to where he's sitting, I lean against the mirror on the wall and stare at him.

"You know…" I say with a teasing smile. "You could always work out some of that aggression on me."

His head hangs as I let out a laugh. "Jesus, Charlotte."

"Come on, it's a joke," I reply, stepping toward him. Then his hand latches around my thigh and he holds me close to him. I don't breathe for a moment as I rest my hands on his shoulders.

"You make everything a joke, don't you?"

I shrug. "I find it makes things easier that way."

"It doesn't make anything easier for me," he grumbles lowly.

His hand strokes the back of my leg as I stand between his knees. His touch is like fire, sending a thrill through my body. This forbidden contact isn't just crossing the line—we're pretending that line doesn't exist. And I lean into his touch to send home the message that I want—no, I *need*—more.

"I filled out the form," I whisper.

"Good," he replies.

"You should know I marked a few zeroes."

He lets out a deep chuckle. "A few?"

"Yeah. No shame to those who like the golden shower thing… but not for me."

I'm keeping the mood light because everything else about this moment is tense.

"Good to know," he mumbles.

He's still holding me close, and as my hands drift along his shoulders, I realize that Emerson and I have grown close since I started working with him. But this is the first time we've really touched each other like this.

"Is there any use trying to avoid this?" His head tips back, and he stares up at me as he pulls me closer, and I realize he's about to kiss me. The fingers of his hand drift higher and higher up my thigh. "Because I gotta tell you, Charlotte, I'm a little tired of trying."

I interlock my fingers behind his neck and squeeze him closer. At this angle, I'm so close, I could kiss him if I wanted to, and I want to.

"Then, stop trying."

My face leans in, and Emerson's eyes close, squeezing me tighter. Then just before my lips touch his, the doorbell rings.

We open our eyes and stare at each other.

"Expecting someone?" I ask.

His brows furrow as he pulls out his phone and opens the front door security camera. Then he looks as if he's seen a ghost, jumping up from the bench, practically pushing me away.

"Who is it?" I ask.

He stares at me with wide eyes. "It's Beau."

Rule #21: When possible, remove the temptation.

Emerson

I'VE NEVER PUT MY SHIRT ON SO FAST IN MY LIFE. JESUS, WHAT the fuck is wrong with me? The internal reasoning as to why I should not ever touch Charlotte in that way has slowly deteriorated over time. And just as I was about to give in and do what I've wanted to do for the past two months, Beau literally comes knocking.

Charlotte is behind me as we reach the bottom floor. She fixes her skirt and heads over to her desk to try and act natural as I open the door.

And there he is. I haven't laid eyes on my son in six months, and I might be imagining things, but he looks different, older. He has the same green eyes and tan skin, but that's about all he inherited from me. The rest is his mother.

Sandy-brown curls. High cheekbones and a wide smile, although I really haven't seen that in a while.

"Hey," I mumble like an idiot, opening the door wider to invite him in. He doesn't move at first.

"I'm just here to get that check," he replies. He's keeping his eyes everywhere but on my face. There's a slight shuffle of his feet and a nervousness in the way he shoves his hands into his pockets.

"Of course. Come in," I say, moving out of the way.

He's only one step into the foyer when he spots Charlotte in the office through the glass door. He hesitates, pausing for a moment as he stares at her. Sharp pangs of jealousy assault me. Because, of course, he can't look away. Charlotte is the epitome of beauty, and although I wouldn't have said it when she started working for me, she's the epitome of sophistication now. In fact, she's the best of both worlds. Somehow equally regal and fun. Demure and ridiculous in the best way.

He takes a step toward her.

"Charlotte is an exceptional secretary. Smart and organized. I hope I never have to replace her."

Pride bubbles up as I brag about her to him, and I see the moment his jaw clicks. He doesn't like me talking about his girl as if I know her better, and I can't say I blame him. But this jealousy is a two-way street because I feel it too.

"Come in and say hello," I say, pressing a hand to his back.

When we reach my office, Charlotte stands up and greets Beau with a hug.

"It's good to see you!" she says.

"Good to see you too. You look…"

She waits awkwardly for him to finish his sentence and I wish I could finish it for him.

Gorgeous.

Amazing.

Breathtaking.

Any of these would work, but he ends up using, "Different."

There's a tense smile on her face. "Good different, I hope."

"Yeah, good different."

"Can I get you something to drink? Coffee, soda, water?"

"Yeah, a Coke, please," he replies, without taking his eyes off of her. And I can't stop watching her either, looking for a reaction to his presence. How does she really feel about him? Excited to see him? Eager to please? But no. Instead, she's wearing a tight-lipped grin and looks entirely unnatural in his company.

"I'll get it," Charlotte replies eagerly, moving toward the kitchen. She's trying to leave me and my son together, but he follows her instead of staying with me.

"You two catch up," I say. "I just finished my workout and I need to go change out of these clothes and get cleaned up. Son, I'll get you that check when I get back."

"Sure," he says to me, and I wish I could say it's like there is no awkwardness between us, but there is. My son seems to have this idea in his head that by owning a sex club, I'm some sort of monster. Both a pervert and a criminal. There's nothing I can do to change his mind or make him see differently, and it's taken half a year of our relationship, but I refuse to believe it's irreparable.

When I come back down about ten minutes later, I hear them talking in the front room. Stopping in the kitchen, I listen in.

"I feel like such a fuckup," he mumbles.

"You're not a fuckup," she replies. "You're going through a rough patch. You have to live with your mom for a while, so what? It's not forever. You'll get back on your feet and everything will be fine."

The comforting sound of her voice makes me smile.

"I lost my job, my place, you…" His voice trails, and I feel the hairs on my neck rise.

And it dawns on me in that moment—Charlotte means something to Beau. Whether they broke up or not, she means something to him. And quite possibly, he means something to her. How could I get in the middle of that? How could I have even done the things I already have?

"You didn't lose me," she replies softly. "We're still friends, Beau." Her voice is so low, they sound close together. There's silence, clothes rustling, movement on the couch, and I wish I could stop myself from listening now.

"Give me another chance," he mumbles, and I can't stop myself. Making my steps loud, I walk out of the kitchen, going straight to my desk. I'm not quite sure what I'm doing. Getting Charlotte back with Beau was what I wanted. It's the whole reason I hired her. It's what was going to make everything between me and Beau better, so why am I trying to stop it?

They scoot apart on the couch, and I glance up to see her face. She's glaring at me, eyes wide with an expression of fear as if she's been caught. And she's trying to gauge my reaction.

"Sorry to interrupt. Let me get you that check." Sitting down at my desk, I reach into the top drawer and pull out my checkbook. While I'm filling it out, Beau stands and walks over to me.

He's positioned a foot or so away. When I glance up at him, I notice his eyes aren't on me or the check; they're on my desk. I follow his gaze and am suddenly filled with horror. The form Charlotte filled out is sitting face up on the desk, open to all of those filthy consent questions. Quickly, I grab it and flip it over, but I catch the way he tenses, his eyes narrowing with judgment. My son is disgusted by me. And at the moment, I can't say I blame him.

Luckily, there's no way for him to know it's Charlotte who filled out that form.

"How much do you need?" I ask.

"My half was one thousand."

My shoulders drop. "How much to get you through the next couple months, Son?"

"I don't need your money," he snaps.

"I'm not giving it to you because you need it. I'm giving it to you because I want to."

"Well, I don't want it."

"Beau…" Charlotte's soft voice breaks through as she comes to stand next to him. "He's just trying to help."

I wince. The last thing I want is for her to take my side, no matter how good it feels. It will only drive him further away from me.

"He thinks he can pay for everything and that it will just solve all of our problems," he says, staring coldly at my face.

"No, I don't."

Charlotte breaks in again, this time with a hand on his arm. "At least he's trying. My dad hasn't even spoken to me in months, let alone tried to help me or my family financially."

Beau looks at her, and his expression softens. *Come on, Son. Do it for her.*

"Fine," he says.

I fill out the check for ten grand and tell him to come back for more when he needs it. It feels like bait, but I don't care. Anything that brings him back into my life. Even if he's mad at me because of it.

Charlotte looks pleased for a moment as I hand him the check, so I don't know why I say what comes out of my mouth next. Self-preservation, I guess.

"Why don't you take Charlotte out for dinner?" I say, and her head snaps in my direction. "If she wants to, of course."

Digging into my pocket, I find my wallet and pull out a hundred-dollar bill. Beau stares at Charlotte with hope in his eyes, but she's still watching me.

I need Charlotte to no longer be an option. If she's really *with* Beau, then I no longer have to resist the urge to have her for myself because the choice would be taken away.

I hate the way she's staring at me right now, disappointment and anger and guilt all rolled into one.

"What do you say, babe? Want to grab some dinner with me?" He squeezes an arm around her waist, and I have to look away.

"Sure," she replies softly, and it kills me.

After she gathers her things, she sends me a small wave goodbye, which is more than my own son can manage. I return her wave with a nod of my head. Watching her walk away with him is torture. But I'm doing this to myself for a good reason. Charlotte is *not* mine, no matter how much it feels like she is.

Rule #22: If you want it, take it.

Charlotte

"Maybe instead of going out, we can order in and go hang out at your place," Beau says, as he puts his hand on my thigh while I drive. He had a friend drop him off at his dad's, which makes me wonder if this was his plan all along. My skin is prickling just from his touch.

I can't tell if Beau's changed, I've changed, or the entire dynamic between us has. But there is no chemistry, no sparks or any kindling of what we had before. This guy I used to be so smitten with, who I let bring me down so low...can't hurt me anymore.

I don't feel like the same girl he broke up with, and maybe I'm not. I like this new version of me, the one Emerson helped build back up.

God, even the thought of his name makes me feel queasy. We had a moment, and I'm pretty sure we were about to have an even bigger moment, but then Beau showed up and Emerson couldn't pawn me off fast enough. It hurt, especially after that whole "you have no idea what I want to do to you" speech. The second his son walked through that door, my hope shattered.

"Umm...that sounds good. Pizza?"

"Sure. We can just order it from your place."

"Okay," I reply with a forced smile.

"So, you really like working for my dad?" he asks.

"Yeah. I do. And he says I could easily work my way up into business management."

Beau scoffs. "Not with that business, I hope."

My hand grips the steering wheel as I pull into the driveway. I don't know how much Emerson makes public about the club, or if he still uses the dating service as a front, so I decide to keep it discreet. "What's wrong with the company?"

"You know what they do there, Charlie. Come on. Don't act stupid."

"I'm not acting stupid," I bite back. Just then, I spot my little sister across the yard, and my heart sinks. She's sitting out front with one of her friends, both of them on their phones as she looks up and spots Beau getting out of my car.

Fuck.

"Hey, Smurf. You want some pizza?" I call.

Her eyes track back and forth between Beau and me before she shakes her head. "No thanks."

Regret hits me hard. Sophie is disappointed in me, and I hate it. She never liked Beau, so she's certainly not going to be joining us for pizza.

"Come on, babe," Beau says, draping an arm over my shoulder, and I can feel Sophie watching us as we disappear into the backyard, heading straight for the pool house. Everything in me is telling me to call this off, drive him home, and forget this ever happened. Beau clearly has expectations about tonight and I really don't want to have to let him down. Because that is *not* happening.

Two hours ago, I thought it was Emerson I'd be cozying up to.

When we get inside my small room, I check my phone, looking for anything from Emerson, but there's only silence. Beau drops onto my bed, and he seems in such a better mood than before that I almost feel bad that I have to break it to him that tonight is not going to end the way he wants.

"I'm going to change out of these clothes," I tell him, walking toward the bathroom, but he snatches me by the hand before I can make it there.

"Charlie, wait."

Suddenly, I'm on his lap. And I don't say anything. *Why* don't I say anything?

"I didn't want to be alone with you just for sex," he says, and my eyes widen.

"Beau, we're not—"

"I really do want another chance. I know I was a shitty boyfriend. I was just going through stuff with my dad."

My shoulders soften, and sympathy floods my system.

"Why didn't you ever confide in me?" I don't bring up the cheating part because that's where things get heated and it becomes impossible to get him to talk or open up about anything.

"I was embarrassed," he replies gently. "I didn't want you knowing my dad was a…freak."

"He's not a freak," I bite back.

"He might as well be a porn star or a pimp, Charlie. His whole job revolves around sex and some really kinky shit. It's not normal—"

"It is normal, though," I argue, trying to get out of his arms, but he holds me tight. I hate that I'm not fighting harder. And it's like he doesn't even hear me as he goes on and on about how terrible his dad is. Bile rises up my throat.

"And I thought that if he was some sex freak…maybe I was too. That's why I…did what I did."

My spine stiffens. "Are you serious right now?" I snap. "You're going to blame your dad for you cheating on me? You letting some new girl at work give you a blow job in the break room was because your *dad owns a sex club*?"

I see the argument building in him, but I feel so hot and angry right now, I could scream.

"I told you that was the biggest mistake of my life. I told you I was going through a lot, and—"

"Beau, we broke up for a reason. We weren't right together—"

"Baby, I need you." He squeezes me closer, nuzzling his face in my neck, and everything feels so wrong. *Baby, I need you?* Since when did he ever call me baby? And he certainly never *needed* me.

This stops now. I finally push myself away from him to stand. He looks disappointed, furrowing his brow and pressing his lips into a tight line.

"You don't need me, Beau. You need to grow up," I argue. "Or maybe you just need someone to finally put you in your place because I'm not going back to the way things were."

"What the hell are you talking about?"

"I'm talking about how you never once made me feel good about myself while we were together. You talk about how hard your life was…well, have you noticed mine?" I ask, waving my arms around.

"You've changed," he says with a grimace, and I laugh.

"Yeah, I guess I did. Because if you think your dad is such a freak, then I am too."

He stands in a rush with his eyes wide. "Charlie…" There's a tone of warning in his voice. "Have you been to that club?"

"Yeah…I have, and I'm not ashamed." It takes everything in me to hold my shoulders back and look up into Beau's eyes proudly as I say it. He's scrutinizing me, letting this new information sink in, like he's literally imagining me doing whatever freaky shit he thinks happens at that club.

I wish I could tell him more, but I realize that it doesn't matter what Beau thinks—not anymore. The Charlie of four months ago would have never admitted to this, and maybe if Beau had told me about his dad while we were dating, I would have thought the same thing he does. But that was before Emerson opened my eyes. Not to the club—but to myself.

I have someone who really treasures me now, who sees something in me when he looks at me that I never saw in myself. Who makes me feel smart and sexy and perfect.

And at the end of the day, I'd rather be Emerson's pet than Beau's girlfriend.

"Tell me the truth right now," he demands. "Are you sleeping with my dad?"

I scoff, shaking my head. "No," I reply with conviction, because I'm not. But I really fucking wish I were. "Beau…" I take a deep breath, before continuing. "I love you. I'll probably always love you because I know there's good in there, but you and I are never going to work. I'm sorry."

I expect him to lash out, but he doesn't. I think he's still reeling from the *Charlie goes to a sex club* information. Instead, he looks defeated. "There's someone else, isn't there?"

For a moment, I'm taken aback. *That's what he got from this conversation?* I don't answer, and it's enough to confirm his suspicions. There's *sort of* someone else. And it may not be a relationship—hell, it may never be a relationship—but it works for me. I watch his expression for a moment to make sure he doesn't suspect that that someone else is his dad, but he doesn't really say anything else. He just looks…sad.

After I broke up with Beau, I was finally alone with myself, and I realized how much I missed…me. Because I didn't exist around him. He existed as the center of my universe, and I was his shadow.

"Let me take you home," I say, touching his arm.

He nods solemnly.

Sophie isn't outside when we leave, but I wish she were. I want her to see him leaving, so she knows this really isn't what it looks like.

In the car, Beau is quiet. His mom's house is on the opposite side of town. She lives in a quaint bungalow. I never met either of his parents before we broke up, but just the idea of meeting her, this woman who was once married to Emerson, makes my skin crawl. As we pull up to her house, he freezes in his seat.

"I think my dad will be disappointed," he says, and I start to panic.

"Why?"

With a snicker, he adds, "He was clearly trying to get us back together, *Charlotte*." He says my name like Emerson does, impersonating his father. And I'm not quite sure how that makes me feel.

Strange. It makes me feel very strange.

"Oh yeah. I got that feeling too." A fact I'm purposefully ignoring for the time being because it makes me too angry to think about.

"Maybe someday I'll get my shit together enough to deserve you," he says with his eyes on the dash, and it shatters my heart to hear him say that. All this time, I thought I wasn't good enough for Beau, and now…everything's changed.

Reaching across the seat, I pull him into a hug. "I'm here for you—always."

He squeezes me back before opening the door and walking up to the front of the house. Watching him leave has me feeling so many things for this family. They are so broken, both Emerson and Beau—at war with themselves and each other. And considering the shitshow that is my family, this says a lot coming from me.

And as I pull away from the curb, I think about what he said, about Emerson clearly trying to get us back together. The more the thought cycles through my mind, the angrier I get.

He thinks he's the only one making a sacrifice here. He acts like denying this attraction is only costing him, but what about me? He thinks he can just push me off on his son, like it's just that easy.

Doesn't what I want count? Isn't he the one who taught me to go after what I want?

The more I think about it, the more I fume. Heading onto the freeway, I find myself skipping the exit to my house and taking the one after it. I might be crazy, but there's no way I'm going home when I have so much on my mind that I'm dying to tell him.

Rule #23: If all else fails, ask nicely.

Charlotte

I'M TREMBLING. IT'S AFTER DARK AND I'M STANDING ON EMERSON'S front porch about to rant at him, and I'm still not one hundred percent sure what I'm going to say. I feel the feelings, but I just don't have the words to go with them. All I know is I'm tired of not having what I want—and I want him.

The light in the foyer comes on just before he opens the door. I hold my head up high and scramble to think of what to say.

"Charlotte?" he asks when he sees me. "Where's Beau?"

"I drove him home."

"Why?"

"Because I don't want him anymore."

"Don't say that," he snaps.

"Did you read the form? I filled it out. Did you read it?"

A small wrinkle forms between his brows, clearly confused by my rambling. Before he can shut me out, I storm through his front door, directly to his office. I hear his footsteps on my heels, and when I spin to face him, I catch the way he's still wearing his work clothes from a couple hours ago, but the white shirt is unbuttoned, revealing his chest and the patch of hair peeking through. God, I want to touch it, run my fingers through it. Am I into chest hair now?

He reaches up to rub his forehead, looking exhausted as he says, "Charlotte, we really can't be doing this. The form, the submission, any of it. We can't."

"Why not?" I snap back. If there was any semblance of me guarding my feelings, it's gone now.

"You are my son's girlfriend!" There's so much desperation in his tone and turmoil in his expression.

"Ex!" I yell back.

"Does it really matter? Does it make me any less of a piece of shit if he's your current or ex-boyfriend?"

"What about what I want? Why am I being denied?" I cry out.

"I never should have hired you. This was all a mistake." He pulls at his hair, staring at the floor, and I'm left speechless. Too sad to be angry and too angry to be sad.

"Why would you say that?"

Suddenly, his body is pressed against me, one hand around my lower back and the other cupping my jaw. His face is only inches from mine as he whispers, "Because I didn't expect you to be so perfect. I had no idea keeping my hands off you would be this hard. And then I walked in that day and found you on your knees…" He squeezes his eyes shut, pressing his forehead against mine. "Jesus Christ, Charlotte. You have no idea what you do to me."

"Yes, I do. Because I love the way I feel when I'm with you. I see the way you want me, how much you adore me. How many people really get to feel that with someone? Why would I ever deny myself something like that?"

"We could never let anyone find out," he replies, his gaze falling to my lips. "It could never be real. You deserve better than being someone's dirty secret."

I know he's right and somewhere down the line, I'll hate myself for this impulsive decision. But at this moment, I don't care.

"I want whatever I can get," I reply. "I want you." I barely get the words out before his mouth comes crashing against mine. It happens so fast we are lost in the nuclear current of lips and tongues and teeth, starving for each other. His mouth tastes like bourbon and he kisses me with long, powerful strokes of his tongue that send butterflies straight to my stomach.

I'm practically levitating, trying to keep up with the ravenous movement of his mouth against mine. And when he growls with my bottom lip between his teeth, I hum softly in return. I need him like oxygen, gasping for air with every swipe of our tongues as our hands grasp and touch each other as much as we possibly can.

As suspected, the firm muscles of his body feel like heaven against my fingers. I cascade my hands up and down his back, reveling in how delicious he feels beneath this tight cotton shirt. There's nothing in this moment that portrays Emerson as a man twenty years older than me. And I don't feel like I don't deserve him because he's out of my league. It just feels like us, a moment months in the making and worth every torturous second of yearning.

My back is pressed against the wall as his mouth travels down to my neck. Emerson barely comes up for air. He's like a man left to die of starvation and finally offered a meal. His hands grip my ass as he hoists me up, wrapping my legs around him as he grinds me into the wall. The rock-hard bulge in his pants rubs against my clit and I explode with sound, crying out for him.

"My girl wants this, doesn't she?" he growls as he does it again.

"Yes!" I cry, pulling him in for another kiss.

"Then get on your knees and take it out."

No one has ever scrambled to their knees faster than I do in this moment. Heat pummels my insides at just the sound of his sex commands. I want more—I *need* more. I want Emerson Grant to dominate me like he never has before, tell me every single dirty thing he wants to do to me and every dirty thing he wants me to do to him. I will obey every single command without hesitation. His voice is like lava dripping down my spine, and I am a gooey mess of a sub, willing to do literally anything he says.

I'm so eager to have his cock in my hand, my fingers fumble with his zipper while his hand gently brushes back my hair. I'm hit with a sudden sensation of *I can't believe this is happening* mixed with *Thank God this is finally happening*, creating one epic feeling of carnal elation and excitement.

When I finally get his button undone and his zipper down, I see the tip of his waiting cock, red and throbbing, poking out the top of his tight black boxers. Gently easing down the elastic, I slowly let this sight sink in. I'm looking at Emerson Grant's cock, just inches away from my face.

Gazing up at him with my sex-crazed doe eyes, I whisper, "Now what?"

He smiles before biting his lip. "What do you want to do with it?"

Mirroring his expression, I bite my own lip. "I want to suck your cock," I say, my sweet tone laced with false innocence.

He leans down and puts his face close to mine. "You have to ask nicely."

"Sir," I breathe, pressing against his lips. "Can I please suck your cock?"

He growls, squeezing his fist in my hair as he kisses me with so much strength it almost hurts.

"You're so phenomenal." And the praise lights a fire in my belly. My panties must be destroyed by now, and I swear it'll take one touch against my clit and I'll be done for. I thought the hallway moment was the hottest thing I've ever done, but that was before I had the full Emerson Grant experience.

With his hand still in my hair, he stands upright and guides my face toward his crotch. Pulling his waistband down even farther, I run my tongue along the length of his shaft, reaching the head and circling my lips around it. He gasps and shifts his hips forward. I love his reactions, and I want to make him do more. So I lick his cock again and again, teasing him just to feel him tense and hear him pant.

When I finally open my mouth and slide him in along the length of my tongue, he moans so loud, the vibrations rattle through me.

"Fuck, Charlotte."

Yes. I need more of that, I think as I bob up and down on his shaft, finding my rhythm and coating his dick with saliva. When he touches the back of my throat, I gag and take a breath, before letting him go deeper and deeper. He stops breathing at one point and I'm almost certain he's going to unload in my mouth. I've never experienced spitting or swallowing before, but I would for him. I would do anything for him.

Instead of coming in my mouth, he lets out a guttural roar and yanks me off the floor.

"Not yet," he barks as he carries me to his desk, kissing my mouth with a fierce hunger.

He drops me on his desk and grabs my blouse at the center. With one quick jerk, he tears it apart, sending buttons flying across the room. There is no pacing himself as he yanks down my bra. I let out a gasp when his mouth finds my breasts.

My hips are writhing against him as his teeth gently close around my right nipple. He massages my other breast with his hand, tugging on the sensitive bud and making my body light up with fireworks.

"Oh my God," I gasp.

Moving his mouth downward, he drags up my skirt to find my panties underneath.

"Lie down," he growls in a sexy command, so I do. Staring up at the ceiling, feeling like I'm drunk as it sways and blurs in my vision, I feel Emerson's face between my thighs. He takes a long inhale through his nose, nuzzled against the moisture of my panties.

I want to be self-conscious. In any other scenario or with any other man, I would be, but with him, I just let myself feel it without thinking too much about the smell, or how it's been a couple days since I shaved, or if the fact that I'm so turned on is somehow embarrassing.

"God, you're soaked," he whispers. His fingers dig under the waistband of my panties, and he tears them off with violent eagerness. And he doesn't hesitate before drawing his broad tongue along the crevice with an edacious moan.

"You taste so fucking good."

I swear he doesn't come up for air, and I have no idea how after at least five minutes of him lapping hungrily at my cunt, he hasn't suffocated. The sounds I'm making are not anything like the sounds I've ever made before. There is no faking or forcing it with Emerson. Everything *feels so good.*

"I'm gonna come," I pant with my legs clenching around his ears. He hums even louder, sending delicate vibrations straight to my core. When he feels my thighs start to tremble, he slides in a finger and sucks eagerly on my clit.

Thrusting one, then two inside me, he curls them just right and I'm reminded of that elusive G-spot that I didn't know even existed until yesterday. It all feels like too much and not enough at the same time, like I can't take another second but never ever want it to stop. I'm going to explode or die or scream or *something.* Then, he picks up speed and growls hungrily between my legs.

My body erupts in pleasure. With my fists in his hair, I come so hard, my hips lift from the desk, and I start to lose track of time. My body is locked in euphoria for hours instead of seconds, and when I start to come back down from the orgasm I never want to end, there is a gentle buzzing in my fingers and toes.

Emerson stands up and wipes his mouth. "You are so beautiful when you come," he groans, kissing my stomach and then my breasts. I'm subtly aware of him opening a drawer and fishing around for something. When I look up, he's already sheathing his cock in a rubber.

"I need to fuck you now," he murmurs against my neck. Excitement strikes my core like lightning. I may have just orgasmed my face off, but I want more. Latching my ankles around his waist, I look him in the eye as I pull him toward me.

"I'm ready."

The blunt end of his cock presses against my soaking center as he drapes each of my legs over his arms. And with one rapid jerk, he drags me onto his cock, impaling me quickly and sinking all the way in. The actual *roar* that escapes his lips is surreal. With his gaze locked on mine, he plunges inside me hard, pausing once he's seated all the way, only to pull out and slam in again. My toes curl and my fingers grip the desk. The pleasure of having him inside me is so intense, I could cry.

He starts to pick up speed, grunting with each thrust, and whatever spot he's hitting inside me feels like he's untapped some hidden code of bliss because I'm already feeling the urge to come again. With my legs in his arms, he slams into me again and again. It's rapture, another onslaught of sensation, but this time different, less intense but more consuming…and so fucking good.

"I'm coming again," I cry out, and he keeps the hard speed while I lie there with my eyes closed, lost in absolute bliss. Pulling me upright, he kisses my mouth with a harsh bite.

"Open your eyes, Charlotte," he commands, and I do. As our eyes meet, he growls, "God, I love fucking you."

I latch my arms around his neck, watching his expression as he pounds into me. I memorize the look of pleasure on his face, the sounds he makes as he grunts and groans with each thrust. *I do this to him*, I remind myself. I drive him crazy and make him act out of control, and he knows it.

With our gazes locked on each other, he slams into me even harder and faster, his groans turning into loud, bellowing cries of pleasure. My nails dig into his back as I cling to his body. When he comes, the room practically rattles with the sound coming out of his mouth.

I'm left speechless, staring up at him without a rational thought in my head. There are only emotions flowing through me at the moment—emotions like contentment, adoration, and desire. So much desire.

I kiss him again, holding his chest against mine, feeling his rapid heartbeat while we both catch our breaths. And as we hold each other, I say a silent prayer in my head.

Dear God, please let this be the only man I fuck for the rest of my life because there's not a chance in hell anyone else could ever top that.

Rule #24: Work is so much more enjoyable when you're fucking your hot boss.

Charlotte

EMERSON CARRIES ME UP TO HIS ROOM. THEN HE CAREFULLY strips me down until I'm standing in front of him naked. His clothes come off next. Before crawling into his enormous bed, he kisses me again, gently this time.

Pulling back the covers, he gestures for me to climb in. As he slides his giant naked body over mine, I smile. How is this happening? And how am I so fucking happy?

As I stare up at him, I think about how much has changed over the past two months. How my feelings for him have evolved. When did I stop looking at him as too old? Too off-limits. Too... Beau's dad?

Because now I only see him as mine. My...something. I don't know. More than my boss, but not just my lover.

My *sir.*

We don't hurry this time. Instead, he rests on top of me, his elbows framing my face as he strokes my hair and peppers my face, neck, and chest with kisses. Our thirst has been quenched, but our appetite has not been totally fulfilled.

He fishes in his nightstand for another condom, and I watch him put this one on, my eyes fixated on the way his fingers move the rubber over his stiff cock. When he lies back on top of me, he gathers me in his arms, squeezing me tight as he slides inside. And the entire time his body moves in languid, sensual strokes, our lips are locked and our hearts are beating in unison.

I must have drifted off to sleep because I wake up a couple hours later, nestled against Emerson's chest. He's awake, stroking my back as he reads something on his phone.

"What time is it?" I ask.

"Just after midnight," he replies, kissing my forehead.

"I should probably go," I say, but even as I say that, my arm tightens around his body, and I can't imagine peeling myself out of his warm bed. When he looks down at me, I see a hint of dissatisfaction in his eyes.

"I understand. I wouldn't want your mother to worry." Something about that makes me feel so juvenile. I'm twenty-one, and while it's a pool house in the backyard, I do still sort of live with my mom. That unsettling feeling of not deserving Emerson comes flooding back.

"I'm sure she's already asleep, so it's not a big deal, but I do have to work tomorrow." I give him a tight-lipped smile, and he grins back, stroking my bare stomach with his soft, large hand.

"You can come in a little late tomorrow, I guess."

"I don't want to. I'll be here bright and early."

"Good."

Finally, I force myself out from under the covers and slip my skirt back on.

"I guess I have to drive home like this," I say, showing him my now buttonless blouse.

"Not a chance," he says with a grimace. Without a shred of clothing on his body, he gets out of bed and pads over to his dresser, where he pulls out a T-shirt. I couldn't tell you what color or size the shirt is because my attention is laser focused on Emerson Grant's naked bum.

He turns toward me, and I do my best not to stare at all of his nakedness. I mean…I just had the damn thing in my mouth. Why would I blush about it now?

"Are you okay?" he asks when he notices me not moving to take the shirt from him.

I pinch my lips together and look up at his face. "I'm fine."

He laughs at me as I pull my blouse off and replace it with his shirt. To my disappointment, he slips on his black boxers before walking me to the door.

"I wish you could stay," he whispers, wrapping me up in his arms. I breathe in the scent of his skin and his shirt that I'm wearing, and I wish the same thing.

"Me too."

"But I do look forward to seeing you on your knees in the morning," he says in a low tone, and a thrill tingles at the base of my spine. I look up at him with lust in my eyes. "Wear something sexy for me tomorrow, Charlotte."

"Yes, sir."

"We're going to have so much fun now," he adds, and those words linger in my mind the entire drive home and even after I crawl into my bed, reliving every perfect moment of tonight.

The next morning, I wear the outfit he loves so much—sheer top and tight skirt. I've probably never been more excited to go to work. But I guess I never anticipated getting railed and having multiple orgasms at work before either.

I let myself in when I reach his house five minutes early. He's not in his office, and I consider searching the house for him, but I know he'd much rather find me waiting for him.

After shedding my coat and my shoes, I grab the pillow from

the chair and set it in the middle of the room. I kneel just as I hear his distant footsteps somewhere in the house.

With my head down, my body lights up in anticipation when I hear the click of his shoes on the floor. He's quiet a moment before walking up to me, touching my chin, and tilting my head back, so I'm gazing up at him—just like he did on that first day.

"Such a good girl," he murmurs, and I breathe it in. Those words are a serotonin boost for my soul. They tell me I'm safe, adored, valued, and have nothing at all in the world to worry about.

He leans down and presses his lips softly against mine. It's a soft, quick kiss and I already want more. After he straightens up, he walks to his desk.

"From now on, you need more sleep, Charlotte. If you're going to be out until one in the morning, you need to stay home until ten the next day, understood?"

"Yes, sir," I purr.

"Although I'd prefer you aren't on the streets at all so late at night. Perhaps you should consider staying until morning."

I smile to myself, my eyes still fixated on the floor. "Yes, sir."

When I am on my knees and he is *sir*, not Emerson, he plays the part so well. Only slightly different from who he is on a daily basis, I love this power he manifests. It makes me feel so...something. I don't know how to put a word to this feeling. Like he is *everything* and nothing exists outside this room. I have no other purpose, which really makes me feel at peace. No other purpose means no other worry. Not a mortgage I have to help my mother cover or a struggling little sister. No estranged dad or broken family. And no ex-boyfriend. In this space, it's just him and me. My tasks are simple and fulfilling—please my *sir*. I don't even care anymore about what anyone would say or think about this arrangement. It makes me happy.

"Come here, Charlotte," he commands, and I crawl obediently toward him. "Stand up."

I climb to my feet, keeping my eyes down. His fingers drift down my blouse, sending a rush of excitement through me in its wake.

He touches one of the buttons, and I seriously hope he doesn't plan to rip this one open like he did yesterday. I'm going to run out of shirts. He slips the first button through the hole.

"I'm going to take this off for the day. Is that all right?"

Eagerly I nod.

"Use your words, Charlotte."

I swallow. "Yes, sir." And my mouth goes dry as he slips open my blouse one button at a time and slides it off my body until I'm standing before him in just my bra and skirt.

"This too?" he asks as his fingers glide along the skin just above my skirt. I have to force myself to swallow again.

"Yes, sir," I reply, this time in more of a whisper.

He gestures for me to turn around and slides the zipper along the back down, letting the skirt fall to the floor. The cool air of his office hits the skin of my ass and goose bumps erupt over my skin.

He's silent for a moment, my back to him as his fingers delicately graze my arm, and I wait for him to give me my orders. I'm pretty much ready for him to bend me over his desk or force me to my knees.

His lips press softly against my left shoulder, sending warmth to my core. "Get to work," he says with a gentle smack on my ass.

"Yes, sir," I reply, biting my lip to keep from grinning too hard.

Focusing on my work proves to be difficult, but I manage to get through a handful of emails and send off the tax documents the accountant needed all within the first couple hours of the work day. I feel Emerson's eyes on me from time to time. He watches me with a hungry gaze, but I never look back, relishing in his attention while I work.

When I bring him his coffee, he touches my bare legs, running his fingers up the inside of my thigh and making me want to explode, but I stay in character.

"Is there anything else you need, sir?" I ask with a slight tremble in my voice. He's driving me crazy on purpose. I don't know if he's not currently screwing my brains out because it's not part of the secretary fantasy for him or if he's just drawing out the tension. Maybe when the work day is done and we're out of character, we can go up to his room and do ungodly things to each other. Although if I'm honest, I sort of hope he'll do it the secretary way. I guess that's a fantasy I never knew I had.

"That's all for now, Charlotte." My name rolls off his tongue like silk gliding through his fingers. I no longer care that he doesn't call me Charlie. It makes me feel like I am his and only his, and I like that.

Before lunch, he drops his pen onto his desk. I glance over at him to see what's wrong. "I'm having trouble getting anything done today, Charlotte. You're distracting me and all I can think about is how beautiful that pussy between your legs is." He leans forward and levels a devious glare in my direction.

A subtle smile lifts the corners of my lips.

"I'm sorry, sir. Is there anything I can do to help?"

"Yes. Why don't you come over here and read this email for me?" he says in a way that tells me I'll be doing a little more than reading an email.

"Yes, sir," I reply, pushing my chair back and walking over. He taps his hand softly on his thigh, signaling for me to sit on his lap.

The moment I rest on his leg, his left hand wraps around my middle, holding me tight to his body. He's already hard, his erection stiff against my ass. I gently shift my hips to get comfortable, knowing it's driving him a little crazy.

With his right hand, he opens up the email.

"Read it," he commands.

I swallow, leaning forward and doing as he said.

"Mr. Grant, the federal withholding form required for your independent contractors is attached. Please see the instructions linked here for more information. Thank you, Miles Ward, CPA."

"Click the link," Emerson adds. His hand strokes my stomach, reaching my breasts and giving the right one a squeeze. I click the link and it opens to a tax form.

"Read it."

"All of it?" I ask.

He pinches my right nipple and I let out a yelp. "Are you questioning me, Charlotte?"

"No, sir," I reply. It's all clearly tax jargon and very boring, so I'm not exactly sure where he's going with this. Does he really need to know all of this now? Like he's even going to retain it.

Still, I do as he says.

"File Form 1099, Miscellaneous Income, for each person in the course of your business to whom you have paid the following during the year—"

The fingers of his left hand slip into my panties and slide across my clit. I freeze because it feels so good after hours of waiting to be touched. My eyes close and I hum against his touch.

"Keep going," he growls, halting his movements.

With a nervous gulp, I open my eyes and obey. "Each person from whom you have withheld any federal income tax under the backup withholding rules regardless of the amount of the payment..." My voice trails off as he dips a finger inside me, sliding easily through the pooling moisture. I let out a tiny moan of pleasure.

"Keep going, Charlotte."

As I read through the next paragraph of dull, legal jargon, I find it almost too hard to breathe, let alone speak. His finger plunges deep while his hand rubs exquisitely against my clit, and every time I try to rock my hips for more friction, he stills my body with a harsh grip on my hips.

I'm barely even reading correctly; I skip words and bounce around because I know he's sure as fuck not paying attention to anything this IRS document has to say, but I know he's trying to test me.

"Read that last part again," he says in a breathless grunt while he fingers me even harder, pounding into me without letting me move an inch.

"For all corporate entities…that are reporting as part of satisfying your requirement to report…" Fuck, I'm caught somewhere between heaven and agony. "With respect to a U.S. account…" My voice cracks. "…for chapter four purposes as described in Regulations section one…four…" I'm coming. My fingers grip the desk and my vision gets blurry.

"Keep reading," he grunts.

I cry out. "Four…dot five…section six."

"Fuck," he bellows. Standing up in a rush, he bends me over the desk. Scrambling for a condom in his drawer, he pulls one out and follows it with unbuckling his belt. I'm panting over his desk, my pussy still pulsing from the orgasm and eagerly awaiting the feel of his cock.

My thin cotton thong comes down with a quick swipe. Then he thrusts in hard, crushing my body against the desk. God, it feels so good being filled by him. My high-pitched cries fill the room while he pounds relentlessly. His fingers dig into my hips as his body crashes against my backside.

"Look what you do to me, Charlotte," he growls, sounding like a man come undone. "Sitting over there in these slutty panties. You do it on purpose, don't you?"

"Yes, sir," I gasp, my body building toward another climax. I love this wild version of Emerson, so different from the proper, serious boss he normally is. And I love that I make him this way even more.

"You want me to fuck you over my desk like a little slut?" His voice is strained, and I know he's getting close. I feel so dirty, loving the way his degradation makes me feel.

"Yes, sir," I nearly yell from the torrent of sensation coursing through my body.

"You are a dirty little slut, aren't you?" he growls.

"Yes, sir!"

"This is what you get for tempting me. Tell me you're sorry, Charlotte." His thrusts grow even more rough and wild, sending me into a tailspin as I come, and I swear my feet leave the ground. My body seizes, my pussy throbbing around his cock.

"I'm sorry, sir," I cry in a breathless moan.

His punishing thrusts slow as he comes with a loud groan. Only a second after he finishes, I'm gathered up into his arms. Still inside me, he turns my upper body and kisses me with so much passion, I nearly melt into the rug. Strong arms wrap around my middle, squeezing me tight.

Is it supposed to feel this good or am I just wishing for too much? Not just the sex, although that's great. But the way Emerson makes me feel, so secure and loved. I mean...he just finished calling me a dirty slut and I still feel as if he never truly talks down to me or makes me feel substandard, even as we play roles where I am *literally* inferior to him.

It all feels so ironically surreal. Like this isn't supposed to work, but it does. And I know this is just a temporary thing, and I'm not supposed to get attached, but deep down I'm holding on to the hope that Emerson will get over the fact that I dated his son and let this thing between us be real.

And I really should have learned my lesson by now when it comes to hoping. It always ends in disappointment.

Rule #25: Give him the opportunity to surprise you, and he will.

Charlotte

"DON'T YOU THINK I'M A LITTLE OLD FOR A PIÑATA?" SOPHIE ASKS, while I'm standing on a ladder in the middle of the skating rink.

"Umm...I'm six years older than you and I'm gonna whack the fuck out of this thing and enjoy every second of it."

She rolls her eyes. As I climb down, we admire my handiwork.

"I think it looks great!"

"It looks like a giant penis with herpes," she replies, and I gasp. She's cracking up as I shove her.

"It's a mushroom! I worked all night on this."

"First of all, they're toadstools, and I think the top part is supposed to be a lot bigger."

"Well…"

"I'm just kidding." She laughs, wrapping her arms around me and squeezing me in a bear hug. "I love it."

"Thanks." I squeeze her back.

"Besides…we're going to whack it until stuff comes out, right? So it might as well be a pen—"

"Sophie Underwood!" I shriek. "You're fifteen years old! Watch your mouth."

She's cackling as she jogs over to the party table where Mom is setting up the snacks and drinks. My phone buzzes in my back pocket, and I fish it out.

"I'm gonna tell Mom what you just said!" I yell to my sister as I swipe open my phone to check my messages.

My heart picks up when I see Emerson's name. And his message makes me pause for a moment.

I need you to come in immediately.

I quickly type out a reply.

Why? What's wrong?
I miss you.
We should talk about you working on the weekends. I can't be expected to read my own emails for two days straight.

My smile stretches across my face, and I know I look like an idiot, standing out here smiling so bright my face hurts.

I'll come over tonight, I reply.
What are you doing right now?

I have to think for a moment about how to respond. I've talked to Emerson about my personal life, but that was when I was just his employee. Everything's changed. I shouldn't be so nervous about sharing a little more with him. It's not like we're dating. We're just exclusively screwing—a lot—and occasionally role-playing some kinky secretary stuff.

But with all the screwing and foreplay, it feels strange to bring in regular life stuff. He wants to see me naked and fuck me over his desk, but does he care about my home life or what I do for fun? I want to say he does, but that's my hope talking.

I'm about to respond with something flirtatious like *Thinking of what you did to me yesterday*, but that's not what my fingers type out. Instead, I send him…

> Setting up for my little sister's birthday party at the rink. She turned fifteen today.

It's quiet for a while. No typing bubbles. No texts or pics.
I take the ladder back to the storage closet and just as I shut the door, my phone vibrates.

> *What time is the party?*
> Three. I'll be done by six, and I'll head over.

I'm sure my sister will be busy hanging out with her friends. She only has a couple friends whose parents let them come to our house for sleepovers and she invited them both tonight, so I know she'll be occupied while I sneak out.

Emerson doesn't answer me back, but the party is about to start, so I hardly notice. Before I know it, I'm handing out skates to her friends and coordinating the hokey pokey on the floor. The rink gets busy on Saturdays, and the perks of being family friends with the owner is we basically get to make the whole place Sophie's party.

When I look over at her and I see her bright smile as she sits between two equally quirky girls, I have to bite back the urge to cry. The shit she has had to put up with these past few years is unfair. Bullied at school. Abandoned by her own dad.

I know my sister worries about me, and I wish she didn't. She saw me through a bad relationship and a long year of feeling like I was a failure. It makes me wonder what she would think of Emerson. Would she approve of him, even if she never knew what goes on behind closed doors? Sure, he treats me like property when I want him to, but when we're not in a scene, he's affectionate and loving.

"What are you smiling about?" my mom asks as she brings me a white plastic cup filled with soda.

"Seeing her smile makes me happy," I say, nodding toward Sophie.

"Yeah, me too." She turns toward me. "You know…seeing you smile makes me happy too."

I turn my attention toward my mother. "Of course it does. What's your point?"

"My point is…you've been smiling a lot lately."

I try to act casual, brush it off. "Well, things are good. My job pays well, Sophie is doing well. You seem less stressed."

"Uh-huh," she replies over the brim of her cup.

"What are you getting at?"

"Are you sure there's not someone…"

"Mom! I literally go to work and come home. Where would I even meet a guy?"

She's laughing with a sly smile as she tries to hide her face from me. "I'm just sayin'. You have the look of a girl who's been—"

"I am *begging* you not to finish that sentence."

"I'm an ER nurse, Charlie. You think a little sex talk makes me squeamish?"

"Jesus." I groan, hiding my face in my hands.

While I'm trying to recover from the mortification of my mother telling me I look like I've been fucked well, she chimes in with, "Men like that don't come into the rink often."

"What?" I ask, lifting my face. My eyes scan the room and my heart skitters to a stop in my chest when I spot Emerson fucking Grant waltzing across the skating rink like it's not the most bizarre thing in the world. "What the—"

For some reason, I duck behind the counter. Shortly after dropping to my knees, I realize hiding was a stupid idea.

"What are you doing? Do you know him?"

If I stay hidden, maybe he'll leave. *Why* is he here? It was a big step even telling him about my sister's party. I sure as hell am not ready for him to meet them! And what about Sophie?

"He's asking around for you," my mom adds. "Your aunt Shelley just pointed this way."

Fuck. *Fuck.* Act natural, Charlie.

When I stand up, I try to appear casual, but his eyes are immediately on my face. Naturally, in his gaze, I delight in the attention. It's like sitting under a sun lamp, absorbing the warmth. His mouth quirks up in a small grin.

"Well, hello there," he says in a casual tone I haven't ever heard from him.

"Hi," I stammer awkwardly.

My mom clears her throat, stuck in the crossfire of our locked gazes.

"Oh, Emerson, this is my mom, Gwen. Mom, this is…my boss…Emerson."

She puts out her hand with an eager smile. "Nice to meet you!"

"The pleasure is mine, Gwen."

My mother enjoys another long moment of gazing up at Emerson like he's a national landmark.

Finally, she glances back at me. "I'm going to see if Sophie needs anything," she says, quickly removing herself from our conversation.

Once she's out of earshot, I level my glare at Emerson. "What on earth are you doing here?"

He laughs, like he knew this would get me all flustered. Like he *likes* seeing me rattled. "You said three o'clock. I know I wasn't invited, but I wanted to see you in your element."

Okay, that's really sweet. Fuck, why is he being so sweet? We had a deal: keep it secret and just have our fun when we can. But now he's met my mother, and he looks so freaking good in that T-shirt and those jeans.

I lean over the lacquered counter and bring my face close to his. "Okay, listen!"

He's still wearing a smug grin, and I want to punch him and kiss him at the same time.

"I'm Charlie here, not Charlotte, okay? No 'yes, sirs' or secretary bit here."

"Of course," he laughs.

It's ironic to me, being the one to boss Emerson Grant around, but I guess we're already so out of our element here that anything goes. And he seems to think it's funny too. Then his gaze falls on my lips. I quickly hold up a finger.

"And none of that. You're my boss."

"Do they know..."

"You're Beau's dad? No, but I'm sure they'll find out eventually."

His face keeps that light, amused expression with a hint of a smile, and it's so weird to me. A far cry from the brooding, serious boss I see every day, but I sort of like it. I've never really seen this side of Emerson, and it feels like just another part of him I get to myself.

"So, let me meet this birthday girl," he adds, tapping the countertop. A small sense of worry fills my gut. I trust Emerson, but what if he's not perfect with her? I have an innate sense of protectiveness over Sophie, but also a fear that if he screws this up, I won't be able to look at him the same way.

He turns and faces the rink where Sophie and her friends have taken to doing laps around the piñata.

"Let me guess," he says. "The one with the blue hair?"

I chuckle. "Yep." I wave at her when she spots us watching, her eyes instantly focusing on Emerson. She doesn't give him the same pensive expression she always gave Beau. Instead, she skates over and rolls right up to the low wall with that bright, freckle-faced smile.

"Hey, what's up?"

"Sophie, this is my...friend, Emerson. Emerson, this is my sister, Sophie."

I watch his expression as he holds something out toward her.

"Happy birthday, Sophie." It's a large purple envelope, and I try to imagine him walking down the aisles of a drug store, picking out a birthday card for a fifteen-year-old girl. A smile stretches across my face.

"Thank you!" she beams. "Can I open it?"

"Of course," he replies.

Sophie tears open the birthday card with purple glittery flowers all over the front and smiles as she reads it. When she opens it, something falls onto the floor. As she's picking it up, I glare at him with wide eyes, assuming he slipped some cash in there for her.

"You really didn't have to do th—"

"Oh my god!" Sophie screams.

As she jumps up holding a piece of paper, I ask, "What is it?"

"Two tickets to the Anime Fest!"

"What?" I shriek, grabbing the papers. And they're not just two regular tickets; they're two VIP tickets. "Emerson!"

"Thank you so much!" Sophie squeals, bouncing on her skates.

"But…how did you know?" I ask, completely baffled.

"You told me about it when you first started."

My mouth falls open. I remember that day, when I was rambling on and thought he wasn't even paying attention. He was actually listening. I have chills running up my arms as I stare at the tickets then look back up at him.

Does he even know how much this means to me? That after having my car fixed, I couldn't really afford to get the VIP tickets any longer, even with the salary he's paying me. Does he know that the fact that he listened to me and remembered after all these weeks means more than anything?

Tears spring to my eyes, and I quickly turn, blinking them away.

"What's this?" my mother asks after hearing Sophie's reaction. I hand her the tickets and Sophie proudly announces that she's going to the Anime Fest. And I'm trying to smile and act normal, but I feel his eyes on me and can't shake this feeling that while this is all so amazing, and he is so incredibly perfect, on some level, I hate him for it.

I hate him because, at the end of the day, I can't keep him.

Rule #26: Don't be afraid of a little dirty talk.

Charlotte

"Emerson, are you joining us for movie night?" my mother asks as he helps carry all of Sophie's gifts out to the car after the party.

My eyes widen. Emerson and I had pretty clear plans for his place after the party, so I shoot him a quick look that I hope translates into *just say no.*

To my utter dismay, he quickly replies, "I'd love to," and my expression morphs into one that says *what the fuck?*

But then he smiles, and I just don't get to see that smile very often, and it's such a nice smile.

"I'll ride with you," I tell him as Sophie and her two friends climb into the back of my mom's sedan. And I definitely don't miss the sly look on my mother's face as I disappear with him toward the back of the lot, where he parked his car. After climbing in, we watch my mom's car drive away before he grabs me by the back of the neck and drags my face to his.

We kiss with the vigor of two people who've been waiting for this exact moment for hours. All of that stored desire comes spilling out in one very hot make-out session over the console of his car. His lips are merciless and demanding, devouring my mouth and barely leaving me without enough air to breathe. Oh well, I don't need to breathe. I just need him.

His hands roam down to my breasts, but when I reach for the bulge at the front of his jeans, he grabs my wrist.

"I don't think that's such a good idea." He growls against my mouth.

"I think it's a great idea."

"You want me to fuck you in the front seat of this car, in front of people passing by, so we both get sent to jail? Because if you touch it, that's exactly where this is going."

"Worth it," I mumble, reaching again.

"Behave, Charlotte." The use of my *other* name makes me instantly obey. Like ringing a bell, he can just tame me with one word and a little change in the inflection of his voice. And just like that, I'm his submissive.

Pulling away with a pout, I lean back in my seat. "You know, we really don't have to go to movie night."

"I know."

"Then why are we doing it?"

He reaches across the console and squeezes my thigh with his hand. "Because I like seeing you around your family, and I like your family."

As he starts to drive away, I want to tell him that he's just making everything worse. We're supposed to be keeping this a secret, and we should be accepting that this will never work. It was just supposed to be sex.

When we reach my house, I tense in anticipation for the moment when he walks inside. I love our house, but it's our family house. It's a little bit chaotic on a normal day, but now there are three very excited teenage girls in it, and this is just not Emerson's speed.

We meet my mom in the kitchen, who is busy making

popcorn and snacks while the girls pile into the living room, picking out a movie. They agree on the Japanese animation *Spirited Away*, honestly one of my favorites, but will Emerson appreciate it? I can't seem to relax because I'm too busy worrying about if he notices the dirty dishes in the sink from breakfast or the pile of laundry still stacked on the stairs, waiting for Sophie to put it away. And my mom's cockapoo won't stop jumping on his leg, sniffing his jeans, and I just want to take him out of this place.

Then, I look at his face. And he's smiling again. Relaxed and laughing with my mom, while she tells him some of her favorite ER stories, the funny ones, of course.

And suddenly, nothing makes sense to me.

All of Emerson's praise, the way he tells me I'm so perfect and flawless and good…it was just him playing the part. None of it was real. And if it was, how does he feel about my real life now? None of this is perfect or flawless. It's a mess. And normally I'm okay with that, but I can't be Charlotte *and* Charlie to him. He was never supposed to see any of this, so why isn't he running for the hills? How can I possibly go back to being Charlotte on Monday, when he knows what the real me is like?

After the snacks are made and the movie is cued up, the girls sit on the floor and my mom takes the recliner, leaving the couch for Emerson and me. He sits on the end, crossing his legs with one ankle on the opposite knee as he leans on the armrest. He's too hot to be in my living room. Way too fucking hot.

As we watch the movie, he seems genuinely enthralled, but I catch his gaze on me from time to time, as if I'm more interesting than the movie. At one point, he rests his arm along the back of the sofa, and I find myself leaning against him until we are actually cuddling, with my mother only a couple feet away.

Like always, she's asleep fifteen minutes in anyway. And once the credits roll at the end, the girls take off to Sophie's room. Emerson turns his head toward me in the dimly lit room. I look back at him, and it's so quiet and such an intimate moment, it feels almost surreal.

He leans forward and presses his lips to my forehead.

Again, I hate him so much. Why is he doing this to me?

As he pulls away, he whispers, "Want to show me your room?"

A small laugh escapes my lips. He's joking. Except he looks like he's actually waiting for an answer.

"Why don't we go back to your place? I can stay the night."

He strokes my cheek. "I want to see your place."

"But it's a tiny pool hou—"

His finger presses over my lips. "Show me."

Without waking my mom, the two of us tiptoe out of the living room and toward the back door. I can't stop thinking of what a bad idea this is and trying to recollect if I put my dirty clothes in the hamper or if they're still scattered across the floor.

As we reach the door of my room, he crowds me from behind, wrapping his hands around my waist and kissing my neck. God, does he think we're going to do it in here? On the same queen-size bed I've had since I was fifteen?

The minute we walk in, he starts looking around, as if he's actually appreciating my space.

"It's not much," I say.

Taking me by the hand, he pulls me to his body and kisses the words straight out of my mouth. He tastes so good, and I want everything about this moment—just not here.

"Why are you so nervous?" he asks, locking me in his arms.

"I'm not nervous… I just…"

"Do you think my age bothered your mom?"

"Are you kidding? My mom is the coolest. Now if my dad had been here…" I say, imagining my dad flipping out at the idea of me with a man a couple years younger than him. Good thing he's never going to find out.

"I figured. How old are your parents anyway?"

"I'm not going to answer that question," I reply, grabbing

his face and pulling him in for another kiss. Regardless of how nervous I am, my body lights up from his touch, eager to have more of him.

But every time I try to pull him to the bed or the door, he stands his ground. Instead, he starts looking through the framed photos on my bookshelf.

Pictures of me…as a teenager.

"Oh God, please stop," I cry, trying to push them down, but he fights me.

"I want to see." Naturally, he wins, overpowering me as he browses them all.

When he lands on a picture of me and Sophie when we went to Disneyland as kids, I turn to ice.

"This is cute. Who's this?" he asks.

In the photo, Sophie was six, and I was twelve. Instead of the blue hair she has now, it was cropped short. With a blue Olaf T-shirt, shorts, and light-up sneakers, I understand why Emerson had to ask who it was in the picture. Because when he looks at the photo, he sees a little boy.

And I can't lie to him.

"That's Sophie," I reply, taking the photo down and staring at it.

I tense, waiting for his reaction. I think maybe he will ask questions or avoid it altogether because it makes him uncomfortable. Instead, I feel his arms wrap around my middle, his lips pressing to my ear.

My eyes stay on the photo, and I let myself go back to that day in my memory. "Our mom and dad took us for her birthday because she was obsessed with *Frozen*. Obsessed. A detail she will deny to this day because, of course, now, it's super cliché."

He laughs against my ear.

But the happy memory sours for me. Because years later, when Sophie changed her name and came out to my parents, it sparked a chasm in my family—one she unfairly blames herself for.

"You're very protective of her," he mumbles like it's something brave or commendable. Like doing the bare minimum, loving someone unconditionally, is so great.

"I have to be. He left us because..." I swallow. God, I don't want to cry, not here in such a good moment, and definitely not in front of him. But something in the way he squeezes me tighter makes me feel safe, like I can bare my soul without vulnerability.

"I don't understand how people can be so bad at love. How could he hurt his own kids because of his own selfish ignorance? How can you claim to love someone and hurt them so badly?"

"That's not love."

I turn my head to look into his eyes. This same brooding man who scowled at me when I read his palm suddenly knows about love. Because of course he does. I've seen the way he works to get Beau back in his life, the way he beats himself up for what he's doing with me.

"I see the way you are with her, how amazing you are with your family, Charlotte."

I quickly shake my head. "No, I'm only doing what I should—"

Cutting me off, he takes me by the face and pulls me close. "Stop it. Stop selling yourself short. I bet your mother and sister don't think that. I'm sure they think you're just as amazing as I do."

Heat floods my body, turning everything in me to mush. Emerson Grant thinks I'm amazing.

"I'm a mess," I argue. "Look at where I live. I'm clumsy and forgetful and messy..."

His lips press against mine as he mumbles, "You're perfect." Then he pulls away and stares at me sternly, his voice taking on a darker, edgier tone. "Now, stop arguing with me."

Instantly, my face relaxes, and the stress slides off my shoulders. I set the picture frame on the shelf as I step into his arms. "Yes, sir," I reply.

"I'm going to make you forget every bad thing you've ever said about yourself. And if I catch you saying anything self-deprecating, you'll be punished. Understand?"

There's a tremor under my skin, from fear or from excitement or maybe I'm just caught up in this moment and everything he's saying to me. I quickly reply with a head nod.

His hands cup my face as he arches a brow and tilts his head down toward me. "Your words, Charlotte."

"Yes, sir."

"Good girl," he whispers, his forehead pressed against mine. Then he smiles, and it feels as if the scene has come to an end, and we're just us again.

As he brushes my hair back, I stare up at him, trying to navigate this place we're in. What are we? Does he feel what I'm feeling? Because right now, my heart feels so incredibly full that it's terrifying. Someday, Emerson will leave me, either because the novelty has worn off or because his son has made his way back into his life and there's no room for me there. I know it's going to hurt like hell when that day finally arrives, and I'm not sure I'll ever be ready for it.

Almost as if he can sense the erratic, fear-laced thoughts running through my head, Emerson kisses me hard. Suddenly, I'm lifted off my feet and carried to my unmade queen-size bed. With my legs wrapped around his waist, he crawls down the center, placing me on the pillows.

"We really don't have to stay here," I stammer. "We can go back to your house—"

His lips trail down to my neck as he grinds himself between my legs, knocking all of the rational words and thoughts straight out of my head. I let out a breathy moan.

"You like that?" he mutters against my skin.

"Uh-huh."

"Want me to do it again?"

"Yes, please." I sigh.

Laying his body over mine, he grinds his hard length against me again, sending a shot of arousal through my body. Something about that action, the way his body moves, the promise of sex, has me in knots, and I moan again.

My legs are locked around his waist as he kisses my collarbone, trailing downward to my chest. Lifting my shirt at the hem, he swipes it over my head.

"Tell me what else you want, Charlotte."

I freeze. Dirty talk? I can't. Just the idea of saying the words out loud has me tensing.

His movements stop, and he sits up, leaving my skin craving his.

"I'm waiting..." he teases. From this angle, his large body hovering over me, hard and intimidating, makes me think I'm dreaming. I *want* him. I want him to take control, to bring me pleasure, but also to use my body to seek his own. And yeah, there are a million things I could think of that he could do at this very moment that I would love, so why can't I express them?

What am I afraid of?

My hands cover my face. I can't believe I'm about to say this... out loud...to my boss...to Beau's dad.

"Charlotte..."

"I want to watch you," I blurt out, my voice muffled by my hands.

"Watch me do what?"

"Ugh..." I groan. This is humiliating. But he literally told me to tell him what I want, so that's what I'm doing. Before I can continue, he leans down and peels my hands from my face.

Taking both of my wrists in one hand, he holds them above my head, pinned to the pillow.

"Charlotte, listen to me. You are a smart, beautiful, confident woman. You don't need me to tell you what you want. I want to hear it from you. You deserve pleasure just as much as I do, and trust me, I want nothing more than to hear you utter the dirtiest words, and then I want to do whatever it is you say. So say it."

I'm staring up at him, my eyes filled to the brim with lust. Goddamn this man. I'm fucked. Ruined forever because there's no chance in hell I'm ever going to find a man my own age who can talk to me like that, make me feel the way he does.

"I want to watch you touch yourself."

"Try again," he says, peering down at me with an arched brow.

I have to make it dirtier. God, why is this so hard? "Stroke your cock for me."

"Not bad, but I think you can do a little better than that."

His voice gives me confidence, so I grind my hips upward as I say, "I want to watch you fuck your fist until you come all over my chest."

His face is only inches from mine, and his eyes widen when my words come out. Jesus, I can't believe I just said that.

"Fuck, that was hot."

Letting go of my wrists, he sits up again. Kneeling between my legs, he keeps his eyes focused on mine as he unbuttons his jeans.

"Take yours off too," he commands. I quickly unfasten my shorts and shimmy them down my legs. After his jeans are unbuttoned, he drags down the zipper. But before he pulls his shaft out, he snaps the elastic on my thong. "These too. Let me see you."

After everything we've done together, why am I so nervous about being naked in front of him? I strip them off anyway, unclasping my bra next, so I'm lying in front of him, sprawled out on my bed, naked in the dim light of my bedside lamp.

He moves to pull his dick out, but he stops. His hands run from my hips all the way up to my breasts, and there's something in the way he's looking at my body. His gaze filled with awe as he devours me with his eyes.

"What are you thinking?" I ask playfully, but he doesn't

answer. Instead, he kisses each of my breasts, making my back arch and my brain forget my own name.

"So you want to watch, huh?" he asks, rising back up.

Pulling down his jeans, he finally pulls out his cock, and I can't tear my eyes away. I mean, I've never really admired a dick before, but something about Emerson's is perfect. Made only more perfect by the way his large hand wraps around it, sliding from the base to the head and squeezing the tip.

With his hungry eyes on me, he licks his palm, getting his hand nice and wet before stroking himself again. I'm squirming against my sheets with need as I watch him.

I shift my hips and bite my lip. "Do that again," I whisper.

I feel so dirty. I can't believe I asked that and I can't believe he's doing it, but since that moment in the hallway, I've gotten a taste of liberation, and it's so good. This feeling of freedom to be sexual and feel good and not bad about that is so addicting. I don't know if I'll ever feel this way with anyone other than Emerson, so I'm going to savor it for as long as I can.

His chest heaves as he moves his hand, keeping his eyes on me as he jacks himself slowly. Liquid heat pools in my belly, and I struggle not to rub my thighs together, no matter how much I want to.

"Faster," I whisper in a breathy plea.

He picks up his pace, and I watch his mouth fall open as he does, his eyes hooded with lust.

"Touch yourself," he barks, taking my hand and guiding it to my open legs. When my fingers graze over my clit, the desire grows stronger. He watches my fingers as I slide them through my wet folds and circle back to my clit. He's practically hypnotized by the movement.

"Fuck yourself," he says, and his fist jerks faster.

As I sink two fingers deep inside me, we groan in unison. Then, I begin to pump in sync with him. "I want to come all over you, Charlotte."

"Do it," I reply. I'm dragging my pleasure out, and I know once I'm ready, I could easily come right along with him.

His free hand drags down my hip to clutch my thigh tightly in his grip, and I can tell he's forcing himself not to come. And more than anything, I want to watch his face when he does let go and unloads all of that pleasure onto me.

"Do it, Emerson," I cry out. "Come all over me." Right on cue, he lets out a heavy grunt, dragging the tip of his cock along my belly as warm jets of cum paint my skin. His expression is perfect, half-agony and half-euphoria.

A few hard circles around my clit, and I come undone right along with him. Biting my bottom lip, I tilt my head back and let the sensation take me away.

Then, he's kissing me again, dragging my face up to meet his. I latch desperately on to his neck and tangle my tongue with his.

"Fuck, that was incredible. *You* are incredible," he pants against my lips.

We both collapse against the mattress, coming down from the high. He jumps up and disappears into my small bathroom, returning a moment later with a warm wet washcloth that he uses to gently clean up the mess on my stomach.

When he returns to the bed, I expect him to button up his pants, kiss me goodbye, and leave. What I don't expect is him dropping his pants, draping them over a chair, and flicking off the bedside lamp as he crawls into bed next to me.

"What are you doing?" I laugh.

"What does it look like?"

"You really don't have to—"

"Charlotte," he snaps in a deep authoritative tone that shuts me up.

There's a shred of moonlight peeking in through the window of the pool house and it's just enough light to make out his features on the pillow next to me. His eyes are open as he stares back at me, his hands caressing my hip and back under the blanket.

And I try to remember if I ever felt as close to Beau as I feel with Emerson right now. I've been telling myself it's just sex. I'm open with him and it makes me feel closer to him, but what if it's not just about the sex? What if it's more than that?

"What are you thinking?" I whisper again as my eyes get heavy and he pulls me closer.

I nuzzle into the comfort of his broad chest and heavy arms as he presses his lips against my ear. Maybe I'm already dreaming because I can't believe the answer that comes out of his mouth.

Rule #27: There's always time for a quickie.

Emerson

"Do I have to remind you to behave today?"

Charlotte bites her lip in the passenger seat as I pull up to the front of the club. We don't open for another couple of hours, but we're holding our first club event tonight and I need to check a few more details before it starts.

It's been a mess at work this week. Too much actual work means I can't spend my days fucking my secretary over my desk like I want to. In fact, we've both been so swamped, we hardly get to even touch each other until after five, when I can usually manage a quick fuck upstairs while the phone rings off the hook in the office.

The other part of my week, affected by the workload, is the plan I had for Charlotte. There are so many things I want to teach her, things she's eager to learn as my sub. And I don't know who fucked with this girl's head so much to make her believe she's never good enough, but there are some techniques I had in mind to change that.

When we step into the club, it's chaos. I hear Maggie yelling something in the back of the room, Drake is looking stressed as he barks orders at his men to fix one of the cages on the side of the stage, and when Garrett gets one look at me, he actually smiles.

Which is what Garrett does under stress, he makes a joke out of everything. It's infuriating.

"Contrary to how it looks now, I can assure you, everything is under control," he says with brimming confidence.

"Bullshit," I reply.

"Yeah, it's a mess. That cage on stage right still rattles, two of the girls called out sick, and the city is threatening to revoke our liquor license, so Maggie is having a mental breakdown."

"What can I do to help?" Charlotte asks before I can say a word.

"Well…what are you doing tonight at seven?" Garrett asks with a waggle in his brow.

I grit my teeth and push her behind me. "No."

He replies with a laugh. "Relax. It was a joke. But I mean… let me know if you change your mind. The members would bid a pretty penny for you, sweetheart."

He tugs at one of her brown curls, and I've never wanted to hurt my best friend more than I want to in this moment. Knowing Garrett, he's not flirting. This is just what he does. He sees people for what they're worth, and it's what makes him good at his job.

But it's never bothered me so much, the way he talks to Charlotte. In his defense, he still sees her as only my secretary.

Charlotte's hearty laugh tears my gaze away from Garrett. "You're crazy. You don't want me in your auction. It would be crickets."

My irritation quickly morphs from Garrett to her as I furrow my brow in her direction. I know she means it as a joke, and she can laugh all she wants with him about it, but I know what lurks behind that humor, and it makes me grind my molars just thinking about it.

"That's enough," I bark, silencing both of their laughs. I march straight into the club, tearing off my jacket, ready to fix all this shit that seems to be falling apart. "Let's get to work," I call back to them.

We put out one fire at a time, and honestly, this is my favorite part of my job. It takes me back to my early days, running events, coordinating vendors and publicists and schedules, before I spent my life sitting behind a desk, waiting for something fun to come along.

Every few minutes, I catch Charlotte running around, and I mostly give her over to Maggie for the day. I'm strangely aggravated with her for some reason. Okay, not with *her*, but that one comment this morning has been grating on my nerves all day.

How the fuck can such a brilliant, beautiful girl think so badly of herself?

That piece of shit father of hers never wanted to treat her right, so now she can't seem to wrap her head around the idea that she's worthy of anything. I wish I could face that fucker right now. I'd like to knock his ass out for what he did to Charlotte and Sophie.

"What do you want to do about tonight's lineup?" Garrett asks, while I'm standing in the office, going over the contracts.

"How many do we have?" I ask.

"Seven."

Damn. It's our first auction, the most highly anticipated event at the club, according to the PR firm. They've been raving about this since the club opening was announced, which is great, but also has that fucking criminal investigator breathing down our necks. The girls are auctioning off their time, not sex. At least not publicly. What they do during their date is up to them.

Seven feels a bit dismal for our first auction.

"Talk to the girls we have. Maybe they have some friends. Up their cut to sixty percent, and let's aim for at least a dozen," I say, hoping it's enough.

"You know…" Garrett replies, leaning against the doorframe. The hairs on my neck stand up as if I already know the bad fucking idea he's about to vocalize. "I meant what I said about Charlotte."

"No."

He waits a beat before adding, "You sound awfully protective..."

I raise my eyes and glare at him. I don't normally hide things from Garrett. We've been friends for years, but I've never really had a secret to keep before. I'm not even sure I'm keeping this one very well. And I'm not even sure why I still am.

"She's only twenty-one."

"They're all practically twenty-one."

I busy myself by pretending I'm actually reading these contracts in my hands, sifting through the papers methodically.

"Emerson Grant...are you getting attached?"

"Knock it off," I mutter.

He holds his hands up in surrender. "Fine. You don't have to tell me. Just let me put her up on the stage...auction off an hour of her time tonight. If she agrees, of course. You and I both know she'll rake in a good crowd, not to mention a lot of money."

It's not about the money. But something about what he just said makes me pause.

Charlotte would get a lot of attention tonight. Perhaps then she'd finally see what I see. But I obviously can't let anyone win an hour with her. And I instantly think of our wealthiest member...

"Is Ronan Kade going to be here tonight?"

"You can count on it," Garrett replies.

Fuck. This is going to cost me a fortune.

"Sign her up," I reply quickly.

"Don't you think I should ask her first?"

"I'll talk to her," I bark as I storm out of the office.

Charlotte is helping Maggie stuff envelopes for the event. The girls are chitchatting about something, and I notice the way Charlotte's smile fades and she sits up a little taller as I approach.

"A word, please?" I say, gesturing for her to follow me to a private room where we can talk. The minute I shut us in, I realize my mistake. Her eyes light up, gazing slack-jawed at the black silk bed with handcuffs, silk ties, and ropes hanging from the wall.

"I thought you were too busy today," she says, turning back to me and running her hands up my chest.

Fuck, I am too busy, but the way she's responding to this room right now has me thinking I could just blow off work, the event, my entire fucking job at this point. I'd love to see her pretty pale skin on that black silk, tied to this bed, letting me do ungodly fucking things to her.

"No," I say, shaking my head. "I brought you in here because I really do need to talk to you."

"Oh," she replies, pulling away, but I don't let her take her hands off me. We may need to talk, but I still need to touch her. Grabbing her by the elbows, I pull her against me.

"You're going to be in the auction tonight," I say, like ripping off a bandage.

She tenses, glaring up at me with wide eyes. "I can't—"

Walking her back until her legs hit the bed, I gently push her until she's lying down, and I drape my body over hers. I can't fuck her now, no matter how much I want to, but there will be time later to have a little fun in here.

"Emerson, I really can't be in your auction. I'm sorry—"

I silence her with a kiss and grind my hips against hers. She hums in response. God, I love these soft lips of hers. I could never get tired of her kisses.

"You can and you will."

Her hands drift up my sides, pulling me closer as she reaches up for another kiss. "What exactly am I auctioning off?"

"An hour of your time."

"That's it?" she asks with a tilt of her head.

Glaring down at her, I pinch my brow together. "Did you have something else in mind?"

"Well, anyone can bid, right? Which means anyone can win."

"Yes…"

"So you'd be okay letting me spend an hour with some man I don't even know?" She's searching my features, trying to gauge just how much I care about her talking to other men, which, for the record, is a lot, but she doesn't know that, and I can't let myself grow any more attached to Charlotte than I already am.

"You're not obligated to do anything with them, you know. And it's entirely up to you what you want to auction off."

She hesitates again. "So other girls are auctioning off more?"

I kiss her soft pale neck. "Yes. Some girls will auction off time in a room or a public display of some sort."

"Isn't that…"

"Loopholes and fine print, Charlotte." My cock is getting painfully hard behind my slacks as I grind against her again.

"Oh…" she moans, trying to wrap her legs around me.

"We don't have time for this," I mutter uselessly against her chest, dragging down the deep neckline of her blouse.

"What if I told you I got my test results back?" she says in a breathy moan.

I pull away. "What test results?"

"You said I had to turn in negative test results in order to be a member of the club, so I did. I'm good."

My blood begins pounding so hard through my veins that my cheeks flush and my focus goes hazy, all from the image of sinking my fat cock into Charlotte without anything between us. "Fuck…" I stammer through clenched teeth.

In a quick motion, I flip her onto her stomach, grinding against her from behind.

"We can be quick." She moans, but I'm already one step ahead. I rip her skirt up above her hips, shove her panties to the side, and quickly unleash my cock from my pants in five seconds flat.

The sight of her perfect ass has me feeling wild. I give her backside a quick slap, making her yelp, then knead the flesh with my hand. She squirms against me. Fuck, I love seeing her this needy, and I love that it's my cock she craves. Bending down, I take a ravenous bite of her right ass cheek. She squeals, driving her face into the mattress.

"I should make you wait," I growl, standing up and pulling her hips back, lining up the head of my dick with her wet pussy lips. She groans loudly into the satin sheets. "But I want you leaking my cum in your panties while you're onstage."

I plunge myself inside her, and it's like heaven. Her moans and the sight of her soft hips in my hands is enough to drive me mad, but it's the tight heat of her cunt that makes me crazy. Charlotte was made for me. This pussy was molded for my cock, swallowing me up so eagerly like it's putting a fucking spell on me. Making me never want another pussy again, which I don't.

"Harder," she gasps, pushing backward, her delicate fingers grasping the black satin tightly in her grip. I give her what she wants, slamming into her harder and harder, wondering if I could be hurting her, but she doesn't look like she's in any pain. The expression on her face looks more like ecstasy.

"I wish I were fucking you every minute of my day, you know that?"

"Yes."

"I love fucking you, Charlotte. You take my cock so well."

"I love it," she cries.

"I want your pussy to be sore when you're up there. I want you thinking about this."

"Faster, Emerson. I'm going to come," she moans in a high-pitched plea. God, I love that she asks for what she wants during sex now.

I pull her hips up and slam into them, grunting with each lightning-fast stroke. Her beautiful cunt squeezes my shaft tightly as she comes.

Holding her hips in my hands, I let her body relax from her orgasm as I start to unload inside her, watching her intently and imagining her body soaking up everything I'm giving her.

When I finally pull out, I glance toward the door. If there was any doubt about me fucking my secretary, it's gone now. Even if they didn't just hear me, since these walls are pretty soundproof, we've been in here "talking" for a while now.

I pull up Charlotte's panties and adjust her skirt. She stands up and fixes her blouse.

Before she moves toward the door, I grab her waist and pull her against me. I need her lips, one quick taste before we walk back out there, and she goes onstage, letting random men bid money for her time. I need to fool myself for just a little longer and pretend she's mine.

If I were a smart man, I'd let someone else win Charlotte tonight. I should let him impress her with his money or promises of sex, and if she decides she'd rather be with someone who could love her for real, I should let her go.

But even I know, that's impossible now. I don't think I'll ever be able to let her go.

Rule #28: When he tells you you're worth it, believe it.

Charlotte

I THINK I'M GONNA BE SICK. THIS CAN'T BE HAPPENING. SOMEHOW, I'm standing among a horde of thirteen other women, all of them supermodel gorgeous and in their underwear—if you could call it that.

I'm doing this for Emerson. I can't tell if he's telling me to do this because he needs me to or because he wants me to. Is he really going to let someone else win an hour with me, assuming anyone even bids? Do I mean that little to him?

I can't stop wringing my hands when my gaze locks with the throne-room woman, Madame Kink herself. With her long black hair and disarming green eyes, she struts over to me with a warm smile.

"Hello again."

"Hi," I stammer, trying to keep my eyes on her face and not on her breasts, which are covered only by pasties. I've never felt more ridiculous for wearing clothes.

I straighten my spine and try to pretend I'm sexy and confident. Though I'm not sure it's working.

"You're not nervous, are you?"

"Nervous? No…" Yeah, I'm definitely not selling it. She replies with a smile. "Yes, I'm a little nervous," I continue. "This is not really normal for me."

"What's your name?" she asks.

"Charlie, er, I mean Charlotte."

Grinning, she says, "I'm Eden."

"Nice to meet you," I whisper, still wringing my hands.

"May I?" She touches the buttons of my blouse. Looking into her kind, green eyes, I let out a deep breath and nod. There's something about *her* taking off my clothes that makes me feel a little more relaxed about them coming off in public in the first place.

"Oh, this is cute," she says, noticing my black lace bra under my shirt. "You should definitely show this off." She slips my white blouse off my shoulders. Then, standing behind me, she unzips my skirt.

"How long have you and Emerson been together?" she asks casually.

"We're not. I'm just his secretary," I correct her.

There's a small giggle as she leans forward and presses her mouth next to my ear. "You have a bite mark on your ass cheek, Charlotte."

I gasp, drawing the attention of the girls around me. "Oh my god." I try to hide my mortification, but Eden just slides her hands over my shoulders, trying to comfort me.

"Relax. It's hot as fuck."

"Is it really noticeable?" I ask, trying to cover it with my hand. She moves in front of me, nodding her head.

"Very. So Emerson didn't do that?"

I can't even try to hide it at this point. Twisting my lips, I give a little shrug, and she nods knowingly. "You don't think he's too old for me?" I ask, trying to read her expression. But she only laughs.

"No, I don't think he's too old for you. Do you?"

I shrug. "It's complicated."

"I've known Emerson for a few years, and I've never seen him give someone as much attention as he gives you."

It makes me feel better, but only for a moment. I focus on her face and dread swims through me as I ask, "Wait…you and Emerson have never…have you?"

"No," she answers plainly. "Emerson is very dominant…and so am I."

"Oh." I feel like such an idiot here sometimes, like I don't get any of this and maybe I never will. It's like I'm stepping into a foreign world that I will never truly be a part of. I exist only on Emerson's arm, only here as his accessory, and not really here as myself.

Eden must sense my apprehension because she takes my hands in hers. "Relax, Charlotte."

And then I ask what I've been dying to ask since she started speaking to me. "Can I ask you a question?"

"Of course."

"Are you going to…sleep with them tonight?"

She smirks and glances past the curtain to the men and women waiting on the main floor. Then with a shrug, she says, "I'm at the club, aren't I?"

I'm filled with dread again. What the fuck has Emerson signed me up for?

———

I watch from the sidelines as the girls go, one by one, onto the stage, where they strut around half-naked while men and women in the crowd bid for their time. Some of the girls have offered up their company for drinks while others, like Eden, have promised time in a specific room.

They start the bidding at one thousand dollars, and most girls are going for over five, and my jaw nearly hits the floor when a man in the back wins a night with Eden for fifty grand.

My heels click against the stage floor as I make my way into the spotlight.

Be sexy. Be confident. Be Charlotte.

The MC introduces me, and I barely hear a word he's saying as I scan the crowd. Everyone is staring at me with warm, curious expressions. They're making me a little more comfortable, even though they all look like they want to devour me—it's better than looking uninterested or bored.

I instantly notice a familiar man in front. He's in a black suit, sipping on a glass of something amber brown. He's the same man who was playing poker on the first night in the club, with a woman kneeling at his side while he petted her head. Something about him terrifies me. He exudes power and wealth, and I can only assume he would be equally as terrifying in bed.

Looking up, I catch a glimpse of Emerson standing near the back wall. His arms are folded tightly in front of him, and there's something about his body language that seems off. He's tense.

"Give us a little turn, darlin'," the man with the microphone says, and I force a bright smile as I circle the stage, letting the crowd see my ass, complete with bright-red teeth marks.

Thanks, Emerson.

"Ten thousand," a dark voice calls from the floor, and I spin in surprise, searching for the source.

The man in black winks at me as he takes a sip of his drink. My body floods with heat. This man will pay ten grand to spend an hour with me. Will he be disappointed if I don't have sex with him? Surely, he must know he's just winning my company. I *can't* sleep with him. Emerson wouldn't let that happen…would he?

"Ten thousand for Mr. Kade. Do I hear eleven thousand?"

Movement in the back of the room catches my attention, and I squint through the spotlight to see Emerson raise a hand. We lock eyes for a long, tense moment. He has to win. What if Mr. Kade outbids him? I'm trying not to let my panic show, but I'm shivering in my heels up here. *Why would he do this to me?*

"Mr. Grant for eleven thousand," the man calls.

"Fifteen," the man up front barks.

"Twenty," Emerson replies. I can barely move as the men volley back and forth, the room thick with tension as they continuously outbid each other. When the man in black shouts fifty with a smug grin on his face, I want to cry. I'm about two seconds away from telling them to stop. I'm not worth this much money. They can't possibly be willing to pay this much for me.

I shake my head at Emerson, making it so subtle I hope no one notices, but I think I might lose it if he actually coughs up over fifty thousand dollars just for an hour with me.

"Please, don't," I whisper, although no one can hear me. I know he can read the words on my lips.

He clenches his jaw and glares at me in anger.

The man in black looks back at Emerson, waiting for him to bid. I cover my cheeks, praying that this will end. I'm a nobody, not nearly as sexy as Eden or half as beautiful or as interesting as any of the other women that came up here. How can he just throw away money like that?

"Fifty thousand, going once…"

"Seventy-five," Emerson says, staring at me as if he's angry at me. My eyes are wide as saucers, and I must be pale as a ghost.

The man in black laughs loudly. "You're worth every penny, sweetheart, but I think Mr. Grant wants you to himself."

I'm still staring at Emerson with my mouth hanging open, trying to wrap my head around seventy-five grand.

"Sold!" the announcer yells. "For seventy-five thousand dollars to club owner Emerson Grant!" The crowd begins to cheer, and I catch Eden clapping with a bright smile, while sitting on someone's lap in the back of the room.

Before I know what's happening, I watch Emerson march toward me, looking more irritated than elated at his win. Is he mad at me? Did I do something wrong?

"I'm—I'm…sorry," I stammer as he takes me by the hand and tosses me over his shoulder. "What are you doing?"

The reactions around us are a mixture of laughter and cheers as I'm hoisted across the room with my bare, bite-marked ass slung over Emerson's shoulder. He doesn't stop as we disappear down the hallway on the right. It's not the voyeur hall, but the one with the room we were in today, where we had that quickie on top of the bed.

"Where are we going?" I shriek.

It's dark back here, but I hear a door close behind us as we reach the dimly lit room with the black bed I remember. My stomach clenches in both excitement and fear.

"I paid for an hour of your time, Charlotte." He tosses me on the bed and stares down at me with a look of masked anger. "It's time to collect what I won."

His large hands grip my ankles and yank me toward him. I let out a yelp. I'm not afraid of Emerson. I trust him, but right now…he seems unhinged. Angry at me for reasons I don't understand, and I can't quite tell if we're supposed to be in a scene or if he's being real.

"Remind me, Charlotte," he asks as something soft wraps around my right ankle. When I try to pull my foot away, I realize it's a restraint. He's cuffing me to the bed. "What did you put on that little list for punishment?"

"I…I don't… What am I being punished for?"

He yanks my other leg and wraps another soft, cushioned cuff around my ankle. My legs are spread, and my heart is starting to hammer in my chest.

"What did you say this morning about the auction? What would happen when you were onstage?"

"What?" He's not making any sense, and I can't seem to shake my nervousness. Plus, the way I'm restrained and the anticipation for what's to come has my brain in a fog. He's so angry and being rougher than usual, and it's so hot and terrifying that my body doesn't know if it's scared or turned on.

"Crickets, Charlotte. You said there would be crickets."

"Um…yeah," I reply.

He moves across the room and opens a drawer. I try to peer around him to see what he's taking out. When he turns back toward me, he has a strip of black silk in his fingers.

"Were there crickets, Charlotte?"

"No," I reply. He stands at the foot of the bed and stares at me with that tense brow of his, gliding the silk through his fingers.

"How much did I pay for this hour with you?"

"Emerson, you can't really pay that—"

"Lie down," he barks in a stern command.

"I don't understand."

He raises a brow, tilting his head at me. "Do you want me to stop, Charlotte? If you're scared, we can walk right out the door."

"No…" I whisper.

"Do you trust me?"

"Yes."

"Then lie down." His cold voice sends a chill down my spine, and I force my lungs to breathe as I recline on the bed, staring at the ceiling. Emerson moves up toward my head and reaches behind me, fumbling with the clasp of my bra. It unhooks and he pulls it off, releasing my breasts. Then, he gathers my wrists together, tying them with the black silk.

There's a subtle shake in my bones, but I do my best to hide it. And I realize now that if Emerson is mad at me, he's going to do something to punish me. And strange as it is, that's what I want.

I watch as he walks back to the drawer and pulls out another piece of silk. "We haven't established a safe word because we haven't needed one yet."

Safe word? My stomach turns.

"If you want me to stop, just say *mercy*. Understand?"

"Yes, sir."

I repeat the word over and over in my head, making sure I don't forget it.

Mercy. Mercy. Mercy.

But I won't need it, will I? He's not really going to hurt me.

"Charlotte, tell me why you think I'm punishing you tonight."

I take a breath, staring up at him. His features have softened, and I focus on the fabric in his hands, knowing that it's going to cover my eyes in a minute and I need to prepare myself for it.

"Because I...um," I stammer. It's because of the money, isn't it? "Because I cost you seventy-five thousand dollars?"

He growls, stepping toward me. As he drapes the fabric over my eyes, he coldly replies, "No." The room goes black as he ties the silk at the back of my head, and my breathing picks up. Everything instantly becomes more intense, my legs wanting to fight against the restraints because I feel so exposed.

When I feel his soft hands stroking my cheeks, I flinch. "You cost me so much money because you are worth it, Charlotte. I put you on that stage, hoping you would see that for yourself, but I could tell as I watched you up there that you still wouldn't believe it."

What? This is about me believing I'm worth so much money? He can't be serious.

"I don't like impact play, and if I remember correctly, you didn't like the idea of being paddled or spanked, correct?"

"Um...yes, I mean..."

He strokes my head. "Relax."

I have to force my chest to inhale. I just want him to touch me again.

"Luckily, there are other ways of teaching you a lesson. And I'll admit something to you..."

I hear him doing something across the room—opening a drawer, moving things around, placing things on the bed. I can't tell what any of it is, but I'm overwhelmed with curiosity.

"What?" I ask.

He brings his mouth close to my ear as he whispers, "I memorized every single thing you wrote on that list."

Fuck. My mind races, trying to remember what I scored those items, but there were over two hundred of them. Could he really have memorized it?

"Deep breath," he mumbles against my ear. Right as I inhale, something clamps down hard on my right nipple, and I let out a shriek, twisting and contorting, trying to move away from the pain, but it won't let up. It takes me a second to realize it's a nipple clamp.

My chest is heaving as I accept the pain, letting it settle in.

"How much did I pay, Charlotte?"

My brain scrambles for an answer. "Seventy-five..." I breathe.

"Do you think that was too much?"

"Yes," I sigh, knowing what's coming before I can even get the word out.

When the second clamp tightens, I don't let out a shriek because it's not as surprising as the first, but it somehow hurts more.

Warm, wet lips press against the flesh of my breasts, and I hum in response. "Do you understand why I'm angry?"

"No," I reply.

His hands draw deep lines down my sides, over my hips, digging under my panties. And I know what's coming before he does it. With a quick jerk, he tears apart my thong, ripping it easily in two. I'm lying naked, bound to the bed, and being punished. It's hot and terrifying, and I sort of don't want it to end.

When his fingers touch me between my legs, I cry out. I'm so turned on already that one touch has me feeling ready to explode.

"Because you are mine, Charlotte. And I don't appreciate when anyone talks badly about something that is mine. Do you think I have bad taste?"

"No..." I gasp. He runs his index finger between my folds, and I ache for more. Then he presses his finger inside me, as if he's playing with me, teasing me.

"Do you think I'm stupid for paying so much for you?"

"No!"

He circles my clit, and I struggle against the restraints.

"Are you worth seventy-five grand, Charlotte?"

I'm trying to lean into his touch, hungry for the pressure. But he eases up every time I get close to my climax. "Answer me," he urges.

"No," I reply, knowing it's not what he wants to hear. And the second the word comes out of my mouth, he pulls away. I could have lied. I knew what the right answer was, but for some reason, I don't want to get out of this punishment.

He disappears for a moment, and I hear him gathering more things, opening drawers and setting something down. Then I hear the unmistakable sound of him lighting a match. The odor of sulfur wafts to my nose. A second later, I hear him blow the match out.

What does he need fire for?

It's quiet for a moment, then I hear the sound of clothes rustling and his belt unbuckling.

"I wish you could see what I see," he mutters, and I feel his weight on the bed next to me. "And I hate to punish you for always talking so badly about yourself, but I'm not going to lie, Charlotte. I'm going to enjoy this."

His mouth lands against mine, our lips tangling as his tongue slips into my mouth. I hum against him, trying to deepen the kiss.

My nipples are numb, and the pain has faded. But something about his kiss has made them ache again.

"Deep breath," he whispers against his mouth, and I do as I'm told, inhaling a warm breath that smells like him.

He has me relaxed and at ease, just as a burning hot pain lands against my chest, making me scream.

"Shh… Don't make me gag you, baby," he mumbles against my mouth.

"It hurts!" I scream, squirming away from the heat, but it's already starting to cool down.

Wax. He just dripped fucking candle wax on me!

"Do you need mercy?" he asks, but it takes my brain a minute to catch up. He's asking if I want to stop. Do I? God, that hurt, but he's doing this for a reason. And aside all of that, my body is awake, sensitive and a little horny behind the pain.

"No," I whimper.

"Good girl." Before touching me again, he sits up and I feel his hands glide up my legs, massaging my hips. "I wish you could see how beautiful you are right now. You are perfection, Charlotte. And I hate to hurt you, but feel what it does to me."

His hips grind against my leg, and I feel his rock-hard erection. He's naked, and I writhe, trying to feel him more.

"Do you want me to fuck you, baby girl?"

"Yes," I cry out.

"Tell me you're worth it. Tell me how beautiful you are."

Emotion stings my throat. *No, no, no.* Please don't get emotional. Please don't fucking cry. This is supposed to be a sexy moment, and I'm about to ruin it because I know he's right. I know I never say anything good about myself, but I can't help it. It doesn't matter how pretty I am or how other people see me. The voice in my head telling me I'm not enough is louder.

I really did not expect all of this to come up right now, but the residual pain and the intensity of being blindfolded and restrained is making everything so hard to keep in. "I can't," I say, but my voice shakes.

"That's okay. You will."

Fire lands against my chest again, and I bite my bottom lip to keep from screaming. It's insane how much this pain makes me feel almost high. The intensity takes me to another plane of existence. Is this subspace?

"Why would Ronan Kade have bid so much to get you if you weren't so beautiful, Charlotte?"

"I don't know," I cry.

"Do you think those other women are more beautiful than you?"

"Yes!"

Hot wax lands against my belly this time, feeling even more sensitive.

"You're wrong, Charlotte."

My blindfold is wet. God, I hope he can't tell I'm crying.

"Say it. Tell me you're worth it."

A sob breaks through, and I use my bound hands to cover my face. Emerson pulls them away and puts his lips against mine.

"Why can't you just say it, Charlotte? Why can't you just admit how wonderful you are?"

"Because I'm not," I sob. "I just mess everything up. I don't deserve you. You think I'm so great now, but you'll realize eventually that I'm not good enough, and you'll leave me. Like everyone does."

I've ruined everything. I'm sobbing, and it's humiliating, and I'm sure he's really done with me now. The room falls silent, and I'm shaking. A moment later, my blindfold is yanked off of my face, and I try to turn my tear-soaked face away. I'm sure I have makeup dripping down my cheeks.

"Jesus, Charlotte."

He takes my face in his hands and holds me close. "Look at me," he barks.

I swallow down the nails in my throat and turn my gaze toward him. "You're wrong," he says with conviction, locking eyes with me.

When I try to shake my head, he stops me. "Say it. Say you're wrong."

"I'm wrong," I whisper.

"Louder," he bellows.

"I'm wrong."

"Louder!"

"I'm wrong!" I cry out, tears trailing down the sides of my face and landing in my hair.

When he kisses me, the dam breaks, a feeling of euphoria

washing over me. Reaching down, he releases the straps around my legs one at a time, and I quickly wrap them around him.

"You're mine," he growls against the skin of my neck, and I lift my bound arms and wrap them around his head. "Forget everyone before me, Charlotte. Just focus on me. I would have paid a million dollars for this hour with you. Do you hear me?"

"Yes," I gasp.

His fingers find the nipple clamps, releasing them, and it's almost as painful as when he put them on. When his lips close around the right one, sucking on the pain, I thrust my hips upward. They are supersensitive now, making my entire body sing as he caresses them with his tongue.

"Please fuck me, Emerson," I beg. I need to know he still wants me after I just made a complete fool of myself.

He doesn't hesitate, shoving my hips down against the bed and driving his cock between my legs. Thrusting hard, he holds me tightly in his arms. "Fuck, look what you do to me, Charlotte. You drive me crazy."

I can't get enough of him. My legs lock around his waist, and I pull his mouth to mine for another kiss. With Emerson, I don't feel so inferior. Somehow, this perfect, amazing man makes me feel worthy, and my heart explodes in my chest every time I think about it.

"I'm addicted to you," he groans while fucking me. "You were made for me, Charlotte. You're mine, and I never want to let you go. Do you understand me? I'd fuck you forever if I could."

My body cries out as he pounds harder and harder, the sensation of what he's doing to my body mingled with the words he's using to break my heart.

"I wish you could," I cry. Looking up into his eyes, I whisper, "I was made for you." The expression on his face makes it seem like he's momentarily surprised by my admission.

Resting his forehead against mine, he drives me to ecstasy, pounding his body into mine as if he's trying to make me believe what he's telling me. When I come, my nails dig into his back, holding him as closely as I can get him. Matching my intensity, he growls into my ear as he slows his thrusts and comes inside me. Gathering me up in his arms, he pulls out and lies on the mattress. I rest on his chest and let the moment wash over me.

He loosens the ties around my wrists. Grabbing a wet washcloth on the table next to the bed, he carefully rubs it across my skin. When I look down, I see splatters of black across my chest and stomach. It stings when he peels the wax from my delicate skin, but after the last hour, it's nothing. And I almost welcome the pain now, like it brings us closer together.

Then he cups my face and pulls me up to his lips, kissing me softly.

"You're not mad at me anymore, are you?" I ask, my voice trembling with emotion.

His face softens. "I was never mad at you, Charlotte. I just wish you could see what I see."

I don't see what Emerson sees, but I wish I could. Maybe I never will. It wasn't just Beau, but I think ever since my dad walked out on us, I built up a wall between men and me, making myself believe that if I wasn't good enough for them from the start, I could never disappoint them. I would never have to live through anyone's disappointment ever again.

"I wish I could too," I whisper, letting him hold me tightly in his arms.

Rule #29: Aftercare is the best.

Charlotte

"CAN I TAKE YOU HOME WITH ME?" EMERSON ASKS, KISSING MY forehead.

"Of course," I whisper, as if that's even a valid question.

"We can continue your aftercare there."

My heart does a little dance of delight because I don't need to ask what aftercare is—I've done my research, after all. And Madame Kink—er, Eden—was very adamant about the importance of aftercare, and I mean...who wouldn't love to be pampered and doted on? As if Emerson doesn't do that enough.

"I sort of thought this was the aftercare," I point out. He's already cleaned off all the wax, made me drink a bottle of water, and cuddled me into cozy bliss for the last hour.

But he looks down at me and brushes my hair out of my face. There's a humorless expression on his face. "You got a little upset. I just don't want to send you home. I'd rather keep you with me all night."

"Oh God." I try to hide my face, still a little humiliated over the way I cried. He won't let me turn away, though, pulling gaze back to his.

"Don't be embarrassed, Charlotte. That's a normal response to pain. I did that to you on purpose."

"You wanted to make me cry?"

He runs his thumb under my eye, which I'm sure is just dripping with mascara from my tears. "Yes. I wanted you to let go of whatever you were holding on to. It was intense, I know. Are you feeling okay now?"

I nod. I feel better than okay. I feel both exhausted and raw but also renewed.

"Good." He kisses my temple. "Let's go home."

After he gets dressed, Emerson gives me his jacket to cover myself with before I retrieve my clothes from backstage. Then, we walk quietly together out the back of the club. The entire time I wonder if Emerson knows what he's doing to me when he says stuff like that. *Home*, as if it's ours. While we had sex, he called me his. He told me he wanted to fuck me forever, which could have been in-the-moment sex talk, but stuff like this keeps going to my head.

I feel like I'm his, and Emerson feels like mine. I've managed to block out any and all thoughts of forever with him and what that would look like because we made a deal two weeks ago when this started that no one could find out. That we would take whatever we could get.

So the deal we made doesn't seem to correlate with the way we're acting now, and I wonder if he notices that too.

The ride to his house is quiet, but he holds my hand over the console as he drives, stroking my thumb softly as the radio plays quietly. I can't silence the questions in my mind, and I'm too afraid to bring them up. If I do and he tells me what he said was just sex talk and that we are just a mostly secret fling, then it will crush me.

I realize what I want is ludicrous. Absolutely irrational and insane. Because I want Emerson to put me first, even before Beau. I want him to tell me he cares more about our relationship than the one he's trying to repair with his son.

It stings to know that is impossible. I'm stupid for even thinking it.

When we reach his place, he takes me straight upstairs. We don't stop in his bedroom either. Instead he pulls me into his giant bathroom. There's a glass shower, and with one hand still laced with mine, he uses the other to turn on the water.

Then, without a word, he begins stripping me of my clothes. His ministrations are slow and deliberate, as if I'm sick or hurt and he's trying to pamper me. When he pulls my blouse off, he kisses the black-stained skin where the candle wax fell. When he releases my bra, he kisses the red marks from the clamps. And when he pulls down my skirt, he gently presses his lips against the spot where he bit me earlier.

They're not heated kisses. He's not trying to get me warmed up for more sex. It feels more like he's trying to heal the hurt, and I want to tell him there's nothing to mend. Nothing physical at least. But if he can quiet these voices of doubt and fear in my head, that would be great.

Once I'm naked, he opens the shower door and whispers, "Get in."

Then he takes off his clothes and follows me. We stand together under the hot spray, letting it wash over us both. Wrapping my arms around his waist, I rest my face against his chest. Emerson is tall enough that I can nuzzle myself against his neck, and I love how well our bodies fit together. He's just soft enough to be cozy and strong enough to be chiseled. I seriously don't think a man's arms have ever been so inviting.

We stand like that for a while, and I bite back everything I want to say or ask. This moment is too fragile, and one word of apprehension could have it all crumbling down around us. What would happen to me after that? What will my life look like after Emerson Grant and the Salacious Players' Club? I could never go there without him, could I? Date another man? Call someone else *sir*?

It all feels so impossible now. More than impossible—unfathomable.

When I pull away and reach for the soap, he stops me. "Let me."

I watch as he fills his palm with shampoo, lathering it into my hair, slowly and sensually. He washes my hair like I'm the most delicate thing in the world. Like I mean everything to him, and I close my eyes to ward off the sting from that thought.

God, I'd give anything to feel like the most important thing in Emerson's life. To be his whole world.

When he rinses my hair, I gaze up at him. And maybe he sees the redness in my eyes, but he pauses, looking down at me.

And he doesn't say a word.

I swear he can feel what I'm feeling and knows what I'm truly afraid of, but he doesn't tell me everything will be all right or that he will keep me forever. He just leans down and kisses me against my lips.

Then, he runs his fingers through my hair, applying conditioner before lathering up a washcloth and gently scrubbing every inch of my body.

"None of this was what I expected," I mumble as he gets on his knees and runs the washcloth with precise attention up and down my legs.

"What did you expect?"

"Well, I thought I was the one who was supposed to please you," I say, running my fingers through his hair.

"You do please me." He says it with such cool confidence, as if it's obvious. I'm not quite sure how I please him. He's already had to punish me twice, and I don't feel like I do enough for him anymore.

"Then why are you the one on your knees?"

He gazes slowly up at me, his hands still on my ankle. "You think because I'm the Dominant that I can't take care of you?"

"Sort of," I reply with a shrug.

"But you're mine to take care of, Charlotte." He lifts my foot to his thighs as he lathers soap bubbles under my arch and between my toes. "This relationship is a give and take, not a one-way street. Not to mention, when we are not in that Dom/sub mode, I don't want you to submit to me. I want you to let me worship you and..."

His voice trails off, and my heart hammers in my chest while I wait for him to continue. But he doesn't. And my mind is left to wander and replay every word, trying to figure out where he could have been going with that.

When he stands up, I let him rinse the suds from my body, but when he begins to clean himself, I grab his wrist.

"You said it was a two-way street." And I see him start to argue, but he stops himself.

He has to bend a little to let me soap up his hair, and it makes us both laugh. I let my fingers glide slowly through the sparse strands of gray and I try to remember what it was like when I thought Emerson was so much older than me. I mean...he still is so much older, but it doesn't feel that way anymore. That gap in our ages once felt like a wall between us but is now gone.

After rinsing his hair, I lather his body, taking my time to learn the curves and textures of his physique. This feeling of intimacy washes over me as I explore every inch of him, not finding a single spot I don't love. The broad slope of his shoulders. The patch of hair across his chest and the small line leading down his abs. That delicious V-shape of his hips and the thick muscles of his thighs.

This is dangerous. Getting so accustomed to his body—too attached, really. People who just have sex don't do this. They don't look at another person's hands and arms and back and think *this is mine.*

"You're mine to take care of too, Emerson," I whisper as I drag the washcloth down his legs.

I'm being reckless, but my filter can only hold back so much.

I just want him to know that two can play at his game. If he thinks it's fun to toy with my emotions, then I can toy with his too.

And as I drop to my knees, like he did in front of me a moment ago, he strokes his hand over my head. I gaze up at him, and I see a hint of tension there.

"When was the last time you let someone take care of you?" I ask.

I'm not blind. I can see the way his cock is hardening right in front of my face, but I'm not paying attention to that yet. I'm still looking up at him. I need to know if Emerson acts this way around every girl he's with, or if I'm somehow different and if any truth rings in those sweet words he tells me.

"A very long time," he mutters, stroking my head.

"I want to take care of you," I whisper, and I hope he knows I mean it as more than just making him come in this shower. Call it wishful thinking, but I know I'm disguising my actual feelings under promises of sex.

He blocks the shower spray from me, letting it hit his back and cascade down his body. I set the washcloth down and run my hands up his thighs, each time stopping before I reach the top. His breathing picks up as he gazes at me.

"I should be the one taking care of you," he says, without pulling me to my feet.

"Well, maybe I want to spoil you," I say in a light, almost joking manner. "Maybe I want to make you so dependent on me that you never want to leave me. I want to be so good for you that you keep me forever."

Disguise those feelings, Charlie.

"Then show me how good you can be." With a gentle nudge, he guides his cock to my lips, and I gaze up at him as I run my tongue around the head. The feeling of butterflies assaults my insides at his words and the way he teases me with that tone.

He hums, low and gravelly, as I wrap my lips around him. I play with the head of his cock first, licking into the slit and letting my teeth graze the underside. His hips jolt forward, and I tease him a bit more before letting him slide in deeper.

Relaxing my throat, I pull him in farther and farther each time. Wrapping my hand around the base, I stroke in rhythm with my mouth, moving faster and tighter, waiting for his groans or words of praise. I'm dying to hear his pleasure.

Finally, he lets out a tight, "Oh fuck, Charlotte."

For that, he gets a reward, and I suck even harder, giving his cock head a little more attention.

He shudders and squeezes a handful of my hair in his grasp. "Keep doing that." So I do, moving from the base to the head, twisting and squeezing and practically swimming in the grunts and groans of pleasure my actions are eliciting.

I reach my other hand between his legs and gently knead his sac, watching his expression change as I do. His free hand slams against the wall to hold him upright and his eyes close.

"That's my girl," he groans, and I light up inside.

My movements pick up speed, and I know what's coming when his mouth falls open and his head falls back. "I'm gonna come, baby."

And maybe that was meant to be a warning, but when I don't move or take my mouth away, he seems to pick up the hint.

"Are you gonna swallow me down, Charlotte? You gonna take my cum like the dirty girl you are? *My* dirty girl."

His voice is strained and he barely gets the last word out before I feel the salty jets hit my tongue. I expect to be grossed out by it, but the minute I taste him, I realize this is him. This is my Emerson, and I want it all. I love everything about him.

So as he fills the back of my throat, I eagerly swallow before pulling my mouth off. Strings of cum hang from his cock to my lips when he moves his body, letting the water wash it all away. Then, I'm lifted abruptly from my knees and pressed against the wall.

His hand is under my jaw, pressing my face upward to see his.

"That was so fucking hot," he says, kissing me. I try to push him away out of fear that he could still taste himself on my tongue, but he doesn't let me. His mouth assaults mine with fervor. When he pulls away from our kiss, his words come out with conviction. "Just when I think you can't get any more fucking fantastic, you do. You keep surprising me, Charlotte. And not just with sex. You are so perfect for me, and I do want to keep you forever."

My mouth falls open as I stare up at him, thinking this is it. The moment he finally tells me he's going to put me first and tell Beau everything, so he and I can be together for real. For the long term.

But then he buries his face in my neck as he mutters, "God, I wish I could."

And all of that hope and elation goes down the drain.

Rule #30: Give it all to her—she can take it.

Emerson

"I'M A LITTLE EMBARRASSED IT TOOK ME THIS LONG," GARRETT says, as he walks into the back office of the club where I'm going over the numbers from last night.

"To do what?" I ask without looking up.

"To look up your new girlfriend online."

Well, that gets my attention. My head snaps up, looking at my partner holding out his phone, which is open to Charlotte's Instagram page. You don't even have to scroll far to find pictures of her and Beau together. There's not a single picture of me on there, for obvious reasons, but it still grates on my nerves.

I freeze, looking at the photos and waiting for him to say something.

He puts his phone in his pocket as he says, "I'm certainly not one to judge."

"That's good," I reply coldly.

"Why didn't you tell me?" When I notice the hurt look on his face, I feel the guilt I probably should have felt two weeks ago.

"No one was supposed to know."

He lets out a laugh. "Well, you blew that whistle yourself last night when you got in that bidding war with Kade and carted her off the stage like a caveman."

"I'm aware," I grumble. "But I don't need everyone knowing her connection to Beau, so if we could keep that under wraps..."

"You got it," he says, holding up his hands. As he comes farther into the office, taking a seat in one of the chairs, I know he's not about to drop the topic. "So I assume you didn't mean for this to happen."

"Of course not." I lean back in my chair. I'll admit...it feels good to finally have this out, at least to Garrett. I don't need the rest of them knowing, but not being able to talk to my best friend has been difficult. Especially in these last two weeks when my feelings for my son's ex-girlfriend have gotten even more complicated.

I let a lot of things slip yesterday. I was in the moment, and when I'm with Charlotte, I feel as if I can say anything, and that is dangerous because she suddenly has me telling her I want to fuck her forever.

She must think I'm insane. First, I said it would just be temporary. Then I start showing up at her family's events and begging to see her on the weekends. Even today, I'm forcing myself to work to keep from texting her.

"So what happened?" Garrett asks.

"She and Beau broke up. She came over one day looking for a security deposit from their apartment I cosigned for him, and I mistook her for one of the girls you send."

"Oof," he says with a grimace.

"Yeah."

I let a moment linger while I think back to that day, the first moment I saw her in my office, the way she dropped to her knees, how I knew in that moment that this one was different. That in just five seconds flat, I knew she was somehow made for me.

"I offered her the job. I made it *very* clear that it was just a regular secretary job, but then…I crossed every little line one at a time until we started fucking two weeks ago."

"Jesus."

"I know…"

"I assume Beau has no idea."

"He's still not really talking to me, but I'll be honest…after things started up with Charlotte, I haven't been calling him as much."

He watches me while I keep my eyes averted, letting this whole shitshow run through my mind again. How did I let this happen? I tried to be so careful. I set strict rules for myself, but she has me breaking all of them.

When I finally look up at him, there's more sympathy on his face than judgment. "What the fuck is wrong with me?"

"I don't think anything is wrong with you."

"But…"

"But…" He shifts in his seat. "I can tell you really like her. Maybe more than like?"

I'm not going to answer that. If I put that thought into words, I'm risking so much. Letting myself believe this thing with Charlotte is more than muddled emotions and hot-as-sin sex makes everything a lot more serious than I intended.

I rub my hand across my forehead. "I do like her. I mean… you've seen her."

He nods, unspoken words clearly on his lips.

"What's that look for?"

After a moment of deliberation, he lets out a sigh and leans forward. "Emerson, I've known you for over a decade. I've seen you with a lot of girls. All of them were beautiful. This is different."

"I know it is, but there's nothing I can do about it." I can't seem to hide the subtle frustration in my voice. He's pointing out the obvious but failing to see the problem. It's not as simple as to just admit that I have serious feelings for Charlotte because, no matter what, I can't have her.

"Why not?"

I have to give my friend a minute of grace because he's not yet a father, so he has no idea what it feels like. This torment, struggling with the idea of losing my son forever.

"Because no matter what I do, I lose one of them. What kind of father would I be if I choose..."

The rest of the sentence hangs on my lips as I let out a frustrated sound, and my friend doesn't have a response. We sit in tense silence for another moment before he says, "Just my opinion, so take it or leave it." He holds his hands up as he continues, "But Beau is an adult, Emerson. He's not a kid anymore. He might be mad at you, but it's not something you can't work out if he was to actually speak to you. I think you're a great father to want to give him so much, but you seem actually happy with this girl, and I'd hate to see you throw that away."

He's right. I know that, but it's just not that easy.

"And the longer you let this secret go on, the harder it will be to tell him."

"I know."

"But don't take too much advice from me. I have neither a girlfriend nor a child, so I could be the world's biggest idiot, but I do know you. And I like you a lot more since she's come around."

I let out a small laugh. "Thanks," I mutter as he stands and claps a hand on my shoulder.

"Whatever you choose, I'm here."

I nod at him, the gnawing ball of anxiety in my gut growing even more from this conversation.

"How was the convention?" I ask as Charlotte curls up on my chest on the couch upstairs. Some true crime show plays quietly in the background.

"It was a blast. Sophie was in heaven."

"Good," I reply, kissing her cheek. "Are you hungry?"

"Not really. We grabbed something to eat after it closed. What did you do all day?"

"Missed you." Inwardly, I wince. I really have to keep shit like this to myself.

"I missed you too," she replies without looking at me. There's a growing tension between us. This unspoken argument about Beau and our future keeps expanding, pushing aside all of the elation we felt a week ago when all of this was new and fun. Now, I'm afraid it's all too real. And I want it all too much.

As soon as she got here, we climbed on the couch together. Usually we'd be coming by now, her screaming my name as I fuck her on various surfaces of my house, but neither of us reached for the other's clothes. Yet.

"You're good with your sister," I mumble, kissing her temple. I love the way she wraps her arms around me and how snugly she fits against my chest. I love that no matter how we're feeling, she's comfortable touching me first, instead of waiting for me to make the move.

"She's a good kid."

"Do you want kids someday?" I ask because…I don't know. Self-sabotage, maybe. Because that conversation with Garrett earlier has me feeling like I might as well end it before it even begins. And what better way to do it.

"I don't know," she answers casually. "I could see my life with them or without them."

Not exactly the answer I expected.

"What about you?" she adds. "Would you ever have more?"

I clench my molars. "Had a vasectomy years ago."

She tenses. "Oh."

A cloud of disappointment hangs in the air. And for some reason, I just want to hammer this nail in the coffin.

"Considering my only child won't speak to me, I'd say it's for the best."

She lifts her head and stares at me. "Stop that. I see how much you care about him. You're a good father."

"Yes, so good I'm fucking his ex-girlfriend."

She doesn't respond right away, but she stares at me skeptically. She can tell something is up, and she seems to be working through feelings of her own.

"That was a little harsh," she murmurs quietly.

"I'm sorry." Brushing the hair out of her face, I kiss her forehead.

Instead of laying her head back on my chest, she rises to a sitting position and fiddles with the hem of her shirt in her lap. "Do you mind me asking what happened? Why is Beau so mad at you?"

"He's not mad at me. He's disgusted by me."

Her eyes dance in my direction. "Because of the club?"

I nod. "For most of his life, I worked in various fields of entertainment. When I started up Salacious with Garrett and the others, I told him it was a dating service. Then, it became a dance club. Suddenly, he was twenty-one, and he found out that I'd been lying to him for years and that my dance club being built was really a kink club. Something he just couldn't accept."

She swallows. Talking about my son with her sends a cool tremor down my spine because she knows him so well, probably even better than I do. And right now, I can see the thoughts brewing behind her eyes. I'm both dying to hear what she's thinking and dreading it.

"What is it?" I ask, reaching for her hand.

"I just…I think Beau is wrong to judge you so harshly. But that's just who he is. He rejects what he doesn't understand, and he's quick to pass judgment on others—"

"Charlotte, stop."

She quickly closes her lips. Her brows are raised and there's an apologetic look on her face, one that kills me. But I can't listen to her talk about him like that. He has his faults—I will bear the burden of those flaws and he can be mad at me for however long he wants.

"I think he just needs his own time to get over things…"

I glance at her again. I think I know what she's alluding to. Taking her hand in mine, I touch her knuckles to my lips, wanting to kiss away the sadness I feel creeping in. It's because I'm a coward, and I don't have the heart to kill the hope I know she's begging me for. So I choose silence instead.

But this is Charlotte…or rather, Charlie, and I love all of her young stubbornness and inability to let things slide.

"The sooner we tell him, the sooner he'll get over it."

"Charlotte."

"We have to at least try. If he finds out later, it won't make anything better."

"I can't," I argue, but she doesn't stop.

"What happens when he finds out before you tell him? It would make everything worse."

"Charlie, stop." My voice comes out in a low barking command, and she gapes at me, my words hanging in the air. I can't stand another minute of her hurt expression, so I jump off the couch and pace the room in frustration.

I called her Charlie. And she's probably hurt more by that than anything else. Like I've just stripped her of her name. Glancing back at her on the couch, I watch her chew on her bottom lip. That's not the girl I found on the floor of my office two months ago. Have I built her up only to break her down? Why am I fucking this up so badly?

Two months. That's how long it took this one girl to walk in and fuck my head up so much that I don't even know myself anymore. It's hard to remember a time before Charlotte. And it hurts to think of a time after her.

"I wish you'd just tell me what you're thinking," I say, looking at her from across the room. "I hate to see you holding back."

Her eyes well up with tears as she takes a deep, steadying breath. "I don't want to."

"Why?"

"Because...I just want to make you happy."

It hurts to swallow down the lump in my throat. "I'm not your *sir* right now. Don't try to please me, Charlotte. Just be honest."

She stands up and walks over to me, stopping only a foot away. After another deep breath, she squares her shoulders, and I can't help but admire her from this angle. The hardheaded, tough, beautiful girl who refuses to believe she's absolutely perfect.

"You think letting Beau find out about us would make you a bad father, but, Emerson, you're already sleeping with me. You've already done it, but it doesn't make you a bad father. It makes you human. Neither of us expected this to happen, but it did. And it's a lot more serious than either of us expected.

"You think you're a bad father for wanting me but you're not. You're actually good to a fault because you're willing to forfeit your own happiness to spare your son's hurt feelings, but you need to let him deal with the hard stuff on his own. He will get over it, but...I don't know if I ever will."

"Don't say that. Of course you will." My raw, aching heart claws at some sort of relief to offer her. "You're only twenty-one, Charlotte."

"I won't," she argues, those threatening tears finally spilling over. This is two nights in a row I've seen her cry, and I can't stand it. My arms find her waist, pulling her close as if my touch alone could fix any of these problems.

"I'm forty, baby," I murmur gently into her hair. "You have no future with me."

"I don't care how old you are. It doesn't matter to me." She's sobbing in earnest against my chest now. That nagging anxiety in my gut from before has turned into a gaping, bleeding wound, but it's better this way. Get the feelings out. No secrets. And we'll move past them.

I pull her face up so she can see my eyes. "You understand it's not because I don't want you. You know that, right?"

"Then tell me you want me," she cries.

"I want you. Of course, I want you."

She reaches up, finding my lips for a desperate kiss, and I know I shouldn't, but I kiss her back. I think we've established that I do not make wise decisions where this girl is involved, and I don't want to.

She wraps her arms around my neck and I pull her up by the thighs, letting her wrap her legs around me. I'm done talking. All we've established is that we both can't have what we want, but at least we can have this. In this house, with no one else around, there's only us. Her and me and this unexplainable connection. You're lucky enough to have something like this once in a lifetime, so if this brief, heated phase of our lives is all I'm going to get, then I'm going to squeeze every last drop out of it.

I carry her over to the couch and drop her onto the cushions.

"I need you," she cries, clawing at my shirt. Sitting up, I pull it off quickly and work on my pants, tearing them off while she squirms out of hers. Once we're naked, I drape my body over hers, ravaging her precious, pale skin with my mouth, nibbling and kissing every square inch. When I reach the apex of her thighs, she writhes against me, moaning while she pinches her nipples.

It's not enough. Pulling my mouth away from her perfect pink folds, I grab her by the waist and flip us, so I'm lying down and she's on top. Then, I grab her by the back of the neck, pulling her in for a bruising kiss, and whisper, "I want you on my face."

Her eyes widen, and I see her about to protest, but I don't give her a chance. Hoisting her up by the hips, I position her over my face and pull her down until I have her pussy in my mouth.

She cries out in delight as my tongue slides deep inside her. And I gaze up at her as she finds her pleasure, grinding herself against my lips.

Staring up at her, consuming her while feeling entirely consumed *by* her, I wonder briefly if this makes me a monster. Corrupting this perfect, young woman, making her mine and ruining her, so she can never feel this way about another man. But I don't care. If I'm a monster, I'm a monster. I can live with that.

She grinds harder against me, giving up on the hovering and finally settling her weight down on my mouth. I suck eagerly at her clit, and she screams, her knuckles turning white as she grips the couch.

"Oh my God, Emerson. Don't stop, don't stop, don't stop."

Her spine curves inward as she comes, her cunt pulsing against my lips and her thighs clenching around my head. I lap up every beautiful drop like it's the last time I'll ever be able to devour her this way. I refuse to believe it is. Even if we aren't meant for forever, I'm not done with her yet.

Once her muscles relax and she slumps over, I pick her up again. My cock is aching for her. Shifting into a sitting position on the couch, I guide her soaking core to my shaft, watching her face as she slides down over me.

"Fuck, Charlotte," I groan, grasping her hair at the scalp and dragging her lips to mine. She hums with our kiss, tasting herself on my tongue. "Ride me."

With her haunting brown eyes focused on mine, she holds me by the back of the neck and bounces herself on my cock in hard, deep thrusts. She's fucking me the way I fuck her.

Watching her, I realize…I love her. If this isn't what love feels like, then it must not exist.

It doesn't mean I can give Charlotte everything she wants— everything *I* want. It doesn't make my choice any easier, but I feel freer being able to admit that to myself. After twenty years of waiting, this is the one that has finally shattered the belief that I would never find this. Never find love. But I have…because of her.

And I want to tell her so badly right now, but I can't. I refuse to make any more promises to this girl that I can't fulfill. If I tell her I love her, it will only make her hope even more, and I'm crushing her already as it is.

Grabbing her hips tightly, I slam her down even harder, and she hangs her head back, filling the room with those delicious sounding moans of ecstasy.

"I want to come inside you. I want you to take it," I groan.

"Give it to me."

It only takes two more bounces on my cock before I'm grunting out my release, my cock pumping into her. She hangs from my arms, spent and beautiful. So I pull her body to my mouth, kissing the spot where her heart pumps in her chest.

She's panting for air more than usual, her heart pounding from exertion. There's a sheen of sweat across her back.

"Was I a good girl?" she whispers with her mouth inches from mine.

A smile creeps across my face as I gather her into my arms. "You're always a good girl."

Rule #31: Nothing good lasts forever.

Charlotte

WHEN I HEAR HIS APPROACHING FOOTSTEPS ON MONDAY morning, a sense of calm washes over me. There is something in that sound. The repeating click-click-click cues a response in my body, a serotonin boost that puts me in an instant state of serenity. The anxiety I've wallowed in since waking up in his arms yesterday morning dissolves as I hear him walking into the room.

He strides up to where I'm kneeling and gently strokes my head.

"Good morning, Charlotte," he says with the same inflection that he would say, *Good morning, beautiful.* Or *I love you, Charlotte.* And maybe I'm imagining that last one, but it sounds right in my mind.

"Good morning, sir."

We fit into these roles so effortlessly, like puzzle pieces clicking into place. Not a word was said since Saturday night about Beau, our secret, our future, or our feelings. It's like the conversation scared us both into silence. We came so close to ending everything, so rather than face the music and admit what we both know is coming, we slid right back into the roles we were playing before.

Keep it secret.

Deny our feelings.

Don't think about the future.

It doesn't feel *right*, per se, but since I'm still here, kneeling on the floor for him, it feels like enough. Two weeks ago, I told him I would take what I could get, and that's still the truth.

As he sits in his chair, I wait for instructions. Normally, he tells me to work at my desk or to come sit in his lap as he works. But minutes go by in silence as I wait. The urge to see what he's doing is strong.

Finally, he mutters, "Crawl to me." I bite my lip to keep from smiling as I move onto my hands and knees, looking up at him as I move. His chin rests on his hand, leaning against the arm of his chair as he watches me. There's a subtle look of approval on his face, and I breathe it in like it's keeping me alive.

As I reach his chair, I settle back into a kneeling position. His fingers reach out to stroke my cheek, and I lean into the touch.

"I don't want to work today," he mumbles softly. And when my lips tighten, fighting back a smile, he continues, "I want to play."

"Yes, sir," I reply sweetly.

"On the desk," he commands, tapping the solid surface in front of him. Climbing to my feet, I sit down in front of him, and he instantly spreads my knees, moving between them. I'm wearing a knee-length dress today, black with buttons down the front and small white polka dots. It accentuates my curves well, tight around my breasts and hips. Underneath the dress, I have on a pair of light blue lace panties.

Emerson's hands run up my thighs, and a throbbing arousal hits me as he reaches the edge and carefully pulls them down. Bringing the blue, silky fabric to his nose, he inhales, keeping his eyes on me. I bite my lip as I watch him.

Then he opens his desk drawer and drops the panties in. I watch as he pulls something else out. It's a familiar pink silicone, and my breath hitches as I recognize it.

"I found this in your desk," he says. "Remember this?"

"Yes, sir."

I watch as he wipes the toy clean and dries it. It's hard to hold so still while waiting for something as rewarding as that toy because I know what's about to happen. After it's clean and dry, he holds the blunt end up to my lips. "Open."

Dropping my jaw, I welcome the toy, and once it's seated against my tongue he says, "Suck." And I do, coating the silicone in my saliva. He then gently pulls it out and lifts my dress.

I can hardly breathe as I watch him. Pulling my hips to the edge of his desk, he slowly works in the round, spit-covered end, and I have to swallow down my gasp. The intrusion is different when it's someone else inserting it, and the way he's doing it feels almost clinical. It's an erotic, almost dirty sensation—and I sort of love it.

Once it's all the way in, he admires his work, touching me and running fingers over my folds. I can't tell if he's hard yet, and I keep trying to sneak a peek. I already know today is going to be torturously long, but at the end, when I finally have him, it will be worth the wait.

When he pulls out the small black remote I remember from last time, I smile. With one little click, the toy begins humming against my clit and G-spot, and I try to slam my legs together, but he won't let me.

"Let's see how long you can take it before you come."

I want to protest, but I can't. He's *sir* today, a little different than last time. The vibration is low, but it's almost worse that way, building me slowly toward a climax. And the fact that I can't react much makes it worse.

Tugging my bottom lip between my teeth, I clench my eyes closed and force myself to breathe. Then he begins stroking my thighs, running his hands up to my breasts, pinching each nipple between his fingers.

"You're getting close, I can tell," he says, and he's right. My body writhes on his desk, and my breathing turns into stunted gasps. "Right...there."

Suddenly, the vibration is gone. Just as I was about to crest the peak of my orgasm, he made it stop. I feel a bead of sweat across my forehead as I take in a long, heavy breath. When I look back at him, he's grinning, pleased with himself.

"Was I right?"

"Yes, sir," I reply.

"You're not being punished, but I'm going to do that to you all day. If you're a good girl, you'll be rewarded at the end of the day. Understood?"

"Yes, sir."

He leans forward and presses his lips to a soft spot on the inside of my thighs. "I'm going to keep your panties in my desk. Try not to make a mess on your chair."

Then he gently pats my ass and sends me to work. He spends the next couple of hours teasing me with steady vibrations, taking me to the edge and bringing me back down. I wish I could say I hated it, but so far, it's not so bad. I like the buildup, anyway. And I love his attention most of all, which is what I'm getting today.

"It's beautiful out," he says, while I'm in the middle of an email to Maggie. "Let's walk to the deli together." *Oh, Emerson,* I think to myself. *Of course you want to get me out in public with this thing inside me.*

But do I argue? Nope. I simply smile, nod my head, and answer him accordingly. "Yes, sir."

"I'll give you a foot rub tonight," he says on the one-mile walk back, glancing down at my heels. These are a little more comfortable than the last ones, but I'm not going to turn down a foot rub.

In the deli, he had me almost crying as he tortured me. It was packed in there, people milling around in all the open spaces as he flipped the toy on, making me cling to his arm for support, afraid I would crumble to the floor at any second.

He found so much humor in it, but I could also tell he was aroused too. So much so that he had to hold me in front of him the whole time to block people from seeing his hard length as we ordered our sandwiches. There I was ordering a turkey sub with Emerson Grant's hard cock pressed into my back while a vibrator nearly made me orgasm in the middle of the word *mayonnaise*.

If people didn't notice how strange we were behaving, it was a miracle, or they were blind. But we didn't care. We ate our lunch in a small booth in the back with smiles plastered on our faces. *This could work*, I thought to myself the whole time. I could be his secretary as a front, and his girlfriend in secret, and no one would need to know. It would be enough.

But as we reach his house, and I see a familiar figure standing on Emerson's front porch, all of that idiotic hope comes crashing down around me.

"Beau?" Emerson calls out, spotting his son. When he spins around to answer his father's call, I freeze. I don't know if Emerson feels the same wave of guilt as I do, but seeing Beau now feels like a punch to the gut. And he looks…good. Better than last time. He's cut his hair, has a smile on his face, and doesn't look like he wants to murder his own father.

"Is everything okay?" Emerson asks, rushing over.

"Yeah, I'm fine."

"What are you doing here?" I ask.

There is a look of skeptical surprise on Emerson's face, his attention laser-focused on his son, and I can't believe the rising jealousy that courses through me when I notice. *It's his son, Charlie. Of course he's going to give him his attention. Over you.*

"I was working in the area. I saw Charlie's car here, so I thought I'd come hang out for a bit."

Come hang out? Glancing toward the road, I notice his white truck parked on the curb. How did I not notice that before? He must have used the money his dad gave him last time to get it fixed.

None of this feels right, but I don't say anything as Emerson opens the door to let him in. He looks so elated to see his son again, I can't be the one who takes that away. So I act casual as we walk inside together. Emerson empties his pockets at the front entryway table, dropping his keys into the bowl.

"Are you hungry?" he asks Beau.

Beau shakes his head before turning toward me.

"So where were you guys at?" he asks. My eyes dance between the two men for a moment, trying to get a second of Emerson's attention, but he's too guarded, too scared.

"We went to the deli down the street. Are you sure you're not hungry?" Emerson replies.

"Nope, I'm good. I got a new job," he adds in, and the smile on his face feels almost contagious. If I wasn't so uptight in this scenario, I might actually feel an ounce of joy for him, but I'm too unsettled. I keep waiting for him to notice that Emerson and I are fucking, as if he could read it on our faces.

I mean, I wish I could read Emerson's face right now, but he's being so guarded that it's impossible.

"I'm going to grab some drinks. You guys go sit in the front room and I'll be right out. I want to hear all about your new job," Emerson says, turning toward the kitchen.

"Yes, sir," I answer out of habit, immediately wincing as the words tumble out of my mouth.

Emerson freezes in the doorway, and I try to play it off as nothing out of the ordinary, waltzing straight over to the sitting room at the front of the house.

"Sir?" Beau replies with a laugh.

I laugh too, trying to shrug it off, but I feel so fake. Almost mechanical, like I don't even know how to behave normally. We make small talk while we wait for Emerson to return, and Beau doesn't seem to suspect a thing, which should make me happy but only makes me feel a little nauseous. Then Emerson returns with three beers clutched between his fingers, and Beau looks at them skeptically.

"I figured we could have one drink to celebrate your new job."

Beau gives him an easy half smile, taking one of the beers and dropping into the oversized leather chair. Emerson looks momentarily pleased with himself as he hands me my bottle, and it almost shatters my heart into pieces. Look at how happy he is. Beau is here and he's actually smiling and they are about to repair their relationship. I can feel it.

How can I possibly take this away from him? And how can I be so selfish to expect Beau to just *get over it*? What is wrong with me?

With my eyes on Emerson sitting in the chair opposite his son, I drop slowly onto the last chair, and the minute my butt hits the seat, my eyes go wide.

The vibrator.

I completely forgot it was in there. And now I have to sit here with a remote-controlled dildo and *no panties* on while we pretend that everything is fine and we aren't fucking behind Beau's back. I can hardly hear a word they say over the chanting sound of shame echoing through my head—*this is all my fault*. Luckily, neither of them seem to notice.

In fact, for the next thirty minutes, neither of them notice I'm here at all.

I'm hanging on to the way Beau is looking at his dad. Between sips of his beer, he tells him about the new job as an apprentice for some big landscaper in the area. Then I catch the look of contentment and pride on Emerson's face, and I sit here and question how the hell this happened.

A minute ago, things were so easy. Emerson and I could carry on our secret relationship under the guise of me being his secretary. And no one would get hurt. And just like that, Beau shows up, a cruel reminder that nothing is ever easy, and nothing good can ever last.

"So you like working here?"

It takes me a minute before I realize it's Beau talking to me. With a swig of his beer, he stares at me and waits for my answer.

"Oh, um, yeah. It's a good job."

I can't look at Emerson. I literally can't bear it, but I feel his gaze on me momentarily. Probably the most he's looked at me since Beau showed up.

"Good," he replies with a nod of his head. "Well, next time I'm working in this part of town, I'd like to stop in again. Maybe we can all do lunch or something." The way he's looking at me, as if he's hanging on to hope for something, is so hard to look at I have to gaze down at my beer bottle, which I've completely peeled the label off of because of my nervousness.

"That would be great. I'd love that," Emerson says, standing up.

Beau is still looking at me, but I'm frozen, my gaze locked on the cool drops of condensation on the brown glass of the bottle.

When Beau stands up, I breathe a sigh of relief. I just need to be alone with Emerson. We don't have to go back to the way we were before lunch, but maybe we can just talk through this. There is something to salvage here…unless he wants to break it off now. I'm sure that with how good things seem to be with Beau that I don't mean anything to him anymore.

No, I can't think like that.

Beau hovers near the front door, and they make more small talk. When I see his hand reach for his keys he dropped next his dad's on the front entryway table, I see something familiar sitting next to them. Heat floods my cheeks, and I start to panic when I spot the black remote, just inches from Beau's hand.

He'll just grab his own keys and leave. He won't notice the remote.

When I glance over at Emerson, he seems unfazed, so deep

in conversation with his son that he doesn't even see what he dropped on that table in plain sight. I quickly stand up, hoping to get to the gadget first.

"All right, I should get going," Beau says casually. I freeze in my steps across the room when his hand closes around his keys *and* the black remote, which looks so much like his truck remote it's uncanny. In his fumble to pick them up, the remote goes clattering to the floor.

When Beau reaches down to pick it up, he must hit one of the buttons because the sudden, intense vibration between my legs is unwelcome and *all wrong*. I let out a scream and clamp my hand over my mouth, squeezing my face in a pained expression as I turn and try to run away. I have to take it out *now*.

The energy in the room changes immediately, like someone just flipped off the lights on a seemingly bright, sunny day. Beau stares at me curiously, waiting to understand why I would react like that, but what could I possibly say?

His eyes pause on me, the remote still in his hand. "What's wrong?"

Suddenly, there's a scuffle, and I turn to find Emerson yanking the remote out of his son's hand. With one quick click of the button, the vibration is gone.

"What is going on?" Beau yells.

I should leave. I need to get out of this room, this house, this entire situation, but I'm stuck—caught in Emerson's gaze as he stares at me with a loaded, apologetic expression.

This is it, I think. This is the moment when he can finally admit to his son that he fucked up, when he can finally admit that I mean something to him and that everything he said to me in private was real. I wait on bated breath for the moment that I can already tell isn't coming. Not the way I want it to at least.

"Someone say something, please," Beau barks out after a moment of tense silence.

How on earth could we possibly explain our way out of this?

There is no innocent way to talk our way out of me wearing a remote-control vibrator. And it's at that exact moment when Beau's eyes shift from the remote in his dad's hand to the spot between my legs, where I'm squeezing my thighs together and clutching my dress in my fist.

"I knew it," he mutters in anger, suddenly realizing his suspicions were right all along.

"It's nothing," Emerson stutters with those enchanting green eyes on me.

I swear I'm watching this play out in slow motion, the moment when he tries to actually deny what's obvious. When he tries to deny *me*, or rather, us. My jaw drops as I glare back at him.

"Nothing?" Beau snaps, his gaze bouncing between the two of us.

"Yeah, nothing," I mumble to myself before spinning on my heel and marching out of the room. The walls might as well be collapsing around me. Right now, it feels as if they are. And maybe I shouldn't be so mad. I mean, it's his son. I shouldn't expect him to admit this so easily, but as I march through the office, I see everything that's happened in the last two months play out—except this time in a different filter.

I see me, naive and hopeful, being everything Emerson Grant wanted me to be. I see myself changing for him. Kneeling for him. Lying and sacrificing myself…for *him*. I hear the slightest praise from his lips and how easily I caved and salivated for it, giving up everything I believed in just to hear it again and again. As if my entire worth hung on those two beguiling words: *good girl*.

The conversation between them grows heated, but it's behind me in a muffled chatter I can't translate. I'm too lost in my own haze of rage and desolation. I grab my phone from my desk, trying to focus on my surroundings through my blurred, teary vision. When I spin around and march toward the door for my purse, a warm, calloused hand clamps around my arm.

I look up to see Beau's face stretched in anger. "Tell me the truth. Did he touch you?" he yells, and I can't answer. I don't even register the question. Shaking him off, I continue my march toward the door.

"Where are you going?" Emerson asks, blocking my path. As I bend down to retrieve my bag, a tear shatters on the shiny black surface of my high-heeled shoes. And I stare at them for a second. Who even am I? I lost my identity the minute I walked through that door. I gave it to a man who doesn't even care about me.

It's nothing, he said. About me. About us. Every single hopeful, lovesick, enamored thought in my head suddenly seems foolish.

God, I'm so fucking stupid.

When I tear open the door, he blocks me again. "Don't go," he says, and I hear the tone in which he says it, expecting me to follow it with an obedient, *Yes, sir.*

I keep my gaze away from his face as I obstinately mutter, "No."

No, to your commands. No, to your promises. No, to your praise.

There's another scuffle between them, and I'm able to work my way around Emerson. All my mind registers is the need to leave. So the minute the door is open, I disappear through it, and I don't dare look back. The next second, I'm in my car and a moment later, I'm cruising down the highway toward my house. I manage to make it all the way to my bed before I sob hysterically into my pillow.

Rule #32: During a hard breakup, refer to Rule #4—tacos and margaritas are always the answer.

Charlie

"GET UP," SOPHIE SAYS, SLAMMING THE DOOR TO MY ROOM AS SHE marches in. It's been eight days, four hours, and thirty-two minutes since I walked out of Emerson Grant's house for the last time. And I haven't done much but create a Charlie-size indent on my bed, binge an entire Netflix true crime series, and eat my weight in Swedish Fish.

And cry. A lot.

When I look back at the last two months, I feel a sting of grief and shame. I can't help but miss the way things were and the way I felt when I was with him, but it was all an illusion. I literally played a part, and I played it well. The things I did for him just to win his attention—it's humiliating.

But then I remember the feel of his arms around me when I wake up and the look in his eyes when he gazes down at me. That shattering night on Saturday when he confessed how much he cared about me… It's hard not to feel like I'm throwing that love away. But he loved Charlotte, not Charlie.

"It's Taco Tuesday. Let's go fill up on chips and salsa and eat until we can barely walk."

I grumble into my pillow. "Are you paying? I don't have a job, remember?"

"If you sneak me a sip of margarita, I will."

I force out a laugh. As much as I want to roll over and ignore her invitation, I can't do that to Sophie. It's not her fault I'm a loser who falls for all the wrong guys.

"Fine…let me shower." My voice sounds like gravel and my head is pounding from the bottle of white wine I destroyed last night. Maybe a margarita will help me feel better.

An hour later, Sophie and I are scarfing down carne asada and queso. I mean, it doesn't exactly solve all of my love life woes, but it sure does help. You can't be unhappy in a Mexican restaurant.

About halfway through dinner, I notice the booth across from us. It's a family with two teenage boys, and I instantly notice the way they're staring at Sophie. When I hear them muttering to each other, followed by laughter, I grip my margarita glass so hard, I'm afraid it'll shatter.

Sophie must notice because she stares at me over the top of her soda and whispers, "Just ignore them."

Looking up at her, I realize…shouldn't I be the one saying that to her? I mean, we're used to it by now, and we've all learned to ignore the ignorant assholes of the world, but how is my little sister somehow braver and more confident than I am?

"I wish I had an ounce of your confidence, Soph." I suck down what's left of my drink and switch to water. Sophie freezes and glares at me with a furrowed brow.

"What are you talking about? Where do you think I learned to not give a shit what people think?"

"Language," I joke. "And what do you mean 'I don't give a shit what people think'? I *always* worry about what people think."

"Well, you don't show it. When I came out to you, do you remember what you said to me?"

I stare into my glass and try to remember. I feel like I said a million things to her that year, saying any and everything I could to get her through it. "Remind me."

"You said what people think in their heads is a *them* problem. Don't make it yours."

"Damn. I said that?"

"Yep. I thought you were the most confident person in the world."

"Ha!"

"Then you started dating Beau…" Her voice trails off, and I watch her twist her lips with worry.

We sit quietly for a moment in the white noise chatter of the restaurant as I wait for her to finish that sentence.

"And?"

"And you just didn't seem as happy. It was like you lost all of that confidence. Especially after Dad left."

I let out a heavy sigh. "I just keep ending up with the wrong guys, don't I?"

"You know…I know Emerson is his dad, right?"

I nearly suffocate myself, letting a gulp of water go down the wrong pipe. "You do?"

"Well, let's see…" she says in a sarcastic tone, "I was with you the day Beau gave you his dad's address. Two days later, you had a new job. And a month later, you bring this mysterious older man to my birthday party. Doesn't exactly take Sherlock Holmes to figure it out, Charlie."

I drop my head, rubbing my forehead. "Does Mom know?"

"I assume so."

"Why didn't you guys say something?"

"You were happy!" she snaps. "The happiest I've seen you since before Beau."

"Don't you know how wrong that was? Dating my ex's dad?"

She tilts her blue-haired head as she adds, "You mean, will people think it's wrong? That sounds like a *them* problem."

I can't help but chuckle. "Touché, Smurf. But Beau found out, making it *all of our* problem."

"Did you guys…break up?" she asks.

Solemnly, I nod. "But it wasn't just about Beau. It's… complicated."

"Shoot. I can handle it."

I laugh again. "Okay…here's the PG-13 version."

Sophie screws up her nose, making a disgusted expression. "Yes, please."

With a tight smile, I tell her everything. How Emerson was always in charge. How I had to change my entire identity to be with him. How I would have done anything to please him. And how toxic it became.

And instead of agreeing with me or commiserating with me, she stares at me as if she has something to say. "What's that look for?"

"Nothing," she says with a shrug. "It's just that…I don't think you changed your identity. From my perspective, it was like you got all of that confidence back. Did he really make you change, or did he let you be yourself?"

My head is a mess. I know on some level she's right, but something is blocking me from seeing it that way. It reminds me of that first day I started as Emerson's sub and how he said, 'On some days, I want you just to be Charlotte.' What did he mean by that? Did he like the regular me enough or did he just not want to deal with the hassle of teaching me on non-sub days?

Did he let me be myself? It was *my* idea to take on the sub-secretary role. I was the one wandering down dark hallways in the club. I was the one eager to learn it all.

And I'm the one who really wants to go back to that club.

"Dad left because he couldn't accept me as I am. He would have rather seen me unhappy than accept the change I knew I needed. But you found a guy who *wants* you exactly as you are."

"I wish he wanted me, Sophie. But he has to put his son first…and that leaves no room for me."

She rolls her eyes. "Tell Beau to get over it."

A laugh bubbles out of my chest again. "Trust me, I would if I could."

———

That night, I lie in bed and stare at the eight texts from Emerson I've left unanswered.

Can we talk?
I just want to apologize.
I made a mistake.
I miss you.
I understand you need time. I can wait. My front door is always open.
Beau knows everything now. He's mad, but we can work that out.
I'm not choosing him over you. I'm sorry for ever implying I would.
Please, Charlie.

Tears prick the back of my eyes as I read through each one. There are also six missed calls and a few voicemails that I don't have the heart to listen to. He's right—I do need time. I need to come down from the Emerson Grant high so I can think clearly. Maybe some space will help me figure out what I really want.

There's not one from Beau—which is surprising. No scathing judgment. No invasive questioning. He just disappeared from my life. Probably better that way. I don't even know what I would say to him.

Just then a new text pops up, and I stare at it for a moment before realizing who it is.

Hey kiddo. Hope you're doing okay.
We had a photographer at opening night. These pictures

won't be published online, but I thought you might like to see this one.

Garrett. I can tell just by the tone and the way he called me kiddo. Not that he's called me that before. But he's just that playful. Beneath his first text is a photo. It's taken in the dim club. The people around us are blurred, but Emerson and I are in the middle. My gold and blue dress is pressed against his sapphire suit. We're on the dance floor, and while I'm looking away at something, Emerson's eyes are focused on my face. There's a warm, adoring expression in his features. A hint of a smile that reaches his green eyes.

It's hard to look at. It's no secret that Emerson thinks I'm beautiful, but there has to be more in a relationship than that. And definitely more than being called a good girl because I give good head or kneel at his side like I'm supposed to as his sub. Does Emerson see more than that in me?

Tossing my phone down, I let out a cry of frustration. I wish I could trust my own judgment. If I knew anything about love and relationships, I could actually find the right guy, but I don't. I'm just a naive, desperate girl that craves a ridiculous amount of praise and attention and is stupid enough to do anything for it.

But that's not Emerson's fault. That's mine.

Rule #33: The truth hurts like a bitch.

Emerson

I ONCE LOVED THAT MY DESK FACES HERS. I COULD WATCH HER profile as she worked, admiring the slope of her nose and the way she bit her lip while typing or rested her head on her desk at the end of the day. Now, the desk is painfully empty.

And it's all my fault.

The day Beau found us, he didn't even bother to stay and yell at me. We're just back to the silent treatment again, and I really wish he would have let me have it while he was here. I'd rather my son yell at me instead of ignore me.

I've practically worn out the digits on my phone screen, texting both of them. I try to spend most of my days at the club now, but even there, her memory haunts me. Garrett tells me not to give up, to give them both time, but I don't know how long I can do this.

I want them both, and maybe that's selfish and unrealistic, but I don't fucking care anymore.

Today I'm stuck at my desk. It's been two weeks since she left, and I have no plans to replace her anytime soon. Or ever.

Garrett, Maggie, and Hunter have been trying to cheer me up, and I *hate* being cheered up. Right now I want to wallow in my pity, knowing that I may never see her or speak to her again.

And that's it for me. I don't want another sub or another girlfriend. Charlotte is about as replaceable as Beau, which means not at all.

I find myself tracing the lines on my palm, remembering how she said I had a long heart line, how I'd have great love in my life. Have I turned into the world's biggest sap? Apparently.

A knock on the door breaks my attention from my hand. It's probably a delivery or Maggie bringing me something. Still, I rush to answer it and let out a sigh of relief when I find my son on the porch, waiting for me.

"Beau," I say quietly.

He only looks me in the eye briefly before averting his gaze. "I want to know more. I can't stop thinking about it, and I want to know what really happened between you two."

I force myself to swallow down my nerves. "Of course. Come in."

We find a place to sit in the front room, and I offer him a drink or food, but he shakes his head. His knee is bouncing as he stares at the floor. Bracing myself for what might be the hardest conversation of my life, I take a seat across from him. "Ask me anything."

"Did you sleep with her?"

My jaw clenches. "Yes."

His lips tighten, and his clenched jaw mirrors mine. "The whole time?"

"No, just recently."

"Did you hurt her?" he asks in a vitriolic tone.

"Never. I would never hurt her." My answer is confident and certain. I know what he's thinking…that I manipulated her into sleeping with me. That I played a power role over her and forced her into something she didn't want. I'm one-hundred-percent confident that that's not what happened.

"Did you take her to the club?"

Tension looms over us as he brings up the club, the very catalyst of his disdain for me. My son refuses to believe that I'm not some sleazy pervert because I've given people a place to express their sexual needs safely. I wish I could make him see, but it's not exactly a comfortable conversation between father and son.

"Yes, I did."

He shakes his head. "She's not like that. You've spent all this time corrupting her. No wonder she wants you and not me."

"Now wait a minute," I interrupt. "I didn't corrupt her at all. You think she's not like that, but I promise you, she is. Charlotte is a grown woman and can make her own decisions. I didn't coerce her at all, but I did give her a place to find herself, and I've spent the last few months watching her grow."

He scoffs.

"Second of all," I add. "She never chose me over you. You two were already broken up—"

"Oh, shut up," he barks. "Don't rub that in my face."

"I didn't mean to." I hold my hands up toward him. "I'm only pointing out that she was fully aware of what she was doing. And before you perpetuate this belief that my club is a dirty, shameful place, I promise you, it's not. We take all health and safety precautions. Everything is consensual, and women have even more power there than men do, so please stop telling yourself how bad I am."

He's quiet for a moment, staring at the floor as he wrings his hands and thinks to himself.

"Do you love her?" he asks without looking up at me.

I hesitate. The word *yes* rests on the tip of my tongue, dying to come flying out, but I'm not sure that's what he wants to hear. "It doesn't matter," I reply, holding back my disappointment. "If you don't want me to pursue her, I won't."

His head snaps up in my direction. He's reading my expression before forcefully biting out, "I don't want you to."

I have to remind myself to breathe. My heart, which was just beating a million beats a minute, has now crashed to the floor. That's it then. He said no, and I can't break that. I need him to trust me again.

"Okay."

"You didn't answer my question," he adds. "Do you love her?"

This time I let him hear my response. "Yes. Very much."

His face morphs into part disgust and part pity. With his eyes closed, he shakes his head. "She's only twenty-one. You're forty. That's fucked up."

I shrug. "I'm sorry." There's no point in telling him how happy we were. How we stopped seeing each other for our ages and more for what we offered each other. Charlotte made me laugh and saw right through my emotional armor I've been wearing for twenty years. She always seemed to know exactly what I needed.

"So if I really told you not to see her again…you wouldn't?"

Leaning forward, I rest my elbows on my knees. "You're my son, Beau. Your happiness comes before my own. If you don't want me to date your ex, how could I?"

His brow furrows even deeper as he scrutinizes me. "I should go."

The air deflates from my lungs. "Don't go, Beau. Don't be mad at me anymore, please."

As he stands from his chair, the heavy weight of disappointment burrows itself into my throat, making it hard to swallow.

"I just need time…to figure this out."

"Come over anytime. We can talk about whatever you'd like. I'll do anything," I plead, staring at his back as he walks away, feeling like a fool. But I don't care. I'll act a fool just to get him back in my life.

As the door closes without another word from him, I stand there for a while replaying everything in my head. Then, I somberly make my way back to my desk, where I continue to be completely unproductive and stare at nothing while my mind replays all of my mistakes.

Opening the top drawer, I see those light blue panties she left the day it ended. On top of them is the black remote. Both of them stare up at me as a reminder that I will never see Charlotte again. Not as long as Beau has a problem with it.

Picking up the panties, I toss them in the trash can next to my desk. Then with the remote in my hand, I imagine the way she looked when I played with her. That bright smile and gorgeous brown eyes.

"Fuck!" I bellow, tossing the remote hard against the wall and feeling instant gratification as it crashes to the floor in pieces.

Ignoring the mess I made, I grab my keys off the table by the front door. I have to get the fuck out here, and there's only one place I want to go. I'm tired of moping and feeling lonely. Bile rises in my throat as I think about it, but I need some company tonight. Maybe, if I'm lucky enough, I can fuck away how much I miss her and recover some semblance of the man I used to be.

Rule #34: When you're a member of an exclusive sex club, there's really no reason to stay home alone on a Friday night.

Charlie

TURNS OUT LEADING A GROUP OF EIGHT-YEAR-OLDS ON ROLLER skates in the Cupid Shuffle isn't enough to cheer me up. I can fake a smile, and I can look the part, but on the inside, I just want to go home and crawl into my bed.

After the song is over, I skate back to the front desk, where I pass out skates and sell glow sticks. When it's quiet, I remember the two times Emerson came to the rink—the first time to shock the hell out of me, and the second time to shock me even more. I can still see him standing here, talking to Sophie and my mom, and it only makes me miss him more.

When the front door opens, I catch a glimpse of a man walking in, silhouetted by the sun behind him, so I can't make out who it is. The body and gait of his steps is so familiar, my heart nearly stops in my chest.

He wouldn't come here, would he?

But then the man walks in a little farther, and I make out those sandy-brown curls and slightly thinner frame. What the hell is *Beau* doing here?

He spots me behind the counter and gives me an awkward wave. Oh God...this is going to be awful. I haven't exactly faced my ex-boyfriend since he found out I was screwing his dad.

As he approaches the counter, I sort of expect him to be irate and start ranting at me and calling me names, but he doesn't.

"Hey," he says.

"Hey."

"Sorry to bother you at work. Do you have time for a break?"

"Umm..." I stammer. Getting yelled at by my ex isn't exactly how I'd like to spend my break.

"I'm not mad," he says, obviously reading my mind. "I just feel like we should talk."

"Uh...sure." Turning away from him, I go back to the office where Shelley is working and ask her to cover while I'm on break, which she does. I take off my skates and slip into my slides. Then, I walk with Beau out to the parking lot. It's early May, which means it's warm, a little windy, and not a cloud in sight.

If there was any weather suitable for this conversation...I guess this is it.

When we reach his truck, he flips down the tailgate and I climb up. We used to do this a lot between shifts at work or for lunch. It makes me feel like the old me, not Charlotte, the girl who wore stilettos and played a sexy secretary for her boss.

Beau and I sit in silence for a few minutes.

Finally, he glances my way and says with a grimace, "My *dad*, Charlie?"

Fuck this. I hop off the tailgate and start my march back to the front door.

He calls after me before I can reach it. "I'm sorry, just come back."

"I'm not going to spend my break getting guilt-tripped by *you*."

"I'm not guilt-tripping you!" he argues. "I just want to hear your side of the story."

"My side?" I ask, spinning around. "Did you talk to him already?"

"Yeah. I just came from there."

I'm frozen in place, asking myself if I want to hear what Emerson had to say. "No, I can't hear it."

"Charlie, come back. I'm serious. I'll be nice."

Before overthinking it, I turn around and walk slowly back to Beau. "So if you already talked to him, what do you want to hear from me?"

"I just want to make sure he didn't…"

I watch as he stumbles over his words. "Didn't what?"

"You know…force you into anything."

My eyebrows pinch together as I stare at him in shock. Is he serious right now? "Force me?"

"Yeah…he's your boss, Charlie. Not to mention *my dad.*"

"Ugh!" I groan, throwing my arms up. "No, Beau. He didn't force me or manipulate me. I appreciate the concern, but your dad was actually *nice* to me. Probably the *nicest* boyfriend I've ever had, if I'm being honest. If anything, he was the one pushing me away for weeks."

"And you go to that…club?"

"Don't act so holier-than-thou, Beau. I was actually happy with him there."

"This just isn't like you," he adds with his chin up and his shoulders back, body language that I'm used to seeing on him to mean he thinks he knows more than me.

My blood is starting to boil, and it's taking everything in me not to just walk inside and ignore him all together before I do something really stupid.

"Beau…how would you know what I'm like?"

"We dated for a year and a half, Charlie. I know you."

I shake my head, staring at the ground. I don't want to keep arguing with him. I thought we were over this.

"Were you really happy with him?" he asks.

"Yes, but he was never going to commit to me. Not if he ever wanted you back."

"Did you guys really think I was going to just be okay with this?" He sounds appalled, and the urge to run away is fierce again.

"Yes, Beau. It has nothing to do with you. For once I figured you'd be able to accept that not everything is about you!" I snap.

"He's my dad, Charlie! Not to mention he owns that...club. Look at it from my perspective. You act like you're so much happier with him than you were with me."

My jaw nearly hits the floor. I'm done. Done sparing his feelings. Done putting up with his gaslighting and blaming and patronizing ways.

"Maybe because I was! Even when he treated me like property, I felt more valued, more...liked when I was with him," I yell.

"Are you implying I didn't treat you like I liked you?" He jumps off the tailgate and steps up toe to toe with me.

"Yes, Beau. That's exactly what I'm implying. Emerson never once made me feel stupid or acted like I messed everything up. He never *cheated on me*."

"This again?" He throws his arms up.

"Forget it. What is the point?" I ask, spinning around to leave him in the parking lot.

"He told me he loves you. Did you know that?"

His words stop me in my tracks. My spine straightens as I let this news sink in. Did I know that Emerson loved me? Maybe somewhere deep down I did. I certainly know I love him. This news should excite me. It should be the best thing I've ever heard, but it only hurts me more.

"Like I said...it doesn't matter anymore." With that, I leave Beau in the parking lot, shoving the past behind me where it belongs, so I can't see what might have been anymore.

When things slow down at the rink around seven, Shelley cuts me loose. But it seems every time I drive home, I get a restless buzzing in my bones. I feel like I'm crawling out of my skin. The walls of the pool house start to close in on me in a matter of minutes. I've never hated being home as much as I do now.

But I literally have nowhere else to go. Sophie is at a sleepover. Mom is on nights, and I'm all alone. This is pathetic.

Grabbing a bottle of wine from the kitchen, I take up the living room couch to myself and flip the TV onto the trashiest show I can find. Then, I proceed to drink half the bottle and scroll through my phone, paying *no* attention to the show that's playing.

The scrolling gets boring after a while, but at least the wine is keeping the restlessness away. I mindlessly flip through Insta-stories, noticing how everyone I know seems to be having a much better time than me tonight.

Then I click on a story that makes me pause. It's Eden taking a selfie in a dimly lit room with bright pink light cascading across the black brick wall behind her. I'd know that wall anywhere. She doesn't tag her location in the story…I mean, it wouldn't be much of an exclusive club if everyone knew where it was, but she's giving away just enough of her location as if she's trying to show off to a small crowd of people. People like me, who know about Salacious.

Members of Salacious…like me.

Yeah, too bad there's no way I'm going there tonight.

Nope. That's insane. I don't even belong there. I only went because I was with Emerson. What would I even do if I went alone? People will be busy all screwing each other, and I couldn't…

Before I even know what's happening, I'm in a sleek black dress with a plunging neckline and a hem above my knees. The Uber app is pulled up on my phone, and I'm waiting outside, trembling in my stilettos because the wine buzz is wearing off and I realize now just how insane this is.

The old Charlie would have never done this. I'm not sure

the current Charlie would either. But Charlotte—she definitely would. So as the car approaches from the end of the street, I remind myself that I'm Charlotte for tonight. Nothing needs to happen. I'm just going to hang out, maybe do a little watching in the hallway again.

Maybe bump into him... No.

He won't even be there. He doesn't like to go to the club at night unless there's an event happening. So if he is there, then maybe he's there to find someone or kill some time. That invasive thought settles unpleasantly in my mind, but I try to brush it away as I climb into the car.

When the driver pulls up to the front of the club, I wave goodbye and march my nervous ass up to the door. Surprisingly, I feel a little calmer as I walk through the front door to the small, dark lobby. The young blond girl behind the counter takes one look at me and smiles. I wish I could remember her name, since she obviously remembers me.

"Good evening, Ms. Underwood," she says in a warm greeting.

"Good evening," I reply politely. It feels weird to be back, and I'm caught between feeling comfortable, as if I still work here, and feeling like an imposter.

Be Charlotte. I remind myself.

The girl waves me in, and I smile up at the bouncer who opens the dark curtain and heavy soundproof door for me. "Have fun," he mutters quietly.

Before stepping out into the main room, I press my shoulders back as far as I can, and I lift my chin. It feels like feigning confidence, but honestly, what's the difference between real confidence and fake confidence? Probably nothing. So with my clutch nestled under my arm, I strut into the room and notice that it's so much busier than I've seen it. Even on opening night and auction night, there weren't this many people here.

After taking a quick scan of the room and only noticing a few vaguely familiar faces, I make my way to the bar. The bartender tonight is Geo, the nicest supermodel-hot person I've ever met—almost too nice to be a bartender. His eyes light up as he spots me, and I smile in return, suddenly feeling a little more comfortable. People recognize me. I belong here.

Sort of.

"I wish I had my camera," Geo says by way of greeting. "I would have recorded the way you just walked into this room. Like you owned the fucking place."

I laugh, trying to hide my blush. "I did not."

"Yes, you did" a familiar, warm voice joins in, a soft arm looping through mine. Turning my head, a wave of relief washes over me when I recognize Eden pressed against my side. "I'm so glad you're here," she whispers softly in my ear.

"I need a drink," I reply, because it's the only thing right now that makes any sense to me.

"Get this woman a beverage," Eden says to Geo, who shakes his head with a smile.

"What would you like, my queen?" He's patronizing me, but it's amazing how quickly I feel comfortable here. With Eden on my arm and the nice bartender sort of flirting with me, although I know that he and I do not play on the same team, all of my nervous trembles are gone.

Oh, and that giant blond construction worker, who sometimes likes to make my life hell, is grinning at me from across the bar. When he sends me a wink, I shake my head in his direction. It's a good thing there's a two-drink limit because I would not trust myself around him if I was any degree of tipsy.

"I'll have a vodka seltzer with lime, please," I say to Geo, and he turns quickly, getting to work making my drink.

Eden and I make small talk. She seems to be sipping on a cranberry juice without alcohol, while I subtly scan the room. I want to know if Emerson is here, but I also don't want to know because if he is and he's in one of those rooms, I will be sick.

I recognize the same familiar man from the opening night of

the club, who was staring at me, and tonight, he's wearing a harsh, skeptical glare. It makes my skin crawl, especially since I'm about ninety percent sure this isn't someone I met through Emerson or the club.

Oh well, I have every right to be here, and he's not going to make me feel uncomfortable. Turning away from him, I look at Eden.

"Can I tell you something?" I ask after I'm halfway through my first drink.

"Of course," Eden replies with a devious smirk.

"I recognized you from your blog."

Her eyes widen in response and a bright smile stretches across her face. "I didn't know anyone actually read that thing. But I like writing it anyway."

"Are you kidding? I was obsessed. After I learned about this place and first met Emerson, it was your blog that made me feel...I don't know...like I wasn't so weird."

"Good," she announces, placing a hand on my leg. "That was the intent. Do you think men ever feel bad for the stuff they like? Do they get called sluts or depraved or nasty? No. I think we're all tired of being shamed and shoved into these quiet, perfect little innocent versions of ourselves while men can be as deviant as they want."

I can't help the grin that takes over my expression. "I think I love you," I reply.

She quickly clinks my glass in cheers before announcing, "Good. We could all use more love, right?"

"Right," I reply, sucking down what's left in my glass.

"Geo, someone needs another," Eden announces when she notices the look on my face growing somber.

After Geo sets down my drink, I let out a heavy sigh. Eden must be reading my mind because she leans in and says, "He's here, but I haven't seen him with anyone. He's probably in the office."

Or in one of the rooms with someone else.

"I don't know why I came," I mutter quietly to myself.

"I do," she answers immediately. "To show him what he's missing."

"By sitting here alone at the bar?" I laugh.

Eden is staring at me with a calculating expression on her face. "Tell me, Charlotte. Have you ever been with a woman before?"

My eyes widen, as I choke on my drink. She responds with a light chuckle.

"That's what I figured. If I promise to take it slow, would you like to go make your man crazy with jealousy? I don't think it will take much."

Maybe it's the two drinks I've already finished or the excitement of the unknown, but I can't think of a single reason why I'd turn down that offer. Eden is drop-dead gorgeous, and there's definitely an attraction here. We're not talking about full-blown sex, but the idea of drawing Emerson's attention is something I can't say no to.

"Definitely."

"Come on." She grabs my hand and pulls me away from the bar. "Let's go have some fun."

Rule #35: The best place to beg is on your knees.

Emerson

WHAT A WASTE OF TIME. I OWN A FUCKING SEX CLUB, AND I SPEND my Friday night hiding in the office, instead of mingling with members. I actually thought I could find someone here to fuck my depression away with, but I couldn't even muster the desire to look a woman in the eyes. Instead, I'm mindlessly watching the cameras, sipping on my bourbon when Maggie walks in.

"Oh," she says, freezing in the doorway. "I didn't know you were here." She looks strangely flustered, and I narrow my eyes at her. *What's she been up to?* No use in asking, though. Maggie never divulges her stories the way the rest of us do. In fact, she's a mostly closed book, and if she's ever met anyone or done anything, there's not a single member of our group who would know about it.

"Don't mind me," I reply. "I'm just moping."

A sympathetic expression crosses her face. Then she walks in and closes the door behind her, muffling the music thumping in the main room.

"Garrett filled us all in last night when you didn't show up for drinks."

I nod into my glass. I was having drinks…I was just having them alone. "You must think I'm pathetic."

She rests her hip against the desk and stares down at me. "You know what…this is the first time I've ever seen you look so pathetic."

My brow furrows as I pick my head up. "Well…thanks."

"I mean it. In the ten years I've known you, I've never seen you get this bothered by a girl."

"A first time for everything," I joke, holding up my glass.

She lets out a heavy sigh. "So you're not going to go after her?"

"I've tried. She's not returning my calls, and my son has made it very clear that he wants me to stay away from her."

"First of all," she says, taking the drink from my hand, "you're better off asking for forgiveness instead of permission."

I watch as she tosses what was left of my liquor down her throat, wincing as she sets the glass down on the desk. I've never seen Mags shoot the hard stuff. "Second of all, she's here and she just rented room twelve with Eden St. Claire."

I nearly pop out of my chair, easily shaking off the buzz from the bourbon. "What?"

"Just do me a favor and don't cause a scene. We have a business to maintain."

There is a subtle voice in my head telling me that I should not go back there. Charlotte is not mine, and I have no right to stop her from doing anything with anyone, but that rationale dies quickly as I storm out of my office and down the hallway toward room twelve.

Before entering the dark voyeur hallway, I stop myself. I can't go stomping around like this. Maggie was right; I'd be causing a scene and it would not look good at all. So I pause before the entrance and fix my tie, take a deep breath, regroup, and open the door discreetly.

Keeping to the far wall so I'm out of sight, I meander carefully through the crowd of people until I reach the throne room window. And there she is.

Standing in a black dress that shows more cleavage and leg than I'm comfortable with, she's smiling and laughing with Eden. *What is she doing?* She's not going to…

Charlotte is leaning against the wall. Eden is crowding her as she brushes Charlotte's long brown hair off her shoulder and leans in, planting her lips there against her pale white flesh. Charlotte's eyes fall closed in pleasure.

The urge to rush in there and stop this is competing with the desire to watch long enough to see where this is going. Charlotte's hands drift up Eden's sides, and I can't tear my eyes away as she reaches the woman's breasts, and I swear I stop breathing when their gazes meet, both of them smiling.

Eden says something quietly to Charlotte, who responds with a nod and a smile, almost like she was asking for her consent—but for *what?*

My mouth falls open when Eden gently tugs down the neckline of Charlotte's dress, releasing her breasts and running her fingers over them.

God, look at her, I think to myself. There's not even a tremble in her hands as she runs them down the other woman's sides. I've never seen Charlotte look so fucking sexy in all my life. And she's gathering a small crowd outside their window.

Scanning the people assembling to watch, for a moment, my gaze catches on Garrett, lingering near the back, watching the girls with placid captivation. How is he always so content with being a voyeur on the outside? This is driving me wild.

When Charlotte places her hand at the back of Eden's head, she seems to guide her mouth down to where she wants it. And my jaw nearly hits the floor as her lips press against the soft pale flesh of her tits. I almost can't believe what I'm seeing.

Charlotte arches her back and presses her hips against Eden's, her head hanging back in pleasure. Then she slowly rotates her head, turning her focus to the window where the spectators are watching—where *I'm* watching.

I know she can't see me, but I feel like we are staring at each other. How would she feel about me watching this? Did she really come to the club to have sex in a voyeur room with Eden?

Just then, Eden takes Charlotte's face in her hands and pulls her in for a ravenous kiss.

I can't fucking breathe. Their soft tongues tangle as their hands explore each other's bodies, and the second I see Eden's hands grope the mound of Charlotte's ass, tugging up her dress so I see the black lace beneath, I snap.

Moving quickly through the crowd, I make my way to the entrance to the room hidden around the back. As I reach desperately for the knob, I stop myself. *Calm the fuck down, Emerson.*

Then, I hear a high-pitched moan coming from inside the room.

Yeah, fuck calming down.

My skin is buzzing as I tear open the door. The girls flinch, but when Eden turns toward me, she has a sly, wicked smile on her face.

"Emerson!" Charlotte squeals, fixing the neckline of her dress to cover her tits, and I know I should consider the crowd beyond the glass, but all I see is her. Her innocent brown eyes widen as I cross the room, her bottom lip dropping from the top as she stares in shock. But I don't stop.

"Eden," I reply in a gruff tone with my eyes focused on Charlotte.

"Hello, Emerson," Eden replies sweetly.

"Get out."

She replies with a knowing smile before walking steadily to the door. I don't even hear it close behind her before I'm gathering Charlotte—*my* Charlotte—up in my arms. I had other plans when walking in here, mostly involving driving her home, getting her as far away from this place and all of the sins that could find her, but right now, with her in arm's reach, I'm powerless.

My hands scoop her up by the waist, dragging her against

my body as I crash my harsh, unforgiving lips against her supple, delicate ones. For one second, she lets me kiss her, clutching eagerly to my neck, and my body grows hot and tight with anticipation. But it only lasts a heartbeat. One beat. Enough to let me feel hopeful before it crashes to the floor, breaking like glass.

"Emerson, stop!" she screams, clawing at my chest and pushing away with enough force for me to stop. I pull away from our embrace and stare into those familiar doe eyes, begging and pleading with my soul for one more chance. "You can't just barge in here and expect me to run back into your arms."

"Fine," I grumble. "Then you need to go home."

She reacts like I've slapped her, tilting her head in disbelief. "You don't own me," she spits out with enough venom to make the words hurt like daggers. "Not anymore."

As she tries to move around me toward the door, I grab her by the waist, but she struggles against me again.

"I may not own you, but I own this club."

"I belong here just as much as you do," she yells, shoving away from me, but I'm pulled into her gravity, and I can't move away. Before she reaches the door, I corner her and guide her chin up, so I can level her with my gaze.

"What are you going to do, Charlotte? Did you come here to let Eden fuck you for fun?"

"So what if I did? You were the one who made me believe I was sexy and beautiful enough."

The way she's holding her head up, the strength of her convictions, is like ecstasy in my bloodstream, but I hate seeing her directing this animosity toward me.

"You are sexy and beautiful, Charlotte. And you're also *mine*."

"Not anymore," she snaps, but I catch the slightest quiver in her response, enough to make her stay in this spot, in my hands, until she stops saying that.

"Yes, you are," I grumble, grasping the fabric of her dress in my fists.

"You called us *nothing*, Emerson. When Beau stood in your living room and you had the opportunity to tell him everything, you said it was *nothing*." Her voice shakes, and I can't keep my hands away from her face, touching her jaw and neck. The time away from her has turned me into a desperate man, needy for the touch of her skin and the taste of her lips.

"I am not a perfect man, Charlotte, and I let you down. I'm sorry."

"You told me the relationship we built, being your sub, meant that I could trust you, always."

Those words slice through my tough exterior like daggers.

"You can trust me, Charlotte. I was wrong for what I said. Let me make it up to you. I can earn your forgiveness."

"How?"

There is a far better answer she is looking for, but I'm not exactly thinking with my brain at the moment. I'm thinking strictly with my heart and my cock, both of them fighting for dominance, and while this is the dumbest idea I've ever had, it serves us well in the moment.

"What are you doing?" she shrieks as I hoist her up and toss her over my shoulder. Carrying her to the middle of the room, I lay her gently on the throne. Once she's sitting, I unbutton my shirt at the neck, just a couple buttons, so I can move and breathe. Then, I unclasp each cuff of my shirt and roll the sleeves to the elbow. She doesn't leap from the chair and try to escape the room, so I guess that's a good sign.

"Emerson…" she tries to argue.

Resting on my knees in front of her, I glide my hands up her thighs, rucking her dress up to her hips as I do. She tugs her bottom lip between her teeth and watches me with an uneasy yet curious expression.

"I'm on my knees for you, Charlotte. I know I promised to take care of you, and I made a mistake. Let me make it up to you."

"This is hardly enough, Emerson."

"It's a start," I groan, pulling her hips to the edge of the seat. With my face nearly sandwiched between her knees, I breathe in the scent of her heat, and my mouth waters in response. I'm ready to dive in now, lap at her flawless cunt like the animal I am, but I have to bide my time.

She gasps as I kiss my way up her inner thigh, all soft lips and wet tongue, leaving a trail of goose bumps in my wake. When I reach the throbbing, wet apex of her thighs, her nails dig into my hair, tugging my face close to where she wants it.

My fingers find the thin hem of her panties and delicately peel them down her legs. It's at this moment that I remember we have a solid wall of glass behind me and eager patrons enjoying the show. I was so focused on Charlotte and having her back in my grasp that I forgot we're in a voyeur room.

I *could* pull the curtain closed or dim the room's lights for privacy, but when I sneak a peek up at her face, Charlotte doesn't seem to mind the watching eyes so much. In fact, she looks more aroused than I think I've ever seen her. I can see the pebbled outlines of her nipples showing through the black fabric of her dress.

Her hips tilt, and the hand in my hair guides my face closer to where she wants it, a wicked smile stretching across my face. Tugging her hips closer, I bury my face between her thighs, running my eager tongue between her folds. The rumble of her pleasure vibrates through me as I do it again and again, devouring her sex like the depraved and desperate sinner I am.

"Suck my clit," she whimpers, and I almost hesitate. This is the same girl who once struggled with the slightest bit of dirty talk and now she's fucking my face and telling me what she wants. Pride swells in my chest, and I growl in response, latching my lips around her most sensitive spot, sucking it the way she likes.

Her cries echo through the room, bouncing off the bare walls. Reaching up with one hand, I jerk down her neckline, exposing a breast and kneading the soft flesh as I fuck her with my tongue. With the other hand, I easily slide a finger inside her. Her hips thrust upward, and I never want this to end. I'm holding her pleasure in the palm of my hand, a growling, aching reminder that she's *mine*.

Glancing up at her again, I don't see the too-young girl that stumbled into my office that first day. I see Charlotte in a form she was always meant to be—confident, sexual, and happy.

"It's right there," she pants. "Don't stop."

Hooking my finger, I thrust another in and pump hard as I suck hungrily at her clit, feeling the muscles of her petite body tense all around me. Her panting breaths stop as she climaxes, leaving her in shivers when she comes down. She melts like candle wax into the seat, and I gently pull my fingers out, kissing my way along her thighs.

My cock aches in my pants, dying to plunge into her wet heat, but I don't move to free it from its confines just yet. I'm not here to fuck her. I'm here to get her back.

"Come home with me," I whisper, slowly running my hands up her legs, putting her panties back into place.

Her head still hangs back, her eyes closed as she catches her breath. "You really think this is enough to make it up to me, Emerson?"

Opening her eyes, she gazes down at me, stroking my face with her soft hands.

"Tell me what you want, and I'll do it," I plead.

The warmth in her expression drains away, leaving a tight-lipped look of frustration. Then, she stands from the throne, pulling her dress down as she stomps toward the door. I'm on my feet in a second, rushing after her.

"It's not enough, Emerson."

As she reaches for the door handle, I notice her hesitate, her resolve straining, and there's a part of me that wants to see her break—forgive me, take me back against her better judgment, without making me truly pay for the pain I've caused.

And then another part wants to see her stay strong, take all the power and control I've harbored all this time, and do what's right for her. Even if that means leaving me here.

When she does, I'm so proud of her, but it still hurts like a motherfucker.

Standing alone in the dimly lit room, I think about what she said. *It's not enough.* I know what would be enough, but I don't know if I have the heart to do it.

Rule #36: Don't let them shame you.

Charlotte

I couldn't sleep all night. Visions of what happened in the throne room play on repeat in my mind. Kissing Eden…which worked like a charm, like she said it would. He couldn't stay away the second he saw her hands on me.

And walking away from him was pure torture. But I had to do it. Although I spent the rest of my night tossing and turning, wanting to throw caution to the wind and call him. I could go to his house, let him take me to bed, and pretend that consequences didn't exist and there was no risk of me being hurt.

But then it's only a matter of time before Beau shows back up again and I'm pushed aside, ignored and forgotten. What kind of future did I really have with Emerson like this? He would never commit, never marry me. We couldn't live together or plan our lives as long as he was keeping me a dirty secret under his desk.

I deserve better. I know that to be true, but it's still hard to convince my heart that seems to think the only solution to this problem is to ignore my convictions and crawl back to him. Stupid heart.

I'm lying in bed, staring at the picture Garrett sent me a few days ago of me and Emerson at the club on opening night, when I hear a car door slam shut out front. My mom and Sophie are already home, so something about this seems off.

Then, I hear the ominous sound of my name being called by the one person I would least expect.

"Charlotte, get out here!" my father bellows from outside my pool house, and I freeze. *What the fuck?*

Jumping out of bed in my pajama shorts and a T-shirt, I creep toward the door and peer out the window. And there he is. The man I haven't seen in over a year is pacing outside my door with a look of intense rage on his face. I can't move...the feeling of shame and guilt swimming through my veins, although I have no idea what I feel so sorry about.

A moment later, I watch my mother emerge from the house with a look of shock on her face.

"Jimmy, what are you doing here?" she calls toward him.

His fist bangs against my door before he turns the knob, finding it locked and banging again.

"Charlie, get out here now!"

A cold chill runs up my spine as I fumble with the lock. "What—" I start as I pull open the door.

I barely get the door open before he's shouting at me. "I got a call from a colleague of mine. I heard what you've been up to."

"What?" I stammer, my eyes dancing between my mother and him. *A colleague?*

"What are you talking about?" my mother replies, meeting us by the door.

"Of course you don't know what your kids have been up to, Gwen," he says with a biting hatred toward my mother, and I feel the undeniable urge to step forward and defend her.

I have happy memories of my dad. Memories of his laughter and his smiles. His hugs and jokes and cuddles on the couch. But right now...all I see is the face I haven't seen in over a year contorted in fury as he looks at me with an expression that shows more disgust and shame than love and acceptance.

"I'm not a kid," I argue.

"Yeah, well, you're *my* kid, and I won't have you selling your body to a bunch of rich perverts!" he yells, and my cheeks flush hot.

I catch movement behind my mom and notice Sophie stepping out of the house to see what's going on. Swallowing down my nerves, I give her a quick shake of my head. There's a look of fear on her face that shatters my heart, and I don't care about me or getting yelled at by my dad or my parents knowing what exactly I've been up to these past few months. But if my actions bring any pain or fear to her, then I'll never forgive myself.

"Keep your voice down," I mutter through clenched teeth.

"Why?" he replies. "You don't want your mother hearing that you were at some sex club auctioning yourself off for seventy-five grand?"

My mother gasps and covers her mouth. "Is that where your money has been coming from, Charlie?"

"No!"

Behind my dad, I watch Sophie pull out her cell phone, typing something out before disappearing into the house. I just want her away from here.

"What's he talking about, Charlie?" my mother asks, her tone laced with fear.

My shoulders slump as I stare at her. "I'm not a prostitute, Mom," I say, and she takes a deep breath.

"She's been going to some…some…sex club," he says with disgust, and I wince. I didn't need my mother finding out like this. It's not fair to her.

"Is that where you work? Is that where Emerson…"

"Emerson Grant?" my dad cuts in with a bite in his tone.

I can't believe how badly I want the ground to swallow me whole right now. This is beyond humiliating, and I don't have the heart to look at my mother. I notice the way she's shrinking away.

My eyes stay on the ground, trying to drown out the rage-filled man standing next to me. "Emerson owns the club," I say delicately. I wish she and I could have this conversation alone. I hate myself for waiting this long. My mom is understanding; she wouldn't have cared if I could have just told her everything before *he* found out.

"Oh, Charlie," she says, lowering her head and rubbing her forehead.

"But I never *sold* myself," I bite back, this time directing my frustration at him.

"Bullshit!" he yells.

"Let her talk, Jimmy. She's an adult—"

"A guy I work with *saw you*, Charlie! He saw you there three times. He said you got up on stage, in some auction, and sold yourself!"

The dark, scrutinizing eyes of the man I saw last night come back in my mind. I knew I had seen that man somewhere, and now I can see it all so clearly. I had met him when I was younger, and I knew he worked at my dad's law firm. I wince, thinking about him seeing me on that stage in almost nothing, being carted off by Emerson, in the *voyeur room last night with Eden*. I groan at the memory.

"That man who won was my *boyfriend*," I reply, forcing myself to keep my shoulders up and not cower in shame. Over and over in my mind, I just keep chanting: *I didn't do anything wrong. I didn't do anything wrong. I didn't do anything wrong.*

"Oh, your boyfriend," my dad replies. "I heard all about him too. Emerson *Grant*." It's the way he emphasizes his last name that I know what he's about to imply. "Beau's dad, Charlie?"

"Oh, Jimmy, will you leave her alone? She's an adult. You can't just come here and—"

He holds up a hand, pressing it right in her face to silence her, and a feeling of red-hot rage flows through me.

"You have no fucking say anymore, Gwen. I never should

have left them with you. Look how you've fucked them both up. First, it was…" He waves his hand toward the house, and I know he's about to bring Sophie into this. He's about to deadname my little sister, and everything in me wants to explode with anger.

"Don't you dare bring her into this," my mother snaps, stopping him before he even has a chance. "You lost that chance when you abandoned her."

When she tries to shove his hand away from her face, he pushes her backward, and I snap. My dad has never been violent with me or my mom, but he's always dominated the conversation. He constantly silenced her or talked down to her, and right now, the sight of him shoving her away like her voice means nothing has me seeing red.

"Don't touch her!" I scream, trying to force my way between them. But my mother is fighting back too, and he's too busy screaming at her around me that he doesn't seem to care that I'm trying to stop him.

The scuffle between us intensifies quickly. I distantly recognize the sound of more voices from afar, two car doors closing. But I have tunnel vision, focusing solely on getting my dad as far away from my mother as I can. There's so much yelling, though, him shouting at my mother, her screaming back at him.

Suddenly, I can't even believe what my eyes are seeing as two large, broad hands grab my father by the collar and throw him hard against the wall of the pool house.

I must be hallucinating because Emerson has his face in my father's, snarling at him like an angry animal. "Touch either of them again, and I'll fucking bury you."

"Emerson!" I scream.

"Emerson?" my dad echoes in surprise. "You're the asshole fucking my daughter?"

My hand covers my mouth, and I glance toward the house again to make sure Sophie isn't around to hear this.

My mother grabs my hand, pulling me away, and I feel the

way she's trembling. But I can't take my eyes off of Emerson, the anger and hatred dripping from his expression and the tone in his voice.

He looks unhinged as his brow furrows even more. "Watch your mouth, you piece of shit."

"You make me sick," my dad snaps.

"Both of you, stop!" I scream, coming toward them.

"Stay away from him, Charlie. Call the police," my dad snarls, but Emerson shoves him back up against the wall.

"Please, stop," I beg, wrapping a hand around Emerson's arm. When he glances down at me, there's a hint of softness in his eyes. And he seems to struggle with his next breath as he lets out a heavy sigh. Carefully, he pulls his hands away from my dad's shirt and backs away. The moment is wrought with tension as the two men stare daggers at each other.

"Gwen, did you know this forty-year-old man has been doing…God knows what with our daughter?"

"Dad, please stop," I beg, the humiliation washing over me again. A large hand rests against my back, and I lean into his comfort.

My mother scoffs. "Yes, Jimmy, I knew. *He* came to Sophie's birthday party."

There's a brief moment of shock and confusion on my father's face as he looks between her and him and me. I can see all of the things Emerson wants to say to my dad just hanging on his lips.

I feel like I can barely move. Like one wrong word or move and everything between them will explode.

"Why didn't I know about this party?" my dad replies.

"Because you weren't invited," my mother snaps back in a clipped tone. I've never heard her talk to him like that, and I sort of love her for it. *Go Mom.*

"I think you should leave," Emerson growls.

"Me? This is my house, asshole."

"I don't think your family wants you here right now while

you're acting like this," Emerson says with a level tone. "So why don't you leave and calm down. Come back when you can talk like a real man."

Neither of the men move, and it feels like there's a ticking time bomb between them.

"A real man?" my dad replies with a scoff. "You think you're a real man? Manipulating young girls. I know all about your disgusting club, and my daughter deserves far better than you, you sick fuck."

"Hey!" another voice yells from the fence line, and we all turn in unison to see Beau standing by the gate. My mouth hits the ground as I watch him march toward my father with a look of pure rage on his face. "Don't talk to my dad like that."

Emotion claws at my throat, like someone is sitting on my chest, and when I look at Emerson, I see the way his expression changes too. The anger fades and the shame beneath it shows through.

My dad, on the other hand, is *laughing*.

"Your dad?" he asks. "I'm sorry, but weren't you dating my daughter first? You're telling me you're fine with him taking your girl? What kind of fucked-up family are you?"

"Yeah, well, at least my dad calls me and gives a shit about me and didn't abandon me when I needed him most," Beau replies, and my eyes widen in shock. I reach out a hand to calm him, because at the moment, he looks like he wants to punch a hole through my dad's face. But the words coming out of his mouth make me pause. Is he...standing up for Emerson?

"Son," Emerson says, reaching a hand out to calm Beau, "it's fine."

"No, it's not," Beau cuts back. "I'm not gonna stand here and let this ignorant prick treat Charlie like shit, treat you like shit, and act like he's so much better than you."

"You guys should just leave," my dad snaps, and I look over at my mom. She sends me an apologetic look before turning to my dad.

"No, Jimmy. You should leave. Emerson was right. Come back when you're calm and want to talk, but you've caused enough drama for the girls today."

"I'm not leaving you with this pervert," he argues, motioning to Emerson. Beau and I both react with an argument, but Emerson only holds his hand up to stop us.

Then, he looks right at my dad and takes a long, steadying breath.

"You know what, you're right. I do own a club downtown, and I do take your daughter there, but I haven't brainwashed her or manipulated her or hurt her in any way. And I'm not ashamed. You think you know what's right for your daughters, but you have no idea. You just want them to live how *you* think they should live, and you're so self-righteous, you've lost your family because of it.

"I may not be the best father in the world, but I'd choose my kid's happiness over mine every time. And I know for a fact that you could never love Charlie as much as I do. Not if you could stand being away from her for a single day."

I feel the air leave my lungs as those words leave his lips, my heart nearly exploding in my chest. I realize at this moment just how much I love him, how much I've changed since he started loving me, and how everything we've fought about until this moment is trivial. It becomes strikingly clear in this moment—Emerson means *everything* to me.

Rule #37: Don't apologize for shit you're not sorry for.

Emerson

BEAU AND I WERE IN THE CAR TOGETHER, A SMALL MIRACLE IN itself, when we got a call from Sophie. Charlotte must have given her my number after I gave her the Anime Fest tickets for her birthday because she texted me a few days later to thank me for them. Thank God Beau and I were only a few minutes away. Her frightened-sounding voice nearly had me crashing on the road as I sped toward her house. She said her dad showed up out of the blue and was yelling at Charlie, and that she was scared.

She was scared of her father, so she called me. It makes me hate that asshole even more when I think about it.

It's nearly impossible to keep my words to this human piece of garbage civil, but that's what Charlie and her mother and her sister deserve right now. So I tell him everything. We might as well lay it all on the line now.

I'm not ashamed of who I am or what I do.

And I love Charlie.

And…I don't even have the guts to look at her face as the words come tumbling out of my mouth.

"Enough!"

It's Sophie's young voice that breaks the tension, just as her dad opens his mouth, ready to argue with me. We all stare at the feisty blue-haired teenager as she stomps out to the yard. I see so much of Charlie in her—fearless and reckless and smart as hell.

"Dad, Mom's right. You should just leave. I was the one to call Emerson because you scared me when you showed up," she says, staring at him with a look of fierceness in her eyes that makes my chest swell with pride.

Charlie's head snaps up to stare at me in shock. "Sophie called you?"

I nod. When I look at her father, I notice that for the first time since I got here, he looks more remorseful than angry. His eyes are glued to Sophie, and his brows are pinched together. He looks seriously wrung out, but I recognize the emotion written in his features—a father's guilt.

"Dad…" Charlie says, stealing his attention. When he finally looks toward her, his eyes moist and apologetic, she continues, "I'm not ashamed of who I'm dating or what I'm doing, and it may be hard for you to believe, but Emerson didn't do anything wrong. I'm *tired* of everyone acting like they know what's best for me. I'm twenty-one years old, and I'm not stupid or too young to know what I want."

Her small hand finds mine, intertwining our fingers, and it takes everything in me not to gather her up in my arms and kiss her harder than I've ever kissed her before.

"You chose to leave, and you have no right to talk to me the way you did today. If you had been around the last year, maybe you'd see that I have never been happier than I was the last three months."

I can't help myself now. I pull her against me, resting her against my chest as I wrap my arms around her, kissing the top of her head.

"Gwen, you're really going to allow this?" he asks, still putting up a fight, but Charlotte's mother just lets out a heavy sigh.

"Just leave, Jimmy."

"Fuck this," he grumbles in my direction, but I ignore him, inhaling the familiar scent of Charlotte's shampoo and the soft skin of her arms as I stroke my fingers against them. "We're not done," he says to Gwen. "We need to have a serious talk about this later."

I watch him stomp through the backyard toward the side gate, pausing a moment as he stares at Sophie. She holds up an awkward hand toward him as a way of waving, and we all wait in anticipation to see what Jimmy will do.

"Bye, kiddo," he says to her, sending her the same awkward wave before stomping away, and it's hard to miss the disappointment on Sophie's face. The sound of his car engine echoes before we hear him speed away down the street.

Gwen rushes over to Sophie to wrap her up in her arms. I watch as Beau follows behind, setting a warm hand on Sophie's shoulder in a comforting touch.

Pulling away, I look down at Charlie. "Are you okay?"

Those fierce brown eyes gaze back up as she nods. "Yeah. I'm fine."

I wish I could stop myself, but I can't. I still don't know where we go from here or what will happen next, so I take what I can get right now, and I press my lips to her forehead.

"What happened?"

"He came out of nowhere. Said someone he worked with at his law firm told him about me at the club. Me being auctioned off and sleeping with the owner."

Clenching my jaw, I let out a groan. "I'm going to look into this person and have their membership revoked immediately. It's against our policy to disclose other members outside of the club. I'm so sorry, Charlie."

"It's okay," she says, and maybe by instinct, she leans back into my touch, wrapping her arms around me. The relief from having her back is intense, but I'm too afraid to thank my lucky stars just yet. "Why were you with Beau?" she whispers.

"I called him this morning. Told him I needed to talk to him."

"Oh," she replies, looking up at me. "Where were you guys going?"

"To grab a drink. I had something important to talk to him about."

"Oh…" she says again, her eyes lingering on my face, probably wondering what this very important thing was.

It takes everything in me to let her go and slowly pull away. "I have to talk to him," I say, and I watch her swallow. Then she nods. I wish I could convey exactly what I'm thinking right now. I want to tell her I was about to tell my son everything. No more waiting for permission or asking him to accept us the way we are. I want her to know that I'm choosing her now, the way I should have before. But there will be time for me to tell her that later.

"Can I call you later?" I ask.

She nods eagerly. Then I stroke her cheek delicately, fighting the urge to hold her for the rest of the day and for as long as I can. But this has to be taken care of first.

As I leave Charlotte standing outside, I turn toward my son. I can't exactly read his expression. I expected anger and resentment, but it's more complicated than that. He's pensive and guarded but also unsure.

"Come on, Beau," I call, and he follows as I lead him around to the front yard where my car is parked. I distantly remember the first time I came to Charlotte's house, picking her up for the opening night of the club, how sure I felt at that time that I wouldn't let things between us get out of hand. How fucking stupid I was to think that was even possible.

There's no sign of Charlotte's dad, thank fuck. Although, I guess if I want to be part of her life for the long haul, I'm going to have to find a way to deal with him. As bad as he is for her, it's not fair for her to live the rest of her life without a dad because he's so fucking bad at it.

Looking at Beau, I can't imagine how her father could walk

away from them so easily. How delusional does a man have to be to live a life without his own kids? And yet...here I am about to tell mine that I don't plan on avoiding Charlotte just because he doesn't like it.

It's silent between us for a moment as I prepare how I'm going to say this to him. A better man might apologize first, but I can't bring myself to apologize for loving Charlotte. I'm not sorry about it.

When he looks up at me, I can tell he wants to say something, so I brace myself for it. "You know...she tried to warn me. I knew her dad was a jerk, and I didn't listen. When I heard him say that about you...I just snapped."

"I'm sorry you had to hear that. But there will always be people who react that way. Who see things one way and refuse to open their minds to anything else. I'd rather be someone people deem as depraved or sinful than being narrow-minded and hateful."

He nods, his eyes intense on my face. "You really do love her? It's not just—"

"Yes," I answer, interrupting him. "I really do love her. And I never meant for it to happen this way. You know that, right?"

"Yeah."

Then, I brace myself for the hard part. "And you understand that I'm not going to stop seeing her? I should have told you before, and I never should have acted like it was nothing, but I was really afraid of losing you again."

He swallows and stares at his feet, and it strikes me for the first time that my son really is a man now. He's not a kid anymore, not the same gangly teenager I remember or the little kid who looked up at me like I hung the moon in the sky. Beau is as much a man as I am, and it's about time I stop treating him like a kid.

"I still think it's fucking weird," he grumbles, and I have to look away to keep from laughing. "And I don't know if I can really see you guys together, at least not for a while. But...she seems happy with you—a hell of a lot happier than she was with me."

I'm trying not to get too excited or relieved because this is a small step, but it's also major, and it's more than enough. He's not screaming at me or calling me names or threatening to never speak to me again.

So I stay quiet as he continues.

"I don't really like it…I'm not gonna lie and say I do."

"That's okay," I reply quickly.

"But…thanks for sticking up for her."

"Of course. Thanks for sticking up for me," I say with a half smile.

Awkward silence permeates the space between us. And it feels like hours before he finally looks up and gives me the eye contact I wanted. The fact that he's not walking away or telling me to fuck off is enough to let me know we'll be okay.

"Still want to go get that drink?" I ask, nodding toward the car.

He squeezes his lips together and nods. "Hell yeah."

I'm ready to climb into my car and leave. What I'm not ready for is my son taking the three steps to close the distance between us and pull me into an abrupt hug. I wish I could memorize it, and fuck, I try. It's been so long since he really wrapped his arms around me that I wish time would stop for a moment and let me savor this.

All too soon, he's pulling away. "All right, let's go." Then he climbs into the passenger seat, leaving me stunned.

Beau has a long way to go, and we may never see eye to eye on the club or my relationship with Charlotte, but he's still my son and I'm not going to let him walk away that easily.

Rule #38: Sometimes, there are no words needed.

Charlie

WHEN I WALK INSIDE, MY SISTER AND MOM ARE SITTING ON THE couch. There are red blotches around Sophie's nose and cheeks, a telltale sign that she's been crying.

"Oh, Soph, I'm sorry," I say, dropping onto the sofa next to her. It's only 1:00 p.m. and already today has been exhausting. There's still so much to process. Some creep told my dad about me at the club. My mom and dad both know about Emerson and the club and me *being auctioned off*—insert mortification. And the crème de la crème of the day had to be Emerson Grant proclaiming his love for me in front of everyone. Kind of hard to care about the other stuff when that plays over and over in my mind.

"It's okay," my sister mumbles as she rests her head against my shoulder. "I hope you're not mad that I called Emerson."

I lift my head and stare at her in surprise. "Mad? No, of course not. You did the right thing."

"Did you see him slam Dad against the wall?" she asks, hiding her smile as she pinches her lips between her fingers.

Mom and I both laugh. "That was pretty cool," Mom says.

"I'm sorry for not telling you," I add, mostly to Mom, since Sophie sort of figured it out on her own. And I guess this might be a conversation more suitable in private, but I like the idea that we don't keep secrets from each other. At least not anymore.

My mom rubs my knee as she says, "It's okay, honey. It's not like I couldn't tell how old he was. I had my suspicions, but I trust you, Charlie. You're a strong, smart girl, and I know you can take care of yourself."

The emotion in my throat stings as I force myself to swallow and *not cry*. "Thanks, Mom."

Then, she ruffles my sister's hair. "And neither of you have to see him or face him until you're ready. I'm sorry he scared you."

"It's okay," Sophie mumbles.

"Is anyone else in the mood for pj's and movies? I think we need a lazy Saturday," I add playfully.

"You're the only one still in pj's," Sophie says with a laugh.

"So go put yours on. I'm gonna cue up some comfort Disney on the TV and Mom will make the snacks."

"Sounds good," Mom replies, jumping up and heading to the kitchen.

Grabbing the blankets from the basket, I curl up next to my sister with my mom on the opposite side, and we escape reality for the next few hours, singing along to our favorite princess movies and trying to forget about today and all of its drama. As much as I want to just shower and go straight to Emerson's, I need to just be with my family for a while. I need to know they're okay.

About halfway through the second movie, there's a knock at the front door. I peer back to see Beau's shaggy brown hair through the curtains. I let out a heavy sigh. If he's here to give me shit or talk about this anymore, I'm really not in the mood.

"I'll talk to him," I say, standing with a sigh.

"Don't take his shit," my sister says with a bright smile, and my mother's jaw falls open.

"Sophie! Watch your mouth."

I'm still smiling as I open the door. Beau is staring at his feet before lifting his head to look at me.

"Hey," I greet him, which he then replies to with his own lazy "Hey."

Stepping onto the front porch, I close the door behind me. But he doesn't talk right away, and I can tell he's uncomfortable. If he wants to hate me or be mad at me, I'm willing to let go of our past and our friendship, but if Emerson and I are going to give this a try, I need Beau on my side.

"I'm sorry," he says so quickly I almost don't catch it.

"What?"

"For being a shitty boyfriend...I'm sorry," he mutters. His hands are stuffed in his pockets as he averts his gaze from my face. "I never should have cheated on you, and I should have been nicer to you, and I should have known you were unhappy."

Oh, sweet Jesus, please don't let Beau be saying all of this in hopes of getting me back. I do not think I can handle that level of insanity.

"Thanks..." I say with uncertainty as I wait to see where this is going.

"I just want you to be happy, Charlie. You *deserve* to be happy."

A huff escapes my lips. "Even if I'm with your dad?"

He lets out a loud sigh, and I can tell he's struggling with this, but he still manages to nod. "Yeah. Even if you're with my dad."

"I hope you mean that."

"After what I saw today...I don't know I just...see things differently now. Like it's the real thing. He obviously deserves you more than I do."

The radiating sadness on his face draws me forward, and I take his warm, tan cheeks in my hands. "Stop beating yourself up, Beau. You're loved and you're young and you'll be fine. You're gonna find somebody who makes you feel good, someone as happy as you wish I were with you."

Finally, his eyes lift and find mine. When I pull him into a hug, he relaxes against my body. "Is Sophie okay?" he mumbles into my shoulder.

"Yeah, she's fine."

"Good. I know she probably hates me."

"She doesn't hate you," I reply with a roll of my eyes.

"She just scowled at me through the window," he says with a laugh, and I turn in time to see the curtain shutting. We both laugh for a minute before I turn toward him with a sad smile.

"Do you want to come in and watch *Tangled* with us?"

"Tempting...but no. I think I'm gonna head home. Besides, I just left my dad's and I'm pretty sure he's gonna call you or want to see you." I don't miss the look of disgust that flashes across his face.

"Why do you say that?"

"Because he spent the last two hours telling me how much he loves you and isn't going to wait for my permission to date you... openly."

I freeze. "He said that?"

"Yep."

No more hiding. No more lying to Beau or waiting for his approval. It's real this time.

I must show my surprise because he just claps me on the shoulder as he says, "I'm gonna go then."

"Bye, Beau," I stammer.

Then he's in his car and driving away, and I'm practically running to my shower. When I get out, I almost reach for my pencil skirt and blouse but think better of it. When I go back to Emerson's, I want to go as me. He has to take me as Charlie if he wants me as Charlotte.

I'm shaking in my black Doc Martens as I knock lightly on Emerson's front door. It feels like a step backward to be here as a guest. I've walked through this front door at least fifty times over the last three months, but this feels almost like metaphorically starting over, redefining whatever this is. A second chance to do this right.

It doesn't change the fact that I'm craving his nearness like I need it to survive. When he finally pulls open the door, I take in the sight of him, standing on the other side in the same blue slacks and tight gray shirt he had on earlier, but now it's unbuttoned at the neck, revealing a patch of chest hair I know all too well.

Just being in his presence makes everything in the world feel right. That clusterfuck of a morning is a distant memory, swept away as we stand here and bask in the sight of each other. And while there are a hundred things to say, there is also nothing left to say, no words that will make this situation make sense beyond *I want you, I need you, I love you. And that's all that matters to me.*

As if he can read my mind, he does exactly what I want him to do. Reaching a strong hand out, his grip latches on to the back of my neck, pulling me toward him until there isn't an ounce of space between us. Then his mouth is on mine, his lips devouring my lips, and his tongue finding its way to mine until we are fused.

His kiss does not take or claim or steal anything that I'm not willfully giving. He grunts low and gravelly into my mouth as his other hand finds my lower back and molds me against his tall frame. The same hand creeps lower, squeezing my ass hard and making me yelp into his mouth as he lifts me, and I wrap myself around him.

He carries me inside, slamming the door behind him. He tries to make it up the stairs, but we are too desperate, and I'm clawing at his shirt as he sets me on the steps, kneeling in front of me.

"Fuck, I missed you," he groans, digging his hand in my hair and grasping my scalp as his mouth trails down to my neck.

"I missed you so much," I reply, pulling open the buttons of his shirt, so I can reach his skin because I *need* to feel him. And it doesn't matter that we just saw each other last night and I felt his mouth on me less than twenty-four hours ago, because it wasn't like this.

When I finally have his shirt undone, he quickly shrugs out of it, giving me the full, uncovered view of his body, and I wrap my hands around his waist, kissing my way down from his chest to his waist. There's a low vibration through me from his groan as I lick my way across his stomach, teasing the area just above his belt.

"Get naked for me, Charlotte. I want to see my girl." He takes me by the chin, lifting my face until I'm smiling up at him. *His girl.*

"Yes, sir," I reply sweetly. Then I move deftly to pull off my own shirt.

At the first sight of my breasts, he drops his hands from his belt and reaches for me, peppering my body with kisses and ravaging each side of my chest until I'm gasping for air.

"I want to take my time with you, Charlotte," he murmurs against my skin. "But I can't help myself when I see you. You make me fucking crazy. Now I just want to come, and I want to do it inside you."

"Yes," I gasp as I tear at the button on my black jeans. As soon as I have my zipper down, he grabs me by the waist.

"Turn over," he commands, dropping me on my knees a few steps higher and tearing my pants down my legs almost violently. A loud gasp slips through my lips when I feel his mouth on my back, trailing his wet, warm kiss downward until he's spearing me with his tongue, groaning against my sex hungrily. Lapping at my clit in a frenzied daze, he takes me to the edge of bliss before pulling away and shifting his own pants downward.

"You're mine, Charlotte. This pussy is mine, understand?"

"Yes," I shriek, pressing my hips backward, searching for him—his mouth, his hands, his cock, anything—but he holds me at bay. Turning back, I see him stroke himself languidly, staring at my exposed cunt with lust in his eyes.

"Tell me you're mine. Say it."

"I'm yours," I gasp, clutching the wooden step between my fingers, turning my knuckles white. "I don't want anyone but you. I'm yours and you're mine. My...sir," I cry out.

"That's my girl," he groans, and without warning, he fills me, a hint of pain laced with pleasure. I scream while thrusting my hips backward, trying to take more, as much as I can get until I have all of him and he has all of me.

His hands land harshly on the stairs, next to mine, and he covers my body, thrusting inside with each rough cant of his hips. The hot skin of his chest is against my back and his breath is in my ear. With every smack of his hips against my ass, I let out a breathy mewl of pleasure, mixed with his heavy grunts.

He's fucking me fast and hard until we are moving as one toward our climax, and when I scream with my release, he groans and pounds into me one last time, my name on his lips as he comes.

Before I have the chance to collapse onto the steps, he pulls me upright. His cock slides out of me, cum dripping down my legs, as he turns me until I'm facing him.

"I love you, Charlie," he whispers into my mouth, sealing his words with a languid kiss. And I bite onto his bottom lip, making him feel the intensity that's boiling inside me.

When our mouths part, I lick the teeth marks on his bottom lip before whispering in return. "I love you too."

And it's all that needs to be said between us. No more dirty secrets or stolen moments, just this raw expression of everything we've felt over the last three months. Leaving the clothes we shed on the stairs, he carries me to his bed and makes good on his promise to take his time with me, knowing he finally has all the time in the world.

Rule #39: Good girls get happy endings.

Charlotte

HE'S NOT FOCUSING ON THE MEETING AT ALL. THERE ARE THREE potential investors on the call, each of their faces plastered on the screen as Maggie and Garrett walk them through the new programs the club is rolling out in the new fiscal year, and Emerson's eyes are unfocused and furrowed as he stares at the computer screen.

Granted, I am lapping at his cock with my tongue like it's a damn lollipop, and I'm doing it on purpose to drive him insane. With a quick click-click of his mouse, I know he's muted his mic. Then his fingers dig into my hair as he mutters darkly, "Stop being a fucking tease, Charlotte, and suck my cock like a good little secretary."

I whimper as desire trails down my spine, culminating between my legs and soaking my panties. "Yes, sir," I whisper, and I eagerly take his impressive length down my throat. Moaning with each stroke of my lips around him, I coat his shaft with saliva and bob my head up and down in the rhythm he loves.

"I'm gonna come down your throat," he groans, and I hum in response. Just as he promised, the head of his cock tightens between my lips and then he unloads down the back of my throat, spilling and spilling until I swallow it all down.

When I look up at him, he's gazing down at me with love in his eyes. Petting my head lovingly, he smiles as he bends down and presses his lips against mine.

"You are so perfect."

"Aren't you in a meeting, sir?" I whisper.

"I turned off my camera. Garrett has it under control."

"He's going to fire me if you can't focus on work while I'm here." I laugh. He hoists me onto his lap, depositing me on his desk, then rolling his chair until he's settled between my thighs.

"I'd like to see him try."

A few minutes later, as his tongue is buried in my folds and his lips are taking me to another planet altogether, I briefly realize that the meeting is over and it's just Garrett's voice on the line.

"You can't keep ghosting our investors' meetings," he scolds Emerson. The camera is still off, and the mic is still muted, which is a good thing because I'm about two seconds away from screaming my way through my second climax today.

"I know you can hear me, Grant."

Emerson chuckles between my legs. "Better keep quiet, Charlotte." With his free hand, he clicks his screen and I know he's unmuted the mic. Thankfully, the camera is still off or his business partner would be getting a full view of my ass on Emerson's desk.

"I'm working through lunch, Garrett. What do you want?" he asks, his voice muffled. I bite my lip as he sucks eagerly on my clit, making me see stars.

"Yeah, lunch my ass," Garrett replies over the line. "I'm glad you got your girl back, but we still have a company to run, so if you could maybe spend less time getting blown under your desk and more time finding ways to please our investors, that'd be great."

"Someone needs to get laid," Emerson grumbles between my legs. I've managed to hold off my orgasm until he slides two digits inside me at the same time, and I can't help but gasp, rocking my hips to feel him deeper.

Garrett clears his throat over the speakerphone. "Hello, Charlotte. When you two are done, can you please read the proposal I just sent? We need to meet the VIP quota by the end of the quarter or we're fucked. And not literally."

As soon as the line goes dead, I let out a cry of pleasure and shudder through my long-awaited orgasm. I've barely caught my breath as Emerson pulls me in for a kiss. He rubs his wet fingers over the skin of my chest.

"You heard the man," he says against my lips. "You're keeping me from doing my job, Charlotte. If you can't stop being so fucking fuckable, I'm going to have to tie you to your desk."

"That sounds fun," I whisper.

"Yes, it does," he replies.

After we both come down from our post-orgasm highs, we actually get back to work. I print out the proposal Garrett sent and then reply to him with a quick and informal apology. I like Garrett, and I hate to hear him so disgruntled. It's not like him. He's usually so carefree and fun, and he's always been the biggest supporter of my relationship with Emerson. It has me wondering what could have soured his mood lately. Jealousy, maybe? Emerson says Garrett isn't the settling down kind of guy and gets laid enough that he should never be in a bad mood about it.

But maybe seeing his best friend in a happy, committed relationship is getting under his skin.

Part of the compromise I made with my mom last month when I started moving things slowly into Emerson's house was that we had to uphold the Taco Tuesday tradition. She hardly had to twist my arm, especially since Emerson always drives and pays, which means bottomless margaritas for us.

It makes it more bearable since Sophie always has to sit next to him, and tonight, she's stealing all of his attention by showing him her design for the anime she's been drawing for months now. I guess I'd be more annoyed if he wasn't so fucking adorable, acting all enthralled by her sketches.

We're still on our first basket of chips and salsa when my mom wraps her arm around my shoulder and whispers, "Don't be mad at me. I couldn't help myself."

"What are you talking about?" I ask, but then I see him walking across the room.

"I had to invite him. It's family night."

My eyes widen as Beau waves awkwardly at me. I glance toward Emerson, but he doesn't seem the least bit surprised, which means he already knew about this.

"Why doesn't anyone tell me what's going on?" I ask, but no one answers me as my mom gets up to hug Beau. Then Emerson claps him on the shoulder and scoots in so he can take the seat at the end of the table.

Is it awkward having my ex-boyfriend and current boyfriend at dinner together? Of course. The elephant in the room is bigger than this margarita bowl. But this is Emerson's son, so I guess he's technically family now, and families are weird anyway.

"What's going on?" Beau asks awkwardly, and I just keep sucking down my drink, looking for the waiter, so I can have him on standby when I reach the bottom of this one.

"Sophie is showing me the comic book she drew," Emerson answers casually.

"It's called manga," she corrects him with a roll of her eyes, and my mother laughs.

"Cut him some slack, Soph. He's old," Beau says with a smile. And when she nudges her drawings toward him, he looks as amused as Emerson was, and it warms my heart.

Although that could be the tequila.

By the time the waiter is setting the fried ice cream in front of my little sister, I'm spacey and buzzed and all the awkwardness of the table doesn't feel so weird anymore. My mom and I can't stop giggling, and Emerson looks mostly amused by our drunkenness. He, my mother, and Beau are swapping embarrassing stories about me, and I'm focusing too much on the ice cream to care.

While they're all talking, I nudge my little sister with my foot and she looks up at me with a smile. Silently, I mouth the question, "Do I seem happy?"

Her smile is fighting to take over her whole face when she bites her lip and glances at the people at our table, then back at me. She nods eagerly, and I have to swallow down the emotion building in the back of my throat.

And just like that, it's not weird or wrong or uncomfortable. It's just family.

When the check is paid, we all hug Beau goodbye, and Emerson drives my mom and sister home. On the drive back to his place, I'm staring out the window as he reaches across the seat and clutches my leg.

Looking over at him, I bite my bottom lip. "You're real smooth around my family, but if they only knew the dirty things I'm sure you're thinking…"

The wicked smile he's wearing morphs into something much more sinister. "You have no idea."

"So why don't you show me?" I ask.

He laughs. Then as we pull up to a stoplight, he reaches across the seat and pulls my face to his, gripping me hard under my chin. With a wicked whisper, he says, "Red-light fire drill."

A second later, he's out of the car, and my eyes widen. A laugh bursts through my lips as I jump out of the car and run around the back of it, but he's already so far ahead of me that by the time I reach the driver's side, he's already there. Snatching me by the waist, he presses me against the side of the car. We're both laughing and breathless, and it's a far cry from the brooding man I met four months ago.

With his mouth near mine, he mutters, "Baby, every second

I'm around you, I'm thinking of all the dirty things I want to do to you, and you can rest assured I'm going to live out each and every one of those fantasies. Do you think you can handle that?"

My mouth falls open as he licks across my top lip, teasing me with his tongue. "Uh-huh…" I gasp.

A deep chuckle echoes through the dark night as someone behind us honks their horn. "Use your words, Charlotte." He groans, sliding his hand between my legs.

"Yes, sir."

That sinister smile of his returns as he rests his forehead gently against mine. "Good girl."

Rule #40: Make him praise you.

Epilogue
One year later
Charlotte

"I reserved the throne room tonight."

"What's the occasion?" I ask with a smile as I climb onto his lap. We're sitting in the shared office of the club sometime after ten, and I can tell Emerson is up to something. He has that mysterious look on his face—the one that tells me he has some devious plan that usually involves me getting tied up and tortured somehow.

And I love every second of it.

"No occasion," he replies as he pets my hair with one hand, working on his computer with the other. "I love the way you look in that throne. Is that a crime?"

When his fierce green eyes scan toward me, I melt a little inside. "No, sir."

While he finishes his work, I rest my head on his chest, nestled in his lap like a child. The last year has been a dream. Six months ago, I officially moved in even though, by that point, I was there all the time anyway. Living together means that our *play* time is separate from our *real* time. I'm not always Emerson's good girl and he's not always my sir. Most of the time, we're just us, and I can relax and be myself, knowing that I'm treasured for exactly who I am—flaws and all.

But on the rare occasion that he rents the throne room, I know it means he wants to do more than treasure me—he wants to worship me.

He wants *me* to be in charge. He wants me to be dominant and take from him what I want.

He says it's good practice to see things from the other's perspective, but I'll be honest. It's not my favorite. It's just not who I am. I'm no Madame Kink. I'm much more in my element when I'm Emerson's sweet, obedient sub—as weird as that is for me. I just like pleasing him. It's so easy when he tells me exactly what to do, but when I'm in charge I'm too worried I'm *not* pleasing him. Sort of defeats the purpose, if you ask me.

When I get restless waiting for him to finish this email, I start kissing my way up his neck, inhaling his familiar scent and nuzzling my face in the collar of his shirt. My hand drifts over the bulge in his pants, and he tenses.

"Charlotte..." he says in a stern warning.

"I'm bored," I complain.

"Bored? Or anxious to have me at your mercy?"

"I already have you at my mercy," I reply, straddling his hips and grinding myself against him until he stops looking at the computer and puts his arms around me instead.

"You're not being a bad girl, are you, Charlotte?"

"Maybe," I mumble against his lips, which he kisses back with the same ferocity I'm kissing him with.

We moan into the passionate lip-lock until he clutches onto my thighs and stands from the chair, taking me with him as he marches out of the office.

He carries me out of the office and down the hallway to the

throne room while I nibble on his jaw and ear. Once we enter, my belly warms with arousal at the sight of the throne, remembering all the dirty things I've seen and done in here.

He must feel it too because the door isn't even closed before he drops my legs to the floor and we're tearing at each other's clothes.

"What do you want me to do, Charlotte? I'm all yours," he growls while I fumble with the buttons of his shirt.

"Just let me look at you," I reply, shoving him hard against the wall. As soon as the last button is undone, I swipe his shirt off his large shoulders with one move.

He's standing with his back to the wall, and I take a step back, putting a hand out to keep him where he is. Then I let my gaze rake over his bare chest, moving quickly with his heavy breaths.

Will I ever tire of this view—this *man*—who's by some miracle all mine?

"Take your pants off," I say in a command, biting back my smile.

With his hungry eyes on my face, he slips his belt off and moves to the zipper. After slipping his shoes off his feet, he lowers his pants to the floor and leaves them in a pile with his shirt and socks, so he's standing before me in nothing but his tight black boxer briefs, barely hiding the thick erection peeking out of the top.

"Underwear off," I say in quick, loud order that surprises even me.

"Yes, dear."

I swallow as he slips his boxers to the floor, and I have to remind myself to breathe as I stare at him naked and aroused for me. I see him naked every single day, but there's something different about this moment. As he stands there like an offering, giving his perfect tall, strong body to me.

"What now, my love?" he says softly.

What now?

Slowly closing the distance between us, I lift my fingers to his chest, running my touch over the hard muscle of his chest, down the bumpy planes of his abs and through the strip of black hair leading down to his protruding length. He shivers as I tease him.

Then, I turn around and lift my hair from my shoulders.

"Unzip me," I say, and he does.

Giving Emerson Grant orders feels so strange but exhilarating. It's the rarity of it, and the fact that he submits to me from time to time that makes it so amazing. I don't want this every day. But I love knowing that he can—no, that he *wants* to.

After the zipper is down, he leans in and presses his warm lips to my shoulder.

"Tell me you love me," I whisper, staring down as the dress slips from my body to the floor.

He exhales, tugging me closer as he mumbles with his mouth to my ear. "I love you more than anything."

With a smile, I look back toward him. "Tell me I'm a good girl."

He chuckles. "Even when you're in charge, you need praise."

I spin on him and give him a harsh glare. "And you should obey." I muster as much assertive dominance as I can to snap at him. He looks mildly surprised as he replies.

"You're such a good girl, Charlotte Underwood."

Reaching down, I take his hard cock in my hand, and tug him toward me. His brow pinches together and his mouth forms a small circle as he sucks in air with a wince.

I pull him all the way to the throne. Stepping onto the dais, I stand before him.

"Then worship me."

As I release him, he falls to his knees. His face is just at my middle, and his hands are on my waist. Without hesitation, he presses his lips to my stomach and down to my hips, painting my sensitive flesh with adoring kisses. He's ravenous, devouring my body and leaving my skin tingling and desperate for more.

Mid kiss, he tugs my black lace panties down, leaving me naked in his hands.

As I sit down on the throne, I bring him with me. His mouth

never leaves my body as my legs drape over his shoulders. When his lips find my aching core, I gasp. The friction of his beard against my delicate sex is pleasure and torture combined.

He moans hungrily as he laps at my clit. I grip his hair in my fist and pull him closer. "More," I groan. I'm nearly levitating off the seat as he digs in even more voraciously.

"Oh, Emerson," I cry out as his tongue penetrates me. I fidget in my seat, so close to my climax I can hardly breathe. But I'm not ready. So I press a bare foot against his shoulder and push him away.

He stares up at me in shock.

Reaching down, I take his hair by the base of his head and drag his mouth toward mine. "Fuck me," I command with a deeper than normal timbre in my voice. Then, I press my lips to his, tasting myself on his tongue. It awakens something carnal and erotic inside me.

In a rush, he stands and flips me so I'm facing the throne, both hands on the arms of the chair. Tugging my hips back, he enters me with force. Our thunderous moans of pleasure blend into one, a perfect harmony of passion and need.

His hips piston against me as my hands clasp the sides of the chair to keep me in place. His cock strikes a spot inside me that has my toes curling and a warm sensation reaching every extremity of my body. "More," I cry out, thrusting backwards to meet him, to bring him deeper, harder.

"I don't want to hurt you," he replies, and I feel him holding back.

"You won't. I promise," I say, my voice strained and shaking from the climax my body is looking for. "Just do as I say."

Finally, he listens, taking it to the next level of speed and intensity until I'm on the verge of screaming.

Strong arms wrap around my middle, hauling me closer until our bodies are practically one. Then he runs his tongue along the side of my neck, biting my earlobe between his teeth until I let out a yelp. The pain only heightens the pleasure.

Bracing one hand on the throne and the other around my waist, he picks up speed, our bodies slamming together at a pace that sends me flying into euphoria. I lean back against him as I tense and shudder through my orgasm. He hums deeply in my ear as his body is swept under the same current.

We're left panting together, slumped over the throne as our heart beats slow to a normal cadence. With his lips pressed against my spine, he slowly pulls out, and I feel the dribble of his cum down the inside of my thigh.

"I'll get something to clean you up," he whispers before he disappears from behind me. When he returns, he tenderly wipes a soft cloth between my legs, slowly running it through my sensitive folds.

Then he helps me get dressed, carefully threading my legs into my underwear and then my dress. He's being extra attentive tonight, which I assume is just him still in character in our role reversal.

I watch him button up his shirt, admiring the way his fingers nimbly work each one, and I realize he's being strangely quiet.

"Everything okay?" I ask.

He swallows. Then blinks. "Yes," he replies unconvincingly, and I notice his fingers stumble with the last button. Worry settles itself like a sickness in my gut. Is there something he's not telling me? Is something…bothering him?

What could have possibly brought this on? Was it something I did? The sex was phenomenal. He told me he loved me more than anything. Those weren't just words. Emerson doesn't say anything he doesn't mean.

Still, as I turn my back to him, I blink away the emotion that threatens to build at the mere thought that the passion could ever fizzle out between us. My mind is on a rampage of fear and anxiety. What if he's losing interest? What if there's someone else? What if he…leaves me? Who would I be without him?

I know that's a ridiculous thing to even think. I've grown

so much this year, learned so much about myself and found a strength I didn't even know existed. I don't *need* Emerson Grant just as much as I *do need* Emerson Grant. The more I've transformed, the more he's become a part of me. Without him, I would be a woman without half of her heart. Half of her strength and confidence and happiness. I would be a sub without a Dom.

The tears I begged myself not to shed are starting to pool between my lashes. When I turn back toward him, he's dressed and still looking unsettled. Then his gaze locks onto my eyes.

His brow furrows as he quickly eats up the distance between us, running his hand along my jaw and into my hair. "Charlie, why are you crying?"

"Nothing, I just…get in my head sometimes."

"About what?"

I take a deep breath. I decide to be honest because then at least he could settle my nerves. Tell me all the things my worried soul needs to hear. "How hopeless I would be if I ever lose you."

His face softens as leans it closer to me. "You won't lose me. You'll never lose me."

My heart relaxes a little at the sound of those words, spoken with conviction and promise.

As I reach my lips toward his, he pulls away from my kiss. I watch with confusion as he lowers to his knees. With a smile, I try to tug him back to his feet.

"We don't have to do this anymore. The scene is over."

"I want to do this," he replies, and that look is back on his face. Something unsettled and worried.

"Emerson, I can tell you don't like it. You look uncomfortable, and honestly I don't really like it—"

My words come to a resounding halt as he lifts one knee, so he's only down on one. My skin starts to prickle with anticipation as I wait, my eyes going wide. The blood coursing through my veins picks up speed, thrumming in my ears.

When he reaches into his pocket, all of the emotion inside me comes flooding up to my eyes, causing those threatening tears to return, this time spilling over without warning. At the sight of the small square box in his hands, I gasp and slam my hand against my mouth.

This can't be happening.

"Charlie" he whispers, and I let out a yelp, warm tears sliding over my fingers and onto the floor. "This is why I rented the throne room tonight. I couldn't imagine a more fitting place to kneel for you. And the only reason I looked uncomfortable is because until you are officially mine, with my last name, and my ring on your finger, I won't be satisfied. *You* settle me. *You* bring me comfort. You make every day of my life infinitely better, and I will continue to look *uncomfortable* until your name is Charlotte Grant."

Then, he lifts the lid of the box revealing a ring that is simple and beautiful and *perfect*. It shines under the bright light and my finger itches with the sudden need to wear it, as if it has always belonged there.

"Yes!" I squeal, and he laughs before taking my hand in his.

"You have to let me ask the question first."

"Oh shit," I reply with a sniffle. "Sorry, go ahead."

Wiping the smile off his face so all that's left is a sincere expression of hope and love, he proudly replies, "Charlie, *my Charlotte*, will you marry me?"

"Yes, sir," I whisper before biting my bottom lip. I watch his chest move with a heavy breath of relief as he takes the ring from the box and slips it over my finger. It fits perfectly, sitting snug against my skin like a new part of my body.

Then he's on his feet, wrapping his strong arms around my waist and hoisting me off the floor. There's joy in our laughter as we hold each other. And the moment my feet touch the floor, his mouth takes mine in a passionate kiss.

I never want to leave this kiss, so I let our lips tangle until the kiss becomes heated and the clothes that we just put back on are suddenly being shed again. This time when he touches me, it will be as his fiancée. And someday…his wife.

Considering that a year ago, I thought the dream of truly being Emerson's was a fantasy, to realize it's now my reality is more than I could have ever asked for. I have found someone who truly adores me, treasures me, and showers me with all the praise my kinky heart could ever want.

A few minutes ago, I let myself feel what it would be like to lose him. And now he's telling me I never have to.

Keep reading for an excerpt of the second book in the sizzling Salacious Players' Club series from *USA Today* bestseller Sara Cate: *Eyes on Me*

Rule #1: Don't check text messages from your mom at the sex club.

Garrett

THERE ARE ONLY THREE THINGS I TAKE SERIOUSLY—RUNNING, A well-tailored suit, and sex.

I *have* to be serious about that last one; it's my job. Not *having* sex, of course, but knowing everything about it in order to curate an enjoyable and arousing experience for those both doing it and those who want to watch others doing it. I have to know the minute details that turn people on, that make them feel safe, and that keep them coming back for more. The fine line between hot and creepy. Catering an encounter for men *and women* alike.

Being an expert of the ins and outs, if you will.

And right now, I have my eyes on a delicious little couple in room seven, who are doing everything perfectly. The woman is cuffed to the bed, her golden skin catching the dim red light as the man behind her pounds at a perfect rhythm to make her go wild. The angle is sublime, but I make a mental note to pull the bed to the right about ten more degrees, so the spectators can see her face better. Believe it or not, that's what the people really want to see anyway…her face. The look of need and hunger in her slightly pained and wanton expression.

I made a good choice in inviting these two back. I watched them together a few weeks ago, and it was my idea to incentivize the couples who draw a crowd into renting the voyeur rooms again. A little discount on their membership, a few added VIP perks, and in return, I offer them time together in the red-light room where, for one hour, she can feel like a first-class prostitute, selling her pleasure, and he can be the highest bidder.

They put on a hot show. He came strolling in, in an expensive-looking suit, gave her a devilish smile, while she tried to appear unaffected. It was impressive, and the crowd was into it. Completely.

Well, crowd is a bit of an overstatement. It's only a handful of people. The curtain is drawn around the viewing area, creating an intimacy among the small group currently gathered. We can't exactly let a mob back into the voyeur hall; it sort of ruins the experience if you're trying to observe something private in the company of a hundred others, who are also trying to experience something private. This is a classy place, after all. Can't have a horde of horny men stroking it in a crowd like it's some sleazy backroom peep show in a dirty porn store.

And that's where I come in. Knowing exactly what to regulate and how to let it all happen so nothing gets out of control. It needs to appear natural, even though I'm covertly controlling everything behind the scenes.

So far, so good tonight. There's one woman watching alone near the window, biting her lip as she witnesses the woman on the bed climax *again*. There's a couple standing so close to each other that I can't tell if her hand is down his pants or his hand is up her short dress or both. Which means it's just dark enough in here; although I might have them turn down the red light just a hair… it seems to be giving off a glare on all the metal in the room, and it's distracting.

All in all, the energy in the room is spot-on.

My phone buzzes in my pocket, but I don't pull it out right away; it's against the rules to have phones in here or any private areas of the club, even if I am one of the owners.

The red-light couple are wrapping up anyway, so I quietly slink out of the voyeur hall, through the private service door, and head toward the office. Once I'm safely in the brightly lit staff hallway, I fish out my phone.

The notification reads: *You have a new message from Mom.*

Oh, lovely. A message from my mother after watching people fuck like heathens. I'm willing to bet my left testicle this is yet another invitation to join her and my stepdad at the lake house this week.

You should come up. The weather is beautiful this week.

Ha. I was right.

Every year, she and my stepdad stay at their lake house three hours away, and every year, they invite me to come with them. I'd be more inclined to say yes if his twenty-three-year-old brat of a daughter wasn't going too. So every year, I disappoint my mother with a *thanks, but no thanks* response, and this year is no different.

Mia is the bane of my existence. The apple of not only her father's eye but my mother's too; she's spent the last fifteen years soaking up every ounce of their attention and being a serious pain in my ass, and while I'm far too old to complain about sibling rivalries now, I'm perfectly content just pretending she doesn't exist.

"Who are you talking to?" Hunter asks over my shoulder as I linger by the door, staring down at my phone.

"My mom."

He winces as he walks by. "Gross, dude. I can still hear people fucking behind this wall."

"What? Is that weird?" I reply with a laugh.

"Not for you. Tell her I said hi," he says as he disappears down the long hallway, turning toward the office.

"I can't tell if you're being nice or dirty," I shout, my voice carrying down the corridor, and in the distance, I hear Hunter laugh.

The banter between me and the three people I run this company with is half the reason I love this job so damn much. We get along great. It's always fun, sometimes a little stressful, but never too heavy or too serious.

Just how I like it.

I almost forget I'm in the middle of a conversation via text with my mother, but the buzzing of my phone in my hand reminds me.

You haven't been up to the lake in years.

The sting of guilt actually gets me for a second, as I think about disappointing her once again. But I really am busy with work, and it's not that easy for me to just leave the club for several days at a time. I risk losing my momentum, the energy I need to keep everything running smoothly. The fresh ideas, the creative projects, the new events, the incoming clients, and the all-important VIP incentives. There's a lot on my shoulders, and I can't risk letting anything fall. Not for a second.

I'll think about it, I reply to my mom.

You should come. Mia is bored up here without you.

Looking down at my phone, I laugh. The last thing my stepsister is, is bored without me. At peace, maybe. Soaking up the undivided attention from our parents without me around, definitely. But the last thing she is, is bored.

Tempting, I respond. But if I wanted to be hissed at every ten seconds, I'd get a cat.

Be nice.

Ha. Nice? Mia and I haven't been *nice* to each other since the day we met a decade and a half ago, when she was only eight. I was in my early twenties. We really shouldn't have had a problem with each other, considering the thirteen years between us, but as

Mia grew up, she found ways of getting on every last nerve I had. She's been nothing but an entitled brat, who isn't content unless her presence is a constant source of torture for me.

Luckily, I can dish it out just as much as she can. And she's not eight years old anymore.

Besides, I know Paul really wants to see you.

Dammit. She's going to play the Paul card. My stepdad has been in and out of treatment for bladder cancer for the past couple of years. One minute he's doing great, and the next…she says stuff like this. And it makes me worry. I should go over there more and stay in the loop, so they know I care, but life just gets in the way.

"Meet you at the bar?" Hunter asks when he comes back around, pulling my attention away from my phone. "It's Maggie's turn to watch the club this week."

"Ahhh…and be the only single guy in the group again? Sounds fun. I assume Drake is bringing his flavor of the week."

"Not sure he has one this week," Hunter throws back. "So you'll have him."

I tilt my head back and raise my brows, forcing a tight-lipped smile. Hunter's best friend, and the head of construction for the club, Drake, is a known ladies' man and won't be at our table more than five minutes before he declares open season on the single girls at the bar.

Thursday night drinks have been a decade-long tradition for us, but I really don't have the energy for another couples' night with the team. I hate to cancel on them again. It's just… the dynamics have changed so much. It was fine when Hunter and Isabel got married because I still had Emerson. But now, he's blissfully entangled with his secretary, Charlie, which is great. I'm happy for him.

I am.

Acknowledgments

Thank you for reading *Praise*. I wasn't sure I'd ever be able to devote myself to a book again, and this one was like a warm, kinky hug. It was everything I needed, and I have so many people to thank for helping me through this process.

First and foremost, a huge thanks to my readers, Amanda and Adrian, for helping me write the coolest little sister I've ever written. It means the world to me to have your support and input. Sophie and I thank you.

A HUGE love-filled thank-you goes out to my friend and advisor, Amanda Anderson, for walking beside me this year. There aren't enough words, girl. I couldn't do this without you.

I could not do this without my team:

My editor, Rebecca's Fairest Reviews, and my proofreader, Rumi Khan.

My agent, Savannah Greenwood, of Two Daisy Media.

My amazing assistants, Lori and Misty, who work their asses off to make books like this possible.

The Sweetest readers' group in the world.

And my beautiful Sinners.

My best friend, Rachel, for listening to every neurotic message, crazy idea, and twelve-hundred versions of this cover.

To everyone who paved a way of love and support for me this year, saying thank you just isn't enough.

About the Author

Sara Cate is a *USA Today* bestselling author of contemporary, forbidden romance. Her stories are known for their heart-wrenching plots and toe-curling heat. Living in Arizona with her husband and kids, Sara spends most of her time working in her office with her goldendoodle by her side. You can find more information about her at saracatebooks.com.

Also by Sara Cate

SALACIOUS PLAYERS' CLUB
Praise
Eyes on Me
Give Me More
Mercy

AGE-GAP ROMANCE
Beautiful Monster
Beautiful Sinner

WILDE BOYS DUET
Gravity
Freefall

BLACK HEART DUET
Four
Five

COCKY HERO CLUB
Handsome Devil

BULLY ROMANCE
Burn for Me

WICKED HEARTS SERIES
Delicate
Dangerous
Defiant